C☾NTINUUM . .

I0668592

When Sophia Delaney returns to her earthly life following a near-death experience in a car accident, her awareness instantly expands far beyond the three-dimensional world. She soon discovers innate intuitive abilities, enabling her to tap into countless historic events through dreams of past lives, which over time expands her soul's journey.

As Sophia weighs her new awareness against the life she once knew, a mystical Lakota shaman introduces her to a conclave of people from around the world, called the Order of Apeiros, a culturally diverse collection of intuitive sages, seers, and shamans, whose spiritually gifted sensitivities, sacred talismans, and enlightened wisdom raise their vibrational energies in service of the earth and all her inhabitants. They invite Sophia to join them, for they are aware that she has returned to this lifetime as the most powerful oracle the world has ever known. Overnight, Sophia shifts from her everyday mundane existence to many lives of mystic wonder.

Ardyce West's Continuum Series weaves numerous interlinking stories through each book, blending a bit of self-help with metaphysical historical fiction about unsung heroes and sensitive souls from the present day and the past. The task of her dynamic and engaging characters is simple - to shift the consciousness of the world - one thought, one word, one act of love at a time. Their seemingly ordinary lives are, at times, quite astonishing through the mystery and intrigue of their mystical experiences, with interwoven stories and tales told with humor, romance, suspense, intrigue, and timeless universal wisdom.

APEIROS
CONTINUUM BOOK ONE

Writer and artist Sophia Delaney has led an average life of mixed fortune. Now divorced and coping with the impending death of her enigmatic father, Sophia is asking the inevitable mid-life questions of mortality and existence. Then everything changes in a split second on a rain-slick highway. Sophia's car hurtles into the median, and for a brief moment, she leaves her body and enters the mystical ethers of no time or space, where she realizes the wisdom within her soul's journey.

Otherworldly entities welcome her from the next dimension, and she's given a choice to either stay or return to reconcile a life not yet fully lived. Sophia makes her choice, and from that moment on, only one thing is certain - she will never be the same.

What Amazon.com reviewers are saying:

"After reading this book, I became more thoughtful that there is more to this world than our senses can perceive." - Jay

"Rich, dense, expressive, captivating... you really have to take your time to read her story in order to grasp all that she is saying, because it is so much more than a story..." - Jasper

"There were two journeys that took place. Sophia's amazing trek that came from the powerful descriptive words read within this book and my own expedition that I took with her." - Jewels

"This author has a way of writing that is spellbinding and poetic, full of spiritual wisdom and insight." - S. Walsh

"I found myself being Sophia her story is mine. It's like the author Ardyce West channeled me and my journey!" - Carol

"I found myself really identifying with the main character and wanting to be in on her journey." - S. Cobb

"...it was so engaging, it allowed me to reflect on my own life too, which was unexpected." - Mtina

AETERNALIS
CONTINUUM BOOK TWO

Sophia's metaphysical journey through her many past lives leads to the startling revelation of a family she never knew existed. Empowered by her newfound ability to pull back the veils of time and space, Sophia learns the truth about the mother she never knew, and the dark secret her enigmatic father took to his grave.

Sophia embarks on a quest for understanding and forgiveness as the Order of Apeiros unites in Colorado, introducing her to widely diverse and delightful people who share a common purpose. As Sophia learns more about her mysterious past, a persistent vision transports her to the fateful maiden voyage of the RMS *Titanic*, where she found true love and spiritual calling on a passage into destiny.

SÍORAÍ

Also by Ardyce West

APEIROS
Continuum Book One

AETERNALIS
Continuum Book Two

OUROBOROS
Continuum Book Four

I Never Heard You Cry
A Compassionate Journey Through Abortion

Children's Books:

There Once Was a Kitty Named Digit
Book One of Travels With Digit

On the Horizon:

RÉALTA
Continuum Book Five

Available in paperback and e-book formats at Amazon.com,
BarnesAndNoble.com, and other online book stores.

SÍORAÍ

CONTINUUM BOOK THREE

ARDYCE WEST

LoneWolf

Published in the United States of America
First edition published 09.25.2017 by KC LoneWolf
admin@kclonewolf.com
Littleton, CO

ISBN-13: 978-0-9969544-3-3
ISBN-10: 0996954430

EBook edition also available on Kindle and other devices

Author contact information: admin@ardyce.org

For my beloved Kevin,
whom I have walked alongside
for more than time itself.

Prologue

*Síoraí (SHEARee) - (Irish Gaelic) -
eternal, perpetual, unceasing,
continual.*

AETERNALIS

Watching *Titanic*'s horrible demise,
Jocelyn felt a palpable jolt of pain in her
chest, a brutal yank of her own life force as
it left her body. When the tip of the stern
disappeared, in contrast to the thunderous
roar just moments before, the last of *Titanic*
went under in peaceful silence.

What took 3,000 men three years to
build was swallowed by the sea in two
hours and forty minutes...

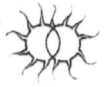

Chapter
One

They took the road less traveled on their way to New Orleans, leaving the Colorado Mountain vistas in the rearview mirror. Darius, Gaston, White Buffalo, and Digit the cat, who loved to go on road trips, all came along. Knowing she would be well cared for, Sophia and Michael decided to leave Digit at the plantation when they went to Ireland on their honeymoon. Everyone loved the tiny black cat, and she returned the feelings as the furry four-legged heat-seeking device curled up from one lap to the next, particularly if that lap was sitting in the sunshine.

They drove through Colorado, crossed the corner of northeastern New Mexico, and on through the great state of Texas. As evening approached, they stopped to eat at a roadside diner that advertised the best chicken fried steak in Texas. The boys decided to test the claim and concluded the chicken fried steak was possibly the best in *any* state, for that matter. At first, Sophia opted for a delicious chicken salad, although it was not long before she couldn't pass up a big slice of Texas toast and yellow chicken gravy, with the thought, *When in Texas...*

Afterward, when they returned to the RV, the vast southwest plains held the sunset, capturing their attention with deep, rich colors of gold, coral, and crimson, transforming each traveler into the silence of eternality.

The solitude of dusk met them as they journeyed eastward along the hilly lush countryside. Along the way, they chased thunderstorms, which left a mysterious thick gray fog that crept among the lower woodlands as the cool evening air settled in. Darkened skies held no lights in the heavens until they breached a hill, where on the far horizon the full moon emerged deep red-orange, as if engulfed in a complete lunar eclipse. The vermilion red orb hauntingly beckoned them on, perfectly framed between columns of tall oaks flanking the road. As the moon rose above the fog, it turned to orange, then on to bright gold, lighting the highway through the quietude of night.

They decided to drive straight through to Louisiana, trading driving duty while the others rested along the way. They passed the time with good conversation, word games, a few road songs, and some rousing trivia challenges that covered everything from 10th century French kings to popular television sit-coms. Having left the cabin at 9:00 a.m., they arrived in New Orleans in the early afternoon the following day, bleary-eyed and quite anxious for the palatial comforts of the MacPhaidin estate.

The last time Sophia and Michael visited the plantation house, Darius and Gaston revealed the truth about the murder of Sophia's parents, which left her with residual, uneasy grief. With the excitement of their wedding now over, and the gathering of Apeiros complete, what laid dormant in her mind now rose to the surface for her to face. She was just beginning to recall moments from that traumatic day when she was three years old.

The list of thoughts and returned memories traversed her mind with irrational whys and what-ifs. *What if I had not been home sick that day, my parents might still be alive. Why did I not stay in the kitchen as Ada told me? If I had done so, my mother might have survived, and my father would not have been killed. Why didn't I just keep my sassy three-year-old mouth shut?*

Wishing for the past to be different spurred on suffering that kept Sophia from releasing pain and uneasiness, consequently holding her healing at bay. All four men were quite concerned, for Sophia's vibrancy at times turned into an unusual level of passivity. Even Digit, the tiny four-legged healer, spent more time on Sophia's lap throughout the drive across the states. She always sensed when her human was in need of greater love and attention. Sophia knew that Digit was a highly evolved spiritual being. Her small but mighty polydactyl Bombay cat could tap into energies beyond Sophia's comprehension.

On the evening following their arrival in New Orleans, Michael spoke up at dinner. "Gaston, when we gathered at Markos' home in Santorini, you told Sophia that you could help her with the memory of her mother. What did you mean by that?"

Gaston smiled as he dabbed his mouth with a napkin. "I'm glad you asked, for it has been on my mind since we were last here. Something I have not mentioned, and I have not done this for years, is that I used to be a practicing medium."

"Is that what the draped room in the back corner of your shop is all about," Sophia asked, "with the crystal ball in the center of the table?"

"It is," Gaston said, "although these days it's there simply to enchant customers and stimulate conversation."

Sophia laughed. "I can see you with a turban, gold hoop earrings, a big colorful shirt with puffy sleeves, and your eyes heavily lined in black."

"A bit too theatrical for my taste," Gaston said, "but in the past I did many readings there."

"I believe a puffy shirt and eyeliner would be quite becoming on you." She looked over at Darius, who had nodded off. "Hey! Sleeping Beauty!"

Darius perked. "Oh? What, dear? I'm sorry. I suppose I'm still a bit ragged from the long drive yesterday."

"Gaston is trying to make an important point here."

"Is he now," Darius said. "Well, wake me if he thinks of something."

"I want to hear about the crystal ball!"

Gaston smiled. "Thank you, my dear, and know this – you are the *only* relative that I have not excluded from my will."

"Thank you, Uncle. Now please?"

"There is so much more to the crystal ball than a simple conversation piece. Now, not to boast, but I was rather well known back in the day for spiritually connecting people with their loved ones. I thought, if you are willing, I might attempt to be an intercessory between you and your mother and father. Willingness - that of an open mind and welcoming heart - is all it takes to tap into the spirit world."

"I'm intrigued," Sophia said.

"Just so you know," Gaston continued, "from where I sit, both of your parents are right here, waiting for you to say yes. Great Spirit, the Divine, the Infinite Intelligence, is always accessible at all times. Some of us come in contact with spiritual wisdom through the angels, entities, and spirit guides. Whatever we call them, or in what form we choose, they are always with us. Most of us just don't perceive them, but that doesn't mean they aren't in our presence. In order to connect, we must invite them in. We must ask for their help."

"Isn't that one of the reasons people come to New Orleans?" Michael asked. "Especially at Mardi Gras - so they can get their palm read - or do that voodoo that you do so well?"

"Cole Porter," White Buffalo said. Michael nodded and touched his nose.

"Come on, you two," Sophia said with a deep sigh. "Don't you think fifteen hours of trivia challenge on the road is enough?" White Buffalo shrugged and gave Michael a wink.

"It is true," Darius chimed in. "La Nouvelle Orléans, since its settlement by the French in 1718, has been the destination to see a medium, or to have one's cards read. Here's a bit of trivia for you: The city was named after the Duke of Orleans, France's ruling regent, until Louis XV took the throne. Over the decades, the mystical city drew people to the Vieux Carré – 'the old city' - otherwise known as the French Quarter, which is the oldest neighborhood in New Orleans. As you know, many are drawn to Mardi Gras in the French Quarter, our famous Bourbon Street, and New Orleans jazz along the mighty Mississippi. Our cultural mix makes the city's flavor like none other in the world."

"I came here to Mardi Gras with some college buddies once," Michael said.

"It's rather an irreverent spectacle, isn't it?" Darius said.

Michael furrowed a brow and rubbed his chin. "I can't remember."

"I *am* in the room, and don't forget that I had quite an adventurous life between the four times we've been together!" Sophia said with a squint in her eyes and half smile.

"Well, yes, perhaps we shall leave that untouched, albeit too late, I might add," Darius said, clearing his throat. "Back to New Orleans - since the French first settled here, old world ways, ancient in origin, still seep between the mortars that hold the city together, sometimes with only a prayer when hurricanes blow through."

"Well, dear," Gaston said, "what do you think? Would you like to try?"

Sophia drew a long sigh and thoughtfully looked at her grandfather, and at each of her beloved uncles. Her gaze then fell on Michael.

"Sounds fascinating," Michael said with a shrug.

"This is all very interesting, and I would like to know more," Sophia said, "but, if you will excuse me, I need to step outside and take a breath of the cool evening air to clear my head."

"Of course," Gaston said.

Sophia stood up from the table and took her leave, but not before she wrapped her shoulders in a woolen shawl. Michael, Darius, and White Buffalo waited patiently, hoping she would say yes to Gaston's reading.

Outside, she walked along the oak-lined cathedral drive under the hanging Spanish moss that dangled from the branches of the 200-year-old oak trees. She took in the multitude of scents and sounds of a land filled with mystery.

Sophia reflected upon the reality of life, which meant

that all occurrences were neutral. Human perception made any situation a solidified mindset, no longer unbiased. But if one could shift from pain and discomfort with a mere changing of the mind, looking at the experience for what it had to teach and inform, the experience could be altered and brought back into neutrality, and therefore healing would take place.

Until she worked her way through the middle of the uncomfortable emotions by feeling the pain, the uneasiness would keep coming up to visit. However, by acknowledging the feelings, knowing they could not bring her any harm, she could take notice of where they resided in her body. She knew that mindfully breathing into the center of that feeling was one way for the body to release its pent-up energy. By seeking the deeper messages and looking for the good that came out of the memories of her experience, she would then come to peace. Sophia knew this well. Where peace is, love resides. It was time to walk her talk - to love herself through her grief. She was in the right place with those who held her in that loving space to help her move through the pain and let it go. Of course, she would gladly take Gaston up on his offer, but they were all a bit too anxious on her behalf, so she decided to delay just a bit longer before saying yes.

Before she walked back into the house and through the narrow black enamel ten-foot French doors, she turned around to marvel at the beautiful countryside, which had been anything but tranquil 150 years earlier. Because the property was a plantation, the bleak shadow of slavery was the one thing that truly bothered her about being Darius' heir. She believed that hundreds of slaves most likely once worked the large plantation.

New Orleans and that part of the Deep South held unfathomable undertones of sorrow and sadness in her history of slavery and the Civil War, countered by its present-day charm of old-world mysticism and party atmosphere. The weather extremes, with hurricanes and tropical storms, influenced the city's planners to build New Orleans as it was. Most everything there was constructed from the effect of extremes - the intensity of human nature and nature itself.

Although more than a century and a half had gone by, slavery was still a relevant, and yet a very touchy subject. Nevertheless, Sophia simply *had* to broach the topic with Darius. Someday this would all be hers, and she would have to find a way to make amends with the spirits of those who suffered at the hands of her ancestors.

Feeling a bit feisty, she used the Greek goddess doorknocker, just because it was there. She went ahead and let herself in the house just as Charles, the butler, met her in the foyer. It was going to take some time for Charles to get used to Sophia's 'northerner' ways. By no means was she a proper southern girl, if there was such a thing anymore.

"Sorry, Charles," she said, "I just love the sound of that door knocker."

"As do I," Charles said in an almost comically deadpan voice. "In fact, I find that I live for its hollow resonance."

Sophia stopped and contemplated his utterly blank stare.

Charles raised his eyebrows. "Rather ghoulish, isn't it?" In a moment, the icy stare turned to a delightful smile with a subtle wink as he quickly spun around and walked a cute two-step back toward the pantry.

Sophia giggled all the way into the library, where the

boys sat in front of a burning fireplace with their favorite libations in hand - Darius with a scotch, neat, Michael with a dark porter ale, Gaston with a bourbon on ice, and White Buffalo with an alcohol-free Tornado Twist.

"May I pour you a drink?" Darius asked.

She pointed to White Buffalo. "I'll have what he's having, but spike it with vodka, please, and a maraschino cherry on top. You know, it's all about the cherry!"

When Darius handed her the tall glass, she thanked him and immediately popped the cherry in her mouth. There was nothing worse, while enjoying a cocktail, when the only thing remaining was the cherry that one had to fish from the bottom of the glass. She stood, facing them with her back to the painting of Maeve, holding her drink in one hand and the cherry stem in the other. "Okay, Gaston, let's see if you've still got it."

They all smiled. "This is going to be great!' Michael said.

"Splendid," Gaston said.

"Get the puffy shirt out of mothballs," White Buffalo said. "I want a picture."

Sophia snuggled next to Michael on the sofa and swirled her drink. "Grandfather? There is something I need to ask that's preying on my mind."

"Oh?" Darius said.

"I simply have to know something, Grandfather. It has nothing to do with Gaston doing a reading for me, but I do think my mind would be more at ease if you could answer a question for me?"

"Why, of course, my dear. What is it?"

"This is such a large plantation – back in the day, were

slaves used to work the fields?"

Darius paused. He took a sip of his Glenmorangie Cellar 13 before he answered. "Well, my dear, I knew the conversation would eventually come to the subject of slavery, but I didn't think we would talk about it tonight. I have to admit, I am a bit taken off-guard by your question, because the answer is not a simple yes or no, but I will be happy to assuage your concerns."

"You are all now undoubtedly familiar with the renowned MacPhaidin Preamble," Gaston said, "as my beloved brother wades neck-deep into uncomfortable waters."

"There is so much more to southern history than slavery," Darius said, tossing a sigh at Gaston, "so I will give you a bit of background of Louisiana, and of your family, to help you weave everything into perspective..."

CHAPTER TWO

Darius lit his pipe and leaned back in his chair. "It is logical to assume this property, as large as it is, would have held slaves. Historically, many large agricultural plantations used slave labor, but some did not. In fact, some of the smaller plantations and farms used no slave labor at all. At the time of the Civil War, this plantation was about one-fifth the size that it is today. The original crops harvested in this part of the South were indigo, rice, and sugarcane."

"Why indigo?" Sophia asked.

"Indigo was highly sought after in France and Spain for the production of bright blue, violet, and purple dyes. Tobacco was a secondary cash crop. In the 1600's and 1700's, there were very few if any black Africans in Louisiana. White indentured servants were contracted for labor here long before slavery arrived."

"Indentured servants? I honestly don't know what they were," Sophia said.

"Indentured servitude was a form of cheap labor," Darius said. "After the settlement of Jamestown, European men and women, seeking a life in the New World, contracted to work for a designated period of years in exchange for transportation across the Atlantic, and for food, shelter, and clothing when they arrived. Many

Mayflower passengers were indentured, some of whom are your direct ancestors, by the way."

"I have Mayflower ancestors?"

"Indeed," Darius said.

With that revelation, something arose just out of reach in the back of Sophia's mind regarding her dreams of Jocelyn Brewster Davis.

"It might also interest you to know," Gaston said, "in the 1750's, the Acadians, descendents of French immigrants, who lived in the maritime provinces of Canada - now Nova Scotia, New Brunswick, and Maine - were expelled by the British due to tension mounting between New France and the British colonies. The British demanded that they adopt Protestantism, and when they refused, the British government burned villages, seized properties, and expelled Acadians to areas between New York and the West Indies.

"Over 5,000 Acadians sailed from New York to New Orleans between 1764 and 1776. They settled in Vacherie - the Acadian Coast or La Côte des Acadeins - on the right bank of the Mississippi. Many were indentured servants here in New Orleans and in the West Indies. The word Arcadia is Greek, meaning *place of peace*. It symbolizes the peace found when fears, insecurities, and trials are released."

"Well then, that's the new definition for me," Sophia said, "since that is what I'm about these days."

"Yes. The Acadians called themselves Cadians," Darius said, "who are now known as Cajuns, two of whom are your uncle Gaston, and your grandmother Lianne."

"I thought you were Creole," Sophia said.

"I am both," Gaston said. "Creoles can be a mix of African, Caribbean, French, Spanish, and Indian heritages. I also descend from Acadian bloodlines."

"In other words, you're American - a mishmash of the world, like most of us," Michael said.

"Indeed! Let us raise our glasses to Americans," Gaston said.

All but one raised their glasses. "To Americans!"

White Buffalo grumbled and deliberately cleared his throat. "Aren't you forgetting someone?" he said.

"Oh my, yes," Darius said, as Sophia and Michael embarrassedly laughed.

Gaston raised his glass to White Buffalo. "To the only *real* American in the room, I bow in reverence."

"As you should," White Buffalo said, raising his empty glass. "Garçon, another Tornado Twist, please."

Gaston complied, bowing several times as he backed away from White Buffalo.

"This is really interesting," Sophia said as she settled back into her seat. "Imagine, I've lived almost half my life not knowing I have such fascinating ancestors."

"In 1619," Darius said, "Dutch traders seized a Spanish slave ship and brought 20 African slaves to Jamestown and sold them as indentured servants to work in the Virginia tobacco fields. There were no Colonial slavery laws yet in effect, albeit slavery existed throughout the world. Any Africans thereafter, laboring as indentured servants, worked off their contracts to obtain their freedom like any other laborer who was indentured. However, by 1660, most every colony established slave laws. Thus, African slavery began in the British Colonies, with

Africans considered as chattel slaves, bought, sold, traded, or inherited as personal property."

"How horrible," Sophia said.

"Yes, it was an atrocious act upon humanity," Gaston said.

"Isn't it true that enforced slave labor was not in full force in the South until the 18th century?" Michael asked.

"In 1790, African slavery existed primarily in the colonies for the farming of tobacco," Darius said. "In this part of the Deep South, there was virtually no slavery. The extent of African slavery did not take hold here until the 1800's. Up to that time, European indentured servants made up the majority of the work force in Louisiana. After we came into statehood, following the Louisiana Purchase in 1803, plantations began to grow more profitable crops, like cotton and sugarcane. Millions of acres turned to cotton production because of the invention of the cotton gin in 1793. Subsequently, greater work forces were in demand for faster production.

"Up to that time, indentured Europeans worked the indigo fields, but they were smaller people and not physically powerful enough to manage the grueling work of the cotton industry. That is when African slavery took hold, for the American South was then the chief cotton region of the world, making cotton an extremely financially viable commodity. Thus, African slavery became the backbone of Southern financial interests."

"The first steamboat arrived in 1812, turning New Orleans into the second largest port in America," Gaston said. "Steam-powered mills followed, increasing the production and processing of sugarcane, and subsequently increasing the demand for more laborers."

"Here in the South, plantation owners could not afford to lose their labor force," Darius said. "Their indentured servants would eventually earn their freedom and some could possibly obtain 25 acres of land, corn, and other sundry items. Retraining new indentured servants took time and resources. Some died from disease contracted on the long, arduous transport across the Atlantic, or from maladies here in the New World, for which they had no immunity. Owners decided that they were too costly, even though the price of an indentured servant was no more than £7 every seven years, whereas the price of a slave was £50. Contrary to popular belief, the majority of the African slave trade did not come directly out of Africa, but from the West Indies, where they were transported from Africa.

"In the 1860's, New Orleans was the fourth largest city in the U.S., and the largest city in the South," Darius said, "with over 50% of Louisiana's population being African slaves. By 1860, there were four million African slaves in the United States - 333,000 in Louisiana.

"At the time of the Civil War, this was a moderately-sized sugar plantation. Sophia, if you remember me telling you, your ancestral grandparents, Alannah and her husband, Connor, were the proprietors of the Hibernia Hotel. They inherited the plantation from Alannah's parents, Maeve and Liam, who built this house in the 1830's after emigrating from Ireland during the Great Potato Famine."

Michael looked up at the portrait of Maeve. "They were quite enterprising people, weren't they?"

"Extraordinarily hard-working," Darius said, "and it was not long before they were well established here in New Orleans. During the war, the 68-room Hibernia Hotel became a hospital for Confederate soldiers. At the same time, Alannah and Connor put themselves at great risk by secretly rendering aid to some of the more seriously wounded Union soldiers, most who were not yet adults. Both Alannah and Connor had family in the North, some of them Union soldiers. They knew the Union men served out of honor and obligation, as did the Confederates. For Alannah and Connor, the only real difference between the two was an attitudinal line of perception that divided the South from the North."

"They would have been considered traitors had they been discovered - a hanging offense," White Buffalo said.

"Indeed," Darius said. "They risked everything to aid the Union soldiers. For a short time during the war, Connor arranged a place of safety for their wounded in an old abandoned barn behind the hotel. There was an entrance on the backside near the woods, not visible to neighboring homesteads. Union physicians brought the men to a well-enough state of health for eventual transportation in the dark of the night to other places of medical refuge until they could return to their homes in the North.

"This property was only one of a handful of plantations throughout the entire South that remained untouched by the Union Army during the Civil War," Darius said. "Most ended up plundered and burned to the ground. The Union Army spared this house because of Alannah and Connor's demonstration of mercy and compassion toward their wounded, but they were not entirely safe from harm, through no fault of the Union troops.

"At that time, Alannah was well into her ninth month of pregnancy. Most women gave birth at home under the care of a midwife, but Alannah was in great need of a physician. Connor rode ten miles into the city and back again by horse and buggy to fetch the doctor, bringing him back just in time for the birth of their daughter, Fiona. In spite of the care of both the midwife and doctor, the extreme strain of the breech birth resulted in Alannah's death."

"It's such a shame," Sophia said. "They were doing so much for others, but no one could save her."

"Life is sometimes unfair, but that little baby girl arrived on her feet and stood tall for the remainder of her time here on earth," Darius said. "Brokenhearted, Connor remained a widower for the remainder of his days, raising Fiona alone. Your life echoes theirs, Sophia." Darius thought of Patrick's unselfish sacrifice in raising Sophia, orphaned at such a young age. "Fiona grew up here, on the plantation, where three subsequent generations continued. Rich in the history that made up the American South, this house itself tells a story of the strong lineage of your family."

"Which begs an answer to my question, Grandfather," Sophia said.

Darius smiled as he tamped out the remains of his pipe in an ashtray. "Sophia, in the same way as Maeve and Liam before them, Alannah and Connor chose to use neither indentured servants, nor African slaves for their labor force to work their crops on the plantation, or for their employees in the hotel."

"And here all the time I thought the entire South used slaves," Sophia said.

"You are not alone," Darius said. "Slavery gave the South a bad name, quite richly deserved, but many of us never used slave labor. Many of my ancestral grandparents' employees came to America originally as indentured servants. During the terms of their indenture, the laborers honed their skills to perfection. By the time Alannah and Connor hired them, they were skilled housekeepers, butlers, gardeners, blacksmiths, cooks, bakers, farmers, and field hands.

"As it was for Maeve and Liam, both Alannah and Connor descended from Irish, Scots, and English, who served as indentured servants as early as the mid-1500's in England, in the English colonies throughout most of the 1600's, and on the island colonies of the West Indies for a good portion of the 1700's. Once they left Britain or Europe, very little news about their welfare made it back to their homeland."

"So, they were not heard from again, I take it?" Sophia said.

"That's right," Darius said. "Because of their family history with the indentured system, Maeve and Liam decided long before they arrived in America that in both their business and personal lives, they would not participate in any form of forced or slave labor. They paid each of their plantation laborers and hotel staff fair wages for a good day's work. For some workers on the plantation, as well as those who served the house, room and board was a part of their pay. They were respectfully treated, and lived in well-built housing.

"Unlike indentured laborers, their employees married and had families if they so desired. Although the hotel and plantation initially made less of an annual profit, both of the businesses steadily flourished in ways that eventually led to greater financial prosperity. Because of their business practices, they not only earned the respect and honor of their employees, but also of their growing number of patrons. Alannah and Connor followed the same principles as her parents, Maeve and Liam, which eventually paid off over time.

"This property was small in comparison to many of the plantations back in the day," Darius continued, "but over the years, subsequent generations acquired neighboring lands, eventually increasing the size of the plantation to one of substantial means as it is today."

Sophia poured herself a bit more to drink and then sat back down next to Michael on the sofa. "Tell me more about the conditions of indentured servants. I didn't know they worked without pay."

"The British colonies established the labor system of indentured servitude in the early 1600's," Darius said, "many years before the colonies implemented African slavery. Colonists in the New World had greater need to manage their agricultural settlements and trades than they had people to tend them. In fact, from 1773 to 1776, ninety-six percent of the immigrants in the lower colonies were indentured servants from England, whereas just under two percent of English immigrants in New England were indentured.

"In Virginia, young men and women were brought over from Europe, primarily from Britain and Germany. In both Virginia and Maryland, for each laborer brought across the Atlantic, the master obtained fifty acres of land, dramatically increasing land holdings and resulting in massive tobacco plantations that developed into today's still-thriving tobacco industry.

"Oliver Cromwell, who later served as Lord Protector of the Commonwealth of England, Scotland, and Ireland, wanted to rid Britain of its Catholics almost to the point of genocide," Darius said. "In the 1600's, he added to the colonies' need for skilled workers by sending them 30,000 Irish prisoners from Britain."

"Some of them undoubtedly *my* ancestors," Michael said.

"Yes, I would not be surprised," Darius said with a laugh. "Cromwell also sent Scots, who were Catholic, along with Quakers and religious refugees - all of them for indenture. Also from the British Colonies, 25,000 indentured Native Americans worked in the plantations in the West Indies from the early 1600's until the Revolutionary War. This was the Colonists' means to rid their properties of the original inhabitants."

"The colonization of America was the downfall for all Native Americans," White Buffalo said.

"Indeed," Darius said. "They did not have a chance against the Europeans. I have to say there actually *were* some benefits of the indenture system, which did help enhance the economy of the colonies and increase ethnic diversity in the U.S.

"Most of those who were indentured came from Britain for the cost of their ship's passage. When their new owner paid the fee, they gave the laborer a set of clothes and room and board to work in the fields or in the business trade until their contract expired, which took from five to seven years on the average. Most were young men from the ages of fifteen to twenty-five. They were required to be unmarried and without dependents before they began their voyage.

"England, at the time, was in a depressed economy, and many skilled laborers were without work," Darius continued. "Moving to the British Colonies offered an answer to their problems. In their minds, they would work hard for years, many times for sixteen-hour days and sometimes longer, with the dream of eventually realizing their freedom. To them, this was their only opportunity to break away from a life of oppression. An entire shipping industry began with the transport of indentured servants from England.

"When Maeve and Liam came over from Ireland, they were among many people on the ship who were laborers intended for indenture," Darius said. "If you remember their story, Sophia, a cotton ship took its load to Liverpool, and upon returning to America, it picked up hundreds of people fleeing Ireland during the Great Potato Famine. Some voluntarily came with their passage paid across the Atlantic Ocean. They had no idea who would buy their indenture, or how they would serve their master for the following five to seven years. For many children in England, their fathers sold them off to the colonies, hoping for a better life than what they were able to provide. Others saw the opportunity to unburden themselves of rearing a family of many children."

"Those poor children," Sophia said, "abandoned by their parents in such a frightful way, and then forced into hard labor for years on end. How horrible!"

"Yes, it is incredulous to think that this country was built on the backs of young indentured servants and slaves," Darius said. "In some cases, a ship's captain paid the fare for each person's passage. On average, the cost of the fare was from five to seven pounds, about $1000 in today's American dollar, equaling four to five years of work in England. The captain sold their contracts once he was on shore.

"The journey across the sea was grueling. For seven

weeks, what little water they *did* drink was stagnant. The overly-salted food caused horrible mouth sores and dehydration, making it even more difficult to eat the poor rations. They lived in putrid, unsanitary conditions in the hull of the ship with no fresh air, which caused diseases such as dysentery. Many didn't even survive the journey.

"Upon reaching the British Colonies, the captain posted the names of those who *did* survive with each laborer's sex, age, and skills. Their contracts were sold to a new owner or master, which stated that during their indenture there were many limitations restricting them from marriage and childbearing for women. A good portion of them lived in squalor."

"Wasn't it called 'white slavery,'" Michael said, "or, the 'Irish slave trade,' because the environments in which they lived were typically no different from the conditions of African slavery?"

"Correct," Darius said. "Most worked in the fields 16 hours a day. Food rations were just enough to keep up their strength. Living conditions for field laborers were oftentimes run-down shacks with little to keep them warm in the winter months, and household servants' quarters were not fit for poverty-stricken folk."

"Some of the women were victims of rape," Gaston said, "forced to have sex with their masters, while others worked in the flesh trade as prostitutes. Many of the youngest and strongest women became breeding wenches, used to mate with African men their masters referred to as 'bucks' - thus creating generations of slaves and free labor for their masters. Mulatto, mixed-race children, came at a premium value in the slave trade."

Darius agreed. "If an indentured woman became pregnant, not forced to be used as one of the breeding wenches, she suffered severe punishment and was oftentimes tortured while her indenture extended into several more years added to her contract. Her children were, by English law, considered slaves and therefore indentured for 30 years, or sometimes for life. Even though the mother might work off her contract, she remained with her children, never to realize her freedom. Many women took drastic measures of abortion to avoid pregnancy. Some mothers suffered the guilt and shame of taking their children's lives so their children would not suffer growing up to live in the same conditions."

"I cannot imagine the horrible decisions they had to make," Sophia said. "What a life they must have lived, and how terribly sad - they endured such tremendous sorrow."

Michael and Gaston shifted in their seats, clearly uncomfortable. White Buffalo sat perfectly still, for he personally knew of the punishments that came to one, not of their choosing, who lived in conditions against his will.

"If their indenture was not sold off to another contract holder or master," Darius said, "and if the laborer did not break any laws, after five to seven years, she or he would be free to begin their life, liberated from their master's tyranny. According to their contract, some laborers earned 'freedom dues,' which was pre-arranged. With the generosity of their masters, they would receive some or all of 25 acres of land, barrels of corn to sustain them for up to one year, a gun, or a new set of clothes. Some masters fulfilled the laborer's contract with only the clothes on his or her back, yet the individual was free to start life again as a farmer or free-laborer.

"One-half to two-thirds of the white immigrants who

came to the Americas from 1609 to 1819 were indentured servants. Before 1660, those who completed their indenture were likely to rise to a comfortable status in society as skilled farmers and craftsmen. Later, the indentured formed a lower class in the colonies. Unable to obtain better parcels of land, because landowners already owned the choicest properties, they had little alternative but to move west into the Appalachians throughout the South, which included the Blue Ridge Mountains, the Smoky Mountains, and the Alleghenies, where the land was not as fertile for farming. The remaining Indian populations thrived there, forced from their homeland along the East Coast, thus making those areas unsafe for the recently freed people of indenture. Some settled to the north in the Catskills and Adirondacks in New York.

"If an indentured contract was sold off to another master, the laborer would be forced to work another five to seven years under their new contract, by which they had no say or control," Darius said. "Many were sold from one master to another, never realizing their freedom. Only forty percent of those who survived the ship's passage lived long enough to complete the stipulations of their contract. The majority of indentured servants never realized their freedom, living as an indentured laborer, in white slavery, for the remainder of their days."

"Yes, conditions of their indenture were what we would consider as tragically poor, here in the United States," Gaston said. "Those indentured in the West Indies suffered even worse conditions and a high death rate at the hand of rough labor conditions and great cruelty of the plantation owners. After Britain abolished slavery in 1833, the plantation owners of the West Indies brought indentured servants from India until it was prohibited in 1917."

Sophia shook her head. "And here we generally learn that slavery ended in the 19th century."

"It exists today," Michael said. "By another name perhaps, but I've seen it in my travels."

"Without a doubt," Gaston said. "While it is supposedly illegal in every country now, the modern slave trade is a billion-dollar industry. India, China, Pakistan – the list goes on. Even here, as our friend Algernon Gillette can attest, there is an alarming rate of human trafficking that exists in the U.S."

Sophia felt a sudden chill at the thought of Gillette. "I'm almost sorry I asked about this."

Darius smiled and reached for her hand. "Because we are able to learn from hindsight, history teaches us about what doesn't work, and what *not* to do. If we learn from our history, both personally and collectively, we make better choices. Maeve, Liam, Alannah, Connor, and on down the line, lived lives of integrity, balancing their material needs with what they knew was the right thing to do for their fellow humans. And so, at last, my dear, my long-winded narrative leads me to state again - no, we were never slave owners."

"Whew!" Sophia broke the tension with a long, dramatic sweep of her brow. "Thank you for taking the time to explain all of this. But honestly, I feel so much better knowing more about the history of this plantation. My concern was about African slavery, but I had no idea of the horror of those who were indentured. Slavery in all forms has been a way of life throughout history - so sad, but true."

"Yes, the right thing is not always easy, but in the long run it pays off with dividends, as it did for Maeve and Liam, on down the family line," Darius said.

"Well," White Buffalo said with resolve. "That was fun." Everyone laughed. "I believe I shall drown my depression in a bowl of extra creamy butter brickle ice cream. Anyone care to join me?"

"Right with ya, Uncle," Michael said. He put his arm around his elder and helped him to his feet. White Buffalo braced himself with his cane in his right hand, and held Michael's arm with his left as they walked out of the library.

Gaston joined them. "I believe I saw a jar of hot fudge in there."

Darius smiled and touched Sophia's cheek. "What we've been talking about tonight emphasizes the importance of our mission in Apeiros. If what we do comes from love, then good will be the eventual result..."

Everyone left the library with another burden released that night. Truly, they were all Acadians - left in a place of peace, released from fear and misunderstanding. Gaston drove to his countryside home, knowing his offering to serve Sophia as a medium would reveal many answers for her. Michael felt as if his good friends were helping Sophia come to an understanding of the family history. And White Buffalo felt truly at peace. When it was time for him to go, he knew he had nothing left unsettled. His friends and colleagues would continue his legacy, as all was well.

CHAPTER
Three

The next evening at dusk, they drove to Gaston's shop, *Nothing but Tyme*. Gaston had prepared the draped back room, arranging the round table and five chairs for everyone's comfort. Clusters of lit white candles, strategically placed on shelves and on top of several tall corner fern stands, left a mystic ambiance in the small room. A French Baroque crystal chandelier hung from the ceiling, radiating soft light over the table.

In the center of the table sat a five-inch-diameter Morganite sphere on a polished brass stand. Soft candlelight reflected the orb's energy with stunning peachy-pink tones, revealing the tremendous beauty of the gemstone. As Sophia entered the shop, the gentle bell attached to the top of the door announced her arrival, and her amethyst pendant began to ring out in high frequency. Michael, White Buffalo, and Darius followed her to the back room, where Gaston awaited.

"I was hoping to see you wear the turban - and where is the black eyeliner?" Sophia said.

"My dear, I wore the puffiest-sleeved shirt I own," Gaston said, shrugging his shoulders. "I will say, occasionally I used to wear one gold hoop earring to catch the eye of the ladies."

"How bohemian of you," Sophia said with a giggle.

They all laughed, but Sophia was a bit nervous as they settled into their seats around the table. Quietly they sat, hearing no sound at all, save the amethyst ringing out in resonance with the crystal ball. Sophia held the amethyst in her hand until the tone faded into the solitude. Stillness welcomed in the spirits, awaiting their invitation to enter the atmosphere, while her amethyst gently vibrated.

"I imagine you might be wondering why I have a crystal ball at the center of the table," Gaston said as he sat back in his chair.

"Isn't it typical for a medium to use a crystal ball?" Michael asked.

"In a Vincent Price movie, perhaps," Gaston said, "but I purposely chose this pink sphere for Sophia because of its properties. It is made of solid Morganite, the pink variety of beryl. The aquamarine in each of our rings is the blue variety. Morganite was discovered around 1910 on Madagascar. J. P. Morgan, the famous American financier, was also interested in metaphysics and mineralogy. He was a passionate gem collector, and Morganite was named after him."

The mention of J.P. Morgan caused Sophia to perk, knowing a bit about him in relation to *Titanic*. "The color is exquisite," she said.

"I'm glad it appeals to you, my dear," Gaston said. "The peach-pink color represents the innocent heart - the state of humility where we best align with the Universe. We are essentially saying that we do not have all the answers, and our hearts are open to receive what will graciously support us. When we are in a state of allowing, we permit the power and essence of the Divine to enter our lives, enabling us to achieve accomplishments unlike anything we could otherwise imagine.

"The metaphysical qualities of Morganite align with our work in Apeiros. Morganite is a crystal of Divine Love, which attunes to the heart and the Heart Chakra, as a stone of healing that resonates at the same frequency of compassion, inspiring one to realize the higher purpose of any challenge. The stone helps cleanse stress and anxiety by releasing ancient wounds. From there, we move forward in peace and confidence. Therefore, Morganite is an ideal stone for the equitability in all associations. It is the stone of lawyers, believe it or not."

"They're not the kind of stones I would think lawyers have," Michael said. He got a smile from the group.

"This stone is excellent for 'scrying'," Gaston said, "a divination tool to discover deep, hidden meaning or future events - which is what you do, Sophia, when you look into the water-filled golden bowl. From there, you enter an altered state of consciousness, which enables you to see into other dimensions. We shall do this tonight."

Sophia smiled and took a deep breath. "I'm with you, Uncle."

"I specifically chose this gemstone," Gaston said, "because Morganite is supportive to girls who do not have a mother. Since you were a small girl when you witnessed your mother's life taken from her, a part of you remains there in the memory of that traumatic incident. Tonight, we are here to support you and the little girl in you who never had your mother to help you grow into your gifts as a healer. We shall fill that gap, and I am certain that both Elizabeth and Tommy are ready and willing to help you do just that. Do you have any questions before we begin?"

"I have no questions now. I may later, but I am ready," Sophia said.

"One of the loveliest qualities of this particular Morganite sphere is its asterism chatoyancy - meaning the cat's eye effect - or star effect," Gaston said. "If it is all right with you, Sophia, may I have your amethyst pendant? The light created by the pendant's resonance with the Morganite will activate the stone."

She pulled the chain over her head and handed it to Gaston. He then attached the golden chain to the crystal chandelier so the amethyst pendant hung directly over the sphere. Immediately, the radiant star shined brightly within the Morganite, its resonant beauty and power mesmerizing to all who sat around the table.

"Love fills this room, yes?" Gaston asked.

"Yes!" everyone said in unison.

"It is so beautiful!" Sophia said, staring into the sphere's mystical star-effect.

"If you will please join hands," Gaston said. "We gather here in support of Sophia, who we greatly love, as we welcome Elizabeth and Tommy. We open up to lift the veils between worlds and allow our hearts to connect." Gaston closed his eyes and breathed in deeply, then pursed his lips and blew out slowly onto the sphere. The candles flickered as the energy in the room clearly shifted. When he opened his eyes, he noticed the look on everyone's faces.

Elizabeth and Tommy were in the room. Sophia gasped at seeing first her mother, and then her father. She stared at their mystical entities, which appeared at the center of the table like that of a hologram. What they all witnessed, with eyes that observed beyond the veils of time and space, was the essence of a beautiful woman and a handsome man.

"Welcome Elizabeth and Tommy," Gaston said.

"My heart is full, knowing you are here tonight," Elizabeth said. They all felt their hearts meld in a love so deep, its power was difficult to fathom. Tommy's energy dimmed while Elizabeth spoke.

"Would anyone like to say anything?" Gaston asked.

"Yes," Darius began, tears flowing down his cheeks. He let go of the others' hands to reach into his pocket for his handkerchief.

"Sophia and White Buffalo," Gaston whispered, "please hold each other's hands behind Darius, to keep him inside the circle."

"Oh, my blessed daughter, I have missed you so," Darius said. "When you left this earth, a light went out in me, which only reignited when Sophia came into my life last year. She is so much like you. It is as if she carries your light - your kind heart and concern for others. She possesses the same fire that you did." He smiled, remembering how Sophia stood up to him when he told her the truth of her parents' deaths. "Whomever she meets, she sees God in them, for she sees deep into their souls. What a blessing she is to me."

Sophia smiled and rubbed her grandfather's back, and then reached out to grasp White Buffalo's hand again.

"My father, you have not changed," Elizabeth said. "It is just like you to speak of another and not of yourself. The goodness of your humble heart has kept you young. Thank you for holding the door open for Sophia to discover her roots. Blessed are our ancestors, who did wondrous works in their day, by which their high vibrations extend into the eternal good. Their hearts continue to affect the world. But most of all, thank you for being my father and bringing me into the world. You and mother raised me well. You were a good father to me. The profound love I felt for you as I grew to being a woman still remains in my heart, for all that you taught me extends into the journeying of my soul. The lives we touch extend far beyond our imagining.

"Father, your wise enterprises have supported millions, helping them to live lives of purpose. With the best of intentions, whatever decisions you make affect the field, whether or not they appear to succeed to fruition or not. You may not see the fruit of all the seeds that you plant, but know that every one yields in some form or another.

"The love I continue to feel for you extends to levels that never cease, for love has no boundaries and no limits. I am with you always. You are ever in my heart, my beloved father, and I am here for you at only a thought's distance away."

"Grandpa Napayshni is here, Granddaughter," White Buffalo said. "All the Ancestors are here as we sit on the back of Grandmother Earth, who smiles at this union tonight. All sing songs of celebration."

"Thank you, Tatanka Ska - White Buffalo," Elizabeth said, turning her ethereal gaze to him. "Yes, I see the Ancestors dancing, and hear their song in celebration of *you* and all that you bring to the world. You must know the good you do not only affects yourself, but also touches all beings eternally and forever. You are a beacon of light for your people - for all people. The Ancestors are smiling. Your heart's work has blessed the Lakota, all Native Americans, and Earth's indigenous people, for you are a spiritual warrior. Being a warrior is a profound calling, as one who is in service to the people, to all beings of the animal kingdom, and to Grandmother Earth. The everlasting effect of your passion reaches out to beings everywhere, for they too feel your heart. The vibration of your slightest thought extends to the farthest stars in the most distant galaxies, and to worlds without end, reaching dimensions beyond your imagining. That is why it is so important to bring love into every thought, word, and deed, for love heals all the wounded places and immediately fills the gaps of misunderstanding. We do not need to know how, but to trust that love is always at work, and this you do so well."

White Buffalo turned his eyes downward in reverence and humility of her words.

"Elizabeth, I am Michael, Sophia's husband. It is a great privilege to be here tonight."

"I know who you are, Michael. I knew of you when you were Yiorgos, and when you were Michel du Nostradame. I have known you as the essence of Yeshua - as the Christ energy."

Michael's eyes widened at her references.

"We are all those who have gone on before us," Elizabeth said. "That is what oneness is - we truly share the essence of everyone and everything that has ever been and will ever be. We are ever becoming a greater version of our soul's evolution, which is God, the Divine, as us."

Michael tried to make sense of what she said. "I am stunned. If I were an incarnation of Nostradamus and, most certainly the Christ energy of Yeshua, would I not have achieved greater success in the here and now?"

"That is your human ego thinking that the material realm is a reflection of your accomplishments," Elizabeth said. "The lives you touch are your legacy, as is every moment. What you do, and the energy in which you do it, affects all there is within the Infinite Field, right now, in this present moment of eternality. And what makes you think what you do has no lasting effect in the world? You are one of a relative few who unearth pieces of history to reveal the mystery of how ancient peoples accomplished such wonders. The heart's passion is a forward motion that generates far more than a person's body of work. It is an extension of the creative force - that of God, the Creator, of Love itself, through the magnificence of you.

"Here is something that very few people comprehend. If what you do is what you love, then nothing can be a greater contribution to the world. Your being happy and content affects everything and everyone. Where you live in the mountains, everything around you thrives - the trees, the plant life, the animals - even the river gurgles a bit more in your presence. Do not the heavens shine their brilliance when you sit in its wonder and glory each night?"

"It is true," Michael said, "we are greatly blessed, but all *that* occurs because of Sophia."

"Yes, she possesses a light that enraptures everyone and everything around her," Elizabeth said. "She is the bearer of the life force. She carries the light of the world, and *you* are this as well, in your own way. Do you not see how you dance between the raindrops? Life regenerates when you enter any space. Peace resides with your every step, and of course, your humor keeps everything light. You are a blessing to the world, Michael. You may not recognize your power, but your soul is on fire, and it knows exactly what to do. Trust that greater part of yourself."

Michael sat still, which was a rarity. For once, he had no smart comeback. Elizabeth's vision deeply touched him.

The entire time, Sophia gently smiled and focused on

the asterism of the Morganite, seeing the spirit of her mother, and hearing her every word. Elizabeth's message was not just for the individual to whom she spoke, but what she said were universal truths for everyone who had ears to hear.

"Gaston, my uncle, how wonderful you are!" Elizabeth said. "Like your father before you, you have kept these pieces of antiquity that contain the spirits of generations gone by. Through these antiques, each spirit awaits the next person to welcome their energy into their homes and hearts. In this way, their spirits may carry forward. A portion of the souls of each artisan who made these pieces is contained in the wood, in the weave of the fabrics, and within each cut in the crystal. A silver cast candlestick carries the essence of that artist into the lives of the next person who will appreciate their gift of artistry. In that, the soul of a long-gone artisan lives on and carries forward. In addition, the owners of these pieces left their essence and a bit of their life force behind. Remember, that which the heart generates is never lost. You are a 'soul provider' for all these beautiful pieces to be preserved for the world. Thank you, Gaston, for opening up, once again, to your gift of divination, for you made this all possible tonight. Because of you, we bridge the dimensions."

"It is truly my honor, Elizabeth," Gaston said.

"The angels, entities, and the Ancestors ask you to assist them in connecting with the many people on the Earth plane who are in need," Elizabeth said. "The answers to their questions are ever available, and we are here to help. All one has to do is think of us and ask for assistance, for it is one of the ways we serve humanity. However, someone must facilitate those who do not believe in the simplicity of things, so they can understand that it is just that effortless. Gaston, will you answer the call to be an intercessory again?"

"How can I possibly say no?" Gaston said. "Yes, of course I will."

"Very well," Elizabeth said. "We thank you for parting the veils, so we can all meet again."

She turned to Sophia. "Sophia, my daughter, you have much to say."

"I have so many questions that have rattled around my mind since I was small," Sophia said.

"I am only a thought away. If more questions arise, I am here whenever you desire," Elizabeth said. "You need not be concerned."

"When my father and I spent weekends at the cabin, I felt a presence that I was certain was you. I now know it *was* you, because the same feelings have returned here tonight."

"Yes, my darling, I have been with you all along."

"Why is it I could feel your presence at its best, there at the cabin?"

"The cabin is sacred to you," Elizabeth said. "There, by the water's edge when you are in nature, you tap in more deeply. It is there where you listen instead of only hearing, where you observe instead of simply noticing. In the peaceful quiet of the wind, the rain, and as you sit by the continuous flow of the river, you become one with nature's surroundings, where you open up to greater dimensional fields. You came into the world this way, Sophia."

"In the safe company of all these people I love most," Sophia said, "I have to ask about what happened the day you were killed. I am so sorry, Mama." Tears welled up as she felt her heart burst with feelings kept hidden since she was three years old. Michael and Darius clasped their hands behind her while she used Gaston's handkerchief to wipe her eyes.

"My darling daughter, my death, as you call it, was not your fault," Elizabeth said.

"Yes, but if I had not tried to defend you - if I had stayed in the kitchen with Ada..."

"You were not the cause," Elizabeth said. "You already know this, Sophia. When we cross that threshold, we choose to remain or to return to our life within our earthly body. Our soul makes that choice, not our human mind. If it had been up to me, as your mother, I certainly would not have left. Even before Algernon hit me with the back of his hand, my soul had already left. My soul knew what to do. My body was there in the room, but I was not. Sadly, you had to witness him hit me, which resulted in me no longer living on earth. My soul was already gone when he struck me, and my body fell onto the hearth, hitting my head. I felt no pain, for I was no longer there. My body appeared to suffer, but *I* did not.

"And let me further say, every choice we make is either life-giving or not," Elizabeth said. "Each choice creates energy, in and of itself. So, consider your choices carefully, Sophia, and ask yourself, is this a life-giving choice - one that is good for everyone involved? If the answer is yes, then proceed ahead. Whatever we think, say, and do, affects everything around us - and I say 'us' because my dimension affects your field of awareness, as yours affects mine.

"My soul finished its contract for that lifetime. Its job

was complete," Elizabeth said. "My soul no longer needed Elizabeth's body to do its work on Earth. Nothing you did caused my death. What occurred were circumstances in the making for a long time.

"When I left, my absence created a series of events, causing everyone involved to make choices for their best good, which is what happens when transitions occur. What is left is a void that fills with new activities - where creation takes hold. Patrick took you to Colorado, where you could both start over. My father, Darius, dug into his work in the hotel industry and built an even greater enterprise, serving people throughout the world. Uncle Gaston developed his skill even more so, as a spiritual medium, in the attempt to reach out to Tommy and me, and as a result, he served thousands of people with his gift. White Buffalo grew closer to the family, and became an even greater teacher, which eventually led you to one of his lectures. You all extended your ancient lifetimes of wisdom into your work in the Order of Apeiros.

"And you, Sophia. Look at who you have become! Aren't you a glorious woman! Have you ever given thought to that day's events, being that your defense of me ignited the Infinite Power within you, in the form of a small three-year-old girl? Could it be that you would not be who you are today, had that not happened?

"Oftentimes, we as humans wonder why we suffer so, especially as children when there is no right of choice and no defense. Every occurrence that tests us brings us back to center, and sometimes those events happen to teach us how *not* to be in the world. They ignite our passion so we make better choices how not to participate in such negativity, and then we catapult into our greatness *because* of the gift that challenge brought to us. This is how Patrick did so well as the father who raised you, because of how he lived his life. Both your father, Tommy, and I came to Patrick in his dreams to assist him in raising you to be a good woman. Here you are - the Divine Feminine - as an example of the feminine spirit in all its glory and fortitude, and it all began on that momentous day."

Sophia looked into the eyes of her mother and finally felt the heartfelt connection that she sensed when she was a child. A tear welled in her eye. "I wish I could put my arms around you."

"Every time you embrace your grandfather, I embrace you. Each time you feel the deep love for Michael, you love me. Whatever you do, I feel. How you go about your day affects the field - the atmosphere - the literal and figurative Universe - like a pebble thrown into a still pond that creates tiny ripples that move out until they reach a barrier, which absorbs the energy and transforms it into something greater. This is the greatest lesson humanity is here to learn - we come to Earth so we can again remember who we have always been, which is Love - the love of God. We are all one, and in that, our only calling is to first love ourselves wholly so we can graciously extend that love to all.

"You must remember, when you sat at Patrick's side the night he died, he felt your calm energy, and it allowed a part of him to leave. Whereas your disquiet - your anxious attention - pulled him back to you like a magnate. He could not see you, but he felt your presence, your love, your concern. Whether we realize it or not, that is how deeply connected we are in this web of life. We are a part of an intertwining network of oneness."

"May I reach out to him," Sophia said, "to express my

gratitude, now, in the light of my awareness of who he really is?"

"He knows you are grateful. Patrick knows how the love you have for him remains," Elizabeth said, "and sometime soon you can ask for him to meet with you. Tonight, he stands aside for Tommy, your birth father."

"I miss all of you so dearly," Sophia said, fighting the tears.

"Sophia, we are all energy in motion," Elizabeth said. "I am no longer housed in a body, but that does not mean I do not exist. I am here to bring comfort to you and to those who call on me. I am simply here to love. All beings are called to do just that, whether we are yet aware of it or not. When humanity follows through, using love as the vehicle, seeming miracles occur. Then we are not operating from the limited ego-mind, but are in union with Mother/Father/God - the Infinite Intelligence. This is your task, Sophia."

"Since my near-death experience," Sophia said, "I've known that love is all I am here to teach and become. Many times I fail, but I do know my life has changed for the better, simply by making more conscious choices to live in love."

"It is like any other skill," Elizabeth said. "As a toddler, you learned to walk because you no longer wanted to crawl. You learned to master language because only you could understand the toddler gibberish you spoke. Within the Order of Apeiros, all of you are called to a higher level to hold the Earth and all her inhabitants in Love. Over time, you will choose only love, because you will find there is no other way to be. It will happen naturally, as you discover that anything not aligned with love is no longer in service to your evolutionary development.

"It's quite simple, really. By loving yourself wholly, you more easily teach others by example. Recognize that you are a blessed creation of the Divine. You are the only one who has ever been, and will ever be, the individualized expression of God, as you. See yourself as the Divine Feminine, being your best self by developing your gifts and talents, and then sharing them with the world. All your decisions and actions will come from the oneness generated from Love's embrace. It is that feeling of joy, the elegance of grace - the compassionate heart that reverberates to every person, every being, and every circumstance - seeing and experiencing each one as God's expression of their Divine self."

Everyone nodded in agreement as tears welled in their eyes.

"Sophia, I love you from the depths of my soul," Elizabeth said. "I am always here for you. And let me finally say to you all - each tear you shed is the expression of the Divine reaching out to hundreds of souls. Allow the vulnerability of your heartfelt tears to easily flow, for Love's grace is in the center of each teardrop."

Sophia beamed, feeling not only her mother's love, but also Love's presence beyond comprehension.

"If you invite me into your lives again, we will go further," Elizabeth said. "Thank you for allowing me to come to you. The essence of me is the joy I feel for you! Remember, I am only a thought away. My love is ever with you, as I feel your love for me."

"Thank you for being here, Elizabeth," Gaston said. "We will happily welcome you again."

Tommy's essence became vivid as Elizabeth's energy dimmed.

"Tommy, I cannot express how happy we are to see you after all this time," Gaston said.

"Thank you, Uncle," Tommy said in a lovely Irish brogue. "Since time does not exist in this dimension, it truly seems like yesterday since I last saw you. You and Darius look well. The years have been kind to you."

"Tommy, we have missed you so," Darius said. "The impact on our lives at the loss of both you and my daughter, and with Patrick taking Sophia so quickly to Colorado, profoundly affected and dramatically changed us all. I must say to you now, what I never told you when you were here - I loved you like a son, and that love has never faded. You were a good provider and husband for my daughter, and a loving father to young Sophia. You left here all too soon."

"Thank you, Darius. It was truly an honor to be a part of your family. Never did you treat me as a lowly shipman who was less than you were. Instead, you treated me as your equal. The love and respect you gave me remains with me, as mine does for you too. This is how you live life, Darius. You give the best of yourself to those you serve, to those you love, and life gives back to you, among other things, your youthful ways," Tommy said.

He re-directed his gaze. "White Buffalo, I remember well what you taught me: 'Your demons are your problem. You must look at them, move through them, and let them go.' As humans, we can dim our light because we place so much of our concentration on what keeps us small, but when we face our challenges and move beyond what we perceive as our barriers, our darkness is released to reveal what has always been present - our radiant light. I see the shining radiance of you, White Buffalo - the eternal light that exists in all of us."

"Yes, I can see more clearly into your world now," White Buffalo said. "The veils are thin. The Ancestors come to me in my dreams, and they pave the way for my return home."

Everyone became a bit misty at the thought of White Buffalo moving on.

Sophia sat in wide-eyed awe, seeing her birth father, for she had no memory of him. He was tall and dark - extremely handsome - with nearly black hair and hazel eyes. Until then, she did not realize that she had inherited her father's eyes.

"Sophia, you are a beauty," Tommy said. "You look so much like your mother. My only regret is that I was not your father for long, save for the first three years of your life. Patrick raised you well."

"He was a good father to me," Sophia said. She hesitated. "Forgive me, but I'm at a loss for words, but I do recognize you from my dreams."

"That is how I could be in your life," Tommy said. "It was my way of being a favorable presence for you."

"I often thought you were my guardian angel, along with Grandpa Napayshni. Now that I know who you are, I will use my golden bowl to see into your life, for I have much to learn about you."

"You will find you already know a great deal more than you realize," Tommy said.

"I have to ask - in fact, I think we would all like to know how you died."

"As you know, I went to the city jail, where Algernon Gillette was locked up in the infirmary, recovering from the amputation of his leg. I was blind with rage and grief. If I could, I would have beaten down the walls to get to him for taking your mother's life. You were staying with your grandmother and grandfather at the plantation, so I knew you were safe, but I didn't know what to do. I went back to work to occupy myself, in the attempt to find some way to get a grip on my anger and despair.

"That day, we were unloading cargo. I was on the dock, standing safely where I should have been. The crane operator swung a load dangerously overhead, purposely releasing the net and dropping it on me. I instantly knew who was responsible the moment I left this world. In the timeless dimension, we know everything there is to know, because there are no earthly filters that block our awareness.

"The crane operator was one of Gillette's henchmen. I was so grief-stricken that I didn't give it a thought to keep my distance from him, but eventually Gillette would have sought me out. I had a reputation for my fighting Irish ways. Where I grew up, we took care of our own and got even with those who did us wrong. I was young and foolish, and Gillette knew I would find a way to get to him.

"If it helps you, I can tell you I didn't suffer. It was my spirit that knew who was responsible for my death. As a man, I didn't know what hit me. It happened so quickly. Before my spirit left, I saw you asleep, cradled in Darius' arms, and knew you would be alright. Then, I visited Patrick that night in his dreams and told him to come to New Orleans and take you to a place where you would be safe."

"Yes, Patrick called us the next day and said he was coming straight away," Darius said. "We didn't know what he had in mind until he arrived. He did not stay for your double funeral, because he wanted no one other than family to know he was in town. When he arrived, he said he would take Sophia and raise her as his own daughter. As difficult as it was, we knew it was the right thing to do, for her sake. Patrick drove Sophia back to Colorado late that same night. It was as if a hurricane came and whisked her away from us."

"Sophia, my little girl," Tommy said, "I am so sorry I left you. I hope you hold forgiveness for me in your heart."

Sophia finally broke down in tears. "Of course," she said. "You did what any husband and father would do. Please stay for now, but I have to stop for a few minutes. I need to go outside to catch my breath."

"Of course," Gaston said. "Take your time."

Sophia broke away from the circle to get some fresh air outside. While she was gone, Tommy turned to Michael. "Michael, I am grateful to know that Sophia has you in her life. The support of many strong people has been her saving grace throughout her soul's journey, especially in this lifetime. I know you are soon going to Ireland, where I grew up. There, you will find my family. They're good people - the salt of the Earth. Take Sophia to meet them. They will tell her some tales about me in my early days. It will help her fill the gaps."

"How will I know them?" Michael said.

"You already do. Follow your heart, for it is leading you the right direction. Trust yourself."

Sophia returned to the shop, rubbing her arms, having caught a chill outside in the autumn evening. She rejoined the circle and Tommy's loving eyes. "I don't know if I should call you father or Tommy. Patrick was the father I knew."

"It doesn't matter. Tommy is fine, if that is more comfortable for you. I will continue to be here for you, Sophia. Just ask for my support and I will answer. Soon, you will know me as well as you know yourself. Our being here with you tonight may take some time to settle in for all of you. We will come to you whenever you call out to us. We are always here, and please know how deeply you are loved."

At that point, the images of Elizabeth and Tommy were equally vivid. They smiled as they faded into the ethers.

"Goodbye," Sophia said, reaching out for them as she broke into tears again. The candles flickered, and a breeze passed through the room when their energies dispersed.

Gaston rose from the table and removed the amethyst pendant from the chandelier. The chain was almost too hot to handle as he gave it to Sophia, but she did not seem to notice its heat.

They all sat in silence, absorbing their connection with Elizabeth and Tommy.

Sophia held onto the amethyst and rubbed the etchings on its surface. For a brief moment, she slipped into another dimension on the upper east coast at a time when the British were beginning to settle into the New World.

The vision disappeared just as quickly, and Sophia looked back into the room. *Tomorrow,* she thought, *tomorrow I will end this.* She had but one more task to complete this journey so she could begin the next. Tomorrow, she would confront Algernon Gillette...

CHAPTER
Four

Sophia arose before dawn. As she had done so many times during her visits to the plantation, she went out onto the second story veranda to welcome the sunrise. On that particular morning, she felt a great deal of anxiety. Because of what the day might bring, she took extra time to meditate, centering herself by trusting in Divine guidance, rather than dropping into her defenseless wounded heart. What made this morning different from any other was the assurance of her parents' presence, which she now knew was always with her.

At breakfast, Michael and Darius noticed Sophia's uneasiness.

"Maybe we should go after we return from Ireland," she said. "I think I'll be more prepared if we wait."

"We can do that," Michael said, "but the whole time we're there, you'll be preoccupied. You don't want to have this on your mind for the next month, do you?"

"No, but I've carried this for 40 years. Another few weeks won't hurt," Sophia said.

"Okay, sit back, close your eyes, and relax. Try to envision what I'm about to tell you. Okay?" Sophia nodded. "Imagine you're standing in line at the airport, waiting to check your luggage. On your back is a fully loaded backpack. You're carrying a big duffle bag in your right hand, with that big-ass purse of yours hanging off your right shoulder. Already, the weight is more than you can handle. On your left shoulder is your computer case, while tucked under your left arm is your makeup case, and all the time in your left hand you're holding your heavy carryon. All this baggage is stuck to you because you refuse to let go. They were heavy to begin with, but as you hold on, the weight becomes far more burdensome. After awhile, you can think of nothing but all that baggage, wishing there was a way to release your load. Does this remotely sound familiar - like something you'd tell me if the roles were reversed?"

Sophia sighed. "I guess you're right."

"No, don't guess, honey," Michael said. "What you're carrying is 40 years of baggage. Today, you can let some of that go and leave it where it belongs. Now, open your eyes and tell me what you're going to do."

Sophia smiled at her wise husband. "Okay, let's go to Angola."

Darius smiled at how well they worked together. He felt such pride for both of them...

They had to arrive by 11:30 a.m., making a two and one-half hour drive northwest of New Orleans to reach the Louisiana State Penitentiary, otherwise known as The Farm. Angola Prison was the largest maximum security prison in the United States, with a land mass the size of Manhattan. Surrounded on three sides by the Mississippi River, Angola was once a large plantation so named for the African country from where most of the slaves who worked there came. From the looks of the massive, bleak institution, Sophia surmised the energy had not changed much since the days of slavery. The prisoners worked the fields, growing wheat, corn, and four million pounds of vegetable crops per year. Two thousand head of cattle roamed the property.

Sophia was nervous, which was not her typical emotional state. It was important to Michael to accompany her inside the prison, for if she ever needed someone to support her, it was that day. Before they entered the gates, she centered herself, remembering her new calling of Love for the coming year. She thought it appropriate to put her concentration on compassion and mercy for everyone involved. Sophia said a silent prayer to think, speak, and be filled with the energy of God during her visit with Algernon Gillette. She needed all the help she could get.

Gillette was leery, for it was a long time since an unknown visitor came to call. Although he possessed considerable influence from the inside over the years, his power, along with the number of visitors who came to call, had greatly eroded with time. With the recent arrest of his son and his crew, coupled with his severely deteriorating health, Gillette was now alone save an occasional cursory visit from the prison chaplain. He could not imagine who requested a visit, nor did he care, but seeing anybody was better than sitting in his cell. From his bunk, he reluctantly stood up, lifting his prosthetic leg to the floor when the guard came to escort him to the visitor area.

Sophia and Michael instantly felt as if they passed into an ominous underworld the moment they set foot inside the prison walls. The gritty feel and acrid smell of the institution gave off an iniquitous sense of the downward spiral's palpable darkness beyond anything of their familiarity. Once through the entrance, they passed through an ion scanner and metal detector, and then both were thoroughly patted down and Sophia's small handbag was searched for weapons and other contraband. They filled out the proper identification applications, and a large guard resembling a bear, hair and all, led them down several bright, sterile corridors and security checkpoints. Each door through which they passed automatically locked behind them with a hollow metallic clang.

They shared a common sense of despair permeating every inch of the place – even the air was stale and musty with odors unlike anything they smelled in the free world. Disembodied male voices, like malevolent ghosts, echoed seemingly through the walls that separated them from the prison netherworld. When they finally reached the visitation room, the guard opened the door for them to enter. Sophia paused and turned around to Michael.

"Okay, you know I need to do this by myself."

Michael nodded and rubbed her shoulders. "You can do this."

"I hope you understand that I must have the courage to face him alone. This is the last thing I must do so I can move on. This is between him and me."

"I get it," Michael said. "I'll just relax out here and throw up while I'm waiting."

The guard almost smiled and said, in a deep southern drawl, "She'll be safe in there, sir. Prisoners in this section ain't in direct contact with visitors. There's three-quarter-inch acrylic window between her and him, so he gets a mind to misbehave, he can't do much harm."

"He's an old man," Michael said, "how much could he do?"

"You'd be surprised," the guard said. "He may not get violent, but inmates in this unit can get purty disgustin' sometimes."

"Great," Michael said.

"Don't worry none. There's guards everywhere. Mrs. O'Hara, you get a mind to light out, I'll get you outta there in a wink. Mr. O'Hara, you can go in the waiting room next door if ya want – get yourself a soda, or the chicory ain't bad for bein' outta a machine."

"I'll hang out right here," Michael said. He took Sophia into his arms and whispered into her ear. "I am always here for you, my love."

The guard looked at Sophia. "A wild guess, you don't visit prison inmates often."

"There's a first time for everything," Sophia said, the tremble in her voice betraying her pasty smile.

"S'cuse me for sayin', but you two don't look like you belong here."

"Thanks," Michael said. "That's the nicest thing anybody's ever said to me."

The guard nodded and looked Sophia in the eye. "The inmates and, frankly, most of the people visiting them ain't exactly your kind of people, if you get where I'm driftin'. Now, ain't none of my business why you want to see Algernon Gillette, of all folks, but you 'oughta know he's an old O.C. don." Sophia blankly shrugged. "Sorry, that means organized crime boss. He was never wired for your world, even when he was free, and now he's what they call 'institutionalized' – a lifer."

"What's that?" Sophia said.

"He's been locked up for 40 years. In stir that long, he

can't relate to nothin' or nobody from the outside world. On top of that, his health is bad – his mind's been slippin' for a spell now. Like I said, ain't none of my business why you're here, but if you're open to a word of advice?"

"Are you kidding?" Sophia said. "Please..."

"I seen victims come in here lookin' for a chance to vent, maybe settle an old score, maybe desperate for answers. Some folks think maybe just standin' upright might give 'em some satisfaction. I seen a lot of broken hearts come and go. I'm just sayin' don't get your hopes up that you'll walk out of here feelin' any better than you do right now."

"I understand," Sophia said. "Thank you."

The guard led her into the room and sat her in a small cubicle facing the acrylic window. On the other side was a simple metal chair. While waiting for the guards to bring Gillette into view, Sophia looked around the stark, cold room and the long row of cubicles where other visitors conversed with inmates. Several guards patrolled both sides of the glass, and video cameras mounted on both sides of the window monitored every movement. The whole scenario was intimidating, and Sophia instantly felt an urge to run.

"You alright there?" the guard softly said.

Sophia turned and smiled. "I think so. I just want to get this over with."

"Need anything, you just give me a holler."

"I appreciate you holding my hand. What is your name?"

"Jonny Lee Dupree. I know - it rhymes."

She smiled as the guard wandered away. The next few

moments felt like hours while Sophia pensively waited. Then, she perked to movement on the other side of the glass as a guard brought in a very old, emaciated, grey-haired man who limped into Sophia's view. Her heart nearly jumped out of her chest as the guard unlocked Gillette's handcuffs and the old man clumsily sat in the chair. His bright orange jumpsuit bore a series of numbers on his left pocket; on the right the name GILLETTE was stenciled in black. The old man's eyes suspiciously crawled over Sophia as he slowly laid his arms on the table and interlocked his bony fingers.

He bore a nasty scar across the bridge of his nose, and the gruesome incident of her mother's murder suddenly flashed through Sophia's mind. She saw her mother swing a silver candleholder and smash it into Gillette's face. Sophia jerked her head, forcing herself back into the present moment. She sat still while she took in the energy of the man who murdered her mother, seeing a black aura around him. She remembered him to be very tall, but to a three-year-old, everyone was practically a giant. He appeared about 5' 6", if that big, and he was not much more than a skeleton covered with an obvious yellow pallor to his skin. According to what Darius said, Gillette was robust years ago. Clearly, the old man before her was quite ill. The dark image of a murderous giant peeled away to this pathetic troll sitting before Sophia's eyes.

Gillette stared at her with watery gray eyes filled with years of a hard and iniquitous life. His Southern-Cajun accented voice was scratchy and weak. She slowly picked up the phone and put it to her ear, as he did the same. "What are you, some kinda social worker? What do you want?"

Despite Gillette's sad, almost pitiable countenance, Sophia felt something boil up that had simmered from the moment, weeks before, when she decided to confront this man. She simply stared at him. "You don't know who I am?"

Gillette furrowed his brow and squinted, taken slightly aback by her wicked stare. "Should I?"

"We met once before, long ago. My name is Sophia MacPhaidin Delacroix Delaney Gallagher O'Hara."

Gillette tried to chuckle, "Whoo, that's a passel a names. There more than one of you in there?"

"I use all of the names of my family, Mr. Gillette, because for 40 years, I had no family at all. You took them from me."

"Wha?" Gillette said. "Now, how could I a-done that? I been a monkey in this cage for-"

"40 years," Sophia said. "Yeah, I know."

Gillette squirmed in the chair. "Who you say you are?"

"Maybe this will refresh your memory." Sophia reached into her handbag and unfolded a crumpled piece of paper. She angrily slammed it against the glass for Gillette to read:

Little girl

I done paid the price of 40 years in prison. I want you to know I ain't sorry never have been cause she asked for it. Nobody hits me and nobody puts a hex on me neither. I been waiting a long time to find you so you better watch your back cause if I don't get you my boy will.

Gillette could barely focus his eyes on the note, but he instantly recognized his shaky handwriting. He flinched back in his chair. "You that witchy gal!"

"I'm the daughter of Elizabeth MacPhaidin Gallagher," Sophia said with acid burning in her throat. "I was in the room while I watched you kill my mother."

"You that little girl that cursed me. You put a hex on me!"

"Oh, please," Sophia said. She leaned close to the glass and looked at him with daggers in her eyes. "How dare you accuse me of anything, when it's *you* who brought this misery into your own life! I did *nothing* to you. I was only three years old! You murdered my mother right before my eyes. You struck her down to her death after you tried to rape her, and then you tried to kidnap me!"

Gillette looked like a caged rat. He weakly tried to wave her off. "You – I ain't done nothin'-"

"Then you ordered the death of my father. I was an orphan at the age of three because of you. You robbed me of my family. You took my precious mother and father – their lives and their legacy – *my* legacy!"

Gillette drifted into a haze and slowly shook his head. "I just – don't know what you's talkin'-"

"You do too know! So for once in your life stop lying. I saw the look on your face when you saw this note. Wasn't it enough that you terrorized my family 40 years ago? Now you send your son to threaten me?" Sophia stopped and furrowed her brow. "Look at you," she whispered. "Some big mafia crime boss you are. You're nothing but a doddering, pathetic shell."

His eyes slowly wobbled up to her. "You," he said, "you cursed me to hell."

"Oh, you didn't need my help. You created your own hell," Sophia said with a vehemence she did not realize still remained. Her hold on the phone increased to a white-knuckled grip. "I had *nothing* to do with that. *You* cursed your own life with the evil that befalls you, because your choices produced your own world of darkness."

She leaned back from the table, removed the phone from her ear, shifted in her seat, and took a deep breath to gather her thoughts as she looked away from him. In a moment, she picked up the phone again and said, "I came here for a reason, Mr. Gillette. Maybe you understand me, or maybe you don't, but you're going to hear me out. All my life, I didn't even remember what happened that day until a month ago when my grandfather told me how you violently killed my mother. I blocked it from my memory all those years. It was only last night when I found out how you had my father killed."

"How'd you find out about that?" Gillette asked.

"I have my ways, Mr. Gillette. Believe me, I have my ways."

He cowered back in his chair as if her words were a threat.

"It doesn't feel good, does it?" Sophia said.

Gillette nervously rubbed his chin with his left hand, his eyes never leaving the table. "I don't know nothin' 'bout that – feelin' good."

"No, I don't suppose you do." Sophia felt her energy shift away from the blind rage that consumed her just moments ago. "Well, I honestly don't care how you feel, and that saddens me, because I live my life with the intention of caring deeply for everyone. But I'm here today, not only to come face-to-face with you, but also to tell you that I forgive you."

Gillette suspiciously looked at her.

"That's right," Sophia said. "What you did was horrible, and I've lived with heaviness in my heart for 40 years, even though I had no conscious recollection of what you did until now. But I refuse to live with revulsion in my heart. Today, I let it go. I came here to forgive you, because you are the only one left for me to settle with. I am doing this for me, so I can move on. I am not going to waste any more energy on you, because frankly, Algernon, you just aren't worth it."

She put the phone down and stood with resolve and turned to leave. Jonny Lee noticed and slowly walked toward her. "You finished?" he said.

"Yes," Sophia said with a smile. "Absolutely." She walked toward the metal door.

"I'm sorry!" Gillette called out, tapping on the glass with the receiver.

She hesitated and turned around and looked at the old man, who still sat in the cubicle, waiting for her to return to her side of the window. She slowly walked back and sat down, and without saying a word, she placed the phone to her ear.

Gillette leaned forward in his chair and rested his arms on the table in front of him. He gave a heavy sigh as his face softened. "I regret what I done. You didn't have a mama or a daddy all those years because of me. If I could change what I done, I would. Your mama was good to me. She was a fine woman. Your daddy was only doing what any man would do. He didn't deserve his fate."

Sophia looked at Jonny Lee, who backed away to allow them privacy. She leaned forward on the small table top, indicating that she was willing to listen.

"You got no reason to forgive me," Gillette said, never looking away from the table. "Yet, you do it anyway. God ain't gonna be as kind to me as you."

"God's got nothing to do with this. As for me, I accept your apology." Somehow, his sincere apology lifted the veils of darkness that clouded Sophia's heart. "I believe we both can be at peace with this now. From what I know of my parents, this is what they would have wanted."

He began to tear up. "I'm *real* sick. The cancer's eatin' my liver and workin' its way to my brain. The prison doctors say I don't have long."

Sophia showed little emotion. "That must be difficult for you."

"I ain't fishin' for pity," Gillette said. "Just sayin' that, for the first time maybe ever, your forgiveness brings me peace."

Sophia afforded a slight smile of kindness. "You might like to know that I have several friends who recently joined me in a prayer for you."

Algernon quizzically shook his head. "You prayed for me?"

"About three weeks ago. They're very compassionate, powerful, and loving people."

Gillette finally held Sophia's gaze for the first time. "It was 'bout that time I had a dream. A purty blonde woman come to me - she looked kinda like you. She looked jus' like 'lizbeth. She took a hold of my hand, and we walked to the edge of a cliff where we saw mountains across the valley below. They was covered with snow. It was gettin' dark, turnin' to sunset. The sky was many shades of pink and the mountains were purple and white - the purtyest sight I ever seen. I was wearin' a long, heavy coat. It was stuck to me. I couldn't take it off, no matta how I tried. I wore that coat day and night, and even in the summer. Every year, that coat jus' got heavier, like somebody glued it to me with heavy rocks in the pockets or somethin'."

Sophia thought of Michael's guided vision of her holding onto all that heavy baggage.

"But that evening at sundown," Gillette said, now almost in a trance, "it was this woman that helped me take it off, 'cause she was the only one that could do it. All that weight I carried all those years was gone. She helped me heave it over the edge of the cliff. We walked away, and it started to rain. We was in a field of wildflowers, with a tall forest nearby. It smelled so good. It jus' kept rainin', jus' washin' away all that nastiness. I was free again. You know, the funniest part of that dream was this tiny black cat, not much bigger than a kitten, followed us the whole time. From the cliff to the field of flowers, that little cat jus' came right along."

Sophia sat and listened as a smile came over her face. She believed Digit had showed up in his dream as Bastet, the Egyptian Cat Goddess. She recalled how her beloved cat sat on the table the night they prayed for Algernon at the cabin, but instead of the deliverer of wrath to the evil, Digit was the giver of blessings to the good, for Algernon let go of his evil ways.

The old man sitting across from her seemed different from when he first entered the room – or, she wondered, *am I the one who changed?*

"I purciate you comin' to see me, Miss."

Sophia sighed. "Mr. Gillette, I have to say, I'm glad I did. I wish you peace. Godspeed, Algernon." She placed her hand on the window. He met her hand with his. She looked deeply into his eyes, smiled slightly, and hung up the phone. She stood and met Jonny Lee at the door.

Before she walked out, she started to turn and look back but then stopped herself. She looked at Jonny Lee. She smiled at the big guard and walked out the door...

The next morning, Sophia and Michael shared a good southern breakfast with Darius and White Buffalo, their choice of omelets made to their liking, with Louisiana sweet potato pancakes, biscuits, and country sausage gravy. They just finished their coffee when Gaston burst through the front door with an urgent look on his face.

"Good lord, Gaston," Darius said. "You come in here like it's a raid. What could possibly be the matter?"

"Did you see the morning news?"

"What is it?"

"You are *not* going to believe it. Algernon Gillette died last night."

Sophia sat back in her seat, stunned. In another moment, she burst into tears. Michael gathered her into his arms as she sobbed, finally releasing so much of the pain she held onto for most of her life. Finally, it was over. It was as if the spell lifted. Sophia could now move on with nothing to hold her back.

Chapter Five

Sophia and Michael flew into Shannon Airport to begin their honeymoon trek through Ireland, home to so many of their ancestors. To more easily take in all the sights, and not worry about driving on the other side of the road, Michael hired a car and driver he found on an Irish travel web site to take them on a grand tour of the island. They checked into the airport hotel to get a good night's rest and acclimate to the time change, and the next morning they hauled their luggage to the lobby in search of their host. In a moment, they spotted a tall, distinguished gentleman holding a sign that read 'O'Hara.'

"Welcome to Ireland! Pádraig O'Hannigan, at your service!" He spoke in a beautifully lyrical Irish brogue.

"It's so nice to finally meet you," Sophia said. "After all our e-mails, I feel like I already know you. I'm Sophia, and this is my husband, Michael. You know, my father's name was Patrick."

They shook hands. "He must have been a charming, intelligent, and frightfully handsome man."

Sophia and Michael laughed. "He was!" Sophia said. "Modest, too!"

"Yes, I could not have much more of an Irish name," Pádraig said. "Of course, Michael O'Hara rates right up there, you know. And Sophia - isn't that Greek?"

"The man knows his stuff," Michael said.

"I do. The first rule of tour guiding is a thorough understanding of onomastics."

Sophia's eyes shifted to Michael. "What's that?"

Michael shrugged. "Beats me. I don't speak Irish."

"The science of pullin' your leg," Pádraig said with a wink. He grabbed a baggage cart and surveyed the mountain of luggage. "Well now, isn't this a wee bit terrifyin'."

"My wife doesn't exactly travel light," Michael said.

"It's not so bad now, is it?" Pádraig said, straining to hoist Sophia's main suitcase onto the cart.

"It all depends on your opinion of a herniated disc," Michael said.

"I can't travel without all of my essentials," Sophia said.

Michael pitched in and helped stack suitcases, and Pádraig then led them out to the parking lot, where they loaded into his new SUV.

"I'll sit in back, so you can have some leg room," Sophia said.

"No argument," Michael said. He helped Sophia into the back, and then opened the front door on the passenger's side and found the driver's side. "Whoa, wrong country."

"Happens every time," Pádraig said with a laugh.

"I knew I'd do that sooner or later," Michael said, embarrassed. He walked around to the other side and climbed in, and they set off on the first leg of their journey.

"So tell us a little about yourself, Pádraig," Sophia said.

"Well, I'll give you a brief personal history, so as not to get you racked with the explanation. I am a recent widower."

"I'm sorry," Sophia said. "When did you lose your wife?"

"It's been almost two years now, God rest her sweet soul."

"So sorry for your loss," Sophia said.

"Thank you, Miss."

When he called her 'Miss,' Sophia smiled and thought, *Pádraig will be the perfect tour guide for us.*

"Soon after my wife died, I retired from my teaching job in Shannon and sold the home my lovely Molly and I shared. I decided to start over. I love meeting new people, and more than that, I love Ireland and her rich history. So, I bought meself this brand new people carrier touring car so I could do what I love, touring wonderful people I meet from around the world throughout Ireland and Northern Ireland."

"Let me guess," Michael said, "you taught history."

"You're absolutely correct!" Pádraig said.

"I'm an archeologist and an architect. We're all going to get along quite well."

"Well isn't that grand! Now, one price fits all, so I'm at your service for as long as you desire. As we discussed through our correspondence, I'll take ya to some of the finer points of interest about the island, and make suggestions for room and board as we progress. I have your bucket list to be certain ya see everythin' ya came to see."

"We'll be here a couple of weeks, but we may add to that if something comes up," Michael said.

"That works for me. If your plans change, I'm flexible," Pádraig said.

"Wonderful!" Sophia said. "We'd like to drive on

through Shannon and County Clare for now, because we'll see that on our way back at the end of our trip."

"Not a problem! Today, according to your list of must-see sights, I'll take you north to Kylemore Abbey by way of Galway. We'll then swing 'round to Cong, where you have placed a star by its name."

"Oh, yes!" Sophia said. "I can't visit Ireland without seeing where-"

"The Quiet Man was filmed," Pádraig and Michael said in unison. Everyone laughed.

"That's right!" Sophia said. "I guess I'm not the first to request it?"

"And not the last," Pádraig said. "It's a popular American choice, and I am more than pleased to accommodate." He looked over at Michael with a wink. "By that time of afternoon, you'll likely want to find a nice inn for the night. I know of one in that lovely Irish village I'm certain you'll fancy."

"Wonderful! By the way, we're both Irish," Sophia said proudly.

"Well, with the name of O'Hara, I assume you're not Japanese!"

"I told ya, honey," Michael said, "Pádraig doesn't miss a thing."

Pádraig laughed. "You know, most Americans who come here say they're Irish."

"I guess you're right," Michael said. "In America, being of Irish descent is something we celebrate - even those who aren't Irish. We throw parties on St. Patrick's Day, when over here it's a religious holiday, isn't it?"

"It was - years ago," Pádraig said. "More recently,

though, we've caught up with you on the celebratory side. Sadly, these days it's more just a reason for folks to get langered."

"How's that?" Michael said.

"Langered," Pádraig said. "You know – bolloxed – fluthered."

Michael shook his head. "I don't know what that means."

"Sure you do, mate - when you celebrate too much – you know – gee-eyed – hammered."

"Oh!" Michael said. "Drunk!"

"Well, that's one way of puttin' it. We're not gonna have to stop and get an Irish-English dictionary, are we?"

Michael laughed. "Sorry, Pádraig, I'm having a little trouble following your accent!"

"*My* accent? Mate, I'm strugglin' with *yours!*"

Everyone laughed. "The funny thing is," Sophia said, "we're all speaking English."

"That's it," Pádraig said, "the Brits are always to blame! Ah, well, it's nothing to get scundered about – before long we'll be conversin' like we know what we're sayin'."

"I think we're going to get along famously," Sophia said. "How fortunate we are to have found you, Pádraig!"

He blushed and tipped his cap as he drove out of the airport.

Charming! She thought. Already, she was conjuring up in her mind which of her single women friends she could convince to come over to Ireland to meet this charismatic gent. Perhaps they could host an Apeiros gathering there. *Ananta and Yesinia are still single. Shoshana and Irina are involved, but you never know... and Anja could probably use another husband...*

Sophia looked out at the charming villages on the outskirts of Shannon. She rubbed the sleep from her eyes. "I'm feeling a bit disoriented, either from the lingering jet lag, or the fact that we're driving on the left side of the road in a car that has the steering wheel on the right. Pádraig, I've always wondered, why is that?"

"You might as well get used to her barrage of questions," Michael said. "Sophia's mind never stops."

"Not at all," Pádraig said. "Questions make my job more interesting. It keeps me on my toes. Legend has it that we drive on the left because originally, to protect yourself while riding on horseback in battle, you would keep your right hand free to use your sword - like a jousting match from the days of old."

"What if you were left-handed?" Michael asked.

"You'd ride your horse backwards," Pádraig said…

They drove the scenic route, 80 kilometers north along the coastline, to their first stop in Galway City.

"Michael's O'Hara ancestors are from this area," Sophia said.

"Are they now?" Pádraig said.

"Unfortunately, that's about all I know," Michael said. "My dad said his great-grandfather was born here and came to America during the potato famine. I have his name, and his father's name, but nothing else."

"I'm acquainted with several O'Haras, but none live here in Galway," Pádraig said.

"I'm sure it's a common name," Michael said. "I wouldn't

know where to begin to look for my relatives. I don't have any information at all on my mother's side, other than her people were from Ballymurphy, County Carlow."

"That would be due east of here," Pádraig said.

"This is a beautiful town," Sophia said as she snapped pictures from the rear window.

"Do ya want me to stop for your photos?"

"No, not here," Sophia said. "I'll give a yell if I want to get out."

Pádraig drove slowly through Eyre Square and the adjacent shopping areas, past quaint shops, restaurants, and pubs lining the narrow one-way streets.

"Galway is renowned for its enchanting street performers of varied arts," Pádraig said, "with jugglers, poets, dancers, magicians, and musicians of every kind. As you walk along the streets, you hear music spill out from the taverns with the lively harmonies of fiddle, harp, guitar, tin whistle, and uilleann pipes. You might hear the melodious blend of *a cappella*, or it could be ballads of a heartbreaking tale, leaving you wrapped in sorrow and woe."

"These roads are so narrow. I'm glad you're driving," Michael said.

"I see why everyone has compact cars here," Sophia said.

They continued on, northwest along the Irish coastline. The charming countryside held red-door cottages with thatched roofs, and miles of stone walls intersecting properties along the rolling hillsides. Water was everywhere. Rivers and lakes shimmered like millions of sparkling diamonds, as if each sunlit reflection was a mystical portal into a magical parallel world. Sophia thought the musical harmonies they heard in the Galway taverns were a metaphor for the blending of sights and scents of the Irish countryside. All seemed in perfect accord, synchronized in varied shades of green, and dotted by sheep and cattle amongst ancient ruins and country life.

Along the way, they visited Kylemore Abbey, a Benedictine monastery built as a private home in 1871 on the grounds of Kylemore Castle in Connemara, County Galway. Pádraig gave them some history as they walked the property.

"It took 100 men four years to complete this 40,000-square-foot granite lakeside home of 70 rooms for a wealthy English couple," Pádraig said. "The home had 33 bedrooms, four sitting rooms, a ballroom, billiard room, library, study, schoolroom, smoking room, gunroom, and many offices and servant quarters. On the property is also a Gothic cathedral with a family mausoleum and a walled Victorian garden amidst the 13,000-acre estate.

"It was sold to the Duke and Duchess of Manchester in 1909, and in 1920, the property was purchased by the Irish Benedictine Nuns, who fled Belgium during the First World War. The nuns turned it into a Catholic girls boarding school that operated until 2010. Presently, the nuns offer education and retreat opportunities, and the Benedictine community sustains the Abbey and surrounding gardens with local donations."

The trio enjoyed lunch at the Mitchell Cafe, named after the original owners of the property. Afterward, they walked through the Victorian Walled Garden and took photos of some of the estate, now reduced to 1000 acres.

The third leg of the day's journey took them 50 kilometers east to Cong, Mayo County, where Sophia could check off one of her Irish bucket list items. One of her favorite classic films was The Quiet Man, partially filmed in Cong. She wanted to drive through the small town, populated by nearly 200 people, and have a look at the film's several iconic locations.

Pádraig drove into the charming village and down Abbey Street, rounding the corner at Circular Road, where a small, thatch-roofed cottage stood.

"Oh, my gosh, there it is!" Sophia said.

"Faith and begorrah," Michael said. He looked at Pádraig for approval.

Pádraig solemnly shook his head. "I wouldn't say that in public, unless you're lookin' to get kicked and booted."

"Stop!" Sophia cried.

Pádraig slammed on the brakes. "What!"

"I have to get a picture!" She hopped out and clicked away.

"Jaysis, she put the heart crossways in me!" Pádraig said, holding his chest.

"You're aware of her camera obsession by now, right?" Michael said.

"Aye, but I wasn't prepared for the bloodcurdlin' holler."

"It'll happen again. Be alert for her sneeze, too. That will send you right through the windscreen," Michael said.

Sophia popped back into the car. "I just went to heaven! Isn't that the most charming thing you've ever seen?"

"Miss Sophia, that is White O'Morn cottage, which -"

Sophia interrupted, "In the movie was owned by Sean Thornton and his wife Mary Kate Danaher-Thornton, played by John Wayne and Maureen O'Hara."

"Did you get that, Michael?" Pádraig asked.

"Check," Michael said. "John Wayne, Maureen O'Hara, no relation."

"A native of Dublin, I might add," Sophia said. "Her real name was Maureen FitzSimons, and she changed her name to O'Hara because the shorter name fit better on movie marquees."

"Did you know that?" Pádraig asked Michael.

"No. I *do* know John Wayne's real name was Marion Robert Morrison. Try fitting *that* on a marquee."

"Go away out of that! John Wayne's real name was Marion?" Pádraig said.

"Why do you think he was so tough?"

"Age thirteen must've been a livin' hell for the lad."

"'Twas," Michael said.

"Boys?" Sophia said. "Pádraig, do you know where the character Will Danaher's home is?"

"Indeed I do," Pádraig said.

"And the Pat Cohan Bar?"

"Any Irishman worth his salt knows where *any* bar in Ireland is, lass."

"Now we're talkin'," Michael said in a sloppy Irish brogue. "I could go fer a pint of Guinness."

"Alright then," Pádraig said, "let's pull our socks up, shall we?"

"Michael," Sophia said. "You aren't going to talk like that for the next two weeks, are you?"

Pádraig said nothing.

They drove past the house that was used as the home of Will Danaher in the film, and this time Pádraig was prepared when Sophia hollered for him to stop for photos. The highlight of the day's tour came when Pádraig stopped at the famous Pat Cohan Bar. To their delight, Pádraig kept secret that he just happened to be a regular who was warmly greeted by everyone in the pub. He made introductions, and Michael and Sophia suddenly felt very at home.

Colin McPhee, the bartender, set three pints of Guinness in front of Michael, Sophia, and Pádraig. "So, from where in America do you hail?"

"Colorado," Michael said. "It's in the western part of the U.S."

"Ah, we all know about the Old West, having watched every bloody John Wayne picture ever made. Colorado has good skiing, doesn't it?"

"The best in the world," Michael said. "Do you ski, Colin?"

"We have gone skiing in Austria and Switzerland, when me wife and I spent a winter there a few years back. Do you live in the mountains?"

"Yes, as a matter of fact, we do," Sophia said. "We have a lovely home in a mountain valley with a river running not far from the front door."

"Sophia spent her summers there as a child," Michael said.

"Ah, sounds heavenly!"

"If you ever come to Colorado, you're welcome to stay with us," Sophia said.

"Now isn't that a lovely offer," Colin said. "Speaking of

which, since it's getting late in the day, do you have a place to stay tonight?"

"No, not yet," Michael said. "We noticed a bed and breakfast next to the White O'Morn cottage. Is that nice?"

"I know a better one - right upstairs," Colin said. "Why don't you and the missus and Pádraig have your supper, and then you can stay the night here. We have a couple of rooms for guests. We'd be delighted to have you."

"Well, that couldn't be better! Is that okay with you, Sophia?"

"Sounds great! Thanks so much! You know, I'm really hungry. What do you recommend?"

"Tonight, our special is shepherd's pie. Me wife makes the best one around."

"I can vouch for that," Pádraig said. "It's what I'll have."

Colin called out toward the kitchen. "Lily! Come out and meet our guests from Colorado."

A slightly-built woman emerged from the kitchen as she pushed back the stray black hairs that hung down around her face, her fair complexion peppered with freckles. "Welcome!" Lily said. "It's been a long time since we've entertained Americans from Colorado. I understand it's a beautiful state."

"We were just telling your husband," Sophia said, "if you ever come to Colorado, you are welcome to stay in our home."

"They live in the mountains," Colin said.

"Now that's a temptation," Lily said. "Colin, did you invite them to stay with us tonight?"

"I did just that, my dear."

"So what can I bring you for supper?" Lily asked.

They all glanced at each other. "Looks like shepherd's pie all around," Pádraig said, "and, Colin, how about another three pints of Gat all around."

"I'll get some homemade bread and butter," Lily said. "I just took the bread out of the oven."

"Well, I think the luck o' the Irish is with us tonight," Michael said.

"Oh? Are you Irish, like every other American?" Colin asked, laughing in his good-natured way.

"Hey, O'Hara was my father, and my mother was an O'Brien."

"Double cursed!" Pádraig said.

"And Sophia is a Delaney, MacPhaidin, Delacroix, and a host of others."

"We'll settle for Delaney then," Colin said.

"Gallagher," Sophia said. "Don't forget Gallagher."

"Oh, that's right," Michael said with a sly smile. "She is mostly a Gallagher."

"So we both are true Irish folk," Sophia said.

"Well then, that calls for a toast," Colin said. "To the Irish!"

"The Irish!" They all raised their glasses and took a drink, as a dozen other patrons looked up and joined in on the toast with a laugh.

When Lily brought their food to the table, Pádraig stood and said, "Sophia, I believe the time has come for a wee surprise, if you're game."

Sophia quizzically looked at Pádraig. "Surprise?"

Lily suddenly pulled a handkerchief from her sleeve

and raised it to her lips, tears welling in her eyes.

"What is this?" Sophia said. "Lily? What's the matter?"

"Sophia," Pádraig said, "it is truly my pleasure to introduce your Aunt Lily and Uncle Colin. Lily is Tommy Gallagher's sister!"

Sophia's eyes widened. "What? Really? How did you..." She looked at Michael and then at Pádraig, then at Lily and Colin.

Lily burst into tears and hugged Sophia, who clumsily hugged back in astonishment.

"Here comes the water works," Colin said, shaking his head.

Sophia continued to stutter. "You all knew. Did you – Michael?"

"Let's just say that Tommy had a way of letting me know," Michael said.

"Remember, we're Irish!" Lily said, still hugging. "We believe in spirits. Tommy came to you and told you about us, did he?"

"Well, he said to trust my heart and I would find you," Michael said. "I asked Sophia's grandfather if he knew where Tommy was born, and he said Tommy once mentioned County Mayo, but her grandfather couldn't remember what town. So when I began searching the Irish travel web sites for a tour guide, and I saw Pádraig's name and address in County Mayo, we got acquainted online and I asked if he knew any Gallaghers in County Mayo. Well, as they say, the rest is history."

"Pádraig, did you know my father?" Sophia said.

"As it happens, Lily, Colin, and I have been friends for decades. I grew up here. Since we were wee lads, Tommy and I were mates, and our friendship grew even more as the years passed. Tommy was a few years older than me, but I remember him well. All the birds had a crush on him - the handsome, dark Irishman that he was."

Lily finally came up for air. "Welcome to the family, my dear!"

Colin then gave her a warm embrace. "We wondered all these years about you – the poor little girl who lost her family. And look at you! So lovely!"

"I could scarcely contain myself when I first saw you," Lily said. "Pádraig and Michael and their silly surprises made me play along and not grab you up!"

"Ok, my turn, now!" Sophia joined in the tears. "In a year, I've discovered so many people from both sides of my family, when I grew up believing I had no family at all. This is a wonderful surprise!"

"Oh, you sweet girl! You're the spittin' image of your father, my beloved brother. And you have his eyes, God bless ya." Lily smothered Sophia again, and both cried more as Colin rolled his eyes over to Michael.

"You can tell they're related," Colin said.

"I only found out about Tommy just recently," Sophia said. "I didn't know about him, because my uncle, who raised me as his own, took me to Colorado right after my mother and Tommy died."

"God rest their souls," Lily said.

"Yes, Patrick, was it?" Colin said. "We met him once when he came here to Ireland. A good man, he was."

"Really! My father, Patrick, was here?"

"He was. Patrick came to Ireland shortly after his wife passed," Lily said. "He was searching for some of his Irish roots. Tommy told him to look us up, and he came and stayed for a few days. He toured through most of Ireland, as you are planning to do. For a time, Patrick wrote us regularly, I imagine until you came into his life. I would think that he was a good father to you, Sophia."

"He was the best, and now that I know more about him, he rates even higher on my list," Sophia said.

"Tommy thought the world of him," Lily said. "He certainly would have approved of him raising you."

"So I've been told," Sophia said. "But I so wish I could have known him."

"Just look in the mirror, lass," Colin said. "You're fair-haired and he was dark, but it's astonishin' how much you resemble him."

"Here, I have the family album for you to look through," Lily said. "There are many photos of Tommy as a child and young man, before he left for New Orleans. At the back, you will find a few photos of Tommy and your darling mother." Lily handed the thick photo album to Sophia.

"Why did he move to New Orleans? It's so beautiful here; I can't imagine anyone wanting to leave."

"The economy was depressed when we were growing up," Lily said. "For Colin and me, we have the bar, and because of its fame from The Quiet Man, we are never without business."

"Has the pub been in the family since the film was made?" Michael asked.

"No. Lily and I bought the place not long ago," Colin said. "We had an inn not far from here, but when we heard this place was for sale, we bought it straight away."

"As for Tommy, there was not much for him here," Lily said. "He worked as a longshoreman in Clew Bay for several years, with the desire to leave Ireland once he earned enough money for passage. Before we knew it, he set sail for America and settled in New Orleans. He was an adventurous sort, never with his feet planted firmly on the ground. That is, until he met your mother, Elizabeth. She turned his head, and never did he wander again. It's as if she put a spell on him."

"My mother was that kind of woman, from what I'm told. She evidently had a way about her that made a person feel as if they could do anything once they set their mind to it."

"Tommy sent us pictures of Elizabeth. She certainly was lovely. You look a lot like her, too. See, here are a few pictures of Tommy and her." Lily showed Sophia several snapshots.

Sophia's eyes welled up, for the first time seeing pictures of her mother and father together. "My, they were a beautiful couple, weren't they? Michael, come and see these."

"The women in your family are all so beautiful," Michael said. "No wonder we mere mortals become so enchanted by you."

"You're silly, but you can tell me that any time you want, my love," Sophia said. "Lily, would you mind if I take the album to our room tonight?"

"Why, of course not. And I will arrange to make prints so you may have an album of your own."

"Oh, Lily, that would be so wonderful."

"Now, go ahead and finish your meal. Colin, darlin',

why don't you help them with their bags and take them up to their rooms. I imagine they would like some quiet time to look through the album. We'll see you for breakfast in the morning. Get a good night's rest, now." They looked at each other, and again the tears came, followed by another round of hugging.

Colin sighed. "Well, c'mon, lad, let's get you squared away before we get wet."

Pádraig followed them out to the car. "I'll give you lads a hand, for you'll be knackered by all the bags the lass brought."

"Oh, I have so many questions," Sophia said to Lily as she finished her shepherd's pie. "You'll have to tell me everything in the morning."

"If you'd like, I can take you to the cottage where we grew up. It's just around the bend," Lily said.

"Oh, I would love that!"

Lily gave Sophia a final, gentle hug. "Goodnight, lass. May you have sweet dreams!"

The following morning, Sophia and Michael joined Pádraig, Colin, and Lily in the pub for breakfast.

"What can I get you, my dears?" Lily asked.

"Some coffee would be great to start off the day," Michael said. "A couple of eggs, toast, bacon, and potatoes sound good to me. How about you, Soph?"

"Make that two," she said.

"You're not fussy like some Americans that come through here," Colin said.

"I guess we've traveled enough to know better," Michael said.

Sophia still had her nose buried in the photo album, drinking up the images of her parents. When she was small, her father probably did not look much older than he did in some of these photos.

When Lily brought out the coffee, Sophia asked, "Do you know how my parents met?"

"From what I heard, your mother was down on the docks, ready to take a cruise on her then-boyfriend's family yacht. That young man evidently was quite wealthy, from an established old southern family. Tommy was working on the dock, and he got one look at Elizabeth and knew she was to be his girl. He pulled one of the crewmen away from her boyfriend's boat and paid him to take the day off. As an excuse, the crewman told his employer that he was not feeling well. Tommy just 'happened' to be in earshot and offered to take his place. Your father was a very confident, determined lad."

"I get that impression," Sophia said with a laugh.

"Well, Tommy took every chance he could get to talk to Elizabeth during their excursion that day," Lily continued. "He was such a charmer, that lad, and oh, how handsome he was, with that thick black hair, hazel eyes, and a golden tan. Oh, and what a smile he had - not a tooth out of place. No one could pass him by without taking a second look in his direction. Tommy gave her his telephone number, not really thinking she would ring him up, but to his surprise, a week later she did. He won her heart, and soon afterward, she dumped the rich lad for our Tommy. They were married six months later."

"What a beautiful story!" Sophia said with a wistful look in her eyes. "It is so romantic that it makes me think they could never be separated again - and so it goes."

"In the Irish Gaelic, their love was *síoraí* - eternal," Lily said.

"Síoraí - such a beautiful word," Sophia said.

"After you finish your breakfast, I'll take you over to the cottage and show you where Tommy grew up."

Sophia turned to Michael and took his hand. "You never cease to amaze me. How you arranged all this still boggles my mind." She gave him a big kiss.

"Me too," he said. "I had a lot of help."

"Sophia, you must possess the same romantic genes of your father," Colin said, laughing at the two of them.

On the walk to her father's childhood home, Sophia noticed the charming thatched roof on the house. "The cottage is not too different than the one owned by Sean Thornton, himself," Sophia said. "How many were in your family?"

"There were six of us," Lily said, "my parents and us four siblings."

"And you all lived in that tiny cottage?"

"We did. It had only two rooms - a large living and dining area, and a bedroom on the other end. My parents slept in the bedroom, and we children slept on day beds and sofas in the living room. In the warmer months, we spent most of our time outdoors."

"Do your other siblings live here in Ireland?"

"Not any longer. Our youngest sister, Margaret, died of polio when we were children, and Nigel, our older brother, died in a fishing accident at sea. I'm the lucky one. I must say, I count my blessings every day."

"And I count my blessings that she's here to share her

life with me," Colin said, pulling Lily close and kissing her on the top of her head.

They returned to the pub, and Pádraig drove them to other scenic areas nearby. They drove through the countryside, past small farms and through several charming villages. Sophia could easily see herself living here when they retired. Lastly, they went to Clew Bay, where Tommy worked for several years. That evening, they shared another wonderful meal with Sophia's newfound family.

During supper, a member of the local Gardaí came into the pub for a bite. He stood tall, a strong-looking gent in his early sixties, wearing a day-glow green jacket with black slacks and a guard hat, which he hung on the coat rack.

"Ah, good evening to you, Detective O'Hara," Colin said. "What can we bring you for supper?"

"A nice pork chop has been preyin' on me mind," he said, "and a baked potato might just do fine. And wet the tea, if you will, Colin."

"Right away," Colin said.

"Speak of the devil," Pádraig said. "Michael, just yesterday I told ya I'm acquainted with several O'Haras, and here be one of 'em. Detective Geoffrey O'Hara, he is."

Colin returned with a pot of tea. "Geoffrey, have ya met Lily's niece from America – Sophia and her husband, Michael O'Hara?"

"Yes, how are ya," Geoffrey said. He shook Sophia's hand first, and then Michael's.

"Pleased to meet you, Geoffrey," Michael said.

"Pádraig must be givin' you the grand tour?"

"He is," Sophia said. She took a long look at Geoffrey.

"Please, would you like to join us?" Michael said.

"Oh? Well, thanks." Geoffrey pulled up a chair and sat between Michael and Pádraig as Colin put the teapot on the table. "So, Mrs. O'Hara, are ya enjoyin' your visit to the Emerald Isle?"

"Oh, yes," Sophia said, rather distracted as she continued to stare at Geoffrey.

"What part of America?"

"Colorado," Michael said, beginning to take notice of Sophia's attentions.

"Oh, now isn't that grand. I always fancied to ski there someday."

"How long have you been a police officer?"

"With the Gardaí thirty-eight years now. I began in Galway, and I transferred here to Cong just three years past, where I plan to retire."

"The Gardaí?" Michael asked. "I assume that is what we call the police?"

"It is. Gardaí means *the guardian of peace*. My father was also a guard, and my grandfather before him was a guard in the Royal Irish Constabulary, which was the police force back in his day."

"Were you born in Galway?" Michael said.

"I was."

"You know, I'm told my O'Hara family came to America from Galway. I wonder if we might be related."

"Okay," Sophia said, "you'll have to forgive me for staring, Geoffrey, but have either one of you noticed how much you two look alike?"

Geoffrey and Michael looked at each other. "You *are* a

strikingly handsome lad," Geoffrey said.

"Thank you," Michael said. "And you are quite possibly the most handsome man I've ever laid eyes on."

"I'm serious!" Sophia said. "Pádraig, what do you think?"

Pádraig chuckled. "Look at me, lads. Aw, sure look it. You could be brothers – albeit Geoffrey a much *older* brother."

"Whanker," Geoffrey grumbled.

"Now that I think about it," Michael said. "You know, I come from a long line of New York City police officers and firefighters - three great-grandfathers, several uncles from the past, and even a few cousins who are on the job there today."

"That's right! Oh, this is fun," Sophia said, rubbing her hands together.

"Sure look it," Geoffrey said, rubbing his chin. "Now it's quare interestin' you say it, for I have ancestors who emigrated to New York and joined the guard. Do ya recall the names of your kin?"

"Yes. My – let's see – it would be great-great grandfather from Galway came to New York around the time of the potato famine. He was Eamon O'Hara."

"Aw, go way outta that!" Geoffrey said. "Was his father Seamus O'Hara?"

"Yes!" Michael said.

"Born around the 1790's?"

"That sounds right," Michael said. "Yes, because Eamon was born around 1817, and he went to New York at the time of the potato famine in the 1840's."

"My great-great grandfather Clive O'Hara was the son of Seamus," Geoffrey said, "born in 1827. He had three brothers, one named Eamon, who went to America. Was your Seamus married to Catherine Ó Heidhin?"

Michael sat back and extended both hands. "We're cousins! I never would have remembered that on my own, but now that you said it, I do recall that *was* her name!"

"So they were our many-great-grandparents, and your many-great-grandfather Eamon and my many-great-grandfather Clive were brothers!" Geoffrey said.

"I knew it!" Sophia said. "You two look so much alike!"

"Well," Michael said, "we're distant cousins – maybe third or fourth generation."

"And *I* say you look alike," Sophia said, and that was that. "Imagine we *all* find family here in the middle of this lovely Irish pub! What a small world, huh?"

"That it is, lass," Geoffrey said. "So, Michael, do ya know where the name O'Hara originates?"

"Sorry to say, as far as I knew, Brooklyn, New York," Michael said. "After three generations living in the U.S., my family became very Americanized. Neither my mom, nor my dad had much information about our Irish ancestry. We're not even Catholic now."

"Well, nobody's perfect, lad," Geoffrey said. "Now, O'Hara was at one time Ó Eaghra, if I pronounce it properly, which is unlikely."

"The 'O' in many Irish names," Sophia said. "I've always wondered what that means."

"In our ancient ancestry, Eaghra was likely the leader of our family clan. The 'O' means descendant of, or, son of."

Colin pitched in. "Sophia, your father Tommy

descended from the O'Gunn clan."

"What?" Sophia said. "O'Gunn?"

"Aye," Colin said as he looked at Pádraig and Geoffrey.

"Aye, Tommy was a son of O'Gunn," they said together and then laughed, quite satisfied.

Sophia rolled her eyes. "You must sometimes wait hours for that opportunity."

"Aw, sure look it," Colin said, "the tourists love that one, they do!"

"So tell me, Michael," Geoffrey said, "are ya in the guard?"

"No," Michael said. "In my family, Eamon, his son, Edmund, and Edmund's son – my grandfather - Michael were all New York City police officers. Michael was shot and wounded in the line of duty. He retired with a disability and didn't want my father or his two brothers to be cops. They all pursued other careers, and my dad, Hugh, was the first O'Hara in our line to graduate college."

"Michael's grandfather started writing after he retired, and he published over 20 detective novels," Sophia said.

"He must have had many captivatin' yarns to spin," Geoffrey said. "What line of work are you in, Michael? Ya don't strike me as a New Yorker."

"I was born there, but we left when I was an infant. My dad was an archeologist, so I grew up all over the world, you might say. Instead of digging in a schoolyard sandbox, I was at my dad's side, digging up ruins in an exotic desert somewhere. I also had an interest in architecture, and I couldn't decide which I liked more, so I became both."

"That sounds quite interestin'," Geoffrey said, "diggin' up dried-up dead people in nearly unrecognizable ancient ruins. Doesn't sound much different than police work!"

"You're in good company with this one," Sophia said, pointing to Michael. "Oh, yeah, you're definitely related."

"And you, Sophia. What do you do for a living?" Geoffrey asked.

"I'm an artist, a jewelry designer, and a writer. I sell my work in art fairs."

"I'm envious. I'm afraid I don't have a creative flare," Geoffrey said.

"You might be surprised at what you could conjure up if you gave yourself a chance. Do you have family here in County Mayo?"

"My siblings are no longer living. I was the youngest, and I am the only one left. My parents are long gone. Mary Ann, my ex-wife, lives in London, and we get on much better than when we were married. She is one of my closest and dearest friends now that we're not annoying each other all the time."

Sophia laughed. "Do you have children?"

"I do. Both my boy and girl are grown. Timothy lives in Scotland with his wife, Eileen, and two young lads – four and six. They own a small scotch distillery, and I do say they make the finest single malt scotch you ever tasted."

"Sounds like a destination for us," Michael said. "What do you say, Soph?"

"Sláinte!" Sophia said, raising her glass.

"My daughter, Cathleen, now in her early thirties, lives in Dublin with her husband, Daniel, and their two girls. They own a quaint little bed and breakfast. I get to visit both my children every year, and along the way I visit Mary Ann in London."

"Why don't we arrange to stay there when we go to Dublin?" Sophia said.

"I'll give them a call straight away," Geoffrey said.

They spent the rest of the evening getting to know one another and enjoying every minute. Lily and Colin joined them for tea after most of the other patrons dwindled out. At the end of the night, Sophia invited Geoffrey to visit Colorado.

"Lily, Colin, and Pádraig have already accepted our invitation. Please say yes."

"I've never been to the States, but I've always fancied it," Geoffrey said.

"You can go skiing like you always wanted," Michael said.

"Do you think they'll give us a group discount to fly out?" Geoffrey said with a laugh.

"One would hope, but the good thing is you can stay at our house," Sophia said. "We'll give you the grand tour of Colorado, and even better, Michael will be your chef."

"You don't cook, lass?" Lily asked.

"Not if you want to recognize what you're eating," Sophia said.

"Well, until then, I am so pleased that I had a chance to get to know you," Geoffrey said.

"We'll send you an official invitation and a possible itinerary. You must come. Bring Mary Ann. We'll have a party!" Sophia said.

The next morning, following breakfast, Colin helped Michael and Sophia bring down their luggage when

Pádraig arrived. Michael took out his wallet. "What do we owe you?"

"Not a farthing, and don't insult us by askin' again," Lily said. "You're family. We're so happy you came to visit."

"Well, thank you so much. How generous of you," Michael said.

Sophia pulled out a couple of picturesque postcards and handed them to Lily. "I've written down our e-mail, home address, and phone number. We're sincere about you coming to visit us. Come next year! And bring along Pádraig and Geoffrey." She leaned over the bar and whispered to Lily, "I have many women friends who would love to meet such charming men, especially if Mary Ann does not come along. I'll be busy getting all my single friends together for that party we're going to have."

"Sure look it," Lily said with a wink. "Pádraig is not without women wherever he goes, but that one needs a fine woman who'd cherish his tender heart, I tell ya! We may just take you up on that offer. We have not yet been to the U.S., and from what I can tell, Colorado is one of the prettiest states to visit." She then handed Sophia a folder. "Here, we printed the photographs, like I promised."

"Oh, thank you so much, Lily. I will cherish these," Sophia said.

"We really enjoyed ourselves. Thanks so much," Michael said as they all embraced.

"Goodbye, dear Sophia," Colin said, kissing her on the cheek. "I don't know when I've seen Lily so happy, now that she's reconnected to her Tommy."

"I love you both," Sophia said, holding back a tear.

Before Sophia walked out the door, she handed Lily a small watercolor that she painted the night before from a photograph of Tommy and Lily, as children, building a sandcastle on the beach. As Sophia walked out the door, she looked back to see Lily in tears.

"We're off to our next adventure!" Pádraig said, holding the car doors for Michael and Sophia. "See you next time around!" he called, tipping his cap to Lily and Colin...

County Mayo, on the northwest edge of Ireland, was a combination of fields and villages, mountains, forest, and dramatic coastlines, all stunningly beautiful and filled with charm. Sophia took hundreds of pictures each day as Pádraig grew accustomed to pulling over every kilometer or so.

"You take more photographs than anyone else I have toured," Pádraig said.

"I'm an artist," Sophia said. "Oftentimes, I combine photos to create the best subjects for my paintings. I have to say it'll be difficult to choose which of the photos to use, because there's so much to see here." So many of her best photos were of the warm people they met along the way.

Near picturesque Westport, Pádraig said, "Eight kilometers ahead is the conical mountain, Croagh Patrick, Ireland's holiest mountain. It rises to 760 meters above sea level."

"Okay," Michael said, pulling out his phone. He clicked away for a moment. "That's 2,500 feet."

"For 5,000 years, long before Catholicism came to our fair island in the 5th century, people have come here in pilgrimage to climb Croagh Patrick, named after me, of course. From its summit, you can see Clew Bay, where we were yesterday with Lily and Colin."

"Named after you, huh," Sophia said.

"It was way back when I was a saint. On Reek Sunday in July, which is our annual day of pilgrimage, twenty-five thousand people climb the mountain."

"Twenty-five thousand?" Michael said. "On one day?"

"Aye. Last year, a million people showed up, with twenty-five thousand of them making the climb. It's a spectacle – and often a disaster. It can be treacherous on days of inclement weather. The Gardaí coordinates with several mountain rescue teams each year. I've seen times when air rescue helicopters had to take pilgrims off the mountain, and other times pluck them from dangerous ledges. We Catholics are a devoted lot, but some of us aren't too bright..."

Next on the day's itinerary was County Sligo, where they drove to the village of Drumcliff, beneath Benbulbin, the most distinctive mountain in Ireland. Pádraig then took them to St. Columba's Church of Ireland to visit the grave of W.B. Yeats.

"How did you know? Yeats is one of my favorite poets," Sophia said. "Thank you for bringing us here." As she looked up at Benbulbin, she began to quote Yeats, and Pádraig joined in.

"'We can make our minds so like still water that beings gather about us, that they may see, it may be, their own images, and so live for a moment with a clearer, perhaps even with a fiercer life because of our quiet.'"

"That's how I see my greater task within Apeiros,"

Sophia said, "to be the power and depth of still water, so others can see themselves more clearly and thrive within their own importance."

"That you are, my sweet Sophia, that you are," Michael said as he pulled her close...

Donegal was the northernmost part of Ireland, quite dramatic with extremes of rugged seacoasts and high mountains. They took in the view from Slieve League Cliffs, where all three walked single file along the trail, high above the vertical cliffs below, overlooking the North Atlantic Ocean. In contrast, they walked the beach at Rossnowlagh. Sophia was in photographic heaven, capturing Ireland's beauty at every turn. At Balleyshannon, they stayed the night.

For some reason, which Sophia never understood its timing, her past lives came to visit in her dreams. Her recall of Jocelyn's life in the tragedy of *Titanic* returned.

Chapter Six

As captives of the frigid black void, the survivors sat wedged together, floating in small lifeboats on the same waters that swallowed *Titanic* just moments before. The wait - the agonizing wait was just beginning, and already excruciating.

Shock set in from the series of traumas that occurred in short order that night. Witnessing the wail of hundreds of terrified people crying for help and thrashing about in the freezing water caused further anguish among the survivors. It was enough that most of those in the lifeboats lost loved ones or colleagues, but adding to their distress was the guilt and shame of leaving more than 1,500 people behind to perish in the icy water.

Some feared their lifeboat might capsize if they attempted to drag people aboard. Other boats rowed too far from the foundering *Titanic* to return in time to rescue anyone from the sea. They simply could not row back fast enough to save anyone before they either drowned or succumbed to the below-freezing water.

The rounded bottoms of the lifeboats prevented anyone from climbing aboard from the icy sea. They simply could not gain a foothold. After treading in the freezing water for only a few minutes, even the youngest and strongest lost the strength in their arms and legs to pull themselves into a lifeboat. It would have taken two strong men to lift a man into the boat, and at that, the boat may have capsized at the weight and the effort it would take to pull someone out of the water.

As Jocelyn helplessly watched hundreds of people flailing about, a traumatic memory broke free. The momentous ordeal caused her to recall a similar predicament of two people who fell from a small boat into the stormy sea. Jocelyn briefly remembered how they both struggled in terror and panic for survival in freezing cold waters at the ocean's command. She instinctively took a deep breath, as if that would help the woman who was underwater - the woman she saw as herself in an ancient past life.

It was not long before the din subsided, as hundreds of people thrashing about, screaming in terror and crying for help, quickly faded - each victim succumbing to icy death. The chaotic horror of the loss of more than 1,500 people stilled to the motionless shock and anguish of those in the lifeboats. Less than one-third of the passengers and crew who began their journey across the North Atlantic, just four days before, were all who remained, and their fate was dangerously uncertain as they aimlessly floated on the frigid dark ocean. The only thing that took precedence over their vulnerability, grief, and overriding fear of not surviving was the freezing cold. All they could do was sit still in their small lifeboats, packed like sardines in the blackened stillness, wondering if they would survive or die. The replay of the last three hours of horror etched into each person's cellular memory.

There they were, 400 miles south of Newfoundland, unsure of what would come first - death, which would bring an end to the nightmare - or rescue, which could be the beginning of atonement for having survived.

Jocelyn grew numb with shock as she squinted into the darkness. She could barely make out a few white objects bobbing on the still ocean surface – undoubtedly the cork life jackets attached to lifeless passengers. Her mind turned to François Delacroix, the man with whom she made love just hours before – the man with whom she dared to envision a life together. In the attempt to close off all she sensed around her, she clenched her eyes shut. To the best of her ability, she dropped deep into her heart and prayed for François, for he was undoubtedly out there - somewhere.

Stillness reigned, for the last word belonged to the ocean, and nature never played favorites.

The survivors' only choice was to wait in the utter silence - a silence so loud it was maddening. Hundreds of ghostly bodies drifted on the ocean surface like marble statues in their watery graveyard, with far more people and animals that sank into the sea below - no longer fighting for breath - no longer restless for life itself.

The only movement was in the brilliant glimmer of stars in silent epitaph.

Those remaining in the lifeboats sat motionless, in shock and astonishment, mourning the unfathomable while feeling the mounting effects of survivor's guilt. The atmosphere was hushed, with only a few muffled cries heard from the distant lifeboats. Time seemed to cease altogether. Without saying so, many survivors wondered if the frigid temperatures would claim them before a rescue ship arrived. Some secretly hoped that would be the case, with guilt plaguing their thoughts. *Why could it not have been me? Why did I survive?*

Stars, by the countless millions, floated above the horizon line where black met black. Yet, the mountainous iceberg stealthily loomed not far in the distance, visible only because it blocked out the sky's crystal pinpoints of light. It was a ghostly entity; a reminder that what was obvious on the surface was only miniscule compared to the massive power that lay underneath - just waiting.

Thoughts about François filled Jocelyn's mind that segued from one to the next. *My god, what happened to him? Where is he? Unless he made it to a lifeboat, he could not possibly be alive now – he cannot survive out there in the water. If he fell in, the fall most likely killed him. What happened to him if he went down with the ship? He would only have a few minutes in the water before he would freeze. What were his last thoughts?*

The incessant whats, ifs, and whys filled her mind - her preoccupation destroying any sense of hope for her own survival.

Jocelyn was certain she met François for a reason, a greater purpose much more important than just a few days of joy-filled, blissful pleasure and lovemaking. There certainly was so much more to understand about their union, and she could not help but recall every detail - from the lighthearted moment their heads first collided on the dock in Cherbourg - to their last passionate kiss when they parted barely an hour before.

François can't be gone, she thought. *This can't be happening. Our life together was just beginning. He has to be alive. He's out there somewhere, struggling to survive with the rest of us.*

Jocelyn felt imprisoned, unable to move, a captive of irrational thoughts swiftly floating by. She replayed her last sight of François - a metaphor it seemed - as she kept her gaze on him rising into the heavens as her lifeboat lowered down to the sea's glassy surface.

Darkened silence laid preview to the playback of her last few years.

She knew all too well, after the loss of Henry, grief-filled thoughts of guilt and loss kept her wishing life had taken a different direction, but at the time, she thought she had no control over occurrences. Now she knew better. In order to move forward, she had to keep her focus on the present moment and make the choice to look for the good as each moment occurred. From that perspective, the answers would avail themselves, for what she envisioned for her future was true on some level. At least, that was what she tried to tell herself.

And yet, the darkness intruded on her mind, as she asked herself how could she possibly look for the good. She felt trapped in a crowded wooden boat in the cold, dank, and dark, while sitting on the same malevolent sea that swallowed fifteen hundred people just moments before - a sea for which she had held such reverence for its mystical beauty. That very sea took the lives of both individuals and whole families who were beginning life again with a dream of freedom and prosperity.

Some of the world's wealthiest people also perished. Vanquished were many of the grand visions that bridged commerce and technology and nurtured the forward-thinking relations between nations, specifically that of Britain and the United States. In her heart, Jocelyn knew, in some way, good would come from the night's atrocity, but at such an unfathomable cost. If she did survive, Jocelyn wondered how she could ever again witness the beauty of the sea for which she held such reverence. How could she ever love again? The losses were exponential.

Jocelyn knew she was not alone in her anguish. Every survivor who languished in the lifeboats was most likely thinking thoughts similar to hers. Some who lost loved ones also lost everything they owned. On the edge of trauma, their grief was just beginning to settle in, everyone unconsciously wondering how might they live on with the knowledge that they were the ones who survived. Wives without husbands, children without fathers - siblings, companions, friends, and business partners gone. How could the survivors go about continuing their lives after such a traumatic loss? They were spellbound, feeling mesmerized and trapped - all of them in the same dire circumstances.

A mishmash of thoughts ran through Jocelyn's mind, and yet emptiness dominated, as if everything she had ever known slipped into the abyss with *Titanic*. Jocelyn was left in a void from all her losses, causing her to wonder, *If I am left with nothing - without all that I know myself to be - who am I now? What will I become?*

Jocelyn was traumatized and alone in her thoughts, with a sense of abandonment and little hope for survival. As she ruminated about her situation, she began to reason that, if she were going to remain among the living and live well and happy, it was up to her to start right then and not bring blame to anyone else for the state of affairs in which she found herself. Victimization would not work. No attitude of - *the White Star Line is to blame - they did this to me -* would help. In truth, there were no *theys*, for she was responsible for her experience through her own choices. After all, she had to admit to herself, she chose to take this voyage across the Atlantic despite the many intuitive warnings not to do so.

Suddenly, the people in her boat seemed to disappear. The obscurity of perpetual darkness overwhelmed her, emphasizing her feeling of utter insignificance - a tiny human helplessly floating at the beck and call of the vast, cold North Atlantic. In her mind's eye, she was alone in the boat, lingering in her solitude.

Am I going to survive, or will I perish? I have no choice but to wait - the incessant lingering wait - just waiting for grace.

Not yet completely awake, Sophia's heart raced with an emergent sense of panic. She could still see herself as Jocelyn, seated in a crowded lifeboat on the icy waters while surrounded by mesmerizing starlight. She felt the same sense of horror Jocelyn felt that fateful night over a century before.

As the dream faded away, she was relieved to let go of the mindset of Jocelyn. Yet, as Sophia awoke, she realized there was a more profound reason for looking into the window of Jocelyn's world. It was true, the tragic story of *Titanic* fascinated her since she was a child, however there was more for her to know beyond her recall of yet another historic past life. In so many ways, Jocelyn's life mirrored that of her own life, for Sophia felt stuck in a proverbial lifeboat out in the watery abyss of her emotions.

A couple years before, Sophia was healing from her divorce, followed by the death of her father, Patrick. Not long afterward, she and Michael reunited. Months later, she became a member of the Order of Apeiros. Then there were her family revelations, with the big reveal of her parents' deaths still spinning in her mind, which would most likely continue for some time. Patrick, the man Sophia knew as her father was, in fact, her great-granduncle. Darius was actually her grandfather, and Gaston, her granduncle. The thought, albeit humorous, crossed her mind, wondering if her beloved Michael was some long lost cousin, twice, thrice, or perhaps eleven times removed. It would not surprise her... Well, maybe a just a little.

Weeks after learning the truth of her parents' deaths, Sophia and Michael hosted the gathering of Apeiros in Colorado. Their first order of business was to bless the life of Algernon Gillette, by assisting Sophia, Darius, and Gaston in their forgiveness and release of decades-long pain and anguish. During the thirteen members of Apeiros' Colorado tour, Michael surprised Sophia with an unexpected marriage proposal, followed quickly by their beautiful wedding ceremony. The big finale of the gathering was the discovery that their dear beloved sage, White Buffalo, was quite ill.

Shortly after, Sophia and Michael were honeymooning in Ireland, following her highly emotional visit with Algernon Gillette in prison. Getting away gave Sophia some perspective on just how fast her life was moving, even though most everything were positive events propelling her life forward. Nevertheless, Sophia was feeling overwhelmed.

For the past year, Sophia found herself in the question of her life's meaning, with her over-arching biggest concern of all - *Here I've been told that I'm the most powerful of all Oracles, when I have done nothing to earn such a responsibility. I'm not quite sure what to do.*

With all the changes in the past few years, Sophia had reinvented herself into someone with whom she was not yet entirely familiar. Evidently, her beloved Michael, Darius, Gaston, White Buffalo, and the others in Apeiros, could see the bigger picture of who she was, but that vision was not yet apparent to Sophia, herself. The answers would reveal themselves in time, and more likely, they would develop into more questions that might catapult her to *Know Thyself* - the charge left to her by her father, Patrick. Again, she felt rutted in her stuckness, with feelings of, *God grant me patience, but it had better arrive immediately!*

Sophia knew that patience paired with fortitude would guide her through her feelings of frustration, because she was on the cutting edge of even more growth. If she was to create a positive shift in her circumstances, she just had to be patient a bit longer. When she felt such feelings of uneasiness, a breakthrough was about to take place. It was right in front of her, and the wisdom within her knew it was just that simple!

With all these thoughts rattling around in her mind, Sophia quietly slipped out of bed and wrapped herself in her robe, so as not to awaken Michael. At the other end of the room, glowing embers in the fireplace remained. She added kindling until they caught fire, and then some larger twigs and a couple of split logs. From the armchair, she took the seat cushion and placed it on the floor, so she could sit comfortably in front of the fire.

As she sat, watching the fire's mesmerizing golden glow, she breathed in the welcoming scent of burning wood, which reminded her of many fond memories growing up at the cabin. Although she and Michael transformed the small cabin into a beautiful mountain home, she never got tired of the simple things like the warmth and scent of a wood burning fireplace. Finally, in that moment, calmness and serenity cast over her like a warm blanket.

She began to experience a shift from her thinking mind to that of her heart when she remembered the wisdom of White Buffalo.

"We see with the eyes of our focus," he said. "We hear with the ears of our beliefs. We feel with the heart's willingness. The closed heart opens no doors, but the heart that is open connects to Love through the natural world - that of the human heart in union with Great Spirit and all of creation."

She contemplated how Jocelyn's experience affected her own life. She ached, thinking of Jocelyn's despair as she drifted in the lifeboat after everything she knew and loved disappeared in a dark, cold sea. It affirmed to Sophia, yet again, *it is not what happens, but how one responds to what happens that determines the outcome. History continues to teach from those who have gone on before. May I be wise to give attention to lessons learned, and may I live from that expanded wisdom.*

Sophia knew her choices created a ripple effect upon all that she touched, ad infinitum. For a brief moment, several thoughts crossed her mind. *What if my thoughts affected Jocelyn? Could what I know about Titanic transfer to Jocelyn in her time frame? What if some of my thoughts are generated from other versions of myself from other dimensional fields. Could it be that simple? It's possible!*

Having arrived at a sense of inspired tranquility, she held a water-filled bowl in her lap, which reflected the fire on the water's surface. As she looked into the bowl, she said a silent prayer, invoking Spirit's wisdom. As the Oracle, she desired to tap into that greater sense of knowing through the water, as so many oracles before her had done.

Suddenly, the bowl disappeared from her sight, and the firelight faded into an indigo haze. A vision of White Buffalo appeared, facing her while sitting at the river's edge at the cabin.

"Your being the most powerful Oracle of all time has nothing to do with you doing anything," White Buffalo said. "It is not about *doing*, it is about *being - being your Self in the present moment of now.* In this awareness, you are grounded in the vibration of your highest self - that of Absolute Love in the merging of the mind and heart... This is the Sacred Way. Sophia, this is what you already know so well - it is the wisdom your father left you before he left this world - to *Know Thyself* is being.

"Whatever we seek is already within. You know this when you paint, for you are in harmony with the Divine as you create. Your writing is the same, for time does not exist when you allow the words to flow as you put pen to paper, or when your fingers dance upon the keyboard. My sweet Sophia, Love is your only task. You came into the world this way, for it is your soul's calling to share what *you* call an exchange of heart. You are about *being* Love with everyone and all that you engage with in the world. It is your soul's authentic way of being - to reach out from the heart's wisdom. This is the calling for all humanity, but you now know it is yours.

"Your task, now, is to serve - to give of your mind and heart through your gifts and talents, for this is where love resides in the present moment. And, whether you know it or not, the effort you make has an exponential effect upon the world around you. Reach out in love. Speak from love.

See and recognize the person, animal, or situation as God, in form, standing in front of you, no matter what the appearances may be. From the silence of your heart, send them blessings, especially if it is not someone who receives love well.

"You returned from your near-death experience with the depth of awareness, knowing all there was to know, because in that realm you no longer had the human barriers and filters to separate you from your union with the Creator - Great Spirit. You are living your spiritual life as a human, and you must remember that you already know everything there is to know. Since God, as Love, is all there is, you are that as well, as is everyone and everything. No longer do you have to seek more to become who you aspire to be, for you have already arrived. The Star People taught us that we are here on Mother Earth to remember who we have always been. You have been here all along.

"Of course, you continue to learn, for that is what life is - a school of thought and constant education through experience, but what we are doing is tapping into what we have always known. As humans, we learn through the action of doing, but our soul's expression is through our way of being. Your life is no longer about acquisition for the sake of getting more and doing more. It is about allowing yourself to give lovingly from the heart - from your place of center that knows all - as you grow within the greater expansive upward spiral of the soul's evolutionary awareness. Step into your power. Your attempt to protect your wounded heart with walls and barriers of pain is futile. Instead, trust. Be vulnerable through the love that easily flows through your heart. In Love - there is no pain - no fear. Open your heart wide, Sophia. When you *are* Love, there is no tiredness, no ego, no wanting.

"When you agreed to come into this life to love, life presented many situations for your experience that were unlike love. When you remember them from the place of pain - that place of suffering and victimhood - those memories keep you small. But what those heart-wrenching experiences taught you is how *not* to be, for it is not in your purview to bring harm to others in the same way. You made a choice to return to your earthly life to teach love, and sometimes it is difficult to remember that love is ever present when the apparent mud and muck of life's challenges seem to take over. Those experiences continue to teach you to forgive, to live with a compassionate heart, to be grateful for your tremendous blessings, and to continue onward toward a better way of being. From this, we learn how to be kind - we grow into our humility as we experience the beauty of grace.

"Bask in this power of your best self, for because of these experiences, you are a better teacher, a better healer, and you are more wise. Remember the thirteen attributes always exist in all circumstances. By recognizing Love in whatever comes your way, you will find great beauty, peace, and joy - where all of the qualities of Great Spirit are abundantly present.

"You are to answer the call now, Sophia. That call comes each and every day, with each person you encounter, and each situation that arises. With every opportunity, you are wiser than you were the moment before. And so it goes.

"Be ready and primed to say yes to the call. Sense the opportunity to cross the threshold as the door quickly opens, knowing that it is opening for you, as if the red carpet is rolled out for you to take your next step forward. Say yes to the call, for the call is to love - to serve - to be a profoundly heart-filled teacher and sage. Everywhere you go, you meet people, animals - all which live on Grandmother Earth - right where they stand. Each of these blessed beings will show themselves to you, one moment at a time, within the presence of God.

"This is your legacy, one loving outreach of the heart at a time. Your heritage precedes you with a rich ancestry of leaders, shamans, mystics, oracles, and wisdom teachers. Say yes to your calling of *being* the Oracle! Look forward, knowing the upward spiral of eternity is where you and all beings reside in the here and now.

"The rear-view mirror is only for your use when you are at the wheel of your car. That being said, understand that your past lives come to you to teach you about who you are now. Keep your eyes focused ahead, for the light shines on the trajectory of your dreams as you stand in your truth of the present moment - as Love incarnate. Love is where you stand. It is right in front of you. Love leads the way - through the Sacred Way of the Heart - within you and as you. Now go and be your magnificent self. *Be* the Oracle, *be* the bearer of the sacred life force - the sacred, holy vessel of water - the most powerful force on the planet. *Be* the consciousness of the world, *be* the light! Love and *be* loved. By loving, you acknowledge your highest self and the same for everyone you encounter. It is simple, just *be* who you already are, my dear!"

The image of White Buffalo faded. Sophia looked down into the quivering reflection of the fire on the water. The bowl shook in her hands as she carefully placed it on the hearth. Her hands continued to tremble, but it was not a physical shaking as much as an energy that came through her as a radiant quickening - for she was vivified as one who communicated life from the Absolute Awareness that flowed through her being. She finally understood who she returned to her earthly life to *be*. Sophia could feel it course through every cell in her body, through every sense of herself.

She then heard from her lips a resounding, "Yes!"

Chapter
Seven

In the cosmic wonder of it all, Jocelyn could only believe that she survived for a reason beyond what she currently understood. From that spark of awareness, she kept moving forward in her thoughts. She *believed* she would survive.

She remembered a quote from her studies of Aristotle: *Nature abhors a vacuum.* Where there is a void, something must fill the emptiness. Somehow, she knew life would find a way to fill in the blanks, but she wanted to make her own choices. Nothing would get in her way as long as she had any say about it. Jocelyn had stepped into new beginnings when she chose to return to the United States. With François, she thought she completed the picture of how that life could be. Despite only meeting him days before, she sensed that she and François knew each other in some other time, long before their few days of bliss. By his giving her the precious gift of the ammonite, he trusted her to carry on with or without him.

Jocelyn deeply grieved the loss of François, but she could feel a tiny flicker of him in the new life she carried. Although that life was in its early beginnings, Jocelyn sensed their child was a boy. She placed her hands on her belly and said a silent prayer for him to grow up to be healthy, wise, and courageous like his father. In that moment, she decided what the baby's name would be. With this spark of life in her body, she knew she must survive, for she held the responsibility for both of them to live. The tiny new life within her linked to many people of great importance in the future. Of this, there was no doubt in her mind.

Jocelyn held onto the amulet that hung from the gold chain around her neck. All the losses caused her to surrender her thinking mind, oddly creating a sense of inner strength that only humility could fully generate. By letting go, she was renewed by what she recognized was a literal and figurative baptism - a cleansing of all she once knew. Without cognitively putting all the pieces together, she instinctively allowed herself to open up to her intuitive guidance that was available to direct her forward.

You are protected, guided, and sourced. Ask in all things, believing wholeheartedly with your innate sense of knowing that you are deserving of all good. Infuse your thoughts with joy and your dreams with the feeling of having what you desire, for what you seek is seeking you. When you ask, and you trust that it is so, your dreams and desires are already taking form and will be granted in ways beyond your imagining, for as it is promised, 'It is the Father's good pleasure to give you the kingdom.' Your good feelings are evidence of that which you are calling forth. The Infinite Eternal God is ever within the grasp of your heart's knowing, for you are a part of It. You are enveloped in Its ever-expanding, evolutionary wholeness. Allow this eternality to become your life, and you will realize its magnificence as a manifest reality, for it is already within you. In this sacred way, you will serve the world. From you will come goodness and greatness as you touch other lives every day, and your life will be blessed in return.

She sat in the stillness and listened to her powerful intuitive guidance speak to her. She knew that the wisdom she received was the same for François, no matter where he was.

Only two years earlier, she was married to Henry Davis, the man she adored, and with whom she planned to raise a family. They had a wonderful life together. He was a successful steel baron, and she, a celebrated clothing designer in Paris and New York. In short order, they had become members of the society elite in Pittsburgh. Then, that life suddenly ended when Henry died of influenza while they were visiting his family in Wales. Alone and crestfallen, Jocelyn had no choice but to begin life anew.

For two years, she traveled throughout Europe, rebuilding herself, step by step, through her grief. The voyage on *Titanic* was the beginning of a new life in New York. Then François entered to complete that picture, and what a grand picture it was. They both obtained prosperous opportunities to work for *Lucile Ltd.*, the couture fashion house owned by Lady Duff-Gordon in association with Macy's owner, Isidor Straus. François' dream to start over, using his talents and abilities, was just as important as Jocelyn's, but now, in just three hellish hours, that overarching dream vanished.

Did Isidor and Ida Straus survive? Were Sir Cosmo and Lady Duff-Gordon able to board a lifeboat?

Jocelyn promised herself and made a solemn vow to the spirit of François. *I am a survivor. I will make it to New York, and I will begin again as originally planned. No matter what, I will make a new and successful life for myself and for our child - a life that would honor all of those who never completed their journey on Titanic. I will carry on and raise our child well, for love always triumphs.*

Stripped clean of her dreams, and left with an entirely clean slate, she sat adrift in the lifeboat, unable to do anything but think. Once more, she felt the ammonite in her hand, the chambers beginning at its center in miniscule proportion as they expanded exponentially, spiraling to the outer edge. It made her wonder - *could there be something better yet to come?*

With that infinite possibility in mind, Jocelyn looked up at the stars, realizing that she too was unlimited in her energy, which emitted into the cosmos. She was an integral piece in the grand design of all things, as were all the others who sailed *Titanic*. She was an essential aspect of energy - a light that shined - and from this point forward, she would understand how simple it was that everyone and everything had importance and purpose in the world. She was not alone in the universe. On the contrary, she was one with everything and of vital importance in the cosmic scheme of things.

Jocelyn was lost in thought when she suddenly realized the even deeper meaning as to why she was aboard *Titanic*. During the chaos of the last few hours, she recalled the vow she spoke with François - to hold every soul, on this night, in their hearts. From this, she was certain her purpose was to remember all who perished. *How selfish I am, thinking only of myself!*

She closed her eyes and brought herself into the quiet recesses of her inner sanctum. When she was clear, she took several deep breaths in remembrance of those who perished in the icy waters. Each face morphed into the next as she summoned their memory, recalling the location upon the ship where she took notice of each one. She also brought to her recollection those who survived, for she knew her blessing over each soul had no boundaries.

When Jocelyn opened her eyes, she saw faint images of each woman, man, child, and animal who departed from their earthly journey during the maiden voyage of *Titanic*. Each appeared as energy rather than in physical form - not quite visible - but clearly a palpable presence. As they floated above the water's edge, they gathered in a circle above where *Titanic* slipped into the sea. Jocelyn was stunned as she realized each one's sacrifice and selfless-ness. All were peaceful, joy-filled, and glowing in every sense. Each soul was liberated and free, incredibly beauti-ful beyond description. She smiled and briefly thought she noticed some of them smiling back. She blew them a silent kiss, sent with profound and reverent love, for the connec-tion she felt was unconditional and without limitation.

She could see them slowly spread out to circle the lifeboats, surrounding their loved ones, each connecting for one last time. Jocelyn could hear some of the children in the other lifeboats talking to them, and the three dogs that survived excitedly barked in the darkened distance, for they had no filters to block the love that encircled them.

Very few of the adults seemed to stir, as far as Jocelyn could tell. Suddenly, Henry appeared before her so she would know he was ever with her. Her eyes were wide in amazement. She nodded and then smiled as she felt the connection of love between them, knowing that love would always remain, for love never dies.

She then observed each soul transform into a golden streak of brilliant light, vertically extending high into the ethers until they disappeared into what seemed a single pinpoint of light blending into the stars. Although she could no longer discern each individual light, she sensed their presence, a strong union of souls surrounding everyone in the lifeboats, never to leave, but ever a part of the eternality of dimensions beyond worldly perceptions.

At 3:30 a.m., the survivors sighted rockets to the south. It was the *RMS Carpathia* signaling to *Titanic* that she was on her way.

Carpathia was traveling from New York to its first scheduled stop in Gibraltar when its Marconi wireless operator, Harold Cottam, heard that Cape Cod had traffic for *Titanic*. Cottam decided to help, and he contacted *Titanic* at 12:11 a.m., "Do you know that Cape Cod is sending a batch of messages for you?"

Cottam immediately received a distress signal from *Titanic*, unaware of any previous calls, for he was on deck the prior few hours.

"Come at once. We have struck a berg. It is a CQD OM (it is a distress situation, old man). Position 41° 46′ N, 50° 14′ W."

Stunned, Cottam immediately responded, "Shall I tell my Captain? Do you require assistance?"

Titanic responded, "Yes, come quick."

The time: 12:25 a.m.

Cottam and the officer on duty awakened Captain Arthur Rostron, who immediately changed *Carpathia's* course to *Titanic's* last reported position, approximately 58 miles away. In all his years at sea, Captain Rostron had never come to the rescue of any vessel in peril, let alone the largest ocean liner in the world. He ordered the ship's engineer to close down power to all facilities that were not of absolute necessity, including heating and lights in the public areas. This enabled the engineers to increase the steam for her to reach top speed, 3.5 knots higher than normal, reaching maximum speed of 17 km, or 20 mph. Never again would *Carpathia* steam at the same pace across the Atlantic.

At 1:45 a.m., the last signal *Carpathia* received from *Titanic* read, "Come as quickly as possible Old Man: the engine room is filling up to the boilers."

The off-duty crew awoke and immediately went to work, all the while drinking hot coffee to stay awake, alert, and warm. Captain Rostron had no idea how many survivors they would need to bring aboard, so he ordered the crew to swing out all sixteen lifeboats on their davits and make them ready for use. They collected extra blankets and warm clothing to best prepare public rooms to house however many survivors they would take on. Crewmembers helped the galley make hundreds of sandwiches, hot coffee, and hot soup to feed the cold and hungry.

Carpathia had to endure traversing the perilous gauntlet of ice fields and icebergs ahead, some 150 to 200 feet high, to aim toward *Titanic's* last known coordinates. At 3:00 a.m., *Carpathia* called out to *Titanic,* advising her to stay alert for her rocket signals, "if you are there."

Other ships listening in replied, "No reply."

The hours spent on the lifeboats were most likely the longest period of time any of the survivors had ever endured. By 3:20 a.m., lifeboats D, 4, 10, and 12 were converging and crewmen began lashing the boats together. At least four of the portside lifeboats also came together.

By 4:10 a.m., *Carpathia's* crewmen spotted the faint green light of a Roman candle lit by Fourth Officer Boxhall, who was aboard lifeboat number two, but no *Titanic*. They were shocked to discover that the great ship had already slipped beneath the surface.

The last hours of waiting for each person to climb aboard *Carpathia* were the most grueling of all.

During the arduous wait for rescue, it took time and great effort of the surviving *Titanic* crewmen to maneuver around the ice and bring the lifeboats together. *Carpathia* was the only ship that came to the survivors' rescue, even though many in the lifeboats earlier saw lights of two other vessels far to the north. No effort was made by either unidentified ship to come to their aid from that direction, and the ships' lights eventually faded and disappeared altogether.

Most of the other ships that heard *Titanic's* distress call were a farther distance away than *Carpathia*, and although as many as ten turned and began to steam toward the stricken ship, they eventually stopped when *Carpathia* passed along the grim news that *Titanic* foundered and just over 700 survivors were rescued. Over 1,500 had perished. Inexplicably at the time, the vessel closest to *Titanic* when she sank, the cargo ship *SS Californian*, did not respond to the distress calls or rockets. Its captain learned of the sinking only after he awoke at 4:30 a.m.

Extra lights were set up on *Carpathia's* deck to help with visibility in bringing the survivors on deck. The gangway door opened on the side of the ship, and seaman threw out a rope ladder to dangle down to sea level, where the lifeboat crews then rowed up alongside. Jocelyn looked up at the ship, which appeared gigantic, although *Carpathia* was one-fifth the size of *Titanic*.

Suddenly, *Carpathia* disappeared from Jocelyn's sight,

and a distant memory from lifetimes past flashed into her mind of massive, tall cliffs rising above as she sat in a boat on a turbulent sea. The ocean always had the last word, and Jocelyn, so close to rescue, felt a sudden wave of fear lock her mind like a vice grip.

Reality returned just as quickly when the lifeboat banged against the hull of *Carpathia*. Jocelyn shook her mind back. Exhausted and torn by grief, she forced herself to focus on the present danger before her. The ordeal was not over, and she did not want to die so close to her salvation.

The hours spent on the lifeboats were most likely the longest period of time any of the survivors had ever endured, but the last hours of waiting for each person to climb aboard *Carpathia* were the most grueling of all. Each able-bodied adult survivor had no choice but to climb the rope ladder to board *Carpathia* as it swayed in the cold wind. At the same time, the lifeboat shifted about in the choppy seas that developed over the previous couple of hours. When it was Jocelyn's turn, she reacted like most everyone else, in great resistance to making the perilous climb up the ladder. The lifeboats pitched in the chop, making it difficult for her to stand, and the rope ladder flopped about in the wind, making for an unstable ascent through the gangway door.

On her way up the ladder, weary and fearful thoughts crossed Jocelyn's mind: *The events of the last few hours are quite enough for all of us without having to climb up to the ship. My arms and legs are numb from the cold, and I can scarcely pull myself up. Have we not suffered enough trauma and loss to the sea that swallowed up Titanic and our loved ones? Unfortunately, this nightmare, I fear, is just beginning.*

She summoned every last ounce of strength, focusing on the crewmen inside the gangway door above, who encouraged her to climb and not look down. Finally in reach, several pairs of strong hands grabbed her and hoisted her inside.

"All right then," she heard a British crewman say, "I've got you, Miss. Come along now, you're safe."

He wrapped her in a warm blanket, swiftly pulling her through the gangway door.

Once Jocelyn was safely aboard *Carpathia* with a blanket wrapped around her shoulders and a cup of hot coffee in her trembling hands, she stood at the railing, watching the crew as they brought up a cargo net filled with children. Crewmen first put each child in a burlap mailbag with others inside the net before hoisting them up to the deck. Jocelyn took particular notice of two small boys brought up from Collapsible D. One of the boys was about four to five years of age, and the other appeared about two. Once on board, the older boy made sure he wrapped himself and his younger sibling snugly in an eiderdown quilt. Jocelyn noticed that the quilt had the same colors and pattern as the one François took from his cabin.

Where is François? I must not leave this deck until he comes aboard, or until...

She shuddered at any thought other than one of his survival.

A makeshift stretcher, improvised by *Carpathia's* crew, hoisted the injured and elderly onto the ship. Finally, the last survivor came aboard. Jocelyn recognized him as Second Officer Herbert Lightoller, but François was nowhere to be found.

Those rescued were immediately provided blankets,

sandwiches, and plenty of hot coffee. Three men pulled from the sea had died overnight from exposure to the elements, but for those survivors in need of immediate medical care, officers and many First Class passengers willingly gave up their quarters and cabins, where they received care by the ship's three doctors.

Before *Carpathia* set out for New York, a short memorial service took place in the dining room for those who were tragically lost just six hours before. *Carpathia* then set sail for New York at 8:50 a.m.

Some survivors were separated from loved ones on *Titanic* before they were placed in the lifeboats. Others were separated when they were transferred from overflowing boats into lifeboats with more room. After *Carpathia* set course for New York, many survivors searched the boat for hours, frantically looking for their husbands, wives, and friends - most of them to no avail. Heavyhearted, they were exhausted and traumatized, not yet aware of what the next course of action would be once they landed in New York. The only thing to do was get warm, eat a bit of something nourishing, and get some rest.

Jocelyn would scarcely remember her time aboard *Carpathia*. She was in a daze. When they departed for New York without François, the harsh reality of black grief extinguished all hope that he miraculously survived. She *believed* she would see him climb up from a lifeboat. When she didn't, she thought her heart would break in two when they slowly steamed away. All she could see were some of the lonely, empty lifeboats drifting in the wake.

The crew and some of the passengers took note of the large ice field that floated in a southerly direction from the north. This was the very ice field in the perilous waters of the North Atlantic where the *Californian* stopped earlier in the night before *Titanic* collided with the iceberg. That year, approximately 400 icebergs were born along the coast of Greenland. The sheets of ice that made up the ice field were massive flat islands wedged together, floating freely with the current and stretching for miles along the Outer Banks. *Carpathia* spent the first day of its journey to New York carefully traversing these ice fields, with dozens of icebergs in the distance up to 200 feet high.

Carpathia arrived in New York the evening of Thursday, April 18, 1912. Thousands gathered at the dock, not yet aware of their loved ones' fate. Many would not be certain until they traveled to Halifax, Nova Scotia, where the bodies retrieved from the sea were laid out on ice for identification at the Mayflower Curling Rink.

Many who survived had no one to greet them - at least, no one they knew. They were starting a new life in America alone. Groups gathered in throngs to assist the 703 people who set foot ashore. Because she spoke German, French, Italian, and Russian, Margaret Brown remained aboard *Carpathia* and assisted other survivors in reuniting with family members and those in need of further medical assistance.

CHAPTER
Eight

Jocelyn left the *Carpathia* that evening with a heavy heart. She held onto a slight glimmer of hope that she would miraculously find François disembarking the *Carpathia* when they arrived in New York, but her hopes dwindled with every poor soul who aimlessly wandered down the gangplank and into the crowd of thousands of onlookers and newspaper reporters. Even though she had only known François for five days, their souls' connection was so unshakable; it was as if she had known him many lifetimes before.

Jocelyn had no idea if she had a job, not even knowing if Lady Duff-Gordon and Cosmo survived. At the time, she could not remember the name of the concierge Ida Straus recommended to her. She would inquire about Mr. and Mrs. Straus when she eventually called on him. She put up a noble front, conceding that she was healthy, and she had plenty of money to find somewhere to settle in New York for the time being, where she could simply rest and take stock of this enormous tragedy.

She suddenly heard someone call out her name. It was Margaret Brown, disembarking from *Carpathia*.

"Jocelyn, honey! I'm so relieved to see you!"

"Maggie?" Jocelyn said. "Oh, Maggie, you're alive!"

They embraced, Maggie taking Jocelyn in her arms like

a protective mother. "My goodness, so many people we met onboard did not make it, but you look well. Tell me... your young man?"

Jocelyn shook her head with the first tears she cried since *Titanic* sank. Margaret gently pulled her close and handed her a handkerchief as Jocelyn broke down, sobbing. "I'm so sorry, honey – so sorry."

"I fell in love with him, Maggie," Jocelyn cried. "He was such a sweet man. It wasn't supposed to end this way."

"I know," Maggie said. "It's a nightmare we can't wake up from." She looked at Jocelyn and touched her cheek. "Do ya have somewhere to go tonight?"

"I don't know. A hotel, I suppose."

"No, I won't hear none of that. You're comin' home with me. I have an apartment on 5th Avenue with plenty of room. You can stay in the guest room for as long as you want."

"Oh, Maggie, you've been through such an ordeal yourself. I don't want to put you out."

"Stop it!" Maggie ordered. "You're comin' home with me, and that's that! Besides, after all this, I don't think neither of us should be alone right now..."

Jocelyn stayed with Margaret for a week, spending her time in quiet contemplation and allowing herself to grieve over the loss of François. She knew she would be all right. She had no doubt, but it would take time. Margaret was of enormous help, offering a sympathetic ear when Jocelyn needed it, and leaving her to rest in solitude when warranted.

The first few days, Jocelyn slept sometimes for hours during the daytime. The shocking experience of the *Titanic* disaster left her weak and physically drained. By the end of the first week, however, Jocelyn began to feel stronger, rejuvenated by Maggie's seemingly endless energy and positive attitude. For her part, Maggie had already organized a relief fund and collected over $10,000 to assist the more destitute survivors.

"We got brined, salted, and pickled in mid ocean, but now we are high and dry," Maggie said. "We need to get up with our heads held high. Ya got things to do, honey, and François wouldn't want you to give up."

The following Monday, Jocelyn called Lady Duff-Gordon's business phone, and to her surprise and great relief, on the other end of the line was Lucy, herself.

"Oh Lucy, I am so happy to hear your voice!"

"Jocelyn?" Lucy said. "Jocelyn, darling! Where have you been? We thought we lost you!"

"I've been staying with Maggie Brown. And Cosmo – is he-"

"He's safe," Lucy said. "We both managed to get in a lifeboat. I didn't see you on the *Carpathia*."

"I know," Jocelyn said, "everything was so hectic."

"I am so relieved that you are safe and well," Lucy said. "And François?" She awaited a long silence. "Oh no, Jocelyn, please don't tell me."

"He did not survive," Jocelyn said, her voice shaky. "I wish it were not so."

"Oh, my darling, I am so sorry." Jocelyn could hear Lucy begin to cry. "So many good people perished. I am so dreadfully sorry, Jocelyn. Isidor and Ida – they did not make it, either."

Jocelyn could barely speak. "They were the loveliest

people. This is almost too much to bear."

"Can you come see me?" Lucy finally said. "If you are up to it?"

"Yes, of course."

"We need each other now more than ever, darling."

"Are we still-"

"Of course," Lucy said. "Isidor's brother, Nathan Straus, is a co-owner of Macy's, or I should say, he's now the sole owner. Nathan received the telegram from Isidor the following morning after our meeting on *Titanic*. He is aware of our ideas for ready-to-wear and is determined to honor his brother's agreement to expand the departments and accommodate your designs. Let us meet tomorrow at P.J. Clarkes, on 55th and Third."

"Thank you, Lucy," Jocelyn said.

"God bless you. We'll get through this together, dear..."

At their luncheon meeting the next day, Lucy and Jocelyn determined to forge ahead into a business discussion, but they found it difficult not to first talk about their shared ordeal. Newspapers worldwide had picked up on the *Titanic* disaster, every day filled with sensational stories about passengers dying in the icy North Atlantic, and accusations of negligence on the part of *Titanic's* crew and the White Star Line. Jocelyn had not read a newspaper while recuperating at Maggie Brown's home, so she was surprised to hear that the United States Senate had already commenced an investigation when the *Carpathia* docked in New York.

Lucy told Jocelyn about distressing rumors printed in the papers, accusing her husband, Cosmo, of paying off crewmembers to deny Second and Third Class passengers access to their lifeboat. Other false and inflammatory stories suggested the Duff-Gordons and others paid the crewman to not rescue passengers from the water, even though their lifeboat held only twelve survivors - the least amount boarded that night.

"Those despicable newspapermen," Lucy said. "They will print any story they hear just to make the headlines. Cosmo is devastated that anyone would accuse him of bribing those men, or dare to suggest he was a coward for boarding the lifeboat. It seems they wish to vilify any man who survived."

"Where were you when they ordered everyone to the lifeboats?"

"We had just gone to bed. After the collision, we did what we were told – dressed warmly and immediately went to the Boat Deck, which at the time, boarding the lifeboats was strictly considered a precautionary measure. We were in our cabins on A Deck and, being one level below, we were among the first passengers to reach the Boat Deck. I was so frightened to get in one of those lifeboats alone, and I would not let go of Cosmo. That Mr. Murdoch finally forcibly put my secretary and me in Boat One, near the bow of the ship. I insisted that Cosmo come with us, but Cosmo hesitated and waited to see if Mr. Murdoch would put any other women in first. There was no one else around at that moment, so Mr. Murdoch allowed Cosmo and two other male First Class passengers, and then seven other seamen to board. Jocelyn, of the twelve, only two of us were women and *seven* were crew, so why Cosmo is being singled out as a coward is perplexing. Mr. Murdoch was in charge, not Cosmo.

"Our boat, by the way, was one of two of the wooden emergency cutters, with a 40-person capacity, not one of the lifeboats with a 65-person capacity, as people were led to believe. I am sure you know, wearing those boxy life jackets filled up the space on the boat, where not many more people could have fit, even if there were more people on the Boat Deck ready to board. I must say, whoever calculated the passenger capacity in the lifeboats was sorely mistaken, and in my opinion, could not obviously do math in his head. Only two of the lifeboats were filled to capacity, and that happened about 30 minutes before the ship sank.

"Before we were lowered down to the sea, Mr. Murdoch told the crewman to row as far away from the ship as we could. I remember, as we rowed farther and farther, how the gravity of the situation became clear as the bow began to sink. We watched in silence, utterly paralyzed in disbelief when that magnificent ship split and went under. That sound is something I cannot get out of my mind."

"I'll never forget that moment for as long as I live," Jocelyn said.

Lucy shook her head, tears welling in her eyes. "Then, the most awful cries of agony – we could hear them, even from a far distance. I think about it now and wonder if we could have saved anyone, but we were too far away to row back to them before they-" Her voice trailed off as she blankly stared.

"There was some discussion in our boat about going back," Jocelyn said, "but the seaman in charge feared the people in the water would tip us over in panic. We simply stayed put until the terrible screaming subsided."

"Then," Lucy said, "during those long hours in darkness so black, you couldn't see your hand in front of your face. I was so frightened, and I suppose I bothered them about our predicament, and one of them asked why I was complaining. He said they all lost everything – their entire 'kit', as they called it – lost their jobs as well. It made our losses, while quite substantial, pale by comparison. So Cosmo promised the boys money to help tide them over when we were rescued. And he did, Jocelyn. He gave each boy five pounds when we docked - and now, those horrible newspapermen say he bribed them to keep our lifeboat away from those poor dying souls in the water. What kind of man would accuse someone of such cruelty?"

"Only a small mind," Jocelyn said, touching Lucy's hand. "No one will ever know what we endured unless they were there with us."

Lucy pulled an embroidered handkerchief from her bag and dabbed her eyes. "We have much to discuss. We have the future, yes?"

"We do," Jocelyn replied.

Their discussion about upcoming business ventures led to Lucy suggesting that Jocelyn officially begin her employment at *Lucile*, Monday, June 3rd. This would give Jocelyn six weeks, plenty of time to put the Pittsburgh house up for sale, pack everything, and move to New York. Lucy asked, in the meantime, if Jocelyn would create a portfolio, specifically with some ready-to-wear designs for fall and winter, so by June *Lucille* would already be producing her designs on the assembly line. Lucy also wanted some of her designer pieces for those buying for the holidays. Her clients would be anxious for the latest, newest couture fashions by summer's end.

Under normal circumstances, the workload might have

overwhelmed Jocelyn, but she insisted Lucy put her under pressure so she could immerse herself in her work and have no time to dwell over her losses.

"I will begin your salary immediately for all the designs you bring to me in the meantime," Lucy said.

Jocelyn was grateful and agreed to bring new designs to Lucy each time she came to New York during her transition from Pittsburgh, and with the move, she would be more than busy to keep her mind off the loss of François.

After lunch, Jocelyn called on Mrs. Straus' concierge, Mr. Abernathy, at the Plaza Hotel, located at the southeast corner of Central Park, not far from the restaurant.

"Mr. Abernathy, my name is Jocelyn Brewster Davis. I sent you a wire from *Titanic*."

"Why yes, of course. What a relief to see you! How are you after such an ordeal?"

"Well, I am here. I suppose that says it all. I wanted to extend my condolences to you. Mr. and Mrs. Straus were exceptional people. I so enjoyed their company while I was onboard."

"Thank you, Mrs. Davis. Yes, they were truly a lovely couple. I am still shocked by their deaths, and am at a loss without their friendship."

"I understand," Jocelyn said.

"Well, let us turn to happier events, shall we?" Mr. Abernathy said. "After receiving your telegram, I found you a lovely two-bedroom apartment in a brownstone on the upper west side, facing Central Park. It is still available. I think you will absolutely love it."

"Oh, I'm thrilled. I can't wait to see it."

"I know the previous tenants, and they left it in immaculate condition." He handed her a piece of paper with the address and the landlord's telephone number.

"Thank you so much, Mr. Abernathy. You've just made my transition to New York much easier." Jocelyn handed him a generous gratuity for his assistance.

"Thank you, Mrs. Davis. Please call on me if I may be of further help."

"I certainly will. A good concierge is an invaluable resource. By the way, please call me Jocelyn. I have a feeling we will become good friends."

"By all means, Jocelyn. You may call me William."

"Until we meet again, William. May you enjoy the day." Jocelyn took her leave. She would certainly keep William Abernathy in mind, in case she could turn business his way. She immediately walked to her new apartment, where she arranged with the landlord to take possession the following weekend.

The next morning, she traveled by train to Pittsburgh and began the sale of her home. She invited Margaret to come with her, finding her to be delightful company. After her experience on *Titanic*, she no longer had any stomach for society's falderal, realizing how empty it all was. Margaret would certainly add a breath of fresh air to Pittsburgh society's highfalutin, pretentious ways. Jocelyn had a thing or two to learn about how to be *in* the world, and not *of* it, and Margaret was just the person to teach her.

They packed what she needed to set up house in New York and arranged to have it all shipped. Then, they returned to Manhattan via train. When the boxes arrived, Margaret helped Jocelyn settle into her new apartment. While unpacking her valise, Jocelyn discovered a piece of paper with Father Francis Browne's address in Ireland. She shook her head, thinking of that delightful priest who fancied photography. How she lamented, at the time, his bad luck for having to disembark *Titanic* at Queenstown, before the ship's fateful journey across the Atlantic - and here it was, his saving grace. That evening Jocelyn would write him a letter.

As she rummaged further through the valise, she came across François' wallet and passport, and she began to cry.

"Honey, come to me," Maggie said, hugging her tightly.

"How can I ever bear this?" Jocelyn said, clutching the wallet.

"You don't," Maggie said. "You cry it out. It's ok."

Jocelyn showed Maggie her necklace. "He gave me this. It was an old family heirloom that he said would protect me."

"Oh, my," Maggie said. "That is a stunning piece. You will always hold a part of him, and he'll hold a part of you."

Jocelyn then pulled out the teacup and saucer, emblazoned with the White Star Line brand.

"Well now," Maggie said. "Those imbeciles at the White Star Line may want you to pay for that."

Jocelyn turned the teacup in her hand with a melancholy smile. "He asked me to marry him."

"He - oh, now I'm gonna cry," Maggie said. "He did?"

Jocelyn smiled. "When I put these in my valise, he looked at me as if I was mad. I told him that we needed something to remind us of that night. I said it was something that we would tell our grandchildren about someday." Jocelyn looked into Maggie's eyes. "I am carrying his child."

"What?" Maggie said, astonished. "Are you sure?"

Jocelyn nodded. "I am. I will see a physician tomorrow,

but I am certain."

Now Maggie *did* cry. "You won't be alone, honey. He really *will* be with you forever…"

Lucile Ltd. was not far from Jocelyn's apartment, and the next morning she walked to her new place of employment to surprise Lucy with some designs. Lucy suggested a few changes, but for the most part, she was quite pleased. She passed them down the line for production, and she predicted the first samples would be ready within a week. It was a good day. All was falling into place. The next day, Jocelyn would return to Pittsburgh to finish the move, but this day was not over. It was April 30th. Jocelyn had one last appointment to keep.

"Would you mind if I use your telephone to make a dinner reservation?" Jocelyn asked.

"By all means, help yourself," Lucy said.

Jocelyn picked up the nickel-plated candlestick telephone and raised the receiver to her ear. The operator answered, "Number, please."

"Would you connect me with the Hotel St. Regis, please?"

"Yes ma'am," said the operator.

In a moment, a man answered.

"Yes, hello," Jocelyn said. "I would like to make a reservation for dinner tonight, if I may? At 7 p.m., a table for one, please. The name is Delacroix. Wonderful, I'll see you then."

"Delacroix?" Lucy said.

Jocelyn smiled with tears in her eyes. "Before everything fell apart on *Titanic*, François invited me to dinner. He said, no matter what, we should promise to meet at the St. Regis on this night. It will be the last memory I have of him…"

She dressed in her finest evening gown - one of her own Art Nouveau designs - a burnt velvet gown in Ming blue-green, with satin ultramarine blue gloves, and blue satin shoes to match. Her entire ensemble was centered around her wearing the gold chain holding the cast of the golden ammonite, inlaid with the labradorite. Gold dangle earrings complemented the necklace. Over her dress, she wore a floor-length burnt velvet duster with a stunning peacock design in glass beads.

The maître d'hôtel seated her at a table facing a window, taking notice of the stunning woman, and yet there was a deep sadness about her countenance. Jocelyn found herself daydreaming about the plans she made with François as she looked out at the bustling city on 55th Avenue. Her brownstone was just five blocks away. She could have walked down 5th Avenue to get to the hotel, but she decided to take a handsome cab and go in style. She looked across the table at the empty chair and second table setting, smiling slightly, a few tears falling down her cheeks. She dabbed her eyes with her handkerchief before the waiter approached, wondering if coming here tonight might have been a mistake.

"Good evening," the waiter said. His purely American accent seemed foreign to Jocelyn, who had spent so much time abroad. "Are we expecting anyone else tonight?"

"No," Jocelyn said, almost inaudibly.

He handed her a menu. "Would you care to begin with a glass of wine?"

"Not tonight, thank you."

"Very well. Before you make your selection, might I suggest the Sole Almandine, served with lemon butter sauce over rice with a side of Brussels sprouts with bacon and thyme? Another of the chef's specialties is his famous filet mignon, served with glazed carrots and mashed potatoes."

"Do you think the chef could prepare the filet mignon with the Brussels sprouts and bacon, along with the mashed potatoes?" Jocelyn asked, for it was all about the bacon.

"Absolutely, Madame. Might I suggest a wine to pair with the filet mignon?"

She hesitated before she politely refused. "No, thank you, but I *would* like a pot of tea with my dinner - Earl Grey, if you have it."

"Excellent, and might I suggest your filet be cooked medium rare?"

"Yes, thank you."

"And might I suggest sautéed mushrooms in a lovely butter sauce?"

"Well, no, that might be too rich, but... perhaps a small portion?"

"Very good - and finally, may I invite you to have a most wondrous evening?"

Jocelyn looked at him quizzically. His warm smile softened her heart, and she tried to smile. "Thank you."

He nodded and took her menu, slightly bowing before he backed away from the table.

Jocelyn sighed and turned her attention to the dining room, which was busy with happy customers. She had hoped, after a few moments in the restaurant, she might feel more at ease, but that was hardly the case. Her heart ached even more as the empty chair across the table continued to remind her of the emptiness in her heart. She thought about asking the waiter to remove it, and the table setting, but she simply could not. She thought about canceling her order and leaving the restaurant, but she simply could not. Despite the busy dining room around her, she felt more alone than ever, unable to return to the past, and unable to proceed forward. Tears clutched her throat, and she felt like she was back in that cold lifeboat, adrift and alone in a darkened sea.

Jocelyn took a deep breath and bravely turned toward the window, watching the people walk by outside and trying to shift from her grief. After some time, in the window's reflection, she noticed two waiters approach the table from behind. One of them slowly hobbled with crutches. *How odd*, she thought. Her original waiter stepped before her with a smile, holding a tray with an elegant teapot. The waiter on crutches took the pot and poured her tea.

"Tea instead of wine? Now, that is not like you, is it?"

How rude. She turned to look up at the waiter who spoke to her.

A French accent!

At that very moment, her mind went entirely blank.

François!

She gasped, unaware that her hands flew to her face. She instinctively closed her eyes to blink this cruel vision away. When she opened them, François tearfully spoke.

"Jocelyn, mon chéri."

Without any ounce of control, Jocelyn screamed and jumped out of her seat, knocking her chair to the floor...

CHAPTER
Nine

Sophia awoke with tears of joy, knowing that François had survived. At breakfast, she filled in the details as Michael listened to her every word.

Tears filled *his* eyes. "Man, this is so much better than the movie."

Sophia laughed. "That Gaston. Whenever I've tried to push the subject of *Titanic*, he goes into his riddle game!" She used her best namby-pamby voice, "You must search the depths on your own. The answers you seek are adrift in your heart. Oh – my favorite – what appears on the surface is but a tiny portion of what lies underneath."

"That's good. You sound just like him."

"You know what?" Sophia said. "When we get back home, I'm gonna slap him!" She burst out laughing.

That morning, they crossed over the border at Derry/ Londonderry, Northern Ireland. Michael convinced Sophia to take a turn in the front seat, a gesture that earned him a 'noble gentleman' tag. He conveniently neglected to mention that his hips didn't hurt as much on a long car ride when he could stretch out across the back seat. A less noble omission, he confessed to himself, but he estimated it spared him a ten-minute lecture about the sheer joy of doctors, hospitals, and total hip replacement surgery by some knife-wielding kid half his age. Who needed that on such a beautiful Irish morning, anyway?

Along the way, Sophia looked back at Michael with a smile, her eyes hidden by sunglasses, but the rest of her face saying she was fully aware a normal human being doesn't ride in a back seat contorted like a pretzel and squirming like he had crickets in his pants.

Pádraig resumed his role of tour guide. "Here in Derry/Londonderry, you'll notice many painted murals covering the buildings that depict the strained relationships and stories of political and cultural unrest between loyalist - sometimes called unionists - and the republican Irish nationalists."

"Is it my understanding," Michael said, "that the division falls along both religious and political lines?"

"It does," Pádraig said. "Most unionists are Protestant, and nationalists are largely Catholic, but that's not a steadfast rule; and politically, unionists of Northern Ireland are loyal to Britain, while nationalists in the Republic of Ireland support an independent sovereign state, which separated from the United Kingdom under the Government of Ireland Act of 1920."

"It's so beautiful here," Sophia said. "It's hard to picture what it must have been like back during that time."

"Aye –'The Troubles', as it is called."

"I guess we're all around the same age," Michael said. "You were born in the middle of it, weren't you?" Michael asked.

"A bit before, actually. The Troubles was a thirty-year period from 1968 to 1998," Pádraig said. "I'd say I've a few years on you, but my memory is vague during the worst of the civil wars, for I've lived far south all of me life."

"I remember traveling in Belfast only one time when I was a kid," Michael said. "We weren't here long, but I remember my parents were very cautious about where we traveled, and how we behaved."

"It was tryin' times with terrorism and civil war," Pádraig said, "but don't have misgivins' about it now. Since the truce was settled in '98, relations between both sides have become more civil, despite the obvious tender scars you see about. The name of Derry, for one. You may have noticed the road signs in the south said 'Derry,' but when we cross the border, it's Londonderry. Despite our civilized ways these days, you can still get hopped on if you shoot yer mouth off about politics, or venture into the wrong places in the city."

"Not really any different than any big city," Sophia said.

"It's not," Pádraig said. "So, no need olagonin' about the past. We're perfectly safe here, and we'll have us a craic."

Sophia quizzically looked at Pádraig as he drove on, and then at Michael, who simply shrugged.

Eastbound, they drove along the North Antrim Coast, following the gorgeous Causeway Coastal Route, considered one of the top five road trips in the world. Binevenaugh Mountain's dramatic cliffs provided a view over fields of green and edges of coastline before they stopped by Dunluce Castle's medieval ruins. They stopped at the must-see Giant's Causeway, a World Heritage Site, where 40,000 interlocking hexagonal red basalt columns appear like stepping-stones beginning at the base of the cliff. The stones eventually disappear under the North Channel of the Irish Sea, only to reemerge on the Scottish coastline. The area is a haven for sea birds and unusual plants not found elsewhere in Ireland. Sophia could have stayed for hours, taking in the sights. The shape of the stones reminded her of Devil's Tower in Wyoming.

All over Ireland and Northern Ireland was history dating back thousands of years. Along the way, they stayed in small inns and bed and breakfasts, getting to know the charm of the local people.

On their way to Ballycastle, they stopped at the spectacular Carrick-A-Rede Rope Bridge that crossed over a 30-meter chasm to tiny Carrick Island. As they approached the narrow bridge, Sophia noticed Michael's limp was more profound than in the preceding days.

"How are your hips? Do you want to walk over the bridge with me?" Sophia asked.

Michael dutifully followed. "Of course. How often do you get a chance to plunge a hundred feet to your death?"

"Ah, not to worry," Pádraig said, "this latest bridge was raised in 2008 by a fine construction unit in Belfast. She'll hold… maybe."

As they began to traverse the chasm, Michael waited until everyone was well past the point of no return. "You say this was built in Belfast?"

"It was," Pádraig said.

"That's where they built the *Titanic*, isn't it?"

"Oh, yeah!" Sophia breathlessly said as the bridge swayed in the wind. "You just *had* to bring that up!"

From Ballycastle, they took a ferry to Rathlin, Northern Ireland's only inhabited island of about 130 people with a rich traditional cultural heritage and abundant wildlife, including thousands of seabirds. Back on the mainland, they drove along the winding roads of scenic Northern Ireland, through charming, picturesque villages, and then on to the green Glens of Antrim.

Pádraig took a short detour up the peninsula to the Gobbins, where they walked across bridges, through tunnels, up steps, and into caves along the very edge of Northern Ireland overlooking the Irish Sea toward Scotland. There, they witnessed waves crashing on the cliffs below, and felt the exhilarating sea spray on their faces.

On the northern shore of Belfast Lough was the well-preserved 12th century Carrickfergus Castle, built by the conquering Normans in 1177. For several moments while she and Michael wandered through the castle, Sophia slipped into a short vision of having once been there, recalling that the interiors remained much as they were nearly a thousand years before.

Belfast, the capital of Northern Ireland, was a bustling city, dramatically different from the tiny seaside villages they saw along the way. After Pádraig told Sophia that Belfast was also famous for its Irish Linen, she had much greater appreciation for the linen jacquard tablecloths and napkins that Darius handed down to her through her MacPhaidin family line. She rarely used them because they were so elegant, but that was about to change. Why keep them hidden away when she and Michael could enjoy their beauty and quality every day?

Despite the great *Titanic* disaster of 1912, the doomed ship's builder, Harland and Wolff Heavy Industries, Ltd., remained among Belfast's largest employers, world-renowned for marine engineering, naval architecture, ship design and construction, and offshore wind farming industries. Directly adjacent was the Titanic Belfast Museum, where Sophia and Michael spent an entire day, while Pádraig took a day off to relax, visit friends, and shop in the city. Michael took special interest in the building's beautiful design as the symbol of the new Belfast, an iconography of shipbuilding, the iceberg, and the fundamental points of the compass. They enjoyed touring the numerous exhibits displaying everything from the timelines of the construction of *Titanic,* to the aftermath of her demise.

On several occasions throughout the day, Sophia slipped into the life of Jocelyn, flashing on the ship's last five historic days, and stirring up latent feelings of trauma that remained from Jocelyn's horrific experience. It left Sophia wondering what more she needed to do to heal ancient past wounds. She hoped the result of the trip throughout Ireland was the catalyst to help her do just that.

That evening, as they walked along the streets of Belfast, Sophia reflected on the rapid changes throughout Earth and all over the globe. Over the last decade, Northern Ireland had ended centuries of political and religious dissonance to establish independence from British rule. Northern Ireland and the Republic of Ireland – both Protestant and Catholic - came together to honor political and religious differences for the common good.

In the last two decades, the United States unfortunately joined the rest of the world with an increase in terrorism activity and political turbulence. Racial tension was increasing again, and worldwide elections were in chaos, demonstrating how pandemonium takes form when outdated systems die out. Throughout the world, governments developed new reforms to encourage unification between nations. The white-knuckled grip on old regimes was releasing hold, in some cases by force, and in other ways by default.

What Sophia found most interesting was precisely what White Buffalo espoused when he said that Grandmother Earth's back was up with the constant shifting of the tectonic plates causing more violent earthquakes and increased volcanic activity. According to scientists, the amplification of weather patterns through global warming was simply something to which humans must adapt. The world was again at the inception of a new way of life with the Earth mirroring the actions of humanity with the same energetic force.

The Earth herself and the world of humanity was rapidly shifting from old systems that were no longer in service to the current stage of evolution. From a broader perspective, many wondrous changes were coming, beyond the appearances of chaos, for the world was becoming a smaller place, and people were taking action to come together in oneness. For many, like Sophia, Michael, and their beloved companions in Apeiros, their union represented not only concern for survival and preservation, but also for the greater good - from Love.

The deeper pieces that Sophia faced were the old systems within her own history rising to the surface of her consciousness for release. As the carrier of the life force who held a consciousness for the world, whatever she did to heal herself also brought healing to the historic wounds still carried by those around her, and sometimes the healing process was uncomfortable and not easy. This was true for everyone who came to their healing, whether they consciously knew of their power to bring positive change or not.

The Irish were a strong and vibrant people who endured centuries of tyranny and mistreatment. The beauty of the land alone, and the raw nature of the surrounding Irish coastline, was a reflection of the hearts of its people, who were constantly working toward settlement of political and religious upheaval. Sophia was there, as a daughter of the Irish, to tap into the deeper mysteries that held the Irish together. Geographically, Ireland was small, but the great heart of the Irish held the world.

That night, Sophia again journeyed into dreams of Jocelyn.

Jocelyn threw her arms around François, tripping over his crutches and taking them both down to the floor. Not yet aware of the cast on his leg, she scrambled to her knees and kissed him several times, although she knew such a public display of affection was improper. The restaurant guests stopped to watch, most of them amused. Then the dam broke as tears flowed down her cheeks. Jocelyn was stunned, rendered speechless for a few moments. François sat up, laughing, although wincing in pain and quite uncomfortable.

"Oh, my, are you all right? What happened to you?" She reached for his arm, and then quickly pulled back, realizing she had already caused enough trouble.

"Not to worry," François said with that marvelous accent. "I have survived worse, I assure you."

Jocelyn gently pulled him close. "Are you real? Am I dreaming?"

"It would seem that I am, and you are not," François said. "But I do recognize a pattern in the way we continue to meet, no?"

Jocelyn put her hand to her mouth and simply stared, unconcerned that they were sitting on the floor of an elegant New York restaurant. "I - I thought you were dead."

"Over the past two weeks, I was not certain myself."

A distinctive New York accent behind them broke the spell. "Perhaps you would be more comfortable in your chairs?"

They both perked, reluctant to let go. "Oh!" Jocelyn said. "Yes, of course." She attempted to help François up, while trying to make sense of it all - and not doing a very good job of it either. Finally, the waiter stepped in and helped François rise to his feet, handing him his crutches. He then held Jocelyn's chair, and then seated François next to her.

Jocelyn pointed an accusing finger at the waiter with a smile. "You were in on this, weren't you?"

"Just a helpless romantic." He smiled and backed away with a bow. "I'll give you a moment."

Jocelyn took François' hand. "It is a miracle."

"Oui, mon chéri." He pulled his handkerchief from his pocket and handed it to her.

She dabbed her eyes. "What happened? I cannot believe you are here - alive! Tell me - where have you been? Oh, my love, you are here - with me. You are here!" She continued to cry in astonishment.

François smiled, for he could not get a word in.

Somehow, the sheer moment of joy eased his physical discomfort. *How I love her spirited ways. I am pleased to know that nothing has changed.*

"I did not see you on the *Carpathia*. I watched for you while everyone came aboard from the lifeboats. What happened? Where were you?"

"I have yet to clearly recall those moments," François said. "I confess my time on *Carpathia* is shrouded in mystery. As for the remainder of our time apart, I must say this one thing before I tell you my tale."

"Oh, yes, please tell me."

"I am desperate for a glass of wine and a sumptuous meal with the love of my life."

Jocelyn laughed for the first time in what seemed forever.

François waved to the waiter and ordered a drink. "Chéri? A claret for you?"

"No, thank you. I will enjoy my tea."

"Very well," François said. "Bring me a bottle of 1909 Chateau Lafite Rothschild, s'il vous plaît, with two glasses." He laughed with her. "One for my leg, and one for my trembling hands, which have yet to cease since I went swimming in the North Atlantic."

The waiter cocked his head and then politely nodded. "Forgive me, but I cannot help overhearing that you both were on the *Titanic?*"

"We were – at least for awhile, oui," François said.

"My goodness," the waiter said as Jocelyn again found reason to laugh.

"The last time I saw this wonderful man," Jocelyn said,

"he was standing on the deck as my lifeboat rowed away from the ship."

He looked at François. "Do you mean you went down with the ship?"

"Unintentional, I assure you," François said. "A more fitting description is the ship went down with me."

"God bless you, sir. I shall be back with your wine and a menu."

"Let us save time," François said. "I shall have whatever my darling is having, s'il vous plaît."

"Very good." The waiter departed as François looked deeply into Jocelyn's eyes.

They reached for each other's hands. "I feel like I am alive again," Jocelyn said. "I can't describe the anguish I have felt."

"I am so sorry, my darling. I have lost these last few weeks in hospital. My mind only cleared in just the last few days."

The waiter quickly returned with the maître d', a chilled bottle of champagne and two crystal champagne glasses in hand.

The maître d' clicked his heels. "My dear guests, it shall be our pleasure to offer your meals this evening with our compliments. Welcome back."

As the maître d' uncorked the champagne, the diners around them stirred and applauded as the word 'Titanic' quickly spread through the room. Several gentlemen approached their table and offered calling cards, pledging to help in any way possible.

"Merci, your generosity is much appreciated," François

said, addressing the patrons. "We are just reuniting after our ordeal. We are so appreciative of your support, but as we sit here tonight, safe and warm in this lovely place, we must not forget the many brave men, women, and children who perished at sea that night."

"Hear, hear," someone softly said.

The guests settled back at their tables as the waiter poured a glass of champagne for Jocelyn, and then for François, who raised his glass in toast. "To dreams come true, mon chéri!" They toasted, and Jocelyn took a small sip. This was certainly not the time, nor the place for her to explain why she was not drinking.

"Is the champagne not to your liking, chéri?" François asked.

"No, no, it is lovely," Jocelyn said, "but I am already so lightheaded with excitement that I dare say I might fall over if I drink too much."

"Precisely my intention tonight," François said, raising his glass. "To my Jocelyn, my love." His throat grew tight, and his eyes welled in tears. "How I prayed that terrible night, clinging to the railing on that dying ship, that I would see your lovely face again."

Jocelyn grabbed his hand, for some reason fearful to let go. "So, I simply must know, François. You must tell me everything, for during those horrible hours after *Titanic* disappeared, I could scarcely breathe."

"Nor could I," François said, quiet serious now. "It was not until a few days ago that I began to recall what happened, for I was delirious with illness and quite captive to the sedatives they administered for the pain in my broken leg and ribs."

"I'm so sorry I could not be with you in the hospital,"

Jocelyn said.

"When *Titanic* split below the water line, I stood near the stern - at an angle so high in the air I could scarcely hang on. The stern abruptly fell back to the sea, and I lost my grip as the jolt threw me off the ship. I fell perhaps some 15 meters into debris floating on the water."

"Oh, how terrible, my love!"

"All I could see was black," François continued. "The water was below freezing, and I with stabbing pain raging through every inch of my body. It was so numbing cold that I had no idea how badly injured I was, but I knew I had no chance of survival if I remained so close to the sinking hull. My arms were uninjured, thank God, so I swam away as the stern began to upend again. I was terrified of that massive, twisted wreck churning and groaning - I did not want to be anywhere near her when she went down, believing the ship's momentum would take me with her. There were many people drowning around me, and each breath I took in the icy water was shorter and more shallow.

"And then, as panic began to consume me, in the horrible din of people either drowning or already dead, I remembered what you told me, Jocelyn – that living or dying was up to me. At that moment, I felt oblivious to the cold and pain, and my mind began to focus in a way that I have never known before. It was as if I could see everything and every means of escaping death, all in one brief moment of opportunity. At that instant, I knew I was not going to die that night.

"By that miracle, I caught sight of something large floating about 20 meters away. I saw men struggling around it, and as I swam, I saw it was one of the collapsible lifeboats bobbing in the sea, upside-down. Several men were straddled on top, trying to prevent it from capsizing. As I approached, one of the men called at me to keep swimming, and he reached for me. I tried to climb on, but my broken leg was useless, so another man grabbed hold of my collar and hauled me up. When I regained my bearings, I recognized Mr. Lightoller's voice. You remember him?"

"Yes," Jocelyn said, still fighting the tears. "We met him the day he spoke with Captain Smith about the fire in the coalbunker."

François nodded, also wiping tears away. "My guardian angel that night. None of us on that little boat would have survived without his quick thinking. He directed the uninjured to pull survivors from the water, ordering us as to which way to lean so we would not flip over. I was helpless, for all I could do was lay there and shake. I feared my tremors would overturn the collapsible. About that time, *Titanic's* stern finally sank. It sounded like a massive thunderstorm at first, and then the last vestige of her disappeared completely in silence."

"I remember that sound," Jocelyn said. "It will not leave my memory."

"Oui, but in the last moment of *Titanic's* life, she went down almost silently, without fanfare. It seemed almost anticlimactic after two-and-a-half hours of sheer pandemonium. And then, in the darkness, utterly blind, we heard the screaming – like a crowd at a sporting match. I was quite disoriented and wondered if it might be a hallucination. I do not recall how long the screams persisted, but before long, they subsided until they altogether ceased. Then, eternity began."

"I know... the wait..." Jocelyn said.

"I was shivering badly, unaware of anything but the darkness. The cold was excruciating, as was the wait. Everyone on that collapsible had come from the icy seas. We were all wet and freezing, so precariously balanced that it was quite difficult to keep from tipping the boat and losing someone off the side.

"There were some thirty of us. Some stood, while others knelt, and I just laid flat on my belly over the middle of the boat, a few of the men assuring me I was keeping the craft centered. Mr. Lightoller kept everyone calm, telling us to remain as still as possible and pray the sea remained still. When the swells later came about, he told the men which way to lean, to keep us from tipping over.

"I do not know how much time passed when Mr. Lightoller called out to another lifeboat, and they eventually found us out there in the darkness. Soon, another joined us, and Mr. Lightoller ordered them to sidle up, one on either side of the collapsible to stabilize us. Those lifeboats were just half-full, each of them."

"Yes," Jocelyn said. "We had 63, but I've read that only two others held as many, while most of the others were one-third to one-half filled to capacity."

"I don't understand," François said. "I am only now hearing the number of dead is over 1,500."

Jocelyn sadly nodded. "So, were you able to get in one of the lifeboats that approached yours?"

"Oui, those who could step into the boat next to ours first did so. Then, those of us who were injured and needed assistance were next. All the time, Mr. Lightoller stood on the collapsible, counterbalancing the boat by shifting his weight to keep her steady. The crew of the other boats steadied the precarious collapsible as well, as survivors helped us board their boats. One poor fellow who had lain next to me, quite delirious all night, was dead." François swallowed a tear and wiped his eyes.

Jocelyn rubbed his arm. "It's all right, my love," she whispered.

"Once I was in the lifeboat, and although in pain and not altogether present of mind, I knew in my heart we would survive despite some talk that a rescue ship might not find us. By that time, we were covered in wool blankets, sitting next to others who helped warm us. I sensed I was slipping in and out of consciousness, for I do not clearly recall the *Carpathia* coming to our rescue, and I have but a vague memory of how I was taken aboard."

"I watched every face that came onto the ship," Jocelyn said. "I recall watching Mr. Lightoller come aboard and someone saying that he was the last survivor."

"I'm told that *Carpathia*'s crewmembers covered me with blankets and placed me onto a makeshift stretcher, which they lifted into one of their lifeboats and then hoisted me up like cargo – appropriate for a stowaway, no?" François gave a slight smile. "I was delirious and barely aware. They put me into a First Class cabin of an American couple who were so gracious to give up their stateroom for me."

Jocelyn resignedly nodded. "So that is why I never saw you."

"I am so sorry, Jocelyn. The doctor gave me a strong sedative for the pain, and I have no recollection of our journey to New York. By then, I grew ill with fever and chills, and I was incapacitated for several days."

"Oh, why did I not think of asking where the injured

were taken? Why did I not think of checking the hospitals?"

"Do not concern yourself, chéri. We are together now, and that is all that matters."

Jocelyn looked François over. "My darling, I probably hurt you earlier. What else is broken, beside your leg?"

"The doctors say I suffered from shock, hypothermia, a broken right leg in two places in my fibula and tibia, three broken ribs, with severe bruising and contusions all over my body. I also had a concussion, by which I am still a bit discombobulated.

"I was in St. Vincent's Hospital until yesterday, when I insisted they release me, for I at last had my wits about me and needed to find you. I simply knew you would come here tonight." He looked deeply into her eyes. "The moment I fell into the sea, your face was before me, Jocelyn. You kept me alive." He leaned forward to take her hand, wincing in pain.

"My dear François, I heard your heartbeat for quite some time that long night, but when I didn't see you onboard *Carpathia*, I convinced myself that the heartbeat I heard was my own. I cannot believe you are here, my love." She looked at him with wide-eyed amazement, still in awe. Trying to be present with him, she changed the subject. "So, since you are just out of the hospital, do you have somewhere to stay?"

"Well, I came here to the St. Regis, and I suppose the lovely manager took pity on my sorry countenance and sad story, for when I told him I was temporarily out of pocket, he graciously offered to accommodate me for a few days while I arrange to obtain funds and more permanent lodging."

"Of course, and remember, before we parted, you gave me your money and passport," Jocelyn said. "I will help you get back on your feet – literally." She simply could not contain her joy.

He took her hand. The candlelight shined on her face, making her even more radiant than he remembered. "You look so lovely tonight. I just wish to sit here and drink in your beauty. I assume this lovely gown is one of your creations?"

"Yes, it is," Jocelyn said. "Tonight, I wanted to dress as if you were waiting to meet me." She smiled and reached over to adjust his waiter's tunic. "And this lovely uniform you're wearing - even though you are on crutches – is quite becoming."

"I could not resist. And, of course, every stitch of clothing I own is now at the bottom of the Atlantic."

Jocelyn tried not to laugh. "It is lucky for you that I have a thing for men in uniforms."

"I hope it is not just the uniform."

She smiled and spoke in a whisper, "Well, in your case, any uniform fits the bill, but it is you who I am attracted to, no matter how you are dressed - or undressed, for that matter."

"Ah, Mrs. Davis, my little coquette. That is truly one of the things I love most about you."

The waiter approached with their meals. Jocelyn and François were content to simply look into each other's eyes while the waiter placed their food before them. He then produced the Bordeaux for François to inspect.

"Darling," Jocelyn said, "I must beg off the wine, as well. Perhaps you would care to have a single glass?"

François nodded at the waiter. "No, no. I believe I shall simply enjoy this fine champagne tonight."

"Very good," the waiter said, backing away.

"I'm sorry," Jocelyn said. "I must be alert tomorrow. I am going to Pittsburgh on the train, and I will be there through the weekend. I sold my house, and I must finish packing. I think it would work out well if you come with me. I can take care of you and feed you good meals while you recuperate."

"I won't be much help, but I cannot wait to be with you, so oui, I am at your disposal."

"I have big burly men hired to do all the lifting for me. They can lift you too, if necessary," she laughed. They enjoyed their meal while talking about their plans for the future. Before long, Jocelyn took notice of François' weariness, and she asked the waiter to order a handsome cab to wait for her.

"We must make this a short evening, my love," Jocelyn said.

François conceded as he stretched his weary back, feeling the strain of his mending ribs. "I dare say I will need a few more weeks of rest before I feel entirely well. But this evening has been magical, no?"

"It has. The beginning of many," Jocelyn said.

They thanked the maître d' and their waiter, leaving a generous tip for their hospitality. Jocelyn then took François up in the newly installed elevator to his room, helping him undress and then carefully tucking him into bed with the promise for greater attention at a later time. Jocelyn smiled and kissed him goodnight.

"I'll be here at 6:00 a.m. in the morning with a cab that

will take us to Union Station. The train leaves at 7:30. We can eat breakfast on the train. Goodnight, my love."

François was smiling, already asleep. The day was complete, and again, all was well.

CHAPTER
Ten

After spending a night in Belfast, Pádraig drove Michael and Sophia to County Meath, just north of Dublin. They spent time at the Hill of Tara, an archeological complex once the seat of the High Kings of Ireland.

Pádraig stopped the car on a rise, where they could survey the terrain. "You see what remains of the pre-Iron Age monuments," he said. "The Hill of Tara was once the capital of political and religious influence during the Neolithic era around 3400 BCE. The site held influence from that time until the 12th century, which held Roman artifacts dating from 100 to 300 CE.

"Ya might be interested to know about the mythical story that many Irish believe makes up the ancient history of Ireland. It begins with the Tuatha de Danaan, which means 'the people of Danu.' They were tall, with red-gold hair, sky-blue eyes, and fair skin - a wise, beautiful, and fearsome supernatural race of gods and goddesses who possessed magical skills, don't ya know. As the story goes, they arrived in dark clouds from above, and landed on the mountains in today's Connemara."

"Oh, I love this kind of stuff," Sophia said.

A master storyteller, Pádraig spoke in hushed theatrical tones. "In their possession were four magical talismans. The first was the Sword of Light, a glowing radiant torch, ya know – it was a torch from which no one could escape once it was drawn against them. The second was Lugh's Spear - a fiery lance that emitted sparks the size of eggs. The third was Dagda's Cauldron, which had the power to bring the dead back to life, also possessing the power that none would go from it unsatisfied. The fourth was Lia Fáil, the stone of Destiny, also known as the Coronation Stone.

"The Danaan placed the stone on the Hill of Tara, where it sits today," Pádraig continued. "It was thought that the Danaan were immortal - they lived forever and were unaffected by illness, for they were ageless and long-lived in comparison to the people of that day. However, the Milesians, perhaps the first Gauls in Ireland who came from Spain, eventually defeated them. The only weapon that could defeat the Danaan was made of iron. At that time, the rule of Ireland split in half. Milesians ruled what lay above ground, and the Danaan below. The Danaan were shielded from mortal eyes with an enchanted mist known as Faeth Fiadha, or the 'Cloak of Concealment.' Over time, the Danaan became known as the Sidhe, Ireland's fairy folk."

"I love it!" Sophia said.

Pádraig slowly pulled away. "As we approach the top of the Hill of Tara, you can see the inauguration mound. There, the High Kings were crowned at the standing stone, Lia Fáil, the fourth talisman of the Danaan. Legend has it, that if the impending King passed a series of tests, the stone would scream when he touched it. The roar from the stone would be so loud, all of Ireland could hear it, and they would know a new king was crowned."

"Like the selection of a new pope," Michael said. "Instead of a screaming stone, the news comes to the world in black smoke if a pope has not yet been selected, and in white smoke when the papal conclave of the College of Cardinals have come to a decision."

"Ya might say that," Pádraig said, "but my story's better."

"Oh, far better," Sophia said.

Michael laughed. "I guess this religious stuff is all smoke and mirrors, and a bit of screaming here and there."

"Some believe the Irish were one of the Lost Tribes of Israel, and the Hill of Tara contained the Ark of the Covenant," Pádraig said.

"Everyone in the western world wants to claim that holy heritage, along with their pursuit of the Holy Grail," Michael said.

"They do," Pádraig said, "but we prefer to think that God is an Irishman."

"Well, of course," Michael said, "that goes without saying."

They drove a short distance to Brú na Bóinne, meaning 'Palace of the Boyne', a Unesco World Heritage Site. Three principal monuments known as Knowth, Newgrange, and Dowth stood among 90 others recorded in the area. Pádraig led them on a walking tour to the largest of the passage tombs.

"Newgrange is Ireland's largest and most significant archeological discovery, built around 3200 BCE during the Neolithic Period or Late Stone Age, pre-dating both Egypt's Great Pyramids, and Stonehenge in England. It is one of the world's oldest intact buildings in existence.

"Back in the year 1699, Charles Campbell, a Scottish settler and proprietor of the property, directed his workmen to use some of the stones piled under the 300-foot-diameter mound, covered with heavy scrub brush. They soon removed a large flat stone from what they thought was a cave entrance.

"Generations of archeologists followed for the next 300 years, eventually discovering a stone-lined passageway leading to the central chamber with the corbelled ceiling, 20 feet high. Only hand-sized cobbles, sod, and soil covered the exterior of the structure, to make up the thirty-foot-high mound without the use of mortar. The building was so well constructed, no rain penetrated the building for over 5,000 years.

"In 1962," Pádraig said, "reconstruction began, as previous archeologists posited many theories as to the origin of the building and its interior passage, which led to the central chamber. They removed all trees and shrubs planted by previous landowners, for the roots would eventually compromise the building's integrity. As you can see, sod, soil, and hand-sized cobbles made up the estimated 181 thousand-ton structure. Over several millennia, the rounded cobbles on the top of the mound's surface fell to the ground. Today's front-facing facade contains the original large round cobbles, finished in white quartz from the banks of the Boyne River, about 80 kilometers south of here.

"Based on the estimated population and the average human age at that time, it most likely took 60 to 70 years, or two generations, to construct Newgrange from tools made of bone, antler, stone, and wood. The Neolithic people of Western Europe had no knowledge to construct tools of metal. The interior chamber is built in the cruciform style, which was common in many European mound structures. At three of the ends of each interior chamber is a large stone basin."

"What was its purpose?" Sophia asked.

"Some believe Newgrange was a burial tomb, because a few human remains were found inside. However, without knowing the Neolithic mindset, it is difficult to define the original purpose of the building. 97 kerbstones around the base of the mound, with carvings astronomically aligned, supported the foundation of the mound. Some stones are decorated with carvings of spirals, zig-zags, and small diamond shapes, called lozenges. In a larger circle, surrounding the exterior of the mound, are twelve standing stones, placed there 1,000 years after the mound's construction."

"Representing the circle of life?" Michael said.

"Perhaps," Pádraig said. "No one knows precisely the meaning of the spirals, but your theory is widely believed. Some suggest they also represent time as circular, as time does not pass, but rotates like the seasons."

Sophia smiled and looked back at Michael.

"The passageway floor that leads to the center chamber is slanted upwards, so the interior chamber floor is even with a light box, located above the entrance. The interior design of the passage undulates, creating light effects that are narrowed both horizontally and vertically. During the three days surrounding the Winter Solstice, the dawning sun enters the light box, and a precise dagger of light penetrates the interior chamber for 17 minutes.

"Obviously, brilliant builders engineered the mound's location perfectly to align with the sun on what we now know as the Winter Solstice - the shortest day and longest night of the year. As I am sure you know, solstice comes from the Roman 'sol', meaning sun, and 'stitium', meaning stoppage. Solstice means *standing still sun*. Once the Winter Solstice was over, the sun returned to longer days with the nights shorter until the Summer Solstice, when the sun reversed its cycle."

"It took tremendous engineering to build these mounds, and to align them so perfectly with astrological configurations," Michael said. "So many ancient cultures aligned their temples and buildings with the Winter and Summer Solstice."

Sophia stood in front of the large, precisely carved entrance stone, briefly recalling that she was there in a previous life, specifically in the celebration of the Winter Solstice. With a smile and a wistful look in her eye, she returned to the present moment. Michael knew she disappeared into one of her past lives for a short time. He took her hand and brought it to his lips. She smiled at her protector, knowing all was well...

Arriving in Dublin, they first visited Trinity College, built by Queen Elizabeth in 1592. Sophia especially desired to go to the Long Room in the Old Library to see the famed Book of Kells, written around 800 CE - the sumptuously decorated version of the New Testament's four gospels, glorifying Jesus' life and message.

"Look at the elaborate detail," Sophia said. "I studied the Book of Kells in college, mostly for its art and design. Its intricacies inspired me to learn how to write in various calligraphic scripts. Seeing these pages in person renews my dream of writing a book in calligraphy, and to illustrate it with my own drawings and paintings."

"Will you autograph a copy for me?"

Sophia smiled. "Why Pádraig, you will be the first..."

For dinner, they joined Geoffrey O'Hara's daughter, Cathleen, and her husband, Daniel McCartney, and their two girls at a popular Irish pub. Cathleen possessed her father's good looks and charm, and she greeted her new-found cousin Michael as if they had known each other all their lives. Sophia thought it almost uncanny how Cathleen, just like her dad, resembled Michael. Afterward, they enjoyed the music before they stayed the night at Cathleen and Daniel's charming bed and breakfast.

The next day, they toured Dublin's St. Patrick's Cathedral.

"This cathedral began as a 5th century Catholic Church," Pádraig said, "and then it became an Anglican church following the English reformation in 1537. Queen Mary later returned it to the Catholics. When the English monarchy changed from Catholic to Anglican, so did the cathedral, which was eventually named Ireland's National Cathedral. Jonathan Swift, who wrote *Gulliver's Travels,* was a dean of the cathedral from 1713 to 1745. It remains today as both Anglican and Catholic. The building went through many transformations over the centuries. Its current Gothic shape and size began in 1220. The interior changed over the years, with the exterior spire added at two different times."

Sophia's artistic eye enjoyed the artisanship of the stunning stained glass windows and mosaic floors. Michael had great appreciation for the spectacular architecture, and spent quite some time walking through the aisles, closely examining the building's fine details.

"You might fancy that the first performance of Handel's *Messiah* took place here in 1742," Pádraig said.

"Is that right?" Sophia said. "I always assumed it was initially performed for the King of England - you know the part when everyone stands when the king entered the room?"

"Yes, that is the tradition, but we Irish are proud to say that the premier was here in Dublin," Pádraig said. "Handel agreed to perform a series of concerts over several months. They were so successful that he decided to remain for an extended stay to perform the premier of the *Messiah*. Monies from the performance were split three ways for different charities, one of which was for the debtor's prison. 127 pounds went to pay their debts, resulting in the release of 142 people - that's the equivalent of over $26,000 in today's U.S. dollars."

"Hallelujah!" Michael sang in his deep baritone voice. He looked around, admiring the echo. "The acoustics in here are amazing."

Sophia and Pádraig blankly stared at him.

"I'm done," Michael said.

Pádraig continued, "That year, 700 people attended the premier. Women were asked not to wear their hoop skirts so more people could attend. The concert was such a success, another was scheduled. Not until a year later was Handel's *Messiah* performed in London..."

A trip to Dublin would not be complete without a tour of the seven-story Guinness Storehouse. Even though Michael had great admiration for St. Patrick's Cathedral, Guinness was his place of worship.

"Arthur Guinness purchased the St. James Gate

Brewery in December 1759," Pádraig said. "He signed a 9,000-year lease for 45 pounds per year for the four-acre brewery site. In 1761, for the first time, he exported six-and-one-half barrels of Guinness to Britain. By 1886, the company averaged 1,138,000 barrels per year in sales, even without advertising or offering their beer at a discount."

"So, Arthur only has about 8,700 more years left on the lease," Michael said. "He may be shocked at the increase in rent."

"He would be, if he were still here," Pádraig said, "but the lease voided when the property was expanded."

They toured the seven floors of restaurants, bars, and the store, complete with every type of Guinness item imaginable. The seventh floor held the Gravity Bar, where they enjoyed a complementary pint of Guinness, or what locals call, 'the black stuff.' From there, they took in the most magnificent view of Dublin.

The next morning, they left Cathleen and Daniel's bed and breakfast so pleased to have developed a greater connection with Michael's family. They drove along a two-lane mountain pass through the Wicklow Mountain National Park that ran from the edge of Dublin, south for 132 kilometers. Cascading waterfalls pooled into lakes through the lush green rolling hills and forested glens.

"Here, we have the peaceful and tranquil village of Glendalough, meaning 'Valley of Two Lakes,'" Pádraig said. "It's set in a deep glacial valley at the southern edge of the park. Originally, it was a 6th century monastic settlement."

They stopped and walked around an iconic, rather medieval-looking tower rising above a cemetery and a lovely green pasture.

"The village centerpiece is this perfect round tower built of stone, rising nearly 100 feet high," Pádraig said.

"What was its purpose?" Sophia asked.

"Bell tower," Pádraig said. "Also, a storehouse, or sometimes a fortress for protection."

Michael couldn't resist yelling from the base of the tower, "Rapunzel! Rapunzel! Let down your hair!" He looked around, quite satisfied.

"You just can't help yourself, can you?" Sophia asked, smiling at her husband while shaking her head.

"Evidently not."

"Well then, I roll my eyes at you," Sophia said.

Michael walked around the tower, marveling at its architecture, built with mica slate and granite. St. Kevin's Church stood next to the tower, also built entirely of stone, including the steep stone roof. A belfry, or more accurately, a miniature tower like the one next to the church, jutted out of one end of the roof. Nearby was a walking trail that followed along a quiet stream.

"I can't get over all the green," Sophia said. "Everywhere you look, it's so lush and beautiful." She thought of Colorado's rugged mountains and high desert plains, the canyons and mesas. "We just don't have green like this. However, I already miss the sunshine. That is one thing we *do* have in abundance."

"I have to say, even though I've traveled the world, I find myself so happy to return to Colorado," Michael said. "The only thing missing is the ocean."

"It sounds lovely," Pádraig said.

"You must come," Sophia said. "Seriously, you are welcome to stay with us. We can then reciprocate and give *you* the grand tour of our beautiful state. You could come with Lily, Colin, and Geoffrey. They're thinking about it."

"Be cautious, for I might just take ya up on that generous offer," Pádraig said.

"Give it some thought. Is it too late to drive to Wicklow? I'd like to visit the Avoca Handweavers Mill."

"Not at all, Miss, but I think we should stay the night there and tour Avoca in the morning," Pádraig said. "I believe you will enjoy Avoca, for it is one of the world's oldest surviving manufacturing companies, built in 1723. They are famous for their throws and blankets, but they now have clothing, perfumes, candles, and tableware."

"Uh-oh," Michael said.

"Get your wallet out, pal," Sophia said.

Pádraig laughed. "They also have world-class cafes in each of their locations throughout Ireland. It's an impressive business, now run by four siblings, whose parents bought the mill in the 1970's."

"Sounds marvelous, Pádraig," Sophia said. "Michael, are you game?"

"Game on!"

They enjoyed breakfast at Avoca the next morning, and following their tour of the extraordinary mill, they bought a shawl and two beautiful throws - one for White Buffalo. In the early afternoon, they hopped in the car and drove to Waterford, Ireland's oldest city with medieval walls, Georgian houses, and cobblestone streets, where Vikings once occupied the land. Before they settled into their bed and breakfast near the river, Sophia and Michael couldn't resist taking a walk, and Sophia took many pictures of the charming buildings lit along the waterfront. They enjoyed a light supper and a glass of wine to finish the evening.

A trip to Waterford was not complete without a visit to Waterford Crystal. From red-hot molten glass to diamond cut crystal, they were amazed at the artistry involved. They bought a set of crystal neon green tumblers and matching decanter for Gaston, and a set of crystal Mad Men Draper Double Old Fashioned glasses and a matching decanter for Darius, because he loved watching the TV show. They shipped both gifts, which would arrive in Louisiana before their return. Sophia spotted a gorgeous pair of champagne glasses, called 'Mixology Talon Red Coupe.'

"We certainly don't need more champagne glasses, but there is no such thing as too much champagne," Sophia said, smiling and mockingly batting her eyes at Michael. "And then there are the Rebel Pink Martini glasses or the flutes. Decisions, decisions."

Michael blinked five times, which among several things signified the calculator ticking away in his mind.

While Sophia was engrossed in other parts of the show-room, Michael arranged with the salesperson to have the Rebel Pink Martini glasses and flutes delivered to the cabin, and the Mixology champagne glasses delivered to Dromoland Castle, in County Clare, where he and Sophia were staying a few nights later. He would arrange with the hotel concierge to have the surprise waiting in the room. Sophia had no idea they were going to stay there. She always wanted to spend the night in a castle, and Michael wanted their stay at Dromoland to be perfect.

In the afternoon, they drove through the gentle charm of County Cork, sprinkled with tranquil seaside villages. Before they drove into Cork, Sophia asked Pádraig to drive to Blarney Castle.

"It is of utmost importance, don't you know, that we kiss the Blarney Stone," Sophia said with a smirk. "Once we kiss it, the stone will bestow upon us the gift of eloquence, and since you and I are both writers and speakers, we can never be too articulate. So, what do you say?"

"Sounds really goodly," Michael said.

Pádraig rolled his eyes.

"Pádraig," Sophia said, "I detect an air of cynicism from you."

"Aye," Pádraig said, "intentional, I assure you."

"And why is that, my good man?" Sophia said.

"Kissin' the Blarney stone," Pádraig said. "Now, don't get me wrong, because, as Americans go, you two are the kindest I've ever known. Ya haven't once said 'Top o' the mornin' to ya,' never once asked if I know any leprechauns, and with the exception of Michael's ill-advised 'faith and begorrah,' ya haven't turned our time together into an Irish cliché festival."

Michael and Sophia laughed. "Well," Sophia said, "that is a relief. But I assume that kissing the Blarney stone *does* fall into the realm of Irish clichés?"

"As American pie," Pádraig said, which garnered an even bigger laugh.

"Well, you must forgive me," Sophia said, "but I am in Ireland, home of my ancestors, and I *will* kiss the Blarney stone, cliché or not."

"And it shall be my pleasure to take you there directly," Pádraig said.

Sophia soon found herself on top of the castle, in the tradition of lying on her back, leaning backwards, upside down, over the parapet while holding onto a vertical iron railing so she could kiss the Blarney Stone. Although there were protective railings, the view to the ground nine stories below was slightly intimidating. Michael did not take the challenge since he suffered from acrophobia. It took everything he had to hold her by the waist, looking the opposite direction, while she leaned backwards to kiss the stone.

"I guess you're not going to be blessed with eloquence and the gift of gab after all," Sophia said.

"Not unless you want it accompanied by a primal scream," Michael said. "Besides, you do enough talking for both of us."

"It's a long drop down there, smart aleck," Sophia said as she whacked him on the arm.

"I'm not worried since I have you to hang onto." He put his arm around her and gave her a hug, making her unsteady on her feet…

They walked through the Scots Baronial style Blarney House and Gardens. Sophia loved touring through the old traditional Irish mansion, admiring the quality artisanship and design detail. In the late afternoon, they drove to Cobh, a lovely village wrapped around Cork Harbour, primarily a naval and commercial port since the Napoleonic Wars. Of the six million Irish who left Ireland for the United States, 2.5 million emigrated from Cobh.

Cobh specifically caught Sophia's interest. Formerly called Queenstown, the lovely seaside village was *Titanic's* final departure port before her ill-fated maiden voyage across the Atlantic.

"The name of Cobh changed over the years," Pádraig said. "The town, originally named Cove, later became the Gaelic, spelled C-O-B-H, yet pronounced the same. In 1849, officials named it Queenstown in honor of Queen Victoria, and in the late 1920's, new authorities of the Irish Free State renamed the city Cobh."

They settled into their hotel room and then walked among the many colorful painted buildings along the harbor. Everywhere they went was a photo-op for Sophia, for Cobh was one of the most picturesque villages yet.

"Above the harbor is St. Colman's Cathedral," Pádraig said, "with its towering spire, 100 meters high, the average height of a 24-story building. The spire houses the largest carillon in Ireland with 42 bells."

After Sophia took several photos, the trio found a small seaside cafe that served the most wonderful fresh seafood.

While sitting and watching the ocean, Sophia's mind wandered. She could not help but recall her life as Jocelyn. The RMS *Titanic* made her final port of call at Queenstown, where seven people disembarked the grand ship, including Father Francis Browne, and 123 boarded before it set sail across the Atlantic toward its demise. Memories of that fateful, frigidly cold black night filled Sophia's mind, temporarily causing her to pause and think of those lost at sea.

"Sophia, are you there?" Michael asked, noticing she had grown pale.

She stared out into the harbor while taking a sip of wine, recalling a memory so traumatic that she could never erase it from her mind. She shook her head, coming back to the present moment, and brought her focus back to Michael's eyes. "I'm fine. I was just having a flashback."

"Waiter, would you please bring the lady a glass of Tullamore Dew?" Pádraig said. "A good shot of Irish whiskey might help, and if it doesn't, Michael and I will have one fer good measure."

"Just the name alone is enticing," Sophia said.

For the balance of the evening, Sophia took in the sights in quiet reverence. She had a fitful night's rest in the city that was once Queenstown, where so many of Ireland's people were lost in the sinking of *Titanic*. It seemed inevitable that, in her dreams, she returned to the life of Jocelyn.

CHAPTER
Eleven

Throughout the weekend, François sat on a chaise lounge, his leg propped up on pillows and thoroughly enjoying the loving attention Jocelyn paid him. From there, he could easily stand with his crutches and hobble around from time to time as his doctor advised. Since leaving the hospital, François felt a bit more at ease with every passing hour. His ordeal aboard *Titanic* and the subsequent two weeks recovering in the hospital left him disoriented and weak. Retrieving some semblance of a normal life – particularly in Jocelyn's company – brought François great comfort, both physically and spiritually. Even now, so soon after being thrust into the frigid North Atlantic with virtually no chance of survival amidst hundreds of poor dying souls, François was beginning to feel as if his life was stabilizing. A long, restful sleep was still elusive, however, for he often awoke in pain and uneasily anxious. In those darkest hours of the night, the sounds, sights, and smells of *Titanic's* demise intruded on his dreams.

Jocelyn offered to set up a small table next to him to eat their meal together, but François insisted on joining her in the dining room. Since that terrible night on *Titanic*, François and Jocelyn found joy in every serene moment they could find. Jocelyn appeared with a teapot on a tray with two cups. She smiled as she placed the White Star

Line teacup and saucer before him.

"Remember these?" she said.

A tear welled in his eye. "Mon Dieu." He picked up the delicate cup. "I've never been so pleased to see a teacup in my life."

"And do you remember what I told you?" Jocelyn asked.

"Oui." He smiled and looked into her beautiful eyes. "A night we shall someday tell our grandchildren about. Perhaps by then I will be able to speak about it with without trembling, no?"

Jocelyn felt tears of great joy coming now. She distracted herself and poured, but she overdid it, and the tea spilled over the cup, into the saucer, and almost into François' lap. "Oh dear!"

François laughed as he squirmed to avoid a rather hot bath. "Not again! Man the lifeboats!"

They both nervously giggled like children as Jocelyn quickly mopped up. "I dare say, Mr. Delacroix, there is something about you that turns me into a clumsy schoolgirl."

He took her hand and pulled her in for a gentle kiss. "Perhaps it is my French schoolboy charm, oui?"

Jocelyn could barely breathe a sigh, for she felt a bit lightheaded. She reluctantly pulled away and sat, this time in full control of the teapot.

"You never mentioned that you are a magnificent cook," François said.

"I haven't cooked for over two years," Jocelyn said, pouring more tea. "After Henry died, I was with his family at first, and then I traveled through Europe and ate at small bistros and cafés. It feels good to get back into the kitchen to create something tasty again. My apartment in the city has a large kitchen and lovely dining room, just right for entertaining."

"With all the famous people for whom you will design clothing, you will have to entertain and feed them well, yes?" he teased.

"Oh, I forgot to tell you I called Lucy this morning before you awoke."

"Mon Dieu, Lucy!" François said. "My mind has been so scattered that I neglected to ask about her and Sir Cosmo. I did read that they survived, yes?"

"They did. And I must say Lucy was simply beside herself with joy when I told her that you are still with us. After we both shed the appropriate tears, she said to tell you – now that you are indeed alive – that she expects you to honor your contractual agreement and come work for her. She also asked that I deliver this –" Jocelyn stood and gave François a loving kiss.

"Mmm," François said. "I must say that Madame Duff-Gordon possesses the most luscious lips."

"Lucy said to tell you that she will contact the firm that originally hired you and reimburse them for the advance you received, plus additional compensation for their having to take extra time to hire another architect. She said she will tend to it first thing Monday morning."

"What a generous woman she is."

"She also said she would reimburse Willborough and Johnson for your fare on *Titanic*." Jocelyn smiled as she watched François squirm.

"Ah, oui," François said. "Now that is – I suppose I

should – I must-"

"I told her."

"You told her?"

"I told her, François," Jocelyn said. "I told her exactly how we met, and precisely who you – and all the other yous – are."

"Everything?" François said. "You mean my stowing away and pretending to be the dock worker, steward-"

"Waiter, and bon vivant gadabout millionaire who stows away on luxurious ocean liners and drinks brandy with captains of industry, yes I told her."

"I see," François said. "This, you told the woman who holds the key to a glorious career for me?"

"She was enchanted," Jocelyn said. "She said it was the most romantic story she ever heard. She also said you may come to work for her whenever you feel up to it."

"Oh! Mon Dieu! Such a relief!"

"May I assume you shall forever remain François, the handsome architect now?"

"Avec plaisir," François said. "I shall be relieved to end this masquerade, but as I said before, I must find a way to someday compensate the White Star Line for my – my-"

"Crimes?"

"I was going to say transgressions."

"Even after they recklessly sailed into a sea of icebergs at top speed, resulting in an accident that left you injured and sure to die in the ocean?"

François shrugged. "Well, perhaps someday I shall repay them for *half* my fare?"

Jocelyn smiled and reached for his hands. "You are an

honorable man, François Delacroix. That is one of the many reasons I love you so."

"And I love you." They simply took that moment to reflect on their good fortune. "I dare say, perhaps I should not feel such joy amidst the horrible tragedy that befell so many, but I cannot help a feeling of such gratitude to be here, safely in this place with you."

"Remember that I held a place in my heart for each and every lost soul aboard that ship?"

"I do."

"Perhaps that is how we both may reconcile any latent guilt we might feel."

François smiled. "You are a remarkable woman, my Jocelyn."

After another moment of silent reflection, Jocelyn took a deep breath and lifted François' spirits. She pointed to the fine dinner before them. "For now, you must eat to regain your strength."

"Oui! You are spoiling me." François rubbed his hands together and then dug in. "This afternoon, I read in the newspaper that the Americans are already holding hearings about the disaster?"

"Yes, in fact they began on the 19th - the day after we arrived in New York," Jocelyn said. "Many of us had not yet disembarked the *Carpathia* before Mr. Ismay and the crew members were served with subpoenas to appear before a special subcommittee of the Senate Commerce Committee."

"They wasted little time, no?"

"Apparently, they wanted to question the British crewman before they went back to England. The hearings convened the next morning at the Waldorf-Astoria, here in Manhattan. The following week, the inquiry moved to Washington D.C. It is so ironic that the hearings took place at the Waldorf, which was owned by John Jacob Astor."

François sadly nodded. "I briefly saw him in the rush toward the stern." For a moment, François' eyes drifted back to that terrible night, but he quickly blinked the images away. "So, did the committee give you a subpoena?"

"No, although some of the passengers *were* questioned. Has anyone contacted you?"

"No, thank goodness," François said. "I doubt they know I exist, and that is fine with me. I do not wish to relive the trauma of that night at the scrutiny of either government, the newspapers, or the public."

"It is terrible what they are saying about Sir Cosmo and Lucy. Lucy told me that they boarded Lifeboat One, the fourth lifeboat to be launched, simply as a precautionary measure, with only twelve people aboard - seven of whom were crewmen. At the time, the crewmen did not appear to realize the ship was doomed until they rowed farther out. By then, *Titanic* was sinking quickly, and they could do nothing but watch in horror like the rest of us. Later, while waiting to be rescued, Lucy said that several of the crewmen complained that they lost all their belongings, not to mention their jobs. Cosmo promised he would help them when they were rescued, and true to his word, he sought out those boys on the *Carpathia* and wrote each of them a check for five pounds."

"I do not understand," François said. "Why would anyone criticize him for that?"

"Somehow, the newspapers turned it into an allegation

that Cosmo offered bribes for the crew not to go back and rescue people from the water. Lucy says that Cosmo is devastated by these false accusations, when all the while he reached out in support of the young men's circumstances. He was under no obligation to them. That much money would most likely be more than a month's wages for those men."

"Despicable," François said. "They are criticizing him because he is a wealthy man who survived. That is the matter at hand."

"Yes, and to the contrary," Jocelyn said, "because Captain Smith went down with the ship, no one criticized him for sailing so fast in a sea full of icebergs. I have read that some captains claim that is a perfectly normal procedure, but I believe that to be quite false. When the *Carpathia* set out for New York after we were rescued, the ship's captain was quite cautious going through the ice fields for the entirety of that first day..."

The *Titanic* sinking generated the first global newspaper storm of its kind. Before she set sail, newspaper and magazine writers went wild with propaganda touting the great liner as 'unsinkable,' but after the disaster, there was no stopping the criticism of Harland and Wolff and the White Star Line printed around the world. The *New York Times* alone devoted the newspaper's first twelve pages to the story, turning the *Titanic* sinking into one of the best-documented man-made disasters in history. Each survivor witnessed only their own personal experience without knowing about the dozens of circumstances and occurrences that converged in one single moment to destroy the largest cruise liner in the world.

To fill in the gaps and be the first source to report the catastrophe, the newspapers printed every wild rumor and unsubstantiated allegation, some with gross exaggerations, making it clear that no one really knew the whole story. In some cases, during both the American and British inquiries, officers and crew often changed their stories and did not corroborate the testimony of the passengers. Many reporters accused crewmen of lying to protect the White Star Line and their jobs.

"You and I both know there were many warnings not to take the voyage," Jocelyn said. "So many events happened to set the *Titanic* on a doomed course from the beginning, starting with the delay in its departure. If the ship had sailed on time, a month earlier, the iceberg would not have traveled that far south into the shipping lanes. Then there was the coal strike, and the near collision with the SS *City of New York*."

"And the coalbunker fire," François said.

"Yes. There is nothing in the newspapers about that," Jocelyn said.

"I do not know if that contributed to the ship breaking up," François said, "but when metal is heated to red hot temperatures, it softens. I wonder if the fire might have rendered the steel weak where the ship split in two."

"I suppose it does not matter," Jocelyn said. "At the rate the ship was flooding, it sank long before *Carpathia* came to our rescue. What is more distressing is there was a ship, the *S.S. Californian*, supposedly just eight miles away, but the newspapers say it was trapped in an ice field."

"That was the light we saw on the horizon?"

"One article reported that one of *Titanic's* officers, his name was Joseph Boxhall, saw a ship turn away when he attempted to signal it with the Morse lamp, but he doesn't believe that ship was the *Californian*. He said he saw more than one ship. We do know, after we overheard Captain Smith's conversation with Mr. Lightoller, the ship was traveling at full speed. Some say, because of her speed and size, *Titanic* had less time to react to the iceberg before the ship turned to avoid the collision."

François shook his head. "So much to consider. I am so saddened to know that Thomas Andrews perished. He was a good man."

"I think you would have become good friends. The two of you got along so well," Jocelyn said.

"I would have also enjoyed getting to know Mr. Astor as well. He was very kind to me - a good man with a healthy sense of humor."

"Leave it to you to befriend the wealthiest man in the world," Jocelyn said with a smile.

François shrugged. "He was quite down to earth in his way. It is astounding, really, as you would expect one so wealthy to be inaccessible, but I found him to be quite unpretentious. And in those final moments before we went down, what did it matter? The wealthiest men in the world perished with the poorest."

"So many good people were lost that night. It is still so hard to fathom," Jocelyn said. "Isidor and Ida Straus – they were so kind to me – it is such a tragedy."

François took Jocelyn's hand. "I was with them. I helped Isidor put Ida in a lifeboat."

"You did?" Jocelyn said. "But, she didn't survive."

"A crewman offered Isidor a place on the lifeboat, because of his age, but he refused, as there were many women and children still about. Ida then stepped out and chose to remain with him. We tried to persuade her to go, but she would have none of it." Tears welled in François' eyes as his voice began to tremble. "Before she stepped back onto the deck, Ida removed her fur coat and placed it over the shoulders of her maid. She told the woman she would no longer be in need of it."

"Oh my, can you imagine?" Jocelyn said.

"Oui, I can," François said.

"Of course. How stupid of me. I certainly do not know what you went through."

"I saw dozens of acts of bravery that night. Theirs was only one - so touching and courageous."

"I read some interesting information about them. Let me see if I can find the article." Jocelyn got up from the table to find the newspaper in the parlor. "Yes, here it is. According to this, Isidor was a German Jew, born in 1845, whose family immigrated to Georgia when he was nine years old. When the Civil War broke out, everything they owned, including the family's dry goods store, burned to the ground. In 1865, they moved to New York, where his father, Lazarus, began an importing business, soon known worldwide for their imported glass, china, porcelain, and crockery. In 1873, he contracted with W.H. Macy to sell his goods in the basement of the 14th Street Macy's store. Evidently, Isidor and his brother, Nathan, carried on the work ethic taught by their father. They became partial owners of Macy's in 1884, and by 1896, they were the sole owners."

"Their success gives me encouragement as I start my life over here," François said.

"There could not be a better example of hard work and

perseverance," Jocelyn said. "From what I understand, part of their success was because the Straus brothers believed in giving back. If an employee was struggling, they found out the cause and provided money, clothing, or medical care. Macy's became the first business in the United States to develop a mutual aid society to provide medical care for their employees, which included a doctor and nurse on the premises. They offered employees low-cost lunches, along with sleigh rides in the winter and company picnics in the summer. Each employee received a Thanksgiving turkey each year. They were devoted to social welfare not only for their employees, but also for the greater Manhattan community, the United States, and for Israel. Evidently, they were involved in nearly every philanthropic organization in New York City."

"Mon Dieu, he was such a well-rounded gentleman, yes?" François said.

"And that is not all," Jocelyn continued. "From 1894 to 1895, Isidor was a U.S. Congressman. He was encouraged to run for re-election, but refused because he wanted to dedicate more time to his family. In 1901, he turned down the nomination for mayor of New York City. And, in 1896, he co-founded the Educational Alliance, a settlement house where Jewish immigrants learn how to acclimate to the American life. On the top of the building is a rooftop garden, where it still serves thousands of people with fresh produce each year. Over the many years, millions of Jewish people of diverse backgrounds have become New Yorkers there. Upon their deaths, Isidor and Ida left a bequest of $101,000."

"The losses *are* unfathomable, are they not?" François said...

On Sunday, May 13, 1912, François and Jocelyn attended a memorial service for Isidor and Ida Straus at Carnegie Hall. Thousands crowded into the Main Hall, with over 300 women and men left standing at the back of the auditorium. Hundreds of people were turned away because the hall was overflowing. Mayor William J. Gaynor spoke, as did Andrew Carnegie, along with other notable dignitaries and personal friends of the couple. In all, twenty thousand came to honor them that day.

CHAPTER
Twelve

Jocelyn and François returned to Manhattan to settle into their lives. After securing a small advance from Lucy, and accepting a loan from Jocelyn, François insisted on paying his way at the St. Regis while he convalesced for another few days.

As Jocelyn busily unpacked and set up housekeeping at her new apartment, she received a package from Father Francis Browne, the Irish priest who had the great fortune of disembarking *Titanic* before her fatal Atlantic crossing. The package contained a letter and several photos of Jocelyn taken on the final Thursday morning in the life of *Titanic*. Father Browne mentioned the five-word note he received from his superior when he requested permission to continue on to New York, ordering him to disembark at Queenstown with the simple order: *"Get Off That Ship – Provincial."*

"I shall keep that note forever," Father Browne wrote.

His photographs of *Titanic* on her maiden voyage were now appearing in periodicals all over the world, but he saved the photos of Jocelyn for her. That was the beginning of Jocelyn and François' long-distance friendship with Father Browne, which would last a lifetime.

During dinner that evening, Jocelyn mentioned to François, "I saved this newspaper article about the *Titanic*

Orphans. Look at the pictures of these precious little boys." She showed him the article. "Are they not the most darling children? They were on one of the lifeboats without either of their parents. The children are evidently French. Margaret Hays, an American woman who speaks French and was also a *Titanic* survivor, began caring for them from the time they were on the *Carpathia* together. Evidently, they will remain with her, under the watch of the Children's Aid Society. These pictures are running in newspapers all over the world with the hope that a family member will claim them. You know, I saw them when they boarded *Carpathia*. The older one wrapped both he and his little brother in a blanket that looked just like the quilt from your cabin."

François read the article and looked at the pictures of the boys. When he finished reading, he sat for a few moments in silence with tears in his eyes, seeing the events on the ship as they flashed through his memory. He then looked at Jocelyn, who could not help but sense the emotion that overcame him. Since he first reunited with Jocelyn, François had not shared much of his ordeal that fateful night, keeping most of his emotions and the distressing details to himself, but the picture of the two boys opened the floodgates.

He simply stared ahead and spoke. "I was there, hoping to climb aboard Collapsible D - the last of the lifeboats. By the time I got to it, there was no more room. I stood on the deck alongside the many men who watched loved ones take their place in the boat. It was quite alarming to realize all my options had run out - that there was nothing more I could do. I stood next to the father of those two little boys."

Jocelyn caught her breath. "Oh, what must have been

going through his mind...through *your* mind."

François continued recalling the events as tears easily fell. "That brave man put his two sons into the lifeboat with the greatest hope that they would be rescued, all the while knowing he would go down with the ship. I could not hear what he told his sons before the crewman lifted them into the boat, but the older boy looked directly into his father's eyes, listening intently to what he had to say. The boys looked so small and innocent in that boat, wedged between an elderly man and woman, and yet they were so brave. The elder of the two seemed excited, as if it was an adventure. I still had my eiderdown quilt, but I would no longer need it, so I gave it to the crewman and asked him to put it around the boys to keep them warm."

Jocelyn took his hand and wept with him.

"Their father then looked at me and, for a fraction of a moment, I could sense the enormity of his world flashing through his mind. Then he kindly said, 'Merci.' Even though I knew my time on this earth was most likely as short as his, I could not help but feel such tremendous compassion for his loss." He looked into Jocelyn's eyes. "I feel grief for them now – and grief for their father who did not survive."

"Oh, my love," Jocelyn said.

"Then, there was a woman who would not get into the lifeboat because they would not allow her dog on the boat. The dog was big enough to take the space of a passenger, so the woman stayed behind. She would not sacrifice the life of her four-legged companion to take the chance for her own survival. I watched her as she calmly walked down the stairs to A Deck below, with her dog at her side. I observed love in a myriad of forms as I witnessed so many selfless acts of courage that night."

"Perhaps one of the reasons you survived was to tell the tale of the heart's courage - to fill your life with such memories of great love. Did you not tell me one time that the word courage is derived from the French *coeur*, meaning heart?" Jocelyn asked.

François now spoke as if in a trance. "Yes, that is true, and there was another - Edith Evans. I will always remember her name - a First Class passenger who was already seated in the same lifeboat with those two boys. There was no more room for her friend, Carolyn Brown, who remained standing with us on the deck. Edith stood up and told the crewman to take Carolyn instead, because she was a mother. When Edith stepped back onto the Boat Deck, she told her friend she would find another lifeboat, but we all knew the collapsible in front of us was the last.

"As the lifeboat lowered onto the sea, we stood there - all men, with the exception of Edith Evans, who sacrificed her life for her friend. Each of us were left with only one thing to do, and that was to pray to our individual god. For a moment - a moment that seemed to last into *aeternalis* - there was nothing but absolute silence.

"The bow was sinking even deeper, lifting the stern higher into the air. I began to hear sounds of buckling metal and splintering wood. I ran back to the stern with the hope that there might yet be a chance to survive. Perhaps my complete surrender to God led me to find another way to live. With the ship tipped maybe 15 degrees, the hull was not designed to support the weight at the stern with the hundreds of tons of water filling her bottom decks. She couldn't take it, and she broke in half."

François stared ahead, holding nothing back.

"I thought what I went through was grueling," Jocelyn said, sensing his pain, "but what you and the others experienced was far more traumatic. François, you sacrificed yourself for me."

"I would like to think I was as courageous as that," François said, "but I, like most of the men who survived, became precisely focused upon living. Over eighty percent of the men stayed behind, knowing they would not live to tell the tale. Quite honestly, until that moment comes, no one knows what one will choose. All I know is that I thought of nothing more than survival, with the picture of you in my mind. Jocelyn, it was *you* who saved *me*. Had I not met you on board, I am quite certain I would have perished with the other 1,500.

"For a brief moment, while I held onto the railing, trying to keep from falling down that slanted deck, Madelyn did come to mind, but I replaced her with thoughts of you. Had I given much thought to her memory, I may have chosen to join her and our child, but I felt compelled to push them from my mind. I never realized, until that moment, that when such choices appear, a fine line separates us from life or death. During my recovery in the hospital, my mind remained with the thoughts of how my choices are either life-giving or not. It is that simple. Evidently, my soul was not finished with its work, and in that, my task on Earth is to join my soul's journey. So, my love, I remain here with you."

"I don't think either of us would have survived if it weren't for the other," Jocelyn said. "In such times, love is the only thing that keeps people alive. I heard your heartbeat, and it kept me hoping for a miracle, and such a miracle you are."

They simply sat in quiet contemplation. François breathed deeply in gratitude for the moment.

"Something I must share with you," Jocelyn said. "When I was in Paris, I bought a book written by an American author - *Futility, or Wreck of the Titan* - which I finished reading on the ship before you and I became acquainted."

"The *Titan*?"

"Yes. It is a novella, published in 1898, with details eerily similar to *Titanic*. The *Titan* sinks after it collides with an iceberg in the month of April."

"How extraordinary," François said.

"In the book, the *SS Titan* is the largest ship of its kind, able to sail at a similar speed as the *Titanic*, the ship has too few lifeboats, and most of the passengers perish. The sinking is not the main plot of the story, which focuses primarily on the life of the protagonist in the aftermath of the wreck, but the similarities are uncanny. The strangest coincidence in the book is this *Titan* sank 400 nautical miles off the coast of Newfoundland."

"Mon Dieu. And who is this magical, prophetic author?"

"I believe his name is Robertson, but unfortunately my copy is securely in the bureau drawer of my suite at the bottom of the Atlantic."

"Oui, an ironic twist of fate, worth millions, if we could only swim down there and retrieve it. I believe, however, the only water I care to see in the foreseeable future is a half-full bathtub."

Jocelyn laughed at that sudden spark of humor she so loved about François.

"I am curious," François said. "Do you think your premonition about *Titanic* was influenced by reading that book?"

"I have wondered that very thing," Jocelyn said, "but when I go into meditation, I disengage from my thinking mind and commune with the Infinite in the eternal realm. Sometimes during meditation, I gain immediate clarity and wisdom, but most of the time it is later when my intuition taps into something I would not normally think of. I was in that mindset when I saw the fate of *Titanic*. And you and I cannot deny that we were *both* guided not to take the voyage long before we boarded."

"Oui, I cannot say how I know such things at times, except that I do," François said, "and with that I should trust what I see and feel. When I do not trust that intuitive guidance, well - you know better than I."

"All too well," Jocelyn said with a sigh...

During the preceding ten years before the *Titanic* disaster, British ships carried 3 ½ million passengers and had lost just 73, according to White Star Line's legal representative, Sir Robert Finlay, in his address to the British Wreck Commissioner's Court in support of the Board of Trade's ship construction rules. 1912 was a most unusual year for sailing the North Atlantic, for there were more than 300 icebergs in the shipping lanes that year, far more than during a typical spring.

In constructing the hull of the *Titanic*, Harland and Wolff used iron rivets to anchor the steel plates instead of stronger steel rivets due to many factors including cost, time constraints, and scarcity of skilled riveters and quality materials where shipbuilders were pushing to produce new liners on time, at a reasonable cost. It took only 5mm of movement for the iron rivets to fail, acceptable under normal operating conditions, but catastrophic in the case of *Titanic's* collision. When the wreck was discovered and examined many decades later, a new hypothesis emerged indicating the iceberg did not slice open the side of the ship as originally believed, but rather it bent the steel enough for the rivets to disengage, allowing more rapid flooding to occur. Samples brought up from the wreckage also indicated that *Titanic's* steel, although the best available by the standards of its day, contained high levels of sulfur, oxygen, and phosphorus, which made it brittle in the icy temperatures of the North Atlantic.

472 spaces aboard *Titanic's* lifeboats were not filled. Two of the lifeboats went back that night, pulling only nine people from the icy waters, of whom three men later died from exposure. Three dogs out of the nine survived, two Pomeranians and a Pekinese.

The exact number of people aboard *Titanic* was never known for a number of reasons. There was no accurate list of crewmembers due to last minute hires. The same was true for the passenger list because of many ticket purchases and cancellations in the final days before *Titanic* sailed. 75% of the women survived, 19% of the men survived, and 50% of the children survived.

The White Star Line hired the cable ship, *CS Mackay-Bennett*, as the first of four ships contracted for the gruesome task of retrieving the bodies. They began on Wednesday, April 17th, and for seven days, they recovered 306 bodies among the more than 1,500 people who perished. 116 were given a burial at sea, while 190 bodies were taken to Halifax, Nova Scotia for identification and burial on land. One of the other three retrieval ships came across the body of a woman holding her baby, and another woman still holding onto her dog.

One of the crew aboard the *CS Mackay-Bennett* was Clifford Crease, a 24-year-old craftsman-in-training. The fourth of the bodies retrieved was a small blonde male infant found with no lifebelt. The crew made sure the boy received a proper burial and grave marker in Halifax's Fairview Park Cemetery, marked as the Unknown Child. On the casket was a brass plate engraved with, 'Our Babe,' the name the shipmates gave the boy. Each year, on April 15th, Clifford Crease visited the cemetery and left a wreath at the grave.

In 2008, 96 years after the *Titanic* disaster, authorities exhumed the child's body with the hope of making a positive identification through modern forensic technology. They discovered one small bone, which the engraved brass plate on the casket protected from decay. A DNA test revealed the boy was 19-month-old Sidney Leslie Goodwin, the youngest of six children of Frederick and Augusta Goodwin. The family of eight sailed in Third Class from England, destined for Fredrick's new job at a power plant in Niagara Falls, New York. The Goodwins were ticketed to cross the Atlantic on a different steamer, but the British coal strike forced them to switch to the *Titanic* at the last minute. None of the other members of the Goodwin family survived, nor were any of their bodies recovered. Today, Sidney's grave marker remains in dedication to the 55 children who were lost at sea aboard *Titanic*.

As the inquiries on both sides of the Atlantic came to a close, the British did not want to lay blame on the White

Star Line, or anything British for that matter, which would have been detrimental to maritime trade, politics, and relations between nations, especially with the U.S. While it concluded the ship hit the iceberg due to "excessive speed at which the ship was being navigated," it fell short of blaming Captain Smith, who according to the commission was at fault for not changing course or slowing down, but did "only that which other skilled men would have done in the same position."

With war on the horizon, it was imperative for Great Britain to utilize the services of the White Star Line, at that time the largest shipping line in the world. Shipbuilder Harland and Wolff employed over 15,000, all Protestants from Belfast, who were true to the crown. Their votes would have great impact on the upcoming elections for Prime Minister and Parliament. Great Britain could not afford to lay blame on either company for numerous reasons. Their emphasis stated, "This enquiry has to do with the future. No enquiry can repair the past."

Contrarily, the American inquiry concentrated on the failures that led to the disaster. It concluded that arrogance and complacency were to blame, pointing the finger at Captain Smith, the shipping industry, and the British Board of Trade for the many failures of *Titanic*, which lead to the deaths of over 1,500 people.

The general public and newspapers on both sides of the ocean reacted with outrage, accusing both the American and British inquiries of whitewashing many details, with ultimately no one held responsible for the sinking of *Titanic*.

Most of the men who survived in the lifeboats received the disdain of public ridicule due to the implied code,

"Without honor is shame," meaning women and children first. Unfortunately, the public outcry called for a reckoning. They wanted someone to take the blame for the loss of so many, and two men were singled out. The first was J. Bruce Ismay, managing director of the White Star Line, and president of the International Mercantile Marine. He boarded one of the last lifeboats to leave the ship, Collapsible C, while so many women and children remained aboard. One newspaper mentioned him as, "The most talked of man in all the world." Much later in life, he died a noble death...

The controversy over the hearings and the general hysterics fueled by the newspapers were not lost on Jocelyn and François, despite their desire to put the tragedy behind them and begin healing.

"I must say, I do not find fault with Monsieur Ismay's decision to board a lifeboat," François said. "Had there been available space for me, and no women or children around, I am certain I would have done the same. In the panic and chaos of those final moments when the ship came apart, only those of us who were there have any right to judge.

"From all I can tell, the men who boarded the lifeboats did so with the permission of the crewmen in charge," Jocelyn said. "Now they are vilified and condemned, when none should ever have been put in that position in the first place."

François agreed. "I was injured and brought out of the freezing ocean, so I am now thought of as a hero. It simply is not true. I saw Monsieur Ismay help many board lifeboats while dressed in just his slippers, pajamas, and overcoat. He was one of the many who were so very courageous.

"Unfortunately, Monsieur Ismay will live with the public scar of being the selfish man who lived," François said. "Only after all the lifeboats were gone did hoards of people from the lower decks rush out onto the Boat Deck. Little did we know we had but fifteen or twenty minutes before the ship was going down. At that point, it was bedlam - utter pandemonium. Panic took over, and everyone was out for him or herself, and naturally so."

"The devastation Mr. Ismay felt that night must have been utterly unfathomable," Jocelyn said. "I have such compassion for his loss. *Titanic* was the largest man-made moving object on earth. She was magnificent. I can only imagine what went through his mind. Not only did so many souls perish, but *Titanic's* sinking will also affect the White Star Line and the International Mercantile Marine. Mr. Ismay's father founded the White Star Line. I don't mean to diminish the loss of so many, but there would have been more chaos for the thousands who work for him if he had gone down with the ship."

"I read that, while he was on the lifeboat, he sat with his back to *Titanic*," François said. "He said, 'I did not wish to see her go down. I am glad that I did not.'"

"The tremendous loss of *Titanic* took the life right out of him," Jocelyn said. "This public disdain, both in the U.S. and in Britain, must be devastating..."

After the fact, the second person offered up as a scapegoat for the deaths of over 1,500 people was Captain Stanley Lord of the *SS Californian*, a 6,000-ton British cargo steamship that stopped for the night, surrounded by an ice field, northwest of *Titanic's* reported coordinates.

J.P. Morgan, owner of the International Mercantile Marine, owned the *Californian* as well. Both inquiries concluded that, if the *Californian* had come to *Titanic's* rescue when the crew first spotted distress flares launched by the great liner, most, if not all lives, would have been saved.

Captain Lord became the scapegoat for the tremendous loss of life, accused of gross negligence by either ignoring or simply not recognizing that *Titanic* was in grave peril. The terse conclusion was drawn due primarily to conflicting testimony given by Lord and several members of the *Californian* crew regarding why Lord did not make any attempt to steam toward the foundering ship. Neither commission apparently gave any rational consideration to the feasibility of the much smaller *Californian* negotiating the ice field and arriving in time to effectively conduct a rescue operation of 2,200 passengers, either from the rapidly sinking 40,000-ton *Titanic*, or the freezing water after the ship went down.

With a capacity for 55 crewmembers and 47 passengers, the *Californian* departed Liverpool on April 5th, bound for Boston with a cargo of cotton goods, 48 crewmembers, and no passengers. On Sunday, at 6:30 p.m., the *Californian* signaled a warning of three large icebergs spotted approximately five miles to the south. *Titanic's* wireless operator delivered the warning to the bridge, although it was not immediately reported to Captain Smith, who was dining with passengers at the time. This was the fourth such ice warning *Titanic* received that day.

At 10:21 p.m., Captain Lord stopped the *Californian* for the night because it had entered an ice field that stretched 30 miles to the north and south, literally surrounding the ship. He decided it best that the ship not commence until daylight. It was Lord's first experience with an ice field. Knowing *Titanic* was in the area, he ordered Cyril Evans, the ship's only radio operator, to send out a message that the *Californian* stopped for the night due to dangerous ice conditions. That message was sent at 11:25 p.m., with the response from Jack Phillips, *Titanic*'s harried radio operator who was trying to catch up on a backlog of passenger telegraph messages, "Shut up, shut up! I am busy. I am working Cape Race." Evans continued to contact Phillips a few more times, interfering with *Titanic*'s contact with Cape Race. Evans listened to *Titanic*'s traffic until 11:35 p.m., when he shut off the radio for the night.

Phillips did not relay the message from the *Californian* to the bridge. *Titanic* hit the iceberg five minutes later.

At 11:40 p.m., *Californian* Third Officer Charles Groves testified he had watched the lights of a large steamship for approximately 30 minutes. He estimated the ship appeared to have stopped approximately 10 to 12 miles away. He informed Lord, who was off-duty and sleeping. Lord ordered Groves to try to contact the ship by Morse lamp. Groves testified he did, but received no response.

At 12:05 a.m., *Titanic* transmitted its first distress call via wireless, and continued a CQD-SOS every few minutes. At that same time, *Californian* Second Officer Herbert Stone took the watch from Groves and testified he also saw the large liner stopped, but he estimated it was eight miles away. He also tried to signal with the Morse lamp, but received no reply.

At 12:55 a.m., Stone observed five white rockets launched over the large ship. Both Stone and Morse lamp operator James Gibson testified they suspected something might be wrong with the liner.

At 1:10 a.m., Stone testified that he notified Captain Lord of five white rockets seen over the ship far to the southeast, one hour and thirty minutes after *Titanic* hit the iceberg, but contrary to his previous claim, Stone testified he told Captain Lord he did not believe them to be distress signals due to their color.

At 2:00 a.m., after observing eight rockets in total, Stone and Gibson noted the lights on the ship disappearing and concluded it was back under way and leaving. Gibson testified he woke Lord, who asked if he was certain the rockets were white, at that time the color used for company identification, while red rockets signaled distress. Gibson said he was certain the rockets were white, and Lord went back to sleep. All testimonies agree that Lord never ordered the wireless turned on to contact the liner.

At 2:20 a.m., *Titanic* sank.

At 3:40 a.m., Stone and Gibson spotted rockets to the southeast, which came from *RMS Carpathia*, notifying *Titanic* that she was on her way. *Carpathia* was one of eleven steamers that responded to *Titanic's* distress calls, and was one of six that immediately turned and headed toward her reported position. She was the first to arrive and picked up all survivors in the lifeboats.

At 4:30 a.m., Captain Lord awoke and went out onto the deck to decide how to proceed through the ice field. Soon afterward, the *Californian* received a message from the *SS Frankfurt* that *Titanic* sank overnight. *Californian* set out at 5:00 a.m., slowly traversing the ice field to the west, and then turned south toward the last known coordinates of *Titanic*. When the *Californian* arrived at the site, the *SS Mount Temple* was also there, but no debris, lifeboats, or bodies were found at that location. The wreck, later discovered by oceanographer and explorer Dr. Robert Ballard in 1985, was actually located 13 miles to the east of the original coordinates sent by *Titanic*.

At 8:30 a.m., the *Californian* arrived at the location where *Carpathia* was bringing the last survivors onboard.

There were two different opinions of the *Californian's* distance from *Titanic*. Officer Stone estimated eight miles, while Captain Lord insisted on 19, and reportedly told a Boston newspaper reporter they were 30 miles away. Clearly, Lord's vessel was closer to *Titanic* than any of the known ships in the area. Lord's apparent complacency, and the watch officers' inconsistent testimonies, were rightfully criticized, however the two inquiries did not acknowledge certain stark realities. Even if the *Californian* had immediately set out at 1:10 a.m. from the eight-mile distance, at maximum speed of twelve knots (22mph), by the time the ship traversed the ice field, she would have arrived at 2:45 a.m. at the earliest - 25 minutes after *Titanic* slipped into the sea. This assumes *Titanic* was located at her reported position.

If, by some miraculous chance, *Californian* had arrived at *Titanic* before she sank, she had only 48 crewmembers to launch six lifeboats, for which 54 crewmen were required to operate the davits and boats. Most of the crew aboard the *Californian* were firemen, engineers, stewards, and lookouts, who were needed to operate the ship. None were seamen trained to operate the ship's davits or lifeboats.

If the *Californian* had arrived at *Titanic* before she foundered, Captain Lord would not have likely rafted the *Californian* alongside to try a daring rescue, for doing so would put his ship and crew at great risk, especially when

Titanic broke apart before she sank. At the angle *Titanic* was sinking, planking between the two ships would have been impossible, with too great an angle for 1,500 people to transfer safely onto the *Californian*. *Titanic* was not afloat long enough to allow the time necessary for the painstaking transfer of people via lifeboat, notwithstanding the obvious fact that the *Californian* had a total capacity of just 102 passengers and crewmembers. A captain's first responsibility is for the safety of his own crew and to that of his ship. None of these facts were ever conceded by either British or American courts in their condemnation of Captain Lord.

Had *Californian's* officers trusted what they were seeing as signals of distress and relayed that information to Captain Lord, especially when they took notice of the rockets firing at regular intervals, he might have awoken his radio operator to have him contact *Titanic*. Assuming he then heard Titanic's call for help, he presumably would have tried to find his way out of the ice fields and set out for *Titanic*, even though it was unlikely that they could arrive in time to be of much help. If not for a series of critical mistakes by Lord and his crew, the *Californian* might have gone down in history as just another of the many ships that heroically attempted to render aid to *Titanic*. Instead, the newspapers conducted a feeding frenzy and vilified Captain Lord, a stain that would haunt him for the rest of his life.

Since 1900, the size of luxury liners increased 400%, and the shipping industry had no way of foreseeing what circumstances could cause such a disastrous sinking until the catastrophe of *Titanic*. Long after she sank, some experts concluded there was an obvious error in the design of *Titanic* and her sister ships. The rudder was too small, for one thing. Had it been larger, more appropriate to the ship's massive size, experts speculated *Titanic* might have steered more easily around the iceberg, perhaps avoiding it altogether.

What came from the most infamous maritime disaster in history were the many changes in maritime law. Rather than requiring a certain number of lifeboats based on a ship's tonnage, the number was soon changed to accommodate the ship's passenger capacity, and lifeboat drills and inspections were mandated. Every ship changed to 24-hour emergency radio operation with a secondary back-up power supply.

The rapid sinking of *Titanic* caused understandable chaotic disorder and pandemonium among passengers and crew, but clearly no one was correctly trained to fire rockets as distress signals. The White star Line provided *Titanic* with 36 of the latest pyrotechnics, designed for maritime application. Each rocket contained a loud detonation, as the rocket signal exploded hundreds of feet above the ship, cascading white stars that fell to the sea. To signal an emergency, the rockets were to be fired in one-minute intervals, recognized as international signals of distress.

However, Fourth Officer Boxhall, under the order of Captain Smith, began firing rockets at 12:45 a.m., and over the next hour and fifteen minutes, he fired eight rockets, but not at one minute intervals. The random firing of rockets signaled to all ships in her view that *Titanic* was experiencing a navigation problem, and to please stand clear. A navigation problem was not unusual and would not cause alarm. *Titanic's* random firing of rockets would not be interpreted as signals of distress.

Neither board of inquiry correctly investigated the facts

surrounding the actual sequence of rockets fired by *Titanic*. Senator William Alden Smith, Chairman of the American inquiry, stated in utter error, on the record, that rockets fired from the *Titanic* were "distress rockets," based on the testimony of Fourth Officer Boxhall, who testified that he was ordered by Captain Smith to fire distress signals.

Lord Mersey and the British Board of Enquiry accepted Senator Smith's statement as fact, adopting the same conclusion, and so the story of the *Titanic* firing distress rockets was adopted as fact, making history, however incorrectly. This "fact" led the blame of *Titanic's* sinking to Captain Lord, who did not respond to the rocket signals.

Prior to the *Titanic* disaster, ships commonly used rockets or Roman candles in various color combinations for identification purposes. By 1912, the wireless radio eliminated the need for rockets, and it was agreed that ships would thereafter use rockets only as a distress signal. Violations would result in a misdemeanor, as would any case in which a ship made no effort to come to the aid of a distressed ship when it was reasonably feasible to try.

In addition, the new construction of ships with a passenger capacity of 100 people or more were built with a double hull and watertight bulkheads raised ten percent above the waterline.

The International Ice Patrol developed the monitoring of icebergs in the Arctic and North Atlantic oceans. No single incident involving a ship and an iceberg has occurred since the IIP came about…

Jocelyn could not help but put all the pieces together with respect to her own understanding of *Titanic's* demise. *Titanic's* maiden voyage was delayed from 20 March to 10

April 1912 because her sister ship, *Olympic*, had to be out-fitted with *Titanic*'s propeller after *Olympic* threw one of her propeller blades during her maiden voyage to New York. Sailing later in the spring put *Titanic* directly in the vicinity of icebergs and ice fields, which flowed unusually farther south in the warmer waters that year.

The fire in coalbunker ten, which started two weeks before *Titanic* left Belfast for Southampton, burned steadily until Saturday, 13 April, creating additional distress to the structure of two of the ship's bulkheads.

Additionally, persistent conspiracy theories spanned the decades regarding the question of whether or not *Olympic* was switched with *Titanic*, which would have been the greatest marine fraud in history, not to mention the murder of more than 1,500 people. No clear, irrefutable evidence to support a lavish insurance fraud conspiracy has ever emerged to change the official story of *Titanic's* demise...

They called *Titanic* the 'Ship of Dreams,' and she carried those dreams of the world with her, whether those aboard were the shipbuilders, passengers, crew, or the people with an intention to someday sail aboard her in grand style. Jocelyn reflected on all the dreams she had while on the ship, but she wrote in her journal, drawing the following conclusion:

> *We are the ship of our own dreams. Our bodies are the vessel. Our dreams are the itinerary. Whatever we desire, we must be clear of its details, envisioning it happening as if it is already a reality. We then take step-by-step*

action, setting the trajectory, feeling as if the dream is already ours. We move about our day focused on those dreams, while at the same time the universe is delivering us to our destination beyond the far horizon. The voyage then becomes the journey of our soul.

On a Saturday in early June, before they began to work for *Lucile Ltd.,* Jocelyn invited François to a sumptuous candlelight dinner served on her best china. François arrived at her apartment with a bouquet of flowers and a bottle of wine.

As they enjoyed an intimate dinner, they spoke of their excitement to begin working for *Lucile,* and of course, an important part of their discussion that night included their plans for the future. They wanted to be together, but had no plans to make a permanent arrangement yet, even though François' gift of the ammonite was a promise of engagement. Time was quickly passing, however, and Jocelyn needed to get to the point. She could no longer wait, for her pregnancy was beginning to show.

"So, tell me, François. When we *do* decide to get married, would you eventually like to have children?"

"Yes, of course," François said. "You remember my wife was pregnant when she died. I so wanted to be a father."

"What would you say if you were a father first, and *then* got married?"

François stopped and simply stared at her. He did not move or speak. Jocelyn's heart raced, for the wait was excruciating – literally, a pregnant pause.

François thoughtfully rested his chin on his hand. "Are we speaking in conjecture?"

Jocelyn leaned back. "That would depend on your definition of the word 'we'."

His face transformed into a huge grin. "Is that why you have been pretending to drink, but not really doing so? You are with child, yes?"

Jocelyn began to laugh. "Yes, I must have expectant tongue - anything with alcohol, among other foods I once liked, no longer tastes good to me."

"How long have you known this?" François asked.

"It was the first night that we made love, I just knew."

"I do not understand. How did you know?"

"It is one of the gifts of being a woman. I just knew. And now that I have seen a doctor, there is no mistake. I am seven weeks along."

He rose from the chair, no longer needing his crutches, and knelt down on one knee with the support of a cane. "Well then, the timing is perfect, yes?" He pulled from his breast pocket a tiny purple velvet ring box. "Would you do me the great honor of being my wife... and the mother of my child?"

"Yes! Yes! Yes, I will marry you, and since I am already the mother of your child, we are half-way there!" Jocelyn threw her arms around his shoulders. He slowly stood and put his hands around her waist, picking her up a foot off the floor to kiss her.

A month later, on a Saturday afternoon, they celebrated their wedding at the New York home of Margaret Brown. Sir Cosmo and Lady Duff-Gordon stood with the bride and groom, and a few other friends were present. For a wedding gift, Jocelyn gave François a sterling silver picture frame with one of Father Browne's photos taken of her standing at the Grand Staircase with the famed *Titanic* clock in the background. The happy couple spent their wedding night at the Waldorf Astoria in the Honeymoon Suite. They made plans to sail to Ireland for their honeymoon, once Jocelyn had the baby, where Father Browne would perform the baptism.

On 15 January 1913, a six pound, seven-ounce baby boy was born, nine months to the day of his conception. They named him François Dylan Brewster-Davis Delacroix, calling him Dylan, which meant 'son of the sea.'

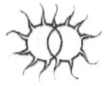

CHAPTER
Thirteen

Sophia and Michael raised their spirits the next day at the Cork Folk Festival, which featured 300 musicians and more than a dozen venues with a variety of performers, including Cajun, Bluegrass, and Traditional Irish Folk music and dance. They danced until the wee hours of the morning, or rather, Sophia danced around while Michael limped, hobbled, and finally sat, pretending there was nothing wrong with his aching hips.

The next day, Pádraig drove them along the rugged Atlantic coastline. Sophia especially enjoyed the views, at the same time wondering how she could be so enthralled by the sea, when she, as Jocelyn, survived the traumatic sinking of *Titanic*. Perhaps it was her soul's way of healing by making peace with the most powerful force on the planet.

In the harbor of Glengarriff in Bantry Bay, they took a ferry to the phenomenally beautiful botanic gardens on Garnish Island. Whichever direction they turned, Sophia found countless opportunities to capture nature's bounty in her photographs. From there, they drove through the 26,000 mountainous acres of Killarney National Park, which included MacGillycuddy's Reeks, the highest mountain range in Ireland, over 1,000 meters high. Early the next morning, they hired a horse-drawn jaunty car to tour the park. One of the sites was Torc Waterfall, and nearby they took in the gorgeous views of the Lakes of Killarney. They toured through Muckross House and Gardens in the afternoon, and enjoyed tea at the Knockreer House. Later that evening, they dined at a charming tavern in Killarney, where they spent the night down the street at a picturesque bed and breakfast.

Killarney National Park was so vast, they could not see it all in a day, so they gave Pádraig a day off, and they traveled by pony and trap - a single horse-drawn two-wheeled cart - through the Gap of Dunloe, which included seven miles of five lakes, connected by the River Loe. Along the trip through the valley, they stopped at the stone Wishing Bridge, where all wishes came true.

Sophia stood on the bridge and made her wish. Michael followed suit.

"So, what did you wish for?" Sophia asked.

"I can't tell you that! If I did, my wish won't come true," Michael said. "What did you wish?"

"Oh, you think you're the exception? What makes you think I'm going to reveal my wish to you, when you won't tell me yours?"

"Well, let's just say, if my wish comes true, it will be a good thing for you, too," Michael said.

"Not mine. My wish is purely selfish," Sophia said with a mischievous Cheshire grin.

"Oh, I see how this marriage is going to go." He grabbed her and tickled her until she collapsed in his arms, giggling uncontrollably. He then held her close and kissed her. "Don't you know, now that we are married, what is mine is yours and what's yours is mine? Underwear excluded, that is."

"You mean I can't wear your big sloppy t-shirts any-more?"

"I guess there are exceptions to every rule."

"Well, now that we have that settled, I wished for you to have your hip surgery, so I don't have to keep bugging you about it."

"That's not so selfish. And, I like the second part."

"Yeah, but the other part of it is - once you're all healed up, we'll be able to do more things together."

"We do pretty well as it is," Michael said.

"I just want to keep it that way, and I truly don't want you to live in pain any longer."

Michael sighed. "You know, White Buffalo needs us right now, and neither one of you need me flat on my back while he's still with us."

"I know," Sophia sadly said. "But, the time is coming when – well, you know."

"Yeah, I do. Okay, when we get back home, I'll check into it, deal?"

"Deal. So, are you going to tell me your wish?"

"Nope."

Sophia laughed as Michael ducked from her attempt to whack him on the arm. As they walked away from the Wishing Bridge, she thought of another metaphor to live by. *Interesting how we are, again, at a bridge, making a decision to take another positive step forward as we link the gap between the life we are living, and the life we would love to live. It's all done one step at a time, enjoying the journey along the way. Feeling grateful that life is truly so good!*

They rode on to see several lakes and loughs. Still traveling by horse cart, they wandered slowly enough for Sophia to capture many photos throughout the verdant valley. It was easy for them to understand how mythical tales developed about Ireland as they traveled through the wild and romantic mountains and valleys.

Michael was excited for their stay the next evening at Dromoland Castle Hotel. Dromoland was the ancestral home of the O'Briens of Dromoland, Kings of Thomond, whose lineage went back 1,000 years to Brian Boru, the most revered High King of Ireland. According to legend, Boru saved Ireland twice, first from the 500 years of political domination of a single great dynasty, the Uí Néill. Brian Boru was the first High King who was not a descendant of the Uí Néill, altering Irish politics for the next 150 years, until the Anglo-Norman Invasion. In 1014, Ireland was saved, yet again, by Brian Boru, from the ongoing 300-year grip of Scandinavian Viking rule.

Sophia had no idea of Michael's plan, because they had typically made it up as they went along, staying at whatever charming inn seemed to fit their traveling fancy.

They had finally circled back to where they began their journey through Ireland, in Shannon, County Clare. The next day, Michael told Sophia he heard of a charming little bed and breakfast he thought they might want to check out. As Pádraig drove them onto the grounds of the Dromoland Castle, Sophia's eyes widened.

"Michael?" Sophia said. "What's this?"

Michael peered out the window. "Wow, I guess it's a little bigger than they said."

From the back seat of the car, Sophia was speechless as she took in the estate's grandeur. She then wrapped her arms around Michael's neck and gave him a tender kiss.

Whenever she had nothing to say, he always knew he struck gold.

The bellman escorted them through a spectacular lobby filled with plush features, including lavish crystal chandeliers overhead. They climbed up the grand staircase to their second-floor suite, and as they walked in the door, Sophia immediately noticed the burning fireplace. On the coffee table was a picnic basket specially prepared by the chef.

"Put on something warm," Michael said. "I have a surprise for you."

"You're just full of surprises today, aren't you?" Over her sweater, she decided to wear a woolen shawl she purchased at Avoca. They walked down to the lake, where a small outboard motorboat awaited.

"Your royal barge awaits, m'lady," Michael said with a long, theatrical bow.

Sophia giggled. "Thank you, kind sir." She took his hand and carefully stepped into the boat. "It's not named *Titanic*, is it?"

"No!" Michael laughed. He started up the engine as Sophia untied the lines. "The guy who rented it to me said it's called *Hindenburg*..."

Once they were out in the middle of the lake, Michael stopped the motor and threw out the anchor. He turned to Sophia and opened the wicker picnic basket, layered with epicurean delights - a plate of small sandwich wedges and several cheeses with sliced homemade bread, a plate of grapes, strawberries, sliced kiwi, and chocolate truffles made by the hotel's award-winning Swiss chocolatier. Lastly was a plate of teacakes that were truly a work of art

- almost too pretty to eat - almost. At the bottom of the basket was a small container that read, 'For the birds.' It contained grasses to throw out onto the water for the ducks and geese to eat, encouraging guests not to feed them 'people food.'

Michael pulled out a chilled bottle of champagne from an ice bucket and popped the cork. He placed the bottle onto the seat next to him. "Here, hold these," he said, handing her the Waterford champagne glasses.

"Oh, Michael, how lovely these are!" Sophia exclaimed, completely surprised at everything he had done for her that day - and, in fact, she was astonished at how Michael had handled every detail since planning their wedding.

"I had Waterford ship them here." He stuck his nose in the air and polished his fingernails on his shirt. "Just saying that makes me a bit of a sport, don't you think?"

"Oh, quite," Sophia said.

He handed her both crystal and red champagne goblets and poured their champagne. "To my lovely bride - may I always be able to bring a smile to your beautiful face."

"So far, I'm grinning every minute." She leaned over to kiss him. "Sport..."

Over the next two days, they took advantage of most every amenity at Dromoland, except for the renowned golf course. Michael wanted to play, but his hips just would not comply. Dromoland offered an archery class, where Sophia proved to be quite adept at hitting the bull's-eye. They also enjoyed the ancient art of falconry and learned how to handle noble falcons, hawks, and owls. For a change of pace, Michael went to the spa for a massage, while Sophia went horseback riding.

Before dinner, they enjoyed cocktails in Dromoland's Library Bar, followed by a scrumptious six-course dinner in the Earl of Thomond's Restaurant. Early the next morning, they went for a sauna, sat in the steam room, and bubbled in the hot tub. They left with grand memories of their royal treatment, and Sophia could finally say that she stayed in an honest-to-goodness castle.

At noon, Pádraig picked them up and took them to the coastline to stay at a delightful seaside cottage in Doolin, along Ireland's Wild Atlantic Way. From their front door, they could see the Cliffs of Moher, the Aran Islands, and Galway Bay.

"Nearby is the Burren, meaning 'great rock,'" Pádraig said, "which is a rugged karst-limestone region, 250 square kilometers in size, bordered by Galway Bay and the Atlantic Ocean. The Burren is famous 'round the world for landscape and flora. A combination of Arctic alpine plants coexist with plants of the Mediterranean, some that live in the limestone, which is an alkaline environment, and others that live in acidic environments. Rare Irish plant species exist here, some found only on the Burren. In the stones are a variety of fossils, corals, sea urchins, and ammonites, and underneath the stones are caverns and underground rivers.

"Also on the Burren is the Poulnabrone dolmen. It's a Neolithic portal tomb, most likely dating between 4200 BC and 2900 BC. "

"What is a portal tomb?" Sophia asked.

"It's a single chamber megalithic tomb - one of 174 throughout Ireland. Each consists of two or more vertical megaliths supporting a large flat horizontal capstone or table - a megalith in itself - originally covering the structure with earth and smaller stones to form a small grass-covered mound, called a tumulus. Over thousands of years, the covering of soil and grass weathered away, leaving the stone skeleton behind."

"Dolmens are ancient burial grounds," Michael said.

"Aye," Pádraig said. "Poulnabrone means 'hole of the sorrows.' Years ago, archaeologists excavated human remains and artifacts around the site that they believe may date back to as early as 2500 BC."

Later, they explored Doolin Cave along the Wild Atlantic Way, where they marveled at the 23-foot-long Great Stalactite, the longest free-hanging stalactite in the Northern Hemisphere, estimated to be older than the dinosaurs from 65 million years ago. Sophia and Michael then enjoyed an afternoon stroll along the Clare Coastal walk, beginning at O'Connor's Pub across the bridge from Sea View House, where they walked a gravel path right up to the edge of the Cliffs of Moher.

The next morning, they took a ferry along the cliffs. Viewing the rugged cliffs overhead, and the sea caves from sea level, gave them a greater respect for the violent coastal erosion of 60-foot waves that constantly wore away the cliffs at the lower levels. The great 67-meter-high stack Branaunmore, once a part of the cliffs, extended farther out into the Atlantic, standing like a singular stone sentinel jutting out of the sea.

The ferry took them on to the three Aran Islands - Inisheer, the smallest island, Ihishmann, and Inishmore, the largest of the three, with a population of about 840. The inhabitants of the Aran Islands spoke Irish Gaelic as their primary language, but most everyone also spoke English.

Before the sun settled in the west, they walked among

some of Ireland's oldest archeological remains of a Bronze Age and Iron Age fort, Dun Aengus, on the very edge of a 100-meter-high cliff. Over three millennia ago, the supporting cliff collapsed, taking with it possibly a third of the original fort and the remaining edges of the fort's two concentric rings. Drystone beehive huts also remained from the early years of Christianity.

Michael was familiar with the era, but had never visited Ireland's ancient historic places.

They stayed the night at a charming traditional inn on Inishmore, where all night, Michael snored as if he had just discovered how, and was trying it out just to see how loud he could be. The following morning, at the adjoining restaurant, Michael and a nearly delirious Sophia quietly awaited their breakfast, when a weary couple entered and sat at the table behind them.

"I didn't want to be a yobbo last night," the man said, "but I was about to shoot through the room and give a gobful to the bloke next door. It was enough to listen to him and his sheila doin' the naughty, but when he fell asleep with his yap wide open, I was about to bust down the door and shove a sock in it."

"Ah, come on now, dearie, why don't you tell me how you really feel," the wife said with a smile, patting her husband on the arm.

"I canna' understand how anyone making that much noise can sleep through all that racket. So, what 'cha havin' for breakfast, love?"

"What's this 'sausage'?"

"That's what we call mystery bag."

"Well, alright then, I think I'll have scrambled eggs,

sausage, and veggies on the side," the woman said.

Michael slowly turned around in his chair, "G-day, mate! You're from Australia?"

"Reckon! Big Smoke."

"Sydney or Melbourne?"

"Both. Originally, she came from Melbourne, me - Sydney. You?"

"We're from Colorado, in the States, but I spent many years down under, and quite a few in Oz."

"What brought you to our fine country, mate?"

"University - Australian National."

"ANU! Good on ya! Same!"

"Beautiful campus. Canberra is a great city. What was your focus?" Michael asked.

"Business Admin. You?"

"Archeology and Architecture."

"You must be in heaven here in Ireland. Been to Dun Aengus yet?"

"Just last night - fascinating place. Have you been to Ireland before?"

"First time. Wouldn't you like to know how people lived in these places so long ago?" the woman said.

"Yeah, to have a window into that world would be quite a talent," Michael said as he took Sophia's hand. She just smiled that knowing smile. "When we were there last night, I think I might have inhaled an evil spirit."

The couple looked at him questioningly.

"We couldn't help but overhear that you couldn't sleep last night."

"Yeah, some bloke needs a muffler," the man said. "His poor sheila, God bless her soul!"

"Yep! She's a good sport, alright!" Michael turned to look at Sophia.

"Oh, sorry, mate! Didn't mean to insult," the man said.

"No worries. I *do* have a big yap, especially when I'm sleeping. Tell me, have you checked out of the inn yet?"

"No, we will after our meal - why do you ask?"

"How about I pay for your stay last night, since I kept you awake."

"Nah, that's not necessary -"

"Please, let me. Then you can go about your holiday and enjoy yourselves," Michael said.

"Well, that's mighty kind of you. Then how about if we pick up the check for your breakfast?" the man said.

"Too right! We can do that. Hey, why don't you join us here at the table, and afterwards, we'll take care of business," Michael said. The four of them enjoyed each other's company, later exchanging contact information. Of course, Sophia extended the invitation to visit them in Colorado.

Later that morning, Sophia and Michael rented bikes to see many of the sights. They enjoyed the untouched Irish traditions and the warmth of a hearty people that lived there for generations under the extreme conditions of the savage weather of Galway Bay. One thing was certain - they had to buy two hand-knitted Aran sweaters made of sheep's wool. The off-white cable knit multi-patterned sweaters were a must-have for the cold Colorado mountain winters. They wanted the original handmade sweaters made to last a lifetime. They were a good deal more costly, but of much greater quality.

The Arans' Irish traditions were unchanged by the modernity of the mainland. Their charming lifestyle remained as it had for many decades. Another evening of traditional Irish music and food was something that Sophia knew she would miss when they returned home to Colorado.

The following day, they returned to Doolin on the mainland. As they headed toward the Cliffs of Moher, an ominous chill overcame Sophia, and not from the cool winds as they traversed the waters to the mainland. She flashed on yet another moment of déjà vu, knowing she had been there before as she witnessed the giant waves smashing on the cliff walls. She recalled herself surrounded in warm aqua blue waters. Usually, she could make sense of her recall, but the last vision was not consistent with the cold and unforgiving waters of Galway Bay. She put the thought aside, knowing in some way she would put the pieces of the puzzle together.

They spent the afternoon at the Cliffs of Moher Visitor Experience, a contemporary subterranean visitor center built into the grassy hillside. Sophia wanted to wait until late afternoon to catch the golden sunlight on the highest cliffs in Europe, rising 702 feet above the sea. It was a clear, cloudless day, perfect for photos of the five-mile stretch of rugged cliffs.

Moher meant 'ruined fort.' In the first century BCE, a fort once occupied the spot where the 19th century O'Brien's Tower now stood. In 1835, Cornelius O'Brien, a descendant of King Brian Boru, built the observation tower with tourism in mind. The tower stood on the cliff's edge, not far from the visitor center. When Sophia began her ascent up the interior spiral staircase, the amethyst hanging from her neck lit up as it always did when in resonance with something of the same calibration, but she could not imagine what that could be. Something niggled away at Sophia's memory about the cliffs and the surrounding area. It finally came to her when she viewed the cliffs from the top of the tower. In the same way that she knew Delphi, Greece, she also knew the Cliffs of Moher. She had not been to O'Brien's Tower, but she *had* been to the fort that once stood there.

That feeling of knowing stayed with her as they walked the cliffs' pathways, observing the three-million-year-old geological formations of Namurian sandstone, siltstone, and shale. Sophia couldn't understand why, but somehow she knew the five miles of cliffs had changed. The coastal erosion of waves constantly crashing into the cliffs made dramatic changes from how she remembered them. Earlier in history, they extended much farther out into the Atlantic. She tried to recall more details, asking herself, *when was I here?*

As the sun set, Sophia took many photos of the richly colored Cliffs of Moher, bathed in late afternoon corals and golden tones, diffusing into violets and blues in every color of the spectrum. She did not see the images through the eye of her camera. Instead, she perceived them with eyes from her past. She briefly stepped into the life of a young girl who was not yet a woman.

In the tall green grasses, young Laurinda danced barefoot, twirling in circles with wide-open arms and listening to the song of birds overhead and the crash of waves far below the cliff's edge. Afternoon sunlight cast warm colors on her ivory skin, enhancing the golden highlights in her long red hair in curls that wildly flew about in the warm summer breeze. Laurinda ran to the abandoned fort built on the cliff's edge. From there, she climbed to the highest point to view the setting sun on the far curve of the sea's horizon.

As a youth, she lived a carefree life, one that obviously remained in Sophia's memory, but Laurinda's life was about to become much more complex.

That evening, Michael and Sophia ate supper at McGann's, one of the local pubs in Doolin. They stayed into the early morning hours, listening to the locals play traditional Irish music with a combination of fiddle, whistle, guitar, banjo, uilleann pipe, accordion, and harp, all kept to the beat of a bodhran. If there was room enough, some people danced. To Sophia's surprise, Michael pulled her to her feet to join the others in a jig. He was in great pain after walking so much, earlier in the day, but he knew Sophia was in the beginning stages of recalling a significant past life. She needed all the emotional support he could give her, and a dance always did wonders to fill her with delight. The pain he felt was worth the payoff.

While they took a turn around the dance floor, Michael asked, "So, tell me, how are you tonight, Mrs. O'Hara?"

He spun her about the floor, and Sophia looked into the eyes of her wise and compassionate husband. "With you, my love, I am always at my best."

He kissed her on the forehead, twirled her about once more, and then dipped her in a romantic pose as the song came to an end. Sophia was glad for the late night spent at the pub, for she sensed her dreams would soon take her into a recollection of one of her most challenging past lives.

She awoke early the next morning with feelings of curiosity. It was clear that it would take many more dreams and perhaps the combined use of her talismans to gain greater insight into the intricate life of young Laurinda. But what she *was* left with was yet another intuitive nudge as Pádraig showed up while she and Michael were eating breakfast.

"Join us, Pádraig?" Sophia asked.

"No thanks, I already ate. So, what are we doing today?"

"Sophia has a small project for us before we move on," Michael said, taking one more sip of coffee. "Let's hop in the car, and she'll tell you all about it."

As Pádraig and Michael loaded up the luggage, Sophia paid for their meal, squared the bill for their stay at the inn, and left a note of thanks with a tip for the person who did the housekeeping in their charming room. As she walked to the car, in the back of her mind, she envisioned them living in Ireland someday, even if it was simply in a vacation home to come to once a year.

Following her intuition, Sophia told Pádraig which direction to drive. Most of the area was private farmland, cultivated for centuries. The landscape she saw in her dreams was wild grasslands, undergrowth of shrubbery, and thick forests - nothing like the surrounding lands she saw that morning. That suddenly changed as they drove over a small rise.

"Stop!" Sophia suddenly cried. "Here! This is it!"

Pádraig slammed the brakes, grabbing his chest as the car skidded to a halt. "Sweet mother earth, lass! Ya gotta stop doin' that!"

Michael laughed. "I think you're starting to get the hang of it, my friend."

"Ya, but I may need something more than aspirin for my heart, plus new brakes if the missus there doesn't quit giving me such a scare."

"Sorry, Pádraig," Sophia said as she opened the door, "but something's calling me over there, on the other side of the road. Let's get out and see what's inside this fenced area. Hey, there's a For Sale sign on the property." Sophia gave a look at Michael that he knew all too well.

"Okay, let *me* now hit the brakes," Michael said.

"You know, when my intuition is right, it's right! Right, sweetie, honey-baby, you handsome, big, strong, virile man of mine?" Sophia batted her eyes.

"What am I missing here?" Pádraig asked.

"I'm sure you know when a woman wants something, and it comes from that women's intuition-thing, well, just get out of her way," Michael said.

"Ya, okay, but I think I can help, if you're actually interested in buying this property."

"We are," Sophia said.

"Maybe," Michael said, rolling his eyes.

"I know the family who owns it," Pádraig said. "The old woman passed away not long ago, and the family doesn't need all this land. I know they would not object if we jumped the fence to have a look. Here, let me give you a hand..."

They wandered the property for a time until they came across an area down the hill by a small outcropping of stones. Sophia curiously looked at the thick forest of tall trees not far down the hillside. The entire area had a sense of familiarity to her.

Instinctively, she ran downhill to the edge of the small forested area, crossing a small stream like a child prancing over the stepping stones to the opposite bank. She wandered through the forest until she came to a clearing - a field of grass with a few remnants of a circle of ancient standing stones. Sophia stood in the middle of the grassy circle and closed her eyes, envisioning herself as a youthful Laurinda, twirling in the midday sun with feelings of great joy. All Sophia could do was smile. When she opened her eyes, Michael was standing directly in front of her.

"You are radiant, my love. These trees - the stones - it's like home to you."

"Home is many places," Sophia said, "at the cabin, in Delphi, Santorini, at the plantation. It's not about the location, but the feeling of love's presence conveyed when I arrive at these places, and when I meet such people."

She reached up and gave Michael a hug just as Pádraig caught up to them. Sophia whispered, so Pádraig wouldn't hear, "I lived here once."

"The way *you* do life, it may be more than once," Michael said. "Do you remember where?"

"I think it was just up that hill," Sophia said, still in a whisper.

"These standing stones are from the Neolithic period," Pádraig said. "This area - all of Ireland - is loaded with such remnants of great historic reference. Of course, I reckon you know that better than I do, Michael."

"I'm familiar with the archeological studies," Michael said with a smile, "but Sophia is the one who truly knows."

"Come, it's up here," Sophia said. Michael and Pádraig followed as she walked back through the forest and up the hill to just below the small rock outcropping.

"Are we looking for anything in particular?" a bewildered Pádraig asked.

"Wait for it," Michael said.

"Here!" Sophia pointed at a small clearing.

"Okay," Michael said. "The foliage here grows in a straight line, perpendicular to the hill, clear across this area." He swept his hand across the terrain. "Something blocked the growth beyond this lower ridge. There may be a wall of rock not far beneath the surface. There are similar patterns of growth throughout this entire area."

"Remember when we were in Delphi?" Sophia said. "I have the same sense here."

"Yeah, I can see by the look on your face that you know this place well."

They took their time walking through the area. Suddenly, Sophia's amethyst pendulum began to ring out its familiar resonance. Pádraig's eyes widened at the sound.

"Pádraig," Michael said, "you know that little spade you have with your tools in the back of the car?"

"Aye," Pádraig whispered, still curiously listening to the pendulum.

"Can I borrow it?..."

By now, Pádraig was accustomed to his unconventional American friends. For once, he thought it best just to stay quiet and observe as Michael adjusted his hat and began digging where Sophia's pendulum indicated its highest vibration.

Michael could not help but notice how the pain in his hips subsided when he was fully involved in what he loved most. When he was with Sophia, enjoying her company, when in ceremony with the others of Apeiros, and when he was involved with a possible archeological find - all the pain went away. In times like these, he tapped into his soul's calling - centered in loving what he was doing and doing what he loved.

Seeing Michael in his fedora with his shirtsleeves rolled up to his elbows, passionately digging into the hillside and backlit by the sunset to the west, reminded Sophia of one of her favorite movies. Her amethyst rang out when Michael's shovel suddenly hit rock. He carefully uncovered a stone the width of a soccer ball, and found the surface carved with triple inter-connecting spirals on the surface. He removed the rock and set it aside as Sophia's pendulum continued to reverberate.

Pádraig stood beside Sophia, watching Michael work. "Can ya tell me, Sophia," he whispered, "what in the world is happenin' here?"

"I could," Sophia whispered back, "but you'd think we were nuts."

Pádraig leaned a wee bit closer to her ear. "It's too late to worry about that, lass."

Michael continued to dig, and soon unearthed a stone slab. He found the edges and dug around them, only to find what appeared to be a well-crafted stone box about the size of a large shoebox. He carefully dug around the box so he, with Pádraig and Sophia's help, could gently lift it out of the ground. He brushed the sides and the lid, which revealed intricate chiseled spiral designs and lozenges etched into the slate surface. In tremendous anticipation, Michael slowly lifted the stone lid off the box. Sophia gasped...

Chapter
Fourteen

Neither Sophia nor Michael wanted to leave Ireland, but it was past time to return to the States. A few days before they were planning to leave, Sophia phoned Darius to check in and detected a slight edge to her grandfather's voice when she asked how White Buffalo was doing. Sophia and Michael then felt a compelling urge to come home after that. As they flew over the island of green, Sophia thought she would never be the same after visiting another place of her soul's heritage - a heritage that extended back at least 17 centuries before. The memories flooded her mind.

For Michael, the trip brought an unexpected gem. His little digging expedition with Sophia and Pádraig revealed much more than personal history for Sophia. If what he suspected was true, he may have discovered the remains of an ancient underground Druid village that directly tied to Sophia's dream of Laurinda. He contacted the head of the archaeology department at nearby National University of Ireland at Galway, who enthusiastically greeted Michael's proposal to conduct a survey of the site. If that went well, the university would pursue a grant to conduct an archaeological dig led by Michael and the professor. Sophia would accompany Michael to give direction toward what they might find, and where.

Sophia left a piece of herself behind, but she was confident that Michael's new venture would bring them back before too long.

They left Pádraig's company for the time being, knowing that he was already a lifetime friend. Most gratifying was their new association with Sophia's Aunt Lily and Uncle Colin, and Michael's distant cousins, Geoffrey O'Hara and his daughter and family. They all got along famously, leaving Sophia with the hope that their 'new' relatives would soon come to visit them in Colorado.

Sophia longingly peered out the airplane window. The island's wild beauty contrasted with the cultivated farmland, sometimes separated by low stone walls along the rolling hillsides. Varied shades of emerald, jade, olive, and forest green surrounded the lakes and rivers, both inland and along the cliffs of the seacoast. Ireland was a land of warm and genial folk resilient to challenges, some gentle, and others with fiery personalities, blended with humor that added texture and color to Ireland's rich heritage. Many were farmers, ship builders, artisans, writers, politicians, musicians, and people of the sea, all with a spirit of survival and the fortitude of poets and rebels - and a bit of Irish magic in each.

For once, Sophia slept soundly on the plane as they flew over the Atlantic Ocean, and then along the Eastern Seaboard of the United States.

Upon their return to New Orleans and the MacPhaidin plantation, Michael and Sophia found that Digit had made herself right at home. As they walked from the car to the house, she greeted them from the upstairs veranda, so excited that her humans had returned. As they entered the house, Digit ran down the stairs, calling out for her humans. Sophia picked up her tiny black cat and cradled her in her arms. They would remain in Louisiana for a couple of days to rest up before driving back to Colorado.

When they joined everyone at the dining table, they were shocked to see how frail White Buffalo had become since they last saw him three weeks earlier. He had lost a substantial amount of weight and was quickly failing, now leaning on a finely hand-crafted tiger maple wooden cane that Gaston gave him. Sophia first gave him a hug so he would not notice her surprise, but nothing slipped past her wise sage. Sophia and Michael agreed they had better get him home soon, where they could better take care of him.

"I'm so glad to see you. We missed you all so much," Sophia said as she kissed him on the cheek.

"Whenever I see you, the sun shines in my heart," White Buffalo said.

The night of their return, Gaston joined them for dinner, and Sophia and Michael caught up with everyone about their honeymoon, relaying their trip's high points of meeting Tommy's sister and brother-in-law, Lily and Colin McPhee. Michael shared the wonderful tale about his chance encounter with his cousin Geoffrey O'Hara, and told them about their archeological adventure near the Cliffs of Moher.

"It's a good thing I found the amethyst in your shop, Gaston," Sophia said. "It has led me to some of my greatest finds. Actually, I had an inkling to walk off the main path to an area down the hillside where my amethyst indicated something that was buried. Michael and Pádraig dug up a rock with a spiral engraved on the surface. A few inches underneath was a stone box, also ornately engraved with a triskele - a triple spiral - that for some reason seems familiar to me." She showed them photos of the stone and the box, along with various shots of the area.

"Perhaps we should go into the treasure hunting business together," Gaston said. "I could be your financier, while you and Michael uncover incredible artifacts. We could all be rich! I see Michael as that archeologist college professor – you know, Indiana Whatzhisname."

"Well, he has the fedora," Sophia said.

"But I don't have a bullwhip," Michael said.

"Oh, I'm certain I could scare one up," Gaston said.

"We do pretty well as it is, Uncle, but thanks for the offer," Sophia said. "Besides, my amethyst only rings out when it resonates with something of the like frequency, which limits the prospects."

"Ah, yes, but when you touch material objects that hold the energy of times gone by, with histories of their own, you are able to recall some of their history through what you now know as psychometrics. You have done this with many of the antiques at the shop," Gaston said. "It puts a whole new spin on what you find. I smell a reality series at the very least."

"To be inside that mind of yours must be a wondrous thing," Darius said.

"It's an extraordinary adventure being me," Gaston said.

Sophia smiled at her uncle and grandfather. "I have a big reveal that you'll find of even greater interest."

"How is that possible, dear?" Gaston said.

Sophia rolled her eyes. "You all know that I have these dreams?"

"Oh, they are more than dreams," Gaston said, "but

yes, you have told us about them. Do you have another you would like to share?"

"Yes, Uncle. In fact, some of my most recent dreams explain who you are."

"Do tell?" Darius said. "You have no idea how long I have waited for someone to put into plain words why Gaston is the way he is."

"I'm a conundrum, a riddle, an enigma wrapped in mystery, anything but plain, as you say," Gaston said.

"I prefer puzzling, baffling, challenging, and obscure," Darius said.

"It is all in one's perspective - how you choose to see me," Gaston said. "In your case, I would suggest trifocals, or better yet, your grandfather's looking glass, for otherwise it's all a blur."

"57 years," White Buffalo interrupted.

"How's that?" Michael asked.

"For 57 years, I have heard these two rattle on. It shall be my final wish on the earth to see that one, if not both of them grow up."

"Ah," Gaston said, "the eternal elixir. With that wish, I dare say you may outlive us all."

White Buffalo waved him off. "Sophia, please take us away from this verbal ping-pong match and please tell us about your dreams."

"Well, Gaston, ever since you gave me the teacup and saucer that came from *Titanic-*"

"You mean the highly valuable teacup and saucer that if *sold* would pay for all of our retirement years, by the way?" Michael said.

"Well, yes," Sophia said, "that teacup and saucer, which you will sell over my dead body, and I would come back and haunt you until you went mad – yes, *that* teacup and saucer."

"Okay," Michael said, "just so we're clear."

"*Anyway,*" Sophia theatrically said, "if I could please continue?"

The boys looked at each other and agreed with a collective shrug.

"Okay, that most valued of all of our possessions, of which we are remiss to not keep it in a safety deposit box, locked up in the bank vault, White Star Line teacup and saucer - ever since you gave them to me, I've been having dreams of a past life on *Titanic.* I was a wealthy American widow, who fell in love with a handsome stowaway from France."

"An American widow and a French stowaway?" Gaston said. "What was your name?"

"Jocelyn Brewster Davis. His name wa-"

"François Delacroix!" Gaston said with such excitement that Sophia jumped in her seat.

"Why, yes!"

"My grandparents!" Gaston said, interrupting her again. "*Your* great-great grandparents!"

"I knew it!" Sophia said. "And you, Grand Uncle, are a perfect rapscallion for not telling me!"

"And ruin the joy of your discovery?" Gaston said.

Sophia shook her head in wonder. "Their child, conceived on the ship –"

"Was my father, Dylan," Gaston said. "Six years later,

along came their other son, Patrick."

"When you told me about my mother," Sophia said, "and you revealed how we are all related, you said your birth name was Delacroix. I had not yet begun the dreams about Jocelyn, because I didn't get the teacup from you until a few days later. It is so funny, but I didn't put two-and-two together until recently. And Dad – Patrick Dad – he never told me his mother and father were *Titanic* survivors!"

"He couldn't, my dear," Darius said.

Sophia nodded. "Because he was protecting me. It's so sad that he couldn't share this heritage with me."

"Until now," Gaston said. "I dare say you probably know more about Jocelyn and François than any of us."

"I know he was a scamp, just like you," Sophia said. "And Jocelyn, what an extraordinary woman."

"Just like you," Michael said.

"Right answer," Sophia said. "See? The fact I married this guy proves I inherited Jocelyn's good sense."

"Well, I must say you didn't inherit her culinary skills," Gaston said. "Gramma was an extraordinary cook. What happened there?"

"Hey, mind your manners, sonny," Sophia said. "You're speaking to your grandmother here!"

It took a few moments for them to absorb what she just said before they all burst out laughing.

For the next hour or so, she enlightened them with the tale of Jocelyn and François aboard the *Titanic*. While Gaston knew his grandparents fell in love on that fateful journey, Sophia filled in many gaps regarding the days they spent together before the sinking. Everyone sat mesmerized as Sophia related with great detail the two agonizing hours after *Titanic* hit the iceberg, and the tragic moment when Jocelyn was forced to part with François. Gaston's eyes grew moist when she told him how François clung to the overturned collapsible, his body battered and broken, until he and some 30 others were pulled from the sea, and he openly wept when she regaled them with the moment François surprised Jocelyn, weeks later, at the New York restaurant.

Gaston dabbed his eyes. "Oh dear, look at me. I am such a patsy for happy endings. I always suspected there was more to their story than we knew. Imagine that – Gramma *knew* the ship was going to sink."

Darius swallowed a lump in his throat and also wiped a tear. "Indeed. François also had a vision of the impending disaster. Remarkable."

"And, in all the years I knew them, they never once mentioned it," Gaston said.

Darius smiled. "They were such dear, gentle people – so humble. They never called attention to themselves and their experience."

"Did they ever give interviews about that night?" Michael asked.

"Oh, no," Gaston said. "They both lived into their late eighties, but never once did they ever talk to the media about it – never discussed writing a book or selling their story."

"And we know why," Sophia said. "They stayed true to their word of honoring the victims, to remember their soul's journey by holding a higher consciousness for them."

Darius agreed. "Oh, but I do regret that I didn't ask

them more questions about that terrible night."

"Grampa was a gregarious man, never at a loss for words, except for what he experienced on *Titanic*," Gaston said.

"He didn't talk privately to you or your father about it?" Michael asked.

"Oh, if you asked, they both talked in generalities, but Grampa was rather reticent," Gaston said. "Like this story Sophia told tonight - we knew he was pulled from the sea, but he never described his experience in such detail. He always brushed it off, joking that he just went for a short swim."

"He was moments from dying in that terrible, frigid water," Darius said, shaking his head, "with hundreds around him drowning or freezing to death."

Gaston again fought the tears. "Gramma told him his fate would depend on the choices he made, so he kept his head and found that overturned lifeboat. The miracle of her words saved his life."

"I imagine he didn't care to share those horrific images and the human suffering that preceded it," Darius said.

"Post traumatic stress," Sophia said. "No one ever heard of such a thing in those days."

"Indeed," Gaston said. "Some called it 'irritable heart,' and starting with World War I, it was called 'shell shock.' Grandpa always seemed uncomfortable with the label of 'Hero' that accompanied historical accounts of the men who were plucked from the sea, while those men who boarded lifeboats ahead of the women and children who died were labeled cowards."

"Although I feel like I know Jocelyn and François,"

Sophia said, "how I wish we could have met."

"You will," Gaston said. "In time..."

They finished the evening with a fine cup of coffee and a bowl of French vanilla ice cream. As bedtime drew near, Michael and Sophia were beginning to feel a bit of sadness at the prospect of the long drive home to Colorado.

White Buffalo looked at Gaston and Darius, who gave him an approving nod. "Sophia and Michael, would it be too much of an imposition if Darius and Gaston returned to the cabin with us?"

"Why, of course not," Michael said.

"We talked it over while you were in Ireland," White Buffalo said. "I know I should know better, but I would like to have more time with them right now."

"It's a wonderful idea," Sophia said. "I should have thought of it myself."

"Are you sure it would be no trouble?" Darius said.

"Of course it would," Michael said, his quivering voice obviously betraying his sense of humor. "Trouble follows you three, but we'd love to have you stay with us again."

Sophia leaned over and kissed White Buffalo on the cheek.

He patted her arm. "You are my family. I am grateful for all of you..."

The next morning, Sophia and Michael joined Darius and White Buffalo at breakfast just as Gaston walked into the house. "Good morning, dear ones," he said. "Michael, dear boy, after you're finished, would you fetch my bags from the Cadillac and put them in the RV?"

Michael looked at Sophia. "Here we go again."

"I brought you a gift, Sophia," Gaston said.

"Oh, how I love presents," she said.

Gaston handed her a blue felt pouch with a flap tied in the front. Sophia untied it and slipped a sterling silver picture frame from the pouch, revealing a photo of his grandmother, Jocelyn, standing on the Grand Staircase of *Titanic* in front of the famous carved wood clock.

"Oh, my goodness! It's Jocelyn!" She showed the picture to Michael.

"Jocelyn Brewster Davis Delacroix, my grandmother, and your great-great-grandmother," Gaston said.

Sophia suddenly remembered herself as the young Jocelyn. "Oh my, wasn't she beautiful!"

"Weren't *you* beautiful!" Gaston said.

"Wait a minute," said the ever-pragmatic Michael. "Who took this photograph? Was it François? And how did it survive?"

"Father Francis Mary Hegarty Browne," Sophia said.

"Yes!" Gaston said. "You remember him?"

"Michael, he was an Irish priest who received a gift from an uncle - a cruise on *Titanic's* maiden voyage, but just from Southampton to Queenstown," Sophia said.

"Sounds more like a winning Irish Sweepstakes ticket," Michael said.

"He had a brand-new camera, and he took many photos of the ship that became famous after the sinking. Oh, look at Jocelyn. Wasn't she something?"

"Jocelyn was a stunning woman," White Buffalo said.

"*You* knew her?" Sophia asked.

"I met her when she was in her 70's, and at that time I thought she was still a dazzling beauty."

"My Lianne looked very much like her grandmother," Darius said, "and she was just as spirited. Gaston, it's a shame your sister inherited all of the Delacroix beauty and left nothing for you."

"Ah, but I have François' charm and sophistication."

"And humility," White Buffalo said.

"Wait a minute," Sophia said. "White Buffalo, how did *you* know Jocelyn?"

"And François," White Buffalo said.

"In time," Gaston said, raising his eyebrows up and down, "all will be revealed."

"Oh, Uncle," Sophia said, "would you just *zip it?* Why can't anybody in this family ever just tell me something without all the theatrics?"

"You've never had a family until now, dear," Darius said. "You are just learning they can often be quite confounding."

White Buffalo chuckled. "We still have some road left to travel together. I have more stories to tell."

Sophia looked longingly at the lovely photo. "Gaston, are you sure you want me to have this?"

"With all your past lives, I thought you should have a photo of who you were in one of them. It's quite astounding, really," Gaston said.

She was touched by his gift. "Thank you, Gaston. I will cherish this forever."

Gaston smiled. "And for you, that's quite a long time."

Sophia smiled as she lovingly looked into her uncle's eyes. "It's true for all of us," she said, and then gave him a big hug and a kiss on the cheek, which always made him blush.

"That thing's probably worth a fortune," Michael said.

Sophia glared at her beloved. "Don't you even-"

"Think about it," Michael said. "Yeah, yeah, I know."

Sophia could see that White Buffalo was already weary, and she decided it would be best if they got on the road. White Buffalo carried Digit as Sophia put her arm around him and walked him to the RV. While she helped him in, Darius and Gaston took pity on Michael and his aching hips and actually helped carry the luggage from the house.

Before long, they took to the highway on a long journey that would eventually lead White Buffalo home.

CHAPTER
Fifteen

*U*pon their arrival at the cabin in Colorado, Sophia found a box on the porch, shipped from Waterford, Ireland. They settled in, and Michael drove down to the market to re-stock the kitchen. In short order, they all relaxed around the table and enjoyed a bowl of chili and freshly baked corn bread, served with Irish butter, honey, and plenty of hot coffee.

Sophia pulled out the package she found earlier, suspiciously looking at Michael.

"It's a surprise," Michael said.

"How exciting!" Sophia said as she opened the box and pulled out four pink champagne flutes, and four pink martini glasses.

"Oh, they're beautiful! Thank you, sweetheart. I'm so glad I made a big deal about these when we were in Waterford."

"I guess I should have kicked up a fuss at the Guinness Storehouse," Michael said.

She didn't even hear him as she held one flute to the light. "They're so different from anything else we have. We'll have to get some dishes to go with them." Sophia began to clear a space at the front of the china cabinet, where they would stand out.

"I won't eat on pink dishes," Michael said. "Pink martini glasses are as far as I go."

The boys sat at the dining table and smiled at the two of them. Digit sat in White Buffalo's lap, contentedly purring.

"They don't have to be pink, just something pretty to complement the color," Sophia said.

"I know - it has to be pretty," Michael said.

"You have him well trained," White Buffalo said.

She smiled and looked over at Michael. "Thank you, my darling. I love them. They are perfect!" She gave him a big kiss.

"Okay, we'll find the perfect pretty dishes."

"You're the best," Sophia said, gleaming at her husband, "just the best!"

"By the way, dear," Darius said, "I forgot to thank you for the cocktail glasses and decanter that you sent."

"Yes, and I have been remiss, as well," Gaston said. "I loved your gift, too."

"Glad you liked them," Sophia said. "I like to think that one can't have too many pretty things. Now, why don't you all settle into the living room while I clean up the dishes."

"No, let us earn our keep," Gaston said. He and Darius helped bring the dishes into the kitchen while Michael helped White Buffalo get comfortable by the fire. They enjoyed a short chat until the others joined them.

Sophia came into the living room, holding another gift. "White Buffalo, we brought you this handmade woolen throw to keep you warm while you're napping this winter. It came from one of Ireland's most famous hand weavers." She draped it around his shoulders.

"Oh, thank you," he said. "I remember the beautiful woolen pieces from Ireland when I went there on a speaking tour. I will enjoy this." He patted Sophia on the arm.

Sleep came quickly for everyone that night, for they were exhausted from the long journey. White Buffalo was delighted to be back at the cabin and in his favorite bedroom, where the river sang to the stars, and the deer he had often seen before the trip to New Orleans still foraged below his window...

The next evening at dinner, Darius asked Sophia what she was researching. "I must confess, I took the elevator tour of the house to the third level this morning before you awoke. I peeked into your library and saw a mountain of books and papers."

"The inner sanctum of chaos," Michael said, raising his eyebrows up and down.

Sophia laughed. "Oh my, I hope you didn't get lost in there."

"No, in fact I was slightly astounded. Admittedly, a bit frightened."

"That's why we built Sophia a studio and a library of her very own, way up in the rafters, to do with as she pleases. I have my neat and tidy man cave right here on the ground level," Michael said.

"It is definitely the domain of the creative mind, and from what I saw, you must be immersed in something fascinating?" Darius said.

"As a matter of fact," Sophia said, "I'm researching Nostradamus. I'm so interested to know he is our ancestor."

"Ah, yes" Gaston said, "the quatrain king."

Sophia laughed. "I've been tapping into the time when he traveled to Genoa, Italy. He fled France when he was about to face the Catholic Inquisition for charges of heresy."

"You must tell us more," Darius said.

"I haven't recalled the entire story, but when I do, you'll be the first. But you both know it was he who gave our ancestral grandmother, Luciana, the hourglass, which she passed down to me."

"Wait, I don't understand," Gaston said. "Don't you remember that *I* gave you the hourglass as instructed by my great aunt, who knew that the rightful owner would eventually come to claim it?"

"Ah ha! For a change, I finally have something over *you*, Uncle," Sophia said, rubbing her palms together.

"Gaston, you must recall the hourglass was first in *my* family," Darius said, "passed down from one generation to the next, but that legacy was interrupted when my great-great-grandfather Connor gave it to the doctor in payment for assisting the birth of my great-grandmother Fiona." For a brief moment, Darius paused. "Ah yes, now I remember - on the interior of the box that contained the hourglass was a silver plate, engraved with a statement of gratitude to Luciana, from Michele du Nostredame."

"Yes, that's true," Sophia said, "but I found a letter underneath the silk lining that held the golden bowl, which incidentally was inside a box, nearly identical to the one which held the hourglass. The letter was penned on parchment, specifically written to me, by Luciana nearly 600 years ago."

Darius and Gaston blankly stared at Sophia.

White Buffalo chuckled and nudged Michael. "I love how she can shut those two up."

"Yeah, she has a way about her," Michael said.

"She wrote *you* a letter?" Darius said.

"From 600 years ago?" Gaston said. "You found it inside the box, with the golden bowl that came from my shop, yes?"

"You are correct, sir!" Sophia said.

"Well, if what you say is true, it certainly took a long time to reach you," Gaston said.

White Buffalo nudged Michael again. "Snail mail."

Michael laughed. "Soph, go get the letter and read it to them. Then they'll understand."

"Give me a minute," Sophia said, "but you will have to take what I read on faith." She departed for the library.

"What does that mean?" Darius asked.

"I haven't the faintest idea," Gaston said. "She's *your* granddaughter."

"Yes, but the talking in riddles, she got that from you."

"Just wait," Michael said. "This is Sophia's mystical way, but believe me, you're gonna love this."

"I don't *always* talk in riddles," Gaston said.

"Oh, please," Darius said. "White Buffalo, would you care to break the tie?"

"Riddles," White Buffalo said.

"Have a look at this!" Sophia said as she came back into the room. It appeared as if she had something in her hand, but nothing was there. Sophia unfolded the pages of parchment that she thought only she could see.

"What are you doing, dear?" Darius said.

"Grandfather," Sophia said, "if you please." She held up what appeared to be her empty hand. "A letter, written in Italian 600 years ago by Luciana Nervetti, our ancestral grandmother. I'm translating it as best I can." She cleared her throat and held her hands out:

My dearest Sophia,

I am your ancestral grandmother, Luciana Nervetti da Genova. I write to you from the coastal port of Genova, Italy, in the year of our Lord, 1541. I see your many lives through the veils of time with the aid of the golden vessel, and now it finally has come into your possession, for you are ready for its power.

It has been necessary for you gradually to come to yourself through your dreams, because no one gave you the appropriate training to receive the rites when you were young. Sages, shamans, and wisdom keepers are gathering to align with you and your purpose. As you know, not all of them come to you from the physical realm...

I, Luciana, had the privilege to know and commune with Michel de Nostredame. If you peer into the golden vessel, you will learn of my relationship with him, which occurred long before his fame...

She read about all the talismans in Luciana's possession, the golden bowl, the hourglass, the golden chalice, the amethyst amulet, and lastly the aquamarine ring, mentioning that other talismans will come into her possession over time.

When used together, these golden talismans shall empower you so you are able to better increasingly perceive the unseen. Your awareness of other dimensional fields will become manifest, allowing you to Know Thyself by distinguishing the larger perspective - the dominion of the Divine...

With these elemental tools, you will be the master practitioner of the elements. They will assist you in serving the earth, as was their purpose when given to us by the Star People. There will be a time when you will join with these beings, for your soul will evolve to dimensions beyond the realm of this earth. From there, your soul will journey onward, never to cease in its becoming.

Know that I am here in the spirit world, as are all who have gone before you. Call on us to assist you. Be still, know, and listen - the answers will come in a myriad of ways - remain open to the possibilities and you will never falter. Ease and grace in all things will come to you, if you inquire with a humble heart. Love surrounds you as you are greatly blessed to know thyself to

be the Sacred Carrier of the Sacred Life Force.
You, Sophia, are the sacred holy vessel of water -
the most powerful force upon the earth.

Your true journey now begins. I send you great
blessings . . .

When she finished, Darius and Gaston simply stared at her in silence.

"May I see that?" White Buffalo said.

Michael, Darius, and Gaston looked at him, thinking he was playing with her, because they could not see nor hear the rustling of the pages in her hand.

"Certainly," Sophia said. "Be careful, the parchment is very fragile."

She handed him the ancient letter. From his breast pocket, White Buffalo removed his glasses and put them on to briefly look over the handwritten pages. "Beautiful calligraphy. Luciana must have been a very powerful seer herself."

He looked over the rim of his glasses at Darius and Gaston. "You know, I think this is the first time in 57 years that the two of you have nothing to say at the very same time."

Gaston looked at Darius, who simply shrugged. "I defer to you, dear brother."

White Buffalo raised his mug of cocoa. "I think we should celebrate this moment in history and make a toast to their silence."

"You can see the letter?" Michael said.

White Buffalo nodded with a shrug. He pointed to Luciana's signature. "Here it reads, 'With Love, Your Grandmother Luciana Nervetti da Genova, on this day of our Lord, Friday, 17 April, 1541.'"

"You also read Italian?" Gaston asked, still not believing what he was seeing - or not seeing.

"You don't know everything about me, roomie," White Buffalo said, carefully folding the letter and handing it back to Sophia. "We Lakota just don't like to showboat."

"Thank you!" Sophia said. "I'm glad *somebody* can see this. Until now, I didn't quite believe it myself."

"I have to say, even though I cannot see the letter, nor can I hear the pages as you turn them, I sense that what you are reading is true," Darius said.

"I remember the same thing happened when Elizabeth read the letter from Alannah," Gaston said. "It just disappeared in her hands. At least, my father and I could no longer see it, even though Elizabeth could. She just folded it back up and put it into her handbag."

"I wonder what happened to that letter," Sophia said. "Grandfather, would you have it at the plantation?"

"The question is, would I be able to find it, if it was only visible to your mother," Darius said. "If it still exists, you might be the only one who would see it."

"Well, dear girl," Gaston said, "all I have to say is you had better get yourself back up those stairs to recall the lives of Luciana and Nostradamus." He looked at White Buffalo. "And you –"

"What?"

"You never cease to amaze - with those powers of yours."

"It is all in the experience of your belief," White Buffalo said, taking off his glasses. "It is faith in the unseen, and in the depth of knowing that right in this present moment creation exists beyond what the world presents. That is where all power lies."

Everyone but Sophia retired to the living room to discuss the marvels of what they just witnessed. She returned to her loft and placed the golden bowl filled with river water on the antique walnut desk in front of the window. Earlier that day, Michael left her a crystal vase with a pink rose on the desk. She smiled at his thoughtfulness, thinking how fortunate she was to bask in the love of such a good man.

Overhead, one of three large skylights framed the moonless sky, overflowing with starlight above. She felt it most appropriate that evening to make the celestial heavens a part of her meditation. From her chair, she placed the golden chalice with the eternal flame behind the water-filled golden bowl. It was just high enough to reflect firelight onto the surface of the water. When she was ready, she turned over the hourglass, which gave her an hour to do her meditation.

She removed the amethyst amulet from her neck and placed her arm perpendicular to the desk. She draped the golden chain over the back of her hand and lightly held the remainder of the chain with her forefinger and thumb. Gently holding the chain, the amethyst swung in circles. If it swung to the right, it was affirmative - to her benefit. Contrarily, if it swung to the left, the amulet indicated the negative. Her aquamarine ring kept her in a circle of protection. On the desk, she displayed her sacred spiritual talismans, used by her family for several millennia. Evidently, according to Luciana, they were a gift to humankind by the Star People.

The darkness of the room enveloped her, except for the firelight coming from the eternal flame, which cast long dancing shadows throughout the room. She looked up through the skylight into the heavens. Starlight beckoned her with beams reaching out from millions of light-years away. She turned and looked down into the bowl, speaking her intention into the room.

"Tonight, I call upon the celestial angels to join in their awareness of my journey of becoming. I open my mind and heart to the wisdom of the ages as I peer into my golden bowl to witness the life of my ancestral grandfather, Michel du Nostredame. I call forth his wisdom as I tap into his timeframe. I seek his knowledge, his mindset, and his spiritual techniques, for Nostredame was one with the Divine in all his wondrous accomplishments. If he was able to heal those afflicted with the Black Death, then I also can heal in ways where only love can avail. I claim this as my truth, as well.

"I give great thanks, in advance, trusting that the wisdom of the ages is mine to use."

She turned over the hourglass. It would be just short of an hour before the sands of the earth came to a halt. She began her meditation by picking up the golden-cast ammonite that also sat on the desktop, which represented the ethers - the invisible nature that permeated everything into eternity. In the middle of the golden cast was the labradorite stone, which revealed layers of Earth's history in its blues, greens, golds, and silver-grays - with just a slight tone of lavender. The labradorescent dimensions played with her perception as she moved the piece in the firelight. Its golden metal of unknown origin - like that of her other talismans - made up the cast of the ammonite, accentuating the chambers of the increasing logarithmic golden spiral of mathematical precision. The labradorite mesmerized her, making her feel as if she traveled on the wings of eagles, viewing the earth below with time swiftly speeding in reverse.

Sophia returned to the life of Luciana, from Genoa, Italia, in 1539, who was an innkeeper by day, and a healer and seer by night. She witnessed herself as Luciana, serving her tenants, one of whom was 35-year-old Michel du Nostredame.

He sat in the darkest corner of the room, not wanting to call attention to himself. With his head in his hands, he faced the rough wooden table with closed eyes, leaving a puddle of tears beneath.

"Monsieur, I thought you might enjoy a plate of stew with fresh bread and a flagon of honey wine."

"Merci, Madame. You might wonder why I am so distressed," he said.

Luciana seated herself at the chair across from his. "I have the time, if you would care to tell me your troubles."

Feeling he could trust her, he began to reveal his story.

"Two weeks past, I fled my homeland of France to avoid the Inquisition by the Catholic Church. Four years ago, my wife, daughter, and son all died of the plague, which is the very disease I have so tirelessly worked for years to heal many throughout my country of France. Consequently, because of the death of my family, the financial support from my community ceased, as well as my patron's benefaction. I have lost everything due to the limited beliefs of those who surrounded me, with the attitude *if the great Nostredame could not heal his own family, he must be in league with the devil.*"

Luciana recognized his grief cloaked in melancholy, resulting from the trauma of tremendous loss. She recognized it well, having been there herself, for it was a level of consciousness where nothing of value seemed to exist within the tedious monotony of despair. Luciana knew she could be of help. She had stepped out of the shadowy abyss from the time when her husband died. If Michel would allow it, she could assist him out of the dark of night into the light of day. It would take time, and her new patron was rich in time, with nowhere to go and nothing to do...

Sophia's vision was deep into the life of Luciana interacting with Nostredame, when the ammonite suddenly slipped from her fingers and dropped into the water-filled golden bowl, causing her instant return to the present moment.

Immediately, the firelight reflecting on the water turned to a brilliant golden white light, surrounded by millions of light refractions expanding from the bowl's edges, blocking her view of everything else but the golden vessel and the ammonite submerged in the water. Sophia's eyes widened.

Celestial angels intoned their heavenly melody. She recognized them as the same entities that sang their pure ecstatic joy during her near-death experience. Sophia was not just looking at the light, she *was* the light - *and* the melody itself. There was no time, no space. Instead, she was everything that ever was and would ever be in the midst of eternality.

In that moment, Sophia realized she had become that of her calling of Love and Absolute Awareness, which included every other attribute of the Divine. She had always been that very nature, as *was* everyone and everything, but she now realized the convergent consciousness of her calling. She began to see and hear the angels and entities speak to her, which up until that moment their presence was comprehensible only during meditation or in her dreams. She immediately became aware that these ethereal beings had always given her direction. They had been with her all along, and with this awareness, she could fully tap into their guidance.

"When you return to this dimension," the entities said, "you must be fully prepared to receive what it is we have to teach you by openly welcoming our wisdom. You may ask any questions of us, and the answers we give will be for your benefit, but you must return to us in absolute trust. It will be necessary that you prepare in advance, cleansing yourself of all negativity to release undesirable trappings of judgment. Find what works for you. The practice of gratitude will enable you to be fully receptive, creating an atmosphere of appreciation for something greater to unfold. It is necessary that you are able-bodied and healthy of mind, so the strain of transition will have less effect on your senses. Meditation and prayer with your sacred talismans will enable you to relax and be in the elegance of calm as you spiritually open to our next bequest. If fully prepared, by opening your heart to us, you will be more than receptive to what we impart."

She had many questions, but she was unable to bring them into logical formation. From what they just told her, evidently she could ask questions at a later time when she was prepared.

The familiar sound of the sacred elemental talismans rang out in a confluence of melodious harmonies. The walls and ceiling disappeared, and Sophia joined with the celestial heavens into the barred spirals of the Milky Way. She no longer had a body, but truly was Absolute Awareness, as consciousness, fully expanded into hundreds of billions of galactic stars, planets, and gaseous formations. She was completely aware of everything in existence and beyond, to infinity. Sophia became the eternal magnitude of the everlasting, expansive spiral universe itself, and beyond.

She became Eternality - *Síoraí.*

Chapter
Sixteen

Michael called out to Sophia from downstairs in the great room, but she did not answer. It was getting late, and the others had gone to bed. Michael was certain she had gone up to the loft, so he took the elevator to the third level. Before entering the room, he noticed an almost unworldly glow inside, causing him to beware.

He immediately halted, for all he saw was a brilliant light emitting from the golden bowl. He stood completely still, as if frozen to the floor, seeing Sophia seated at the desk in front of the bowl in a ghostly image of herself. He reached out to touch her, but his hand went through her as if she were a mere apparition.

"Sophia, return to me, now!" Michael said, his voice booming. He centered himself and closed his eyes, knowing what he must do. He held his palms facing out, gathering his energy within while joining the expansive nature of the Divine Intelligence. He fully embodied the Divine attributes of Health and Well-being, immediately filling the room with the sense of Sophia returning back into her body again. With his eyes closed, and the images in his mind of her in full health, he saw her return without injury. He held the truth of her reappearance to be effortless, graceful, and immediate. There was nothing more for him to do, because with all of his energy, he declared it to be - and so it was.

In that very moment, gravity pulled the sands of the hourglass to finish out the hour. Sophia's meditation was then fully grounded - completed. The brilliant light ceased as Michael began to see Sophia's body re-emerge in the firelight of the eternal flame.

In order to break the energy completely, Michael immediately removed the ammonite from the golden bowl and threw the water onto a rubber plant in the large Chinese porcelain jardinière by the desk. For a few seconds, the plant turned to pure light, each leaf with a golden glow. The leaves then returned to shiny dark green just as quickly.

From Sophia's perception of the experience, she heard Michael calling her back to the earth realm. Simultaneously, she heard most every sound mixed into odd and peculiar melodious echoes, concluding the sound was the whole of earth's pulse returning to her awareness. Multidimensional flashes of her life, in full color and texture, appeared before her as she burst through them, one by one. They were images of everyone she had ever been, including every past life in her recollection, and then some. She felt the pull of her humanity traveling faster than light-speed, as it drew her quickly back into her body, completely grounding her in the earthly realm.

When she arrived fully back into the room, she was white-knuckling the arms of her desk chair as if she had just survived a plane crash. The amethyst pendulum remained in her grip, dangling below the arm of the chair, swinging to the right in full force, evidently indicating her "trip" to be of an exhilarating extremely positive nature. Her eyes, wide with astonishment, stared up at Michael. Then she burst into tears, at the very least relieved by her safe return.

Michael gathered her into his arms and held her close. In that moment, he did the only thing the protector in him knew what to do. He gently rested his cheek on the top of her head, while she stood in his arms, her body trembling from shock. Slowly, his loving warmth and strength seeped into her, helping her return to herself again, safe, secure, and forever changed.

They returned to the great room, where Michael seated her on the couch and then made her a cup of peppermint tea to soothe her nerves. Soon she was asleep, safe in the arms of her protector, but Michael remained awake for hours. He contemplated how his task as her defender and guardian was increasingly becoming an imperative mission.

Sophia slept for the next twelve hours, filled with dreams of her celestial voyage. There, she experienced a visitation from otherworldly beings that filled her mind with knowledge of the ages. They showed her thousands of transparent panels that appeared as vertical thin crystalline sheets etched with the same ancient calligraphy she found engraved on her talismans. When she read one of the crystals, the information filled her senses with sights and sounds, instantly shifting to the next crystalline panel - somewhat like a physical stream of consciousness with no end.

The crystals were not physical, but more an awareness of universal truths, available at her beck and call. All that there was to know, and everything that had ever been was recorded there. What she witnessed transcended the wisdom of the Akashic Records - beyond the intelligence of the known universe. She questioned if she had discovered the Infinite Field in form, but she wondered, *how could that be?*

The beings, originally known to her as the Star People through her past life experience as Roxana, were generous and all knowing, yet gentle - not a combination typically found on earth. They possessed a peaceful confidence, appearing to her that they bypassed the trappings of the human ego. Sophia realized they were powerful ethereal teachers. When she awoke, she had little memory of the physical nature of the beings, but she was certain immense discoveries would be uncovered.

Meditation, with the use of her talismans, enabled her to travel effortlessly through the veils of time, into dimensional fields afar from human conception. She had passed into new territory and into an expansive consciousness. As with her near-death experience, she became aware of everything there was to know, and this time she not only witnessed it all, but also *became* it, in the full comprehension of what oneness meant. Her experience caused her to unite with all beings, for she realized the spiritual truth for everyone and everything in existence. She was not only an integral piece in the immensity of the universe, but she was the entire cosmos itself.

Recognizing the power of God was within her, as her, she could not be anything else, for Sophia then realized that she was one with the Infinite. *If God is all there is, I am that as well, for I am an individualized manifest creation of the Divine.* Knowing this, she could then hold that same truth for every being, especially as she served in community with the other twelve in the Order of Apeiros. What shifted was her absolute cosmic self-awareness of her calling, as love made manifest in the earthly realm, including the eternality of the universe. A portal opened, and Sophia could enter whenever she saw fit.

A few days passed as Sophia began to spend her time writing the knowledge she obtained from those she now called the *Réalta*, derived from the Irish Gaelic for *luminary*. They were incandescent beings, radiant in their physical countenance, while also possessing the intellectual and spiritual brilliance of the enlightened divine awareness. They did not live in time, but rather in varied dimensions. Depending on how she perceived them, they were angels, entities, and godly beings, certainly far more advanced and complex beyond anything human, and yet, they possessed the best of humanity in their very being.

She named her body of work, *The Wisdom Chronicles*. The challenge would be how to communicate such information with ease. Perhaps, she thought, the crystal panels would give her direction to do just that.

One thing she was unable to recall was how to translate the written language from the crystals and the etchings on her talismans. When she was in the same dimension with the Réalta, she could read the calligraphy and speak it as if the language was her native tongue. She was certain that eventually she would remember as she progressed.

Sophia had previously painted enough pieces for her next art fair, so there were no projects to keep her from her writing. Her only other concern was in keeping Darius, Gaston, and White Buffalo content, and specifically watching over the health of White Buffalo. She spent her time adjusting to the new knowledge provided by the Réalta, recording it for future generations. The combined use of her five elemental talismans revealed to her even more powerful ways to tap into different timeframes and levels of higher perception.

To enable herself to be more receptive, Sophia refrained

from activities that drained her energy. She supported herself by meditating daily, along with clearing and centering practices that grounded her, liberating her from distractions. From this platform, she catapulted into greater awareness as the weeks passed. Sophia recorded most of what she recalled as a memoir of her journey.

In the back of her mind, Sophia knew she would later tap into more detail in the lives of Laurinda, Luciana, and Nostredame, for she was certain each obtained secret mysteries that led to knowledge and power beyond that of human awareness. In the same way, an inkling of awareness kept niggling at her dreams as she began to beckon the memory of the advanced race of people from what she knew as Akrotiri, long before the life of Roxana. Sophia now possessed a passionate enthusiasm to seek the greater task ahead, so she could convey these deeper mysteries of the past for future generations to behold.

As the days went by, she had flashes of recall into many past lives just waiting to gather in her memory. One was the life of Cassandra Wilder, who lived in the Massachusetts Bay Colony during the late 17th century. The concept of Aeternalis, and Síoraí became clear - enduring forever, everlasting, and eternal. Sophia realized she had become her own version of Apeiros, being one with the cause of all unity and the measure of all things.

Chapter Seventeen

Sophia realized the connections to her past lives and her ancestry were not about whose blood ran through her veins, or who she was at some point in time - it was about making good on their legacy, which was now hers to pass on. She knew she was here to do what those in her past could not achieve. Therefore, to take action on her birthright, she decided to do a reading for herself, but she first needed to prepare in advance to welcome her life's vision to its fullest. Days before her intended reading, it suddenly sunk in that the golden bowl in her possession was the very same bowl used by Luciana, Rachel, Hypatia, Roxanna, and the many other seers, teachers, and oracles of her lineage. Their energies were infused in the mysterious golden bowl that was now hers to utilize.

For several mornings, as the sun rose to greet the day with golden sunrays, Sophia went to the cove at the river's edge, first to sit in contemplation, and then in meditation. While wrapped in a down quilt, she sat on the large root of a majestic blue spruce, listening to the soft murmur of the wind blowing through the valley of spruce, pine, and fir. Blue shadows of snow and ice muffled the gentle gurgle of the river underneath. Sunrays danced upriver and caressed the groves of majestic white aspen trees, as sunlight filled the narrow valley with golden splendor. The time was ripe for her reading.

Sophia took in the beauty of the early morning as she dipped her golden bowl into the shallow stream, filling it with the river's icy cold waters. Feeling the cold through the golden metal, she breathed deeply and said a prayer to open herself to what the future had in store. She allowed her eyes to relax while looking into the ancient calligraphy etched into the bottom of the bowl. Soon, she began to envision emerging images.

She returned to a time, long before the days of Roxana. There, she witnessed an advanced culture able to use the Earth's elements in ways unknown to Sophia's present world of high technology. Their use of fire, water, and air enabled them to perform tasks that humankind could not possibly understand, at least to her knowledge. They commanded weather, lightning, and the rising seas. Sophia saw some of what this ancient society accomplished, inspired to understand the marvels of their world and learn how to use the powers they possessed.

Then, her mind began flashing images like a digital recording on fast forward, downloading information more rapidly than she could possibly comprehend. Sophia heard familiar voices, and although the language spoken was alien to her human comprehension, she could somehow understand the communication as if it was her native language. She connected with them on a soul-level, within the wider expanse of the all-powerful, ever-present, upward spiral of the Universal Intelligence:

"*Again, Sophia, welcome to our world. Know that the wisdom we convey is understood by you within your level of awareness. Do not concern yourself, for you will soon comprehend all the information you receive. If you continue to daily meditate into the waters, more details will come to you. Just take it in and allow it to fill your mind and heart. In this way, you will more easily prepare for the time when you return to us. Remember to keep your heart open wide. When you live from love, protection from anything you perceive as harm is yours. In this, your intuition will guide you, filling you with the depth of gnosis as the knowledge of the spiritual mysteries. All that you need to live well is easily sourced. Remember to invoke mindfulness - breathe and smile, staying in the present moment. In this mindset, you are always safe."*

Sophia looked into the water, entranced by what she heard. Images came as she envisioned herself writing the compiled wisdom that she gained from the many sages and wisdom keepers - the Réalta. As if by magic, she witnessed herself writing as the words automatically transcribed onto the large crystal panels in permanent etchings that she saw in her earlier meditation. The etchings were the same calligraphy engraved on her talismans.

Again, she heard the Réalta speak:

"Sophia, you are our daughter. You are one of us. Yeshua told you this long ago when you were Rachel. Who you once were, you are now. Who you are now, you will forever be within the evolution of your soul.

"Humanity thinks in terms of horizontal time, which is past, present, and future. Whereas, in the truth of all things, the reality of everything that ever occurred, or will ever happen, is what some might call vertical time. All of life happens within this moment of now. Some indigenous people see it as all the directions coming together. The four directions meet at the center, with the earth and sky at the one point of reality - eternal and endless. This is the point of power, which is the center of the never-ending, expansive spiral that extends outward to all that has ever been and will ever be. It is sacred geometry - in the

Flower of Life - you see it in the physical perfection of a sunflower's center. All power resides in this singular present moment where, to humanity, what seems to be time does not actually exist.

"*Those you have recalled in other lifetimes - and many you have not yet called to mind - discovered this singular truth. All those in the Order of Apeiros understand this truth as their reality. This is the way of being - the Sacred Way of the Heart. Being in the present moment of now is where you heal, create, and fill the Universe with Love. When your father conveyed to you to Know Thyself, he passed on what he finally understood to the depths of his being. This point of eternality is when what seems like miracles occur. This is when inspired ideas come through. It is what the creative artistic mind refers to as 'the zone'- where all things that have ever been merge into that singular moment of inspired pure brilliance. At that point, life emerges from the paradigms of the known - from just moments before - into the expansiveness of eternal creation.*

"*All of the individuals you tap into are you, Sophia, as all beings are one. You will discover more of your other lives as you progress in your work. Their lives will continue to teach you about who you are. Learn from them and love them in return, for they too live on in vertical time to infinity, affecting worlds without end.*

"*Sophia, as you begin to think in these terms, whatever is needed will come easily to you. The limited thoughts of someday or somehow will no longer exist, but instead you will understand how to think from the point of now, where all that is exists. From that frame of mind, you will pinpoint exactly what you desire and bring it easily into fruition, because you are living fully in the present moment where all power exists to infinity. Your thoughts and actions will be inspired, for your intuition and sacred gifts will be a way of life for you, to dimensions beyond your imagining. If you temporarily forget, just remember what your father 'knew' when he left you the wisdom to 'Know Thyself.'*

"Now go. Return to Michael, and soon we will rejoice when you once again visit us. Next time, come to us with all of your sacred talismans, for we have wondrous works for you to do..."

Sophia took a deep breath and looked around. She again witnessed the river flow through the rocks as the golden sun rose in the blue Colorado sky. A brisk winter breeze blew through her hair, bringing her awareness back to the present moment of here and now. Right then, that was all she needed to know.

At dinner, Sophia revealed some of her recollection of Luciana and Nostredame. "Nostredame directed Luciana to leave me the hourglass. She also learned that I would be in company with twelve others, two of which were her descendants – Grandfather and Uncle Gaston, as we all know. She also knew that one of the twelve would become my teacher - a wise sage with an old soul."

Everyone's eyes shifted to White Buffalo. He simply nodded with a smile.

"Nostredame was speaking about you," Sophia said as she grasped White Buffalo's hand. "All this emphasizes how what we do affects not only those around us, but for time ad infinitum."

"Time is an illusion, but infinity is right here, where we live," White Buffalo said. "The way we live affects everything. That is why what we do in Apeiros is so very powerful. And, by the way, you will never guess who called me this afternoon."

"Who?" Gaston said.

"Guess," White Buffalo said.

"Chayton," Gaston said.

White Buffalo's eyes widened. "How did you know?"

Gaston flashed that familiar mischievous smile. "You said I would never guess."

"What?"

"You said I would never guess who called you, so I didn't."

"You didn't what?"

"Guess," Gaston said. "I *knew* he called you."

"How did you know?" White Buffalo asked.

"He called me this morning to inquire as to how you were getting on."

"You could have said that in the first place," Darius grumbled.

Gaston's eyes twinkled. "I told him we were all here together in Colorado, and thanks to the loving care of our gracious hosts, dear Sophia and Michael, you are getting on famously."

White Buffalo awaited any further ramblings. "Okay, did he tell you anything else?"

"Guess."

"Uncle," Sophia interrupted, laughing. "Can we move this along to Chayton? How is he?"

"Getting along famously," White Buffalo said, rolling his eyes away from Gaston. "In fact, he and Irina are engaged to be married."

"Oh!" Sophia said. "How marvelous!"

"Splendid!" Darius said.

"Your matchmaking paid off," Sophia said.

"When I know something, I *know* it," White Buffalo said.

"So, when is their big day?" Michael asked.

"Well, that is something I must discuss with you. They honored me with a request to preside over their ceremony, if I am up to it."

"That would be so lovely," Sophia said.

"I am sorry to say, however, I am afraid my traveling days have come to an end. The journey back here from New Orleans was difficult and a great burden on all of you."

"Would they agree to come here?" Michael asked.

"Of course!" Sophia said. "We could have the ceremony right here by the river!"

"I hoped you might say that," White Buffalo said. "I recall I mentioned that might be an alternative." He flashed that loving smile.

"The wise sage at it again," Gaston said.

"Well, what did Chayton say?" Sophia asked.

"He said yes," White Buffalo said. "If it would not be an imposition."

"Are you kidding?" Sophia said. "It will be grand! Oh! Do you think they would like to invite the Order? Wouldn't that be fabulous if they all could come?"

"Chayton said they didn't want to impose, but I know they would love to have everyone here."

"I think the entire Order *should* come," Darius said.

"Chayton would like to invite his mother and father," White Buffalo said, "and Irina would like to invite her brother and his wife. Would that be alright?"

"The brother who greased him and Irina up, jumped naked into an icy ocean, and hopped a Greek trawler to defect to America?" Michael said. "Oh yeah! I want to meet that guy."

"Since it's winter, the Riverside Inn should have a lot of vacancies," Sophia said. "I'll call Jameson to see what is available. We'll have to contact everyone and see when is the best time for all of them. Oh! I need to call a caterer – I wonder if the Ello sisters could come..."

She wandered off into the kitchen, excitedly talking to herself.

White Buffalo sheepishly looked at Michael. "Such short notice – I hope this isn't too much."

"Please," Michael said. "She lives for this kind of stuff..."

That night, Sophia slept soundly, snuggled up in Michael's warm embrace. She traveled in her dreams to the time of the newly formed British Colonies.

CHAPTER
Eighteen

It was a time of fresh ideas, enterprising endeavors, and new territories in the New World. Yet, religious controls, government oppression, stagnant traditions, and infectious disease froze the mindset of the British colonists in the belief that the devil was at work. In their minds, Satan lurked around every corner, breathing his putrid breath into all that was good and holy. The colonists' means of fighting back was to rid themselves of the threat of evil, but what they created was an even greater foe that haunted them for centuries to come.

Cassandra Wilder was born in Sheffield, England. In 1670, at the age of thirteen, the inquisitive youth sailed with her parents, Cecilia and Richard, to the British Colonies, where they settled in a small cottage at the center of town in Marblehead, part of the Massachusetts Bay Colony. Seven years before, Cecilia's sister, Eva, and her husband settled in nearby Salem Town with their two young boys.

In 1660, Eva married Nathaniel Kimball, a freethinking, audacious adventurer. He took no issue with Eva's special gifts. In fact, he considered her talents to be of great value in their travels, and so they were. Eva was able to predict the best time to sail. Before Nathaniel engaged in business with another, Eva knew which tradesmen were of superior standing, and those who were not, as she was easily able to recognize whether they were a beneficial presence or of ill repute. Because of Eva's intuitive powers, she and Nathaniel could bypass needless encounters and avoid wasted time spent in business dealings and personal connections that did not serve them well. They became quite wealthy in short order, in many ways because of Eva.

Eva was so pleased that her sister and family moved to the colonies. She immediately recognized that her niece possessed gifts similar to those of Cecilia and herself when they were young. Eva was the only one of the two sisters who developed her abilities. Cecilia, on the other hand, was afraid of her powers, thinking they were of the devil, and so they remained dormant, never to be used again. Neither of Eva's sons possessed such an aptitude, but she intended to pass her knowledge on to her niece when it was appropriate.

Cassandra became quickly acquainted with her aunt. Eva was several years younger than Cassandra's mother, and she could not have been more different. Contrarily, Eva and her niece were so alike, as energetic mirror images of the other.

Eva was a lively, stunning beauty, with chestnut hair and eyes of celadon. She held many interests, which were a fine exhibition of her intelligent mind. Possessing the ability to speak several languages, Eva aided Nathaniel in his business ventures throughout the world, where they acquired fine objet d'art for their collections. They owned a library of first editions and literature that would make an archivist jealous. Eva possessed a fine ear for music and played the harp and piano well. However, oddly enough, she could not carry a tune, leaving her singing voice one that should remain mute.

Many an afternoon, Eva spent her time outdoors, painting watercolors of nature, often inviting Cassandra to join her. She found the girl was more like a little sister than a niece. Far from town, in the oaken woods, they created a circle of logs with a fire pit in the center. There, they would often enjoy a picnic lunch unlike any fare from a basket Cassandra had ever eaten. It was there that Eva began to teach Cassandra about many things, one of which was the culinary arts. Away from Puritan eyes, she taught Cassandra about which wines paired with different types of food, specifically French cuisine that Eva prepared earlier in the day. Occasionally, she brought a small bottle of cognac along - quite scandalous for the Puritan new world of old thinking. Cassandra was certainly not going to learn the ways of the world from her mother.

On one occasion, at their secret circle in the woods, Eva attempted to start a fire by striking a flint rock to a medieval firesteel she purchased in a Paris antiquities shop the last time she and Nathaniel traveled to Europe. She was unable to catch a spark. After several attempts, Cassandra offered her help.

"If you allow me, Auntie," she said with determination. Eva watched the girl look intently at the kindling set in the fire pit. Smoke suddenly began to rise. Not long afterward, flames burst forth, leaving Eva to sit back in wonderment. She looked at the girl, who seemed to be her innocent niece, and shivered with fear running through her veins like ice water.

Did she think that fire into existence? What kind of power does this girl possess?

Eva could not leave her curiosity alone. "Tell me, Cassandra, how is it you were able to set the logs aflame?"

Believing she could trust her aunt, Cassandra felt comfortable revealing the secrets her mother admonished her to keep to herself. "Ever since I was quite small, I could start fire when I concentrate my thoughts. If I feel great anger, it comes easily. I can also put out a fire in the same way by snuffing out the flames until they are gone. If I do not like someone, I can play tricks with fire, just to get their goat."

She laughed, recalling a memory. "I once put ablaze the shoe of my tutor who beat me with his book, just because I was late coming downstairs for my daily lessons. It was winter and quite cold. I was ill with influenza, but Mother insisted I was well enough for my lessons that day. After I torched his shoe, he ran around the room, stomping his feet. The other children under his tutorage laughed at him."

"Have you done this often?"

"No. I have learned the hard way that my anger causes more problems than if I mind it well. Rarely do I use my powers in that way."

"In *that* way? What other ways do you use your powers?"

"I also possess the ability to alter physical objects just by thinking of what I want them to do."

"Show me how you do this."

With her arm fully extended in front of her, Cassandra held a fork by the tines out toward her aunt. Simply by looking at the fork, the handle easily bent backwards to meet the tines as if it were a blade of grass bending in the wind. She quickly noticed the astonishment on her aunt's face. "Here let me fix it for you." Just as easily, with her mind, she bent the fork handle back into place.

While holding the fork, Eva could feel the warmth in the metal. "Oh my, what you could do with these powers. We have much work ahead of us. I cannot wait to teach you what I know, and I have much to learn from you as well."

Finally, Cassandra could talk to her aunt about such things. She no longer felt she had to hide her abilities. The two began to spend many days together in a concentrated effort for Eva to teach Cassandra how to hone her unique abilities for the betterment of her life. Cassandra was certainly mature enough to begin her education in the mystic arts, and so they began her training. Cecilia was not aware of her daughter's instruction, and would not have approved, for she thought it the work of the devil. Eva, attempting to avoid any type of conflict with her Puritanical sister, told Cecilia she needed Cassandra to watch over her two boys while she took care of the weekly chores. It was not a complete untruth, because on occasion Cassandra did just that.

The Kimball family happened to live next door to Salem Town's Puritan Church, but they did not attend. For that reason alone, many community members shunned them in contempt. Had they known the townspeople would be so vindictive, they would have lived elsewhere, but Salem Town was a good location for Nathaniel's trading business.

Weeks later, on a sunny Saturday morning, Cassandra discovered how Salem's townspeople were cruelly unkind to her aunt. While she and Eva were leaving the town marketplace on foot, a carriage full of women rode past them.

One of the women spoke in her booming voice so others in the marketplace could not help but hear, "Mistress Kimball, will thee be joining us today for the ladies quilting circle, held at the farm of the widow Wanamaker?" She paused before she continued with a smirk. "Oh, my goodness me - thee was not invited, was thee now?" All the women in the carriage tittered and giggled, looking so far down their noses at Eva that Cassandra thought they might have developed a fear of heights.

Eva looked the other way. "There is no goodness in you," she said under her breath so the women could not hear. She did not want to give any of them the attention they craved. Cassandra just smiled. She would like to be as graceful as her aunt, but it certainly was not going to happen that day.

In that moment, she decided to add a little heat to Salem Town's straight-laced, icy cold, Puritanical ways. Cassandra possessed a good bit of vigilante in her, ever at the defense of the absent or underdog. Just then, a large tree branch gave way above the open carriage, knocking the loud-mouthed woman senseless, and leaving the other women in shock. The startled horses attempted to run from the fallen branch, leaving the women inside the carriage jerked and tossed around until the driver could control the upset team. Eva turned to see a look of satisfaction on her niece's face. She quickly pulled Cassandra by the arm off the street, away from onlookers.

"Cassandra, you cannot do such a thing!" Eva whispered. "It is not up to us to administer any recompense, because what we do comes back to us tenfold, especially when our intention is either a charitable or a malicious act. That is the way of the world. We are responsible for our choice of actions - how we respond is everything in relationship, no matter with whom we are in company. Cassandra, remember this and it will serve you the rest of your days, 'That which you think of me is none of my concern,' because what others think is only generated by their own thoughts, experiences, and beliefs. Their thoughts and opinions have nothing to do with the truth of you - or of me. Do you understand, Cassandra?"

Cassandra looked at her aunt with disdain, as did most young people when dealing with an admonishing adult. She simply did not care that she might have hurt the women in the carriage, but she did remember what Eva said.

Later, in the early evening after eating a light supper at her aunt's house, Cassandra decided to take a slight detour as she walked the four-mile distance to her home in Marblehead. It was a warm summer evening, and a storm was brewing to the west. The smell of rain meant she would probably be soaked by the time she reached home, but Cassandra paid no mind to the upcoming storm. She had other tempestuous concerns in mind.

Since lightning was traveling her way, she decided to give the townspeople something to gossip about, which never seemed to be an issue with all their tongue-wagging. The quilting circle took place at the Wanamaker farm, owned by one of the nastiest women of Salem, who lived on the edge of town. The others in attendance, those that rode by in the carriage earlier that day, were some of the most prominent women of Salem Town, whose chitchat and tittle-tattle oftentimes ended up as harmful rumors.

Cassandra heard the women inside the widow Wanamaker's home, cackling like a gaggle of geese. *Who can possibly understand a word they are saying - all that noise - all that competition among such loud-mouthed old bitties.*

Just then, a thunderclap boomed as Cassandra walked past the property. Since lightning was beginning to strike at regular intervals around her, she took the opportunity to concentrate her anger toward the carriage that brought the women to the widow Wanamaker's farm. Just then, lightning struck nearby and simultaneously, the carriage burst into flames. The horses, still harnessed to the burning carriage, ran down the lane attempting to flee from the blaze, which was already steaming in the cold rain.

"And there thee have it!" Cassandra mocked, slapping her hands together in satisfaction, as if she was brushing off loose dirt.

In a way, she was.

So perfect was her timing, no one could have accused her, were it known she was capable of thinking fire into existence. Needless to say, the women were more than inconvenienced to find their way back into town most likely on foot in the dark of night.

The next day, when Eva heard rumors of the carriage fire, she suspected her niece. When the women goaded her the day before, she felt the heat radiate from Cassandra, and saw such anger in the girl's eyes. Even though Eva snickered to herself at the thought of the women walking home in the dark, trailing the hems of their dresses in the mud and muck and ruining their uncomfortable shoes, she knew she had best be diligent in training her niece how to better use her skills. Cassandra would need to learn how to act in response to people's ignorant comments in a more effective way, for her responses would definitely determine her future.

There was no doubt that her niece had tremendous abilities, but Eva was deeply concerned, having traveled throughout the world and seeing the effects of ignorance many times inflicted on the innocent. With all the witch-hunts that had taken place for 300 years in Europe, she knew the colonies would not tolerate anyone with "special powers." Salem Town was a place of conservative controls. Rampant fears held fast as their strong religious reins bound them to their limited beliefs.

One of the reasons people fled England was to rid themselves of religious persecution, and yet so many were just as extreme in their self-righteous piety on their side of the ocean. In that part of the Massachusetts Bay Colony, there was no tolerance for any thought or tradition other than that of the sanctimonious Puritanical ways.

Sophia awoke with a start, the wind howling outside the cabin, thinking how winter storms could be cold and vicious in the Rockies.

As usual, when she could not sleep, she went downstairs to make herself a cup of hot tea. She was surprised to find White Buffalo seated on the sofa in front of the burning embers in the fireplace.

"Why, hello," she said. "I'm about to make some tea. Would you like a cup?"

"Yes, thank you. Mint, if you have it."

"Coming right up." Sophia brought him a couple of homemade chocolate chip cookies with the tea for him to enjoy. She added a few split logs to the fire, then sat in the big overstuffed chair and tucked her feet up underneath her.

"Don't you know that I get up in the middle of the night, just so you can wait on me," White Buffalo said.

"What is keeping you awake? Anything I can help you with?" Sophia asked as she sipped her tea.

"When I cannot sleep, I come down here. Sitting in front of the fire takes me back to my childhood. My mother always had a fire burning in the tipi when I was a child. It brings me peace."

"If you would like to share with us, we would love to hear about your younger years," Sophia said.

"One day soon, I will take you into my past," White Buffalo said. "Tell me, why are *you* awake at this time of night?"

"Well, you know I have these dreams that take me into my past lives. I just awoke from a dream about a young girl who lived during the time of the Salem Witch Trials."

"I have to say, that would certainly cause *me* to wake up."

"I haven't gotten to the witch trials themselves, but the story is developing. The girl's name was Cassandra. She must have been quite a handful to raise. She was not only precocious, but she possessed psychic abilities. And get this – she was a fire-starter."

"Sounds more like a movie," White Buffalo said.

"Well, that is how these stories run through my mind. It is like an infinite loop that sometimes just won't stop. I would love to meet the characters from my past, and in a way, I guess I do. There are so many of them, and the history is so rich. They just keep coming to my mind." She held her warm cup of tea with both hands, taking a few sips while staring into the mesmerizing flames in the fireplace.

"From our perspective, those who preceded us seemed to have so much against them, and yet they persevered," Sophia said, in philosophical reflection. "We are the evidence of their courage and conviction, and it's important to remember their fortitude and sacrifices. We are so very fortunate. Because we have so much freedom, we have many more opportunities than most people in other parts of the world."

"I often think of how my ancestors prevailed in times when everything was against them," White Buffalo said. "Their belief in Wakan Tanka was sometimes the only thing that kept them moving on toward what impassioned their existence. It is for them that I continue. It is for them that I chose to be a teacher of their ways - to keep their memory alive forevermore."

"You teach more than the ways of your people, White Buffalo. You are a living example as you convey Great Spirit in everything you do."

"I am merely a channel. If I open myself up, what comes through is not me, but rather it is Great Spirit working, as me, in what appears to be my words and actions, but they are not mine."

"Everything I'm about began with your guidance and tutelage. I am the better for it, Uncle," Sophia said, using 'Uncle' as a term of endearment and respect.

"My dear, you were primed long before I came into your life. You just needed someone to open the door so you could enter the eternal vastness of the universe," White Buffalo said. He raised his cup of tea in salutation to Sophia.

"You are such a blessing to me," Sophia said as tears began to well up in her eyes. She quickly segued from the arising emotions. "Well, I don't know about you, but I'm getting kinda sleepy. I'm going back to bed. If you want to, go ahead and snuggle up here on the couch. Sweet dreams, Uncle." Sophia covered him with one of the woolen throws they brought from Ireland, and then kissed him on the forehead. She added a couple more logs to the fire before she returned up the stairs.

"Sleep well, my dear," White Buffalo said.

Soon, Sophia was dreaming again of Cassandra.

CHAPTER
Nineteen

Until Eva came into her life, her young niece was simply not aware of her abilities. For nearly three years, Eva helped Cassandra develop her varied mystical skills, beginning with her intuitive abilities. They worked together on her telepathy, clairaudience, clairsentience, clairvoyance, telekinesis, and prophetic talents, until Eva discovered Cassandra's specific talent for energetic healing. Her aunt particularly aided her wild and strong-minded niece to hone her abilities of moving objects and fire-starting to her benefit, for otherwise, they could be a detriment, as she had already demonstrated.

One ability she taught Cassandra was not commonly known, although everyone used it. During her family's travels to India, Eva worked extensively with a guru to learn about the chakra system and its subtle energies. She learned that the first three chakras, that of the Root, Sacral, and Solar chakras controlled the emotions. The upper three, Throat, Third Eye, and Crown chakras controlled thoughts. The fourth, Heart chakra - located in the middle - controlled feelings. The full use of all three together created what some may call miracles. Simply, that was where powerful manifestation and healing occurred, when the three levels combined as one.

Without knowing it, Cassandra used the three areas to

start fire. Eva taught her fiery niece how to control her angry emotions and thoughts of retribution by quenching them with love's power, through that of empathy and compassion. From there, Cassandra could control her rising emotions and thoughts that seemed to plague her mind by turning it into a form of love, the strongest power of all.

After a year of diligent work together, Eva shared with Cassandra a special golden chalice that she had in her possession, which held an eternal fire. Captivated by its power, Cassandra could not control the flame, finding for the first time in her life that something was much more dominant than she was. Eva found it interesting that the eternal flame humbled Cassandra. Finally, something could tame her wild niece after all.

It was not long before the striking young hazel-eyed redhead drew the attention of several young eligible gentleman callers, enchanted by her charms. Cassandra found that she also had the power to woo any man with the ability to lure him into her somewhat wicked wiles. Courting her many beaus took the place of her time spent with Eva, much to her aunt's dismay. Eva did not feel Cassandra was ready to settle down into domestic life. What she truly wanted for her niece was to travel the world, as she had. She would gain so much by observing other cultures and ways of life, but that was not what Cassandra desired.

By the age of eighteen, Cassandra married Joshua Brewster, the grandson of one of the original surviving families of the Mayflower. Before long, Cassandra gave birth to a baby girl, who they named Aurelia, which meant 'golden.' Cassandra no longer engaged in learning from her aunt Eva, thinking her lessons were of no real importance, but she could not have been more mistaken.

The colonies were struggling. The Puritans were greatly intolerant of other religions. Untamed lands still surrounded them, and their fear of the Indians still prevailed. The Puritans believed the devil could take any form, which in their minds were the diseases that struck most every family.

The plague took its toll in the early years of colonization. Smallpox and yellow fever played no favorites among many of those in the Massachusetts Bay Colony - English or Indian alike. Within a few months, Cassandra lost both her parents and her uncle, Nathaniel, to yellow fever. Cassandra's husband, Joshua, died only two months later. Soon afterward, her cousins, who were Eva and Nathaniel's grown children, also passed on. During the care of her dying family members, Eva had a premonition of her own death, soon to take place.

Eva quickly got her affairs in order, knowing that before long she would also succumb to the disease. Before she showed any symptoms of yellow fever, she met with her solicitor to have her properties and assets transferred into Cassandra's name. When the time came, she sent a note by messenger to have Cassandra come to Salem to meet with her, post-haste.

When Cassandra and Aurelia arrived at Eva's home, they waited at the door for quite a length of time before someone answered. The door opened slightly, and a nearly unrecognizable Eva peeked out, wrapped in a quilt that touched the floor. Eva did not allow them to enter the house. Shocked by Eva's appearance, it appeared to Cassandra that her beloved aunt had aged thirty years since she last saw her just three months before.

"I will not take much of your time," Eva said in a

strained and weak voice. "I do not want you near me. I too have the yellow fever."

"Oh, Auntie, no. It cannot be!" Cassandra said. After all the other deaths in the family, she did not think she had any tears left to cry, but the tears flowed as if a dam broke.

"Momma, don't cry," Aurelia said. The twelve-year-old handed her mother an embroidered handkerchief from out of her rabbit fur muff.

"Cassandra, you must hear me. I have little vigor left to stand here with you. Please listen." Eva propped herself up next to the door jam.

Cassandra wiped her tears and took several deep breaths to calm herself. "Of course, by all means."

"When you leave here today, I want you to go to my solicitor, Phineas Abercrombie, on the corner of Essex and Main, who already has everything arranged. He will have a horse cart loaded with all that I own, which I am leaving to you. You may do what you want with the house, for no one will buy property where an outcast once lived. After all, the people of Salem Town believe I am a witch." With that statement, she paused and gave Cassandra a knowing look.

"Do you mean-" Cassandra said, before her aunt interrupted her.

"You may do what you see fit, but *do* use your gifts wisely, Cassandra. Be discreet, for it is time to teach your gifts to Aurelia and to her children. I sense she specifically possesses the gift of sight and healing. The one thing I have for you today is the golden chalice. It burns all disease from its surface, so it is safe to take with you."

Eva opened the door just wide enough to hand her a

long leather pouch that nearly reached the porch floor-boards. It contained a hinged metal box with the burning chalice inside. Cassandra took the pouch and set it on the porch next to her. She briefly saw the sparse room behind her aunt, remembering how well it once displayed beauti-ful furnishings with wondrous collector's items from their world travels.

Next to the burning hearth, Eva kept only a chaise lounge covered with quilts and a small end table. On top of the table was a burning beeswax candle - its flame flicker-ing wildly at Cassandra's attention, as if a strong breeze blew through the room. She also noticed a single hand-cut crystal cordial glass next to a decanter, most likely filled with rum. Eva taught Cassandra the pleasures of drinking rum and gin, something she would not typically learn on her own while living in Puritan Essex County. Cassandra thought that she would also most likely numb *her own* mind and body if she knew she would not be among the living for much longer. What remained of Eva's posses-sions awaited her at the solicitor's office for Cassandra to transport to Marblehead.

"Wisely care for the golden chalice, Cassandra. It is now your most valued possession - more ancient than your imagining - with powers that are yet to be discovered. Treat the eternal flame with respect, and it will serve you well. Pass the chalice on to someone who will honor its purpose.

"I will be gone by month's end. I am very weary, and I can feel the sickness quickly overcoming my entire being. At least I know there are many on the other side waiting for me to join them, for I will not be alone.

"I always wanted a daughter, and you have filled that space in my heart, Cassandra. Knowing you are well gives me peace. I love you so. Remember, there are countless others who have gone on before that surround you in great love. And there are those who knew your name when only the wind whispered it before the existence of time. Soon, I will join them, but you may call on me when need be. I will reply. Pay attention! The answers will quickly come if you listen well - that is, if you listen with your heart. Now, go and please know how deeply you are loved."

"I love you, Auntie! I will remember you, and everything you taught me." Cassandra could barely speak the words. She reached out to touch the quilt wrapped around her aunt, but Eva smiled and quickly pulled away, shutting the door and leaving Cassandra standing on the porch in tears.

Cassandra and Aurelia walked to the waiting carriage. The driver took them to the business establishment of Phineas Abercrombie. Before they arrived, Cassandra dried her eyes, straightened her hat, pinched her cheeks to bring back the color, and took a deep breath.

"All will be well," she said aloud. "All will be well."

Phineas Abercrombie was a short, rotund man whose large proboscis could have supported much larger spectacles than the tiny ones perched for his eyes to peer through. The amusing caricature of a man had documents ready for Cassandra to sign, which covered the legalities upon Eva's death, leaving all her earthly belongings to her niece.

Phineas handed her a jewelry box filled with gemstone jewelry from Eva's travels throughout the world. He revealed a chest of gold pieces, enough to keep Cassandra and Aurelia financially set for the remainder of their years. Waiting for them outside were two large horse-drawn carriages carrying family furnishings, crates of china, crystal and sterling silver, books, and paintings, all stacked and covered with tarps. Two hired drivers would follow them in carriages to Marblehead when Cassandra was ready.

As Cassandra took her leave, Phineas Abercrombie rose from his chair. "I shall miss Madame Kimball's colorful ways. She possesses a high intellect paired with mystery, unlike the majority of those here in Salem Town. I already feel the impending loss of her death. I wish you well, Madame. If I may be of further service, please do not hesitate to call on me."

"Thank you, kind sir," Cassandra said, about to take her leave. Just then, an inspired idea entered her mind. "As a matter of fact, I am in need of a much larger home to house all that my aunt bestowed upon me. For some time now, I have had my eye on the Smyth House on the coastal road in Marblehead. I understand that the widower Smyth has moved to Boston, and the house is now for sale. Could you arrange for its purchase?"

"It would be my pleasure, Madame," Phineas Abercrombie said. "I have the contract somewhere here on my desk. Let me find it." He began shuffling through stacks of papers.

"I'm pleased to know you can help me in this way. It will make this transition much easier, will it not?"

"Ah, here it is," he said, adjusting his spectacles to peruse the documents. "Yes, as I look it over, it appears that the house is ready for possession today. What luck! I happen to know that Jonas Smyth left it in good order. I am certain it should not take much work to bring it up to your standards."

"Splendid! I believe Aurelia and I will be quite happy there," Cassandra said.

With his quill in hand, Phineas first adjusted his spectacles so he could write in her name and all the needed legalities. "Please sign here, Madame, and with the exchange of some of that gold your aunt left you, you may consider the house yours."

She signed the document, thinking how fortunate she was - but sadly at the cost of her beloved aunt's life. She paid him the asking price plus several more gold coins as a commission for his excellent service.

"Thank you, sir. I so appreciate your professional support of my aunt and uncle. I did not realize that you were also friends. There were not many in Salem Town who took an interest in either of them, outside of their business dealings. May you continue to prosper and have good health. Good day to you, sir." She placed her hand out, and Phineas gently took her hand in his and kissed it.

"Blessings, my dear, and may your lives be peace-filled and bountiful." He walked her to the door and opened it for her to take her leave.

Since Cassandra first came to the Colonies, she dreamed of living on the beach at the ocean's edge. She had set her sights upon that house since she was a youth, but never truly believed it would ever be hers. The carriage drivers helped Cassandra and Aurelia unload their new belongings. A week later, she paid the same two men handsomely, employing them to move everything from her home in town.

She had very little time to grieve the impending loss of her aunt. She and Aurelia spent the next fortnight cleaning their new home, painting walls, and going through all of Eva's belongings. They also prepared the house in town, and arranged for its sale. They completed all the work in their new house just in time for Phineas Abercrombie's notification of Eva's death.

For a year, Cassandra aided her sick husband and both of her parents during their illnesses. She later buried them all when they succumbed to yellow fever. She then went through their belongings, decided what little to keep, sold items of value, and gave away the rest. Other than their possessions, the only thing that remained of value was her daughter, Aurelia. *Thank God for Aurelia,* she thought. She asked a trusted friend if Aurelia could stay with her for a few days while she took time to bury Eva and clear her mind of the grief that not so patiently awaited acknowledgment.

Cassandra hired a coach to take her to Salem Town, where she made funeral arrangements for the service and burial of her beloved aunt. Most of Eva's contemporaries were either sick, or had died from yellow fever or smallpox, leaving a sparsely attended funeral.

Afterward, Phineas Abercrombie kindly offered to take Cassandra to dinner at the local eatery. She wished it were a tavern, but he had a welcome surprise for her. He stealthily removed a silver flask from his inner coat pocket. Under the table, he poured some rum into her glass. He did the same with his own before slipping the flask back into his pocket.

Phineas raised his glass. "To Eva - a fine woman who shall remain in our hearts to the end of our days."

"To Eva," Cassandra said.

They clicked their glasses and drank the fine rum, which warmed them from the inside out. Cassandra enjoyed the company of her newly appointed solicitor, who by then insisted that she call him Phineas, and to him, she became Cassandra. To others, he was a peculiar looking little man, but what she perceived was the true spirit of who he was - his good mind, warm heart, and a captivating sense of humor - all of which brought her great joy. Toward the end of their meal, Cassandra silently gave thanks for yet another dividend left by her aunt in her new association with Phineas. Their friendship would blossom for many years to come.

Over the following few days, Cassandra chose to stay at a nearby inn close to Eva's home. The evening after the funeral, she took a stroll by Eva's house to say her good-byes. She thought it appropriate that a full moon lit up the sky so brightly that the stars faded from their brilliant sparkle. She stood in the park across the street from the house, behind some bushes so as not to call attention to herself by passersby.

Cassandra thoughtfully looked over the home that no longer possessed any life within its walls. There, she spent most of her youth with her aunt who passed along the knowledge of her special gifts. She was so grateful to Eva, for she would never have known how to use her abilities had it not been for her dear aunt's patience and kindness. She thought it such a shame that the Puritan community did not know Eva and Nathaniel well. It truly was their loss. The couple would have gladly given anything to be of support to individuals or the community itself, but the Puritans had little to do with them. Eva taught Cassandra early on that one could only give openheartedly to those willing to receive in the same manner.

Cassandra then overheard the conversation of a couple who walked by. "Have you heard that the sorceress is dead? It must have been she who brought this misery of yellow fever and smallpox to us all. We can now breathe easier, for the devil no longer lives in this house."

Young Cassandra seethed in anger. *Their comments are ignorant and blinded by self-righteousness. Eva and Nathaniel lived a good and decent life. They were wonderful people who suffered tremendous loss of both of their sons, like so many others from Salem Town. Now, all four of them are gone. How is it that these Puritans continue to be so cruel?*

Temporarily erased were the years of Eva's tutelage, which taught Cassandra about the benefits of turning her negative thoughts into compassion and love. Right then, she could not muster up anything for the people of Salem Town but bitter contempt. The sorrow and heartache that churned inside for a full year increased with each loved one she lost. In a matter of moments, those feelings turned to fury and rage.

Although she knew better, she looked intensely at her aunt's abandoned home, and every window suddenly shattered, appearing as if a force from within the house caused an explosion. The large two-story house burst into flames. Cassandra remained hidden in the bushes, watching many people flee in fear. She stayed until the fire brigade arrived to put out the blaze, but by that time, the entire building was an inferno, and the blaze spread to the Puritan church next door. It was done.

It was a cleansing, a clearing of her soul's anguish. *Perhaps Eva is pleased, as well,* she thought. Cassandra felt such relief and release after so much death, and for the time being, there was no remorse or guilt... yet.

CHAPTER
Twenty

Cassandra could not easily resist the guilty pleasure of being the only one in town who knew the facts about what occurred. Fear ran rampant in the Puritanical village, and after hearing the gossip about the fire, she did not mind adding fuel to the town's collective nastiness. Never did she intend to bring physical harm to anyone, however, and she *was* grateful that no one was hurt.

She overheard one woman say, "The devil had his way last night." The Puritans alternately suspected the Quakers, Indians, Dutch, French, and finally, the Baptists - no one could be trusted.

"Anyone of *those others* may have started that fire with the intention of burning down the entire village."

The worst of the speculation blamed otherworldly entities. "Witches were at work last night," one clergyman said, "just waiting to poison the minds of any good soul who approached the vicinity of the witch's lair. That woman and her husband were of no good, she being a conjurer herself. Perhaps she was angry and not yet ready to leave this world, and in her anger, she started the fire. Thank the good Lord, her presence is no longer here. It is good riddance, I tell ye!"

Cassandra left Salem Town, never to return, but not with the satisfaction she expected after setting fire to the house. Something in her was beginning to understand the wisdom Eva taught her.

When she settled into her routine back home in Marblehead, Cassandra soon met a Native woman, Kerayetskyee - or Kera Lightsky, so named by the English. Kera's ancestral grandfather was Nanepashemet, meaning *New Moon*. As Sachem, he was the paramount chief, the highest-level political leader of a confederation of the Algonquian Tribes on the North Atlantic Coast that included the Naumkeag, which inhabited an area near the Salem Town colony.

For 4,000 years, the Naumkeag were a peaceful, productive fishing tribe of the *Massa-adchu-es-et* people, which meant "at the great hill" in reference to the Great Blue Hill, an ancient volcano from 400 million years before. The Naumkeag used wood dugout canoes and fishing weirs to trap migrating fish with their nets. They were the first people in that area to establish maritime trade and commerce. They also developed roads and pathways, and planned sturdily built, sound villages.

The majority of what they survived on throughout the year came from agricultural development. They created a mound of soil, where they planted corn along with herring, used as fertilizer. When the corn was a few inches high, they sowed beans, squash, and pumpkins next to the corn. As the corn grew, the vine wound up and around the stalk. Nearby, they planted melons. The large leaves of the squash and melons controlled weed growth and kept the soil moist during the heat of summer. Most of the corn dried on the cob for later use, with some ground into flour for bread and soups.

For winter, dried squash, dried pumpkin slices, and

beans helped sustain them. They also gathered roots and berries, and hunted deer. In preparation for the winter months, they dried meat and fish to sustain them. Both the communities of Salem Town and Marblehead were located on a portion of the land where Kera's people thrived for many millennia.

In 1615, the plague claimed many lives of the Naumkeag. The Abenaki and Mi'kmaq, also part of the Algonquian Tribes, were coastal raiding Indians from the north St. John River Basin. In 1619, they raided the coastline to the south, and consequently killed Nanepashemet. In 1633, smallpox nearly destroyed what remained of the small community. With very few people left, it took only eighteen years to nearly wipe out the Naumkeag. By the time Kera was born, very little was left of her heritage, but there were more profound reasons why she came into being.

Kera married Matthew Edwards, a wealthy Englishman from the village of Marblehead. They had two children, a girl named Harmony, and a boy named Lukas. Kera wore the clothing and hairstyle of the women of Marblehead to conform to the community's standard of dress, but her remarkable beauty outshined any outfit she wore. Educated by her husband in the ways of the English, the highly intelligent Kera easily learned to read and write. As a family, they traveled to England for business every two years. At one point, they ventured to Paris, Venice, and Florence, where the European elite celebrated Kera's dark mystical splendor.

The townspeople of Marblehead were not as welcoming to Kera, so for that reason alone, Cassandra went out of her way to befriend the Native woman. She and Aurelia took a basket filled with a fresh loaf of bread, churned butter, and elderberry jam as a neighborly gift of hospitality, along with an invitation for the Edwards family to join them for dinner the following Saturday evening. As it turned out, the three adults easily discovered common interests, and Harmony and Lukas, being close in age to Aurelia, enjoyed each other's company immensely. Quickly, they found new friendship in the making.

For the next several years, the two women shared the knowledge of each other's gifts and skills, in addition to the use of their senses beyond the human realm. Cassandra shared with Kera what her Aunt Eva taught her about the chakra system - the subtle energies of the body, mind, and spirit. Kera, in return, taught Cassandra about living among nature's storehouse, steeped in the generations of traditions passed down through her mother and grandmother. Cassandra quickly learned about the medicinal qualities of plants, roots, herbs, and flowers. Many a day they spent gathering flora to dry and mix into herbal concoctions for healing. They learned from each other's perspective about the spiritual gifts beyond the five senses, which enabled them to tap into their innate abilities as healers.

Both were strikingly beautiful women – Cassandra, with her ivory skin, flowing red hair, and hazel eyes, and Kera's olive skin, hickory eyes, and silken ebony hair. Between the two, they became a powerful duo. Before long, many people of Marblehead, Salem Town, and the neighboring Native people came to them for cures of illness and injury when the traditional physician in town was unable to bring them to health.

Mistress Llewellyn, of Marblehead, sought the help of

the two women when both her husband and son came down with influenza. The town physician was overwhelmed with too many patients, and so she turned to them for help. Cassandra and Kera kept cold compresses on their foreheads and torsos to calm the fever. They fed them warmed honey tea, infused with healing herbs to calm their stomachs and digestive systems. The most important task was to keep them hydrated. The malady itself did not kill, but dehydration did.

The boy struggled. His fever would not break, so Cassandra did what she knew best. She laid one hand on his head and the other on his chest, and she lovingly envisioned him well, feeling the life force easily flow throughout his body and mind. In her mind's eye, she envisioned the peaceful, yet strong waters of the river flowing past rocks, branches, and around the bend, eventually streaming easily into the sea and leaving her with a feeling of serene joy and freedom. She then declared aloud that his body return to full health immediately. She felt a shift occur in the boy's energy, and shortly afterward, his fever broke. Two days later, both the boy and his father recovered more quickly than those treated by the local physician.

Joseph Llewellyn and his son spread word of the women's natural abilities to heal, and their practice grew as a result. But after a few weeks, his wife grew tired of hearing their praises, and so she began to ridicule the two women. Mistress Llewellyn, like so many, scorned that which she did not understand, but for a time, the healing works of Cassandra and Kera continued to thrive, serving many with their unconventional healing techniques. Soon, Mistress Llewellyn gathered others into her vicious web, for she regarded the two women a threat and began to tell tales to turn the minds of the community away from them.

"Surely the two would most likely tempt my Joseph into submission with their sorcery had he stayed one more day under their spell," Mistress Llewellyn said. "No man is safe. It is time to rid Marblehead and Salem Town of their evil enchantments."

Jealousy wielded its wicked sword in a destructive downward spiral. Others joined in the persecution of Cassandra and Kera, because unconsciously, they thought it easier to be a part of the collective whole than to dare stand alone and risk public ostracism themselves. They thought a scapegoat could spiritually cleanse them of their woes, for in the midst of their external fears of outsider invasions and disease taking a hefty toll, death knocked at most every door. What plagued them most, however, was the unknown darkness of not facing their fears directly. Thus, people made up tales about that which they did not understand, in the attempt hide their wounded fearful hearts from their own inner demons. In less than a week, only Native people came to the two women for help.

In the early months of 1692, several young girls in Salem Town began to suffer from stomach cramps, convulsions, delusions, and screaming outbursts. Some in the community accused a Caribbean slave named Tituba of witchcraft. Tituba confessed to being in league with the devil and accused several other women in the community of complicity. Over the next two years, 200 people in the 2,000-person community were accused of witchcraft and consorting with the devil. Twenty of those were executed, 19 by hanging and one crushed with heavy stones placed on his chest until he could no longer breathe. Fourteen were women, and six were men.

Many of those convicted were social outcasts, while others were poor beggars, homeless, elderly, and impoverished. One woman was a gossip of ill repute, considered licentious by Puritan standards, but a few were upstanding citizens who were longstanding church members. *If they were witches, anyone could be,* thought the Puritans of Salem Town. Fear ran rampant.

Much of the trepidation during the centuries of the witch trials was due to the rising independence of women. In Colonial America, many were rejecting Puritanical extremes, specifically against women. The natural conditions for growth and change among the surrounding wilderness provided opportunity to move beyond religious rigidity into a greater sense of freedom. Many began to believe in the community of variety, where people could choose to worship as they pleased, honoring differences while living in peace together.

Adding to the fear-based beliefs and paranoia were a variety of issues. The fear of witchcraft continued from 14th century Europe, into the 18th century British Colonies, with the Salem Witch Trials becoming the first American witch hunt. Healers, midwives, herbal practitioners, and alchemists - anyone operating outside the increased regulation of medical institutions - were considered witches, most of whom were women. Many of the accused incurred ghastly torture prior to their deaths by means that were horribly painful and oftentimes disfiguring.

For over four hundred years, thousands, and some say up to a million people, were put to death after being falsely accused of witchcraft, supposedly in league with Satan. Many of those accused were sensitive souls who lived from their hearts and loved greatly. In this, they were sadly misunderstood, as many of them knew themselves and the world well beyond the five senses, through their varied gifts of healing.

In 1689, King William's war - the British war with France in the colonies - left damaging after-effects, with refugees transferred to Essex County in Massachusetts, especially affecting Salem's stores of food. The recent smallpox epidemic and yellow fever, plus the ongoing fear of conflict with Native American tribes, added to the strain. The winter of 1692 was particularly brutal, and cabin fever may have been another factor in the mix, but the Puritans were certain the devil was at work, and someone had to take the blame.

Many of the grains grown by colonists were rye, barley, wheat, and other cereals. When stored in damp environments, the fungus ergot easily developed, especially in rye. Consumption of the damaged grain caused symptoms, such as delirium, nausea, muscle spasms, contortions, and outbursts of screaming and mania. No one was immune to the fungus. Children were the first affected, but soon adults also became sick.

Marblehead was not far from Salem Town, and the Puritans were not about to allow witchcraft in their community. Both Cassandra and Kera feared retribution for misdeeds of which they were suspected but did not commit. Both families prepared to leave the area, having already received many threats. They decided to head west, toward an area where most of the remaining Naumkeag joined with other tribes of the Algonquian.

By that time, Aurelia was seventeen and Lukas was eighteen. Since they first met, the two were inseparable and desired to marry. Harmony was fifteen, quite independent, and more than willing to venture into the wilderness with the rest. Cassandra arranged with Phineas Abercrombie to sell the house and all her possessions. She packed only necessities and items of value for which they would trade when needed. They were readying themselves to leave in two days, but there was one more thing to do. Cassandra invited Kera to her house, while the children helped Matthew finish packing the carts at the Edwards home.

When Kera arrived, Cassandra invited her to sit across from her at the dining table, where the golden chalice burned at the center. "My dearest friend, it is time I pass on this chalice to you. I know there is no one who would honor it more. I have shared with you its history and the powers of the eternal flame as a revolutionary tool that implements change. When used in sacred ceremony for the benefit of others, the fire burns away all that no longer serves, while simultaneously allowing transformative events to develop. Sometimes, time alters and miracles occur. Use the chalice and its eternal flame well. Pass it on only to those you are certain will care for this ancient talisman."

Kera felt deeply touched by the trust of Cassandra. "My friend, I promise to protect and care for it. Let us use it once more to give thanks to the land, to the water, and the animals, for all that they have given us."

"Those were also my thoughts," Cassandra said. "Earlier today, I gathered a leaf from every kind of plant to burn in the fire."

"Do you mind if I gather some seeds from your stores?" Kera asked.

"Help yourself. I am not taking what remains here. All we will take is already on the carts."

Kera took four small bowls, and a large bowl from the shelf. She filled the small bowls, each with a different type of seed, then brought them to the table and set them aside.

The women held hands and sang songs of the Naumkeag, in the Algonquin language, in gratitude to the *Gitche-Manitou*, their name for the Creator. They expressed gratitude for all of their blessings as they placed each leaf into the fire. Kera gave thanks for the generations of people who lived by the sea for thousands of years. She thanked the plants, fish, deer, and animals for the sustenance they provided. She sang songs of gratitude for her ancestors, and for the future prosperity of her husband, Matthew, and that of her children, Lukas and Harmony.

Cassandra gave thanks for having lived in such an atmosphere of beauty. She was grateful for her parents, Cecilia and Richard, her husband, Joshua, and their daughter, Aurelia. Then she spoke of her gratitude for Eva, Nathaniel, and their sons, and for all she learned from her aunt. They both gave thanks for their health and prayed for many blessings as they went forward on their journey. Cassandra wiped tears from her eyes when she finished speaking of her future. It was a ceremony of release of the old, while welcoming the coming of a new way of life on the near horizon.

When they finished, Kera stood at the table, inviting Cassandra to stand with her. "Tonight, we honor the four directions. We can see four in everything when we look with our eyes and heart. We live with the four seasons of spring, summer, autumn, and winter. The four directions are east, represented by the color yellow, south is red, west is black, and north is white." She raised each bowl of seeds with the four colors in each. "There are four parts to the self

- body, mind, heart, and spirit. We have four ways to see the world, through our five senses, through emotion, reason, and spirit. There are four phases of life, which are childhood, youth, middle years, and elder years. As we honor the four directions, we show great respect for all life in its intricate and continual balance and order."

Kera and Cassandra turned to face the west. Kera spoke. "From the west, we honor our ancestors. From the west comes the thunder. The west is the source of all water - rain, snow, rivers, lakes, and the seas. Water is vital to all life. We also pray blessings over our dark brothers and sisters, and we honor all black and dark animals and beings on Grandmother Earth." She raised the bowl filled with black beans to the west, and then poured it into the large empty bowl.

They turned, facing north, while Kera said, "The north is cold and white. The wind comes from the north, which cleanses all in its path. We learn patience and endurance from the north during winter. From the north, we undergo hardship and discomfort, which makes us strong. We give these seeds, in gratitude, and send blessings to all people of white skin. We bless all animals and beings that are white." She raised the bowl of dried pumpkin seeds to the north, and poured them into the bowl with the black beans.

Both women faced the east, as Kera continued. "To the east, we give thanks to the dawn of each new day and ask to receive understanding, to see life as it is. The east provides us with wisdom and helps us live in a good way. We also pray blessings over the yellow people and honor all animals and beings of yellow color." She raised the bowl filled with dried yellow corn to the east, and poured it into the larger bowl.

Lastly, they faced south, as Kera concluded, "The south gives us warmth and growth. All life comes from the south. When I die, I will pass into the Spirit World and travel along the Great Ribbon of Stars overhead to the south, from whence I came. There, I will begin again. For all the red-skinned people, we pray blessings of good over them, and we pray for all red animals and beings." She raised the bowl filled with dried red berries to the south, and then poured them into the large bowl with the beans, corn, and pumpkin seeds. With both hands, she mixed the seeds together. She raised the large bowl and spoke a prayer of peace and harmony for all people and beings on Grandmother Earth.

"We blend all these colors, representing that all beings come together in peace. We give thanks in advance for all people and all beings to live in a good way. May they lead with love in their hearts, may wisdom fill their minds, and may their actions be good for all. We thank you, Gitche-Manitou - Creator - we are so grateful. We go forward now, in Love for all."

Kera poured the bowl of mixed seeds into the fiery chalice where they instantly burst into flames and smoke. The two women looked into each other's eyes with only the flame of the chalice to light their faces. They embraced with a knowing that they had set things into motion and could never look back. Something very powerful had just taken place. For a brief instant, they held the gaze of the other. It was a love of their shared souls, which would last many lifetimes.

Just then, three men with handkerchiefs tied over their faces burst through the door and violently accosted Cassandra.

"You are coming with us!" said one of the men.

Cassandra recognized his voice. It was the physician from Marblehead. Luckily, Kera was too quick for them. She was able to avoid their grip, for it took two men to control Cassandra, who kicked and screamed as they dragged her from her home.

The third man, unable to catch Kera, instead attempted to grab the fiery chalice, but the hot metal burned his hands. He quickly ran outside to the water trough to cool the burns. Kera snatched the chalice from the table, not thinking about the metal burning her. To her surprise, the golden metal was cool to her touch. She grabbed the leather pouch that contained the metal box from the floor next to her chair. She ran through the house and fled out the back door to hide behind the shed, taking a moment to place the chalice in its box and back into the leather pouch. With the fire blocked from view, she safely escaped to the woods far from town.

The two assailants brought Cassandra to the church, where several people, including Joseph Llewellyn, were waiting. Unmasking themselves, the town physician and the parson held her to face her tribunal. The neighbor, with burned hands wrapped in his wet coat, was the last to enter the room. The physician spoke on behalf of the other two and told the town authorities what they witnessed.

"We stood outside her house and remained there for some time, because we heard songs sung in an unknown language. Most likely, they were calling in the devil. When we broke through the door, the two women were standing together, looking at each other in the smoke-filled room. A gold bowl on a pedestal, unlike anything I have ever seen, was sitting at the center of the table, lit with a blazing fire.

The devil was dancing wildly in the flames. Satan's evil was thick with smoke filling the room, and Hell was not far away."

"He is speaking from his fear," Cassandra said, pleading to reason with them. "That is not what we were doing. Please stop and listen to me."

"Silence! A trial will take place immediately," the town magistrate ordered.

Not only did her accusers question Cassandra, they manipulated her responses no matter how she answered, with one more test to take place. They cut the laces on her vest and stripped her bodice away, baring her upper body. She quickly grasped her apron and held it up to cover her breasts, but already the examiner found what he was seeking. On her back were several moles, considered the witches mark. The discovery confirmed that Cassandra was a witch, but in their minds, they were already certain of the fact. Now they had the proof they sought, and found her guilty of witchcraft.

As they dragged Cassandra out the door, Joseph Llewellyn stepped forward and had the decency to stop them and hold out his coat for her. She held her apron over her breasts, and one hand at a time, put her arms in the sleeves. Then, she buttoned the coat to cover herself.

"Thank you for your kindness, sir," Cassandra said.

"You are welcome, Mistress." He nodded his head as he looked deeply into her eyes. "I am certain you are not a witch."

She nodded with a sincere look of appreciation that remained with him.

The magistrate and town officials took her outside to a

dead tree in front of the building. Someone threw a rope over a high branch, as two men forced Cassandra to stand on a wooden box, tying her hands behind her back. They placed the noose over her head and around her neck and tightened the rope. A large crowd gathered to watch the lynching as the mob mentality preceded wisdom.

The magistrate asked Cassandra if she had any last words.

"You can take my body," Cassandra said, "but I will come back to you in your dreams for generations to come, for your fear is what will haunt your minds and hearts, not me. You will remember me. The only devil is the terror you bring on yourselves. If the actions you take are through love - for the well-being of others - you will live on in peace. Until that time, you will continue to suffer."

The crowd mumbled, clearly uncomfortable, and drew away from her as if the witch had cast a spell on them.

"My wish is that you will heal from the fear that plagues you, for that is the true wickedness here. I do bless you, knowing that deep in your hearts you are good people. Live from that place within, the part of you through which God clearly exists. Release these tormenting thoughts from your minds and cease these atrocious actions now!"

Those present that night would never forget the fortitude of strength in her voice, nor the intensity in her hazel eyes.

Then, a whirlwind of unusual events took place. A few tempestuous men took lighted torches and attempted to burn her while she stood on the box. As each torch came close to her, its fire extinguished immediately as if never lit.

At the same time, the crowd engulfed in the frenzy of

mass mentality began to chant, "Hang her! Hang her!" No matter how many times they lit the torches, the flames extinguished. Cassandra put out the fires with her mind. The rope that tied her hands then suddenly began to unravel, and just as her hands became free of their bonds, the box fell to pieces under her feet. She quickly pulled the noose over her head as the crowd reared back in shock, giving Cassandra enough time to run across the square, but not before one of the men seized her.

Several men gathered around in a fury, and with their walking sticks, they beat her down until she laid still on the cold, hard ground with her back, arms, and legs black-and-blue. They tied her, weakened and bruised, to the pillory at the center of town for the night. She would not get away again. The town magistrate ordered everyone to disburse, leaving Cassandra alone for the night, and the next day the authorities would decide what to do with her.

After everyone left, Aurelia crept into the town square to bring her mother a ladle of water and a few bites of food, of which she could eat very little. By that time, Cassandra was so frail in her state of mind, body, and spirit that she was beyond the ability to set herself free from the bonds that tied her hands. Aurelia knelt down in front of her and looked into her mother's eyes. She then frantically began to untie the ropes that bound her mother's hands

"Aurelia, stop," Cassandra whispered. "Leave me be, or you, too, will be accused of witchcraft. You must leave here tonight - immediately! Go with Kera and leave town with the chalice before they find her. I am too fragile to break my bonds. My beautiful daughter, I have known for many months that it is time for me to leave this earth. Go and be well with Lukas. Be happy, and remember me."

Aurelia cried softly, "Mama, you will not see your grandchildren when they come. What will I do without you?"

"Teach your children of your gifts and how to use them well, for you come from a line of great healers," Cassandra said with conviction. "In this, I will be with you. The gifts must live on in you. Treat others kindly, and serve them with your best abilities. Learn from my mistakes. Do not take revenge, for it will take its recompense against you, only to return multiplied. Mind your temper - something which I have not always done."

"Mama, you are a good woman," Aurelia said, fighting back her tears. "People fear you because you live in truth, but the truth frightens them, for then they are forced to look at their own shadow. I know you do not intend any harm. You know about the world as a whole - what most people are not yet aware that they, too, know. If only these people were aware of the love that always resides in their own hearts, what good they could do. I love you, Mama, and I always will. I believe the love I have for you will carry on." Aurelia broke down and sobbed.

"Listen to me, my dear daughter, this is important," Cassandra said, waiting for Aurelia to come to calm. "Tell Kera to pass along the chalice to her people. It will come back, full circle, to our family in three hundred years. Be gone now, my sweet Aurelia. Live and love well, and please know, my sweet girl, how greatly you are loved by me and those who surround you."

"I love you, Mama. You will continue to live on in our family." Aurelia kissed her mother on the forehead and turned away with tears clouding her vision. She ran as fast as she could through the woods, where the Edwards were waiting, ready to leave Massachusetts that night.

Cassandra's heart was breaking. She sobbed, her broken body in a heap at the base of the pillory. Then, she heard a carriage approach. It was Phineas Abercrombie, who came at once when Matthew Edwards rode by horseback to Salem Town to inform Phineas of Cassandra's fate. The round little man wept as he knelt down to look into her eyes. He took his handkerchief from his pocket and wiped the tears from her face and then from his own.

"Cassandra, I have loved you since the moment you came to me. You have brought a lonely man such great joy. Your spirited ways filled my heart and mind with wonder. For years, I wanted to ask you to me mine, but I feared I was not the type of man you could love."

"Phineas, you gave me a cherished friendship," Cassandra said. "I could not have asked for more, but if you had asked me to marry you, I would have said yes, and maybe I would not be here tonight. Please know how dear you are to me. I cannot imagine anything other than you remaining in my heart and soul. I love you, Phineas."

"Oh, my dearest Cassandra, how deeply I love you."

"You must go now," Cassandra whispered, "for you will suffer the same fate if you are caught consorting with me."

"Rest assured, I will see that Aurelia receives the money from the sale of your house and belongings. Regretfully, I do not know what else I can say." Phineas reached up and placed his hand on her face, while looking into her eyes for the last time. "May I kiss you?"

"I was hoping you would."

Phineas gently touched his lips to hers, and all time

stopped for a brief moment.

He then whispered into her ear, "Goodbye, my love. We shall meet again." He took his leave.

Not many who lived around the town square slept peacefully that night while listening to Cassandra cry. Several held great regret for her treatment.

In the early morning hours, a quiet peace came over her. Tranquility settled into the depths of her soul, allowing her to see the heavenly world and those who waited for her to join them. Joshua was waiting, as were her parents. Eva was there, smiling and welcoming her. It was a beautiful sight, and no longer did Cassandra fear death, nor did she feel pain.

Not long after the day's dawning, the parson arrived at the town center to admonish Cassandra for dealing with the devil, except to his astonishment, he found that she was gone. She escaped, using her last bit of energy to break the bonds that tied her hands to the pillory. Later that morning, a fisherman found Cassandra's body lying on the beach in front of her home, having died at the age of 37. She wanted to live and die by the ocean's peaceful waters, and she achieved her wish. She had set her soul free. Cassandra was not forgotten, for the stories of those she healed and whose lives she had touched lived on in ways beyond her earthly imagining.

Those left among the Naumkeag settled among the Ojibwa as part of the Algonquian Tribes, who took refuge and safety in large numbers among the big waters to the north. It was there where Aurelia married Lukas in a Native ceremony. They lived where forests were thick and fish and game were plenty, and raised their family of two boys and a girl in the Native tradition, where the white settlers had not yet taken over their lands. Cassandra became her daughter's guide, ever at the ready when Aurelia called on her mother's spirit. She would ask Cassandra a question into the ethers, and the answer came in ways that Aurelia knew could only have come from the wisdom of her mother.

Kera and Matthew thrived as well. He still traveled some, but only to trade with the Natives. Harmony grew up a beauty like her mother. She was a powerful force and soon married a Dakota, who was the enemy of the Ojibwa. Eventually, they migrated southward, where their descendants, generations later, joined the Lakota in the lands that became South Dakota.

Over the years, the chalice was handed down through the generations of Lakota, to those who were worthy of its power.

Sophia awoke, her pillow wet with tears as she recalled her life as Cassandra. It was difficult to imagine the agony suffered by those accused of witchcraft. She could only imagine how the ones who remained among the living must have suffered to greater lengths, knowing of their complicity in the deaths of those who needlessly died.

Yet, Sophia extended the persecution of that time to the present day, with the understanding of how humanity continued in its judgment and discrimination. At times, people began by poking fun at another, sometimes turning it to bullying and harassment, into the extension of maltreatment or more serious levels of intended harm. The figurative scapegoat never died, after all, because of people's judgments and self-comparison to others' differences of gender, race, sexual preference, politics, religion, age, and levels of wealth or health.

Sophia had to be honest with herself in the reflection of where she was complicit in any of these acts of unkindness, drawing the conclusion that she, too, had her work to do. Her task was simply to teach love by living love, one person, one situation at a time. And so, she reflected even deeper, as to the importance of her individual life mission - and again to the deeper calling of the Order of Apeiros, so they could, together, more effectively hold the consciousness for Grandmother Earth and her inhabitants.

Knowing that Cassandra's and Kera's families lived on and prevailed, Sophia felt tremendous gratitude, because White Buffalo was here as evidence. The golden chalice had even greater significance for her, now that she knew with whom the eternal flame had travelled through time to enhance all that she was called to be.

CHAPTER
Twenty-one

After a few months, White Buffalo settled well into the cabin with his life-long friends, Darius and Gaston. Retired and financially secure, Darius had little worries about returning to New Orleans, for although he was still the CEO of Delaney Hotels, he had long since turned over the day-to-day management to a trusted and competent operations team. He also employed numerous trusted caretakers to look after the plantation while he was gone. Gaston had few financial worries as well, however he did take several brief trips home to check on the antique shop, to be certain his employees had everything under control.

For now, however, home for both Darius and Gaston was Riverside, Colorado. Sophia and Michael had long understood that White Buffalo, Darius, and Gaston were very dear to each other, but only now did they comprehend the depths of their bond. White Buffalo's time on earth was drawing to an end, and although Sophia and Michael avoided the obvious comparison, Gaston and Darius clearly had no misgivings about the fact that they, too, were in the latter years of their long, glorious journey of this life.

It was clear these three sages, for all their playful bravado, loved and respected each other in a way that transcended time and space, and when the first of them made the transition from this earthly plane, it would be both profoundly difficult, and yet magnificent at the same time.

Michael wanted to be sure that Darius and Gaston would stay at the cabin for however long White Buffalo remained, but he knew this was only possible if he did the cooking. With all of Sophia's unique abilities, one would think she could adeptly find her way around the kitchen, but it simply was not the case. Most everything she cooked was a disaster and without a doubt ended up a plateful of multi-textured, sometimes unrecognizable brown something-or-other that only a large quantity of ketchup could rescue. However, on one cold winter evening, Sophia made her specialty - toasted cheese sandwiches, served with potato chips, a dill pickle, and hot cocoa. The meal was a smashing hit.

"Sophia, dear," White Buffalo said, "I believe these are the finest potato chips you've ever served."

"See, on occasion I can do brown quite well," Sophia said as she placed her folded dishtowel over her forearm. "This is a Delaney family tradition, started by my father, I'll have you know. When I was growing up, Daddy fixed us toasted cheese for dinner most every Saturday night, right here at the cabin, complete with potato chips, dill pickle, and hot cocoa."

"I'd wager Patrick is smiling over us right now," Gaston said.

"It's the best toasted cheese sandwich *I've* ever eaten, to be sure," Darius said, "grilled to the most exquisite shade of golden brown, I might add."

"No complaints here, hon," Michael said. "Maybe we should continue the tradition on Saturday nights from this point forward."

"Well, I might break it up now and then with some

spaghetti sauce from a jar, and garlic bread," Sophia said.

"That means you'll be cooking with a color other than brown," Michael said. "This green pickle on my plate is more color than I can handle. I don't know if such a change in tradition can be warranted at this time. We'll have to discuss this at a later date."

Sophia laughed and whacked Michael on the arm with her towel as she cleared the dishes. They bid goodnight to White Buffalo, for he was growing fatigued, and Darius and Gaston settled onto the sofa in front of the blazing fire.

White Buffalo rested in his bedroom that overlooked the mountains to the west and the river below. He covered himself with the woolen throw that Michael and Sophia brought from Ireland. He laid there, listening to the never-ending splash and gurgle of the river as it flowed downstream as he gently fell asleep with thoughts of his childhood. How well life turned out for him as time went on. It was not so for many Native Americans.

White Buffalo was born in the Black Hills, south of Spearfish, South Dakota. The young boy grew up hearing tales of his ancestors and his Native heritage, mostly enjoying the stories about his great-grandfather Tahatan, a very powerful man, whose name meant falcon or hawk.

Tahatan was a Lakota warrior chief, a dream interpreter and medicine man, also known as the *wicasa wakan* - a holy man - who conveyed spiritual messages to the people. He assisted the people by creating a healing atmosphere to welcome Tunkashila - Wakan Tanka, who was responsible for the healing that took place during ceremony.

Tahatan was a warrior in many of the Indian wars, but most notably a survivor of the 1876 Battle of Little Big Horn in his youth, and later the massacre at Wounded Knee in late December 1890. At Wounded Knee, early in the battle, he sustained bullet wounds in both the hip and thigh. The damage to his hip caused him to walk with a limp, but he believed it helped him to remain humble. Whenever he felt pain in his hip, it reminded him to be strong and compassionate - to remember the more than 90 warriors and 200 women and children who did not live beyond that brutal winter day. He felt fortunate to remain among the living for more than 80 years, so he could tell the stories of his great people.

Three years before Wounded Knee, in 1887, Tahatan's daughter, Mika, was born. She was a wild child, ever with the wind at her back and feet loosely planted on the ground. Without the inherent wisdom or clear sight of her father, she possessed the unrelenting desire to run. At fifteen, Mika became pregnant by one of a number of faceless young men and soon gave birth to a baby girl she named Wichahpi. Not a year later, Mika went missing after a band of traders came through the Black Hills heading for Rapid City. At such a young age, she had no desire to be a mother, and she abandoned her infant daughter along with the traditions of her people for what she thought was freedom. Tahatan's wife died when Mika was a small girl, and he had no desire to marry again, and so he raised Wichahpi as his own and taught her the ways of her Lakota ancestors.

Wichahpi was a gifted young girl, also of sighted wisdom like her grandfather. When she was coming of age, she often dreamt of a boy and a man, both with hair the color of the sun, and eyes like that of the sky at midday. Wichahpi envisioned his light hair and blue eyes, unable to know if he was the same person, or two people of the past, or the future. She inquired of her wise grandfather the meaning of her vision.

"My granddaughter, I can tell you what I see of this unusual boy or man, but you must find out who he is for yourself. Even though our people are not to practice our Lakota ways, we still do it quietly. You are now of the age to take your vision quest, to understand oneness with all things, and to gain from the wisdom of the Ancestors and of the Creator, Wakan Tanka."

It took several days before Wichahpi approached her grandfather again, this time with an offering of tobacco to request his counsel during her vision quest. He accepted her gift, which meant he was in concordance with her appeal. Had he not accepted her gift of tobacco, he would have turned away, leaving her to come to the understanding of why he rejected her request.

"Granddaughter, we will prepare for the vision quest to begin four days from now with an Inipi ceremony or sweat lodge. It is a purification rite for cleansing the mind, body, and spirit - for spiritual rebirth. Inipi means, 'to live again.' Many will join us during the ceremony to support you in your first stage of purification. The ceremony will begin when the sun reaches the center of the sky."

To begin her preparation, Wichahpi began fasting at sunrise. For the next four days, she ate no food and drank no water. During that time, her task was to make a continuous string of 405 prayer ties, two fingers width apart. Each contained a pinch of tobacco, a sacred plant, tied in a small square of cloth infused with an individual prayer.

The lodge was a dome made of 16 narrow willow trees bent into a framework and covered in layers of buffalo skins and blankets. They built the structure far enough up the mountain to not call attention to their drumming and song. Since 1882, the U.S. government considered Indian spiritual practices heathen and therefore unlawful, forcing all Native Americans to practice their dances and ceremonies unlawfully and in secret.

For the Inipi ceremony, men wore only loincloths, and women wore long cotton dresses. Everyone's feet were bare, and no one wore any form of jewelry or adornments, so that each person would present themselves in their purest physical form before Great Spirit. At that time in history, few sweat lodges allowed women to enter, but Tahatan believed that women's insights were as valuable as any man's, so he encouraged women to enter the Inipi, and also participate in their vision quest.

The ceremony began as Tahatan instructed them to leave their human thoughts of negativity outside the door, otherwise their experience during the sweat lodge might become quite challenging. He cleansed each person with the smoke of burning sage before he offered a prayer to each of the four directions, to Grandmother Earth, and concluding with the Heavens. Before entering the lodge, everyone gave a gift of tobacco. They placed it on the altar just outside the lodge door, a rounded mound of dirt left from the fire pit dug from inside the center of the lodge floor. The altar held sacred items, among them, a turtle rattle, a fan of eagle feathers, prayer flags, and a stand for the sacred pipe, called a *chanupa*.

Tahatan entered the lodge first, as the wicasa wakan, and sat at the inside edge of the door, followed by the women, one by one. With her prayer ties around her neck, Wichahpi knelt down before the lodge door, which was two feet in height. She crawled through the opening, tipping her head down below her heart, close to Grandmother Earth, in humility before Wakan Tanka. Once inside, she crawled in the sunwise direction around the inner circle on the bed of fresh sage that covered the floor, and sat on the right side of the lodge. She tucked her 405 prayer ties into the willow framework above her head. Others followed suit. The men entered last, sitting on the left side of the lodge.

Since dawn, a firekeeper tended the fire pit outside the lodge, which held many large basalt stones heated to red-hot. When instructed by Tahatan, the firekeeper brought in seven sizzling stones, called 'Grandfathers', one at a time with a pitchfork. They were placed according to the four directions, each into an earthen fire pit dug two hand-widths deep at the center of the lodge floor. Tahatan used deer antlers to arrange the red-hot Grandfathers, the first four placed to honor the four directions. He sprinkled white sage, sweet grass, and cedar onto the fiery rocks to bring purification and blessings, to honor the Grandfathers. The firekeeper then added five more red-hot rocks.

Using a gourd filled with water, everyone blessed the water before the wicasa wakan poured it on the ground around the rocks to honor Grandmother Earth. He then poured water over the red-hot stones to create sizzling steam, further heating up the lodge. The firekeeper closed the flap over the door on the outside, leaving everyone in the heat and complete darkness. The purifying elements of fire, water, and darkness assisted the people in releasing what held them back from their good spirit, while creating a personal deepening into a new sense of themselves through spiritual rebirth.

Tahatan, as the wicasa wakan, called in the Ancestors and the animal spirits. Some beat drums as the people sang songs of the Lakota, which were prayers to Wakan Tanka - Creator - Great Spirit. As the ceremony progressed, the door opened three additional times, each representing the next honored direction, beginning with the west, moving sunwise to the north, on to the east, and ending with the south. As each door opened, the firekeeper placed more red-hot Grandfathers into the lodge for the wicasa wakan to add to the fire pit. For each direction, they sang songs and spoke prayers - opening each prayer in gratitude to Great Spirit, speaking of their personal concerns, and ending with prayers for all who lived on Grandmother Earth.

When the prayers came back around the circle to Wichahpi, the wicasa wakan said to her, "You may offer your prayers, Granddaughter."

Wichahpi raised her head and looked up into the darkness. "Wakan Tanka, this is your granddaughter, Wichahpi. Today, I thank you for this great honor to enter this Inipi and my vision quest so I may see the journey before me. I ask that I may live in a good way. Help me to see with both eyes like the eagle, to hear with both ears like the mountain lion, and to speak clearly with kindness and strength - all coming from my heart center. May my heart be open to the wisdom you have for me. Help me to remember all you have for me to know. Teach me to see and listen to the many signs you leave for me, so I may be receptive to your wisdom.

"If I am to know about the blue-eyed, yellow-haired boy and man, please help me to see who they are, so I may be of service to them. I am so thankful for my life and for all my ancestors, for the Grandfathers, for Grandmother Earth, and for Wakan Tanka. Aho Mitakuye Oyasin."

All responded to her prayer by saying, "Aho."

After the last door, the flap opened and light entered the lodge once more. Tahatan then lit the chanupa with a reed, set aflame from the Grandfathers. He first smoked the pipe, and then passed it to the person on his left. In the sun-wise direction, the pipe passed from one person to the next. Each took the opportunity to smoke the sacred pipe, for smoke was a visible prayer as the breath of Great Spirit. When the pipe came back around to Tahatan, he was the last to smoke the remaining tobacco. He cleaned out the bowl of the pipe and then in place of tobacco he filled the bowl with white sage. The final Grandfathers were placed on top of those in the center. The door closed one more time.

"Granddaughter, this sacred chanupa is now yours," Tahatan said, handing her the pipe, with the bowl in his left hand, and the stem in his right at the level of her heart. "During your vision quest, you are to keep this sacred pipe intact. When you hold the sacred chanupa, keep the bowl - the feminine - in your left hand, and the stem - the mascu-line - in the right. The two joined together represents union, balance, and harmony. Keep the two pieces connected as one until you return to the concluding Inipi ceremony after your vision quest is complete."

Tahatan spoke, not as her grandfather, but with words of wisdom beyond his own, as the wicasa wakan. "Wichahpi, your name means 'star.' Your spirit is pure. Visions come to you beyond that of Grandmother Earth, for your sight soars far beyond the light of the sun. The Ancestors come to you with the sight, long before your days here on Grandmother Earth. In the same way, your vision of the future will show you that life will be far different than it is now. You already know, when we say 'Mitakuye Oyasin,' or 'All my Relations,' it means 'I acknowledge my relation to everything in creation: stones, plants and trees, all people, every animal - all beings that live on Grandmother Earth, the sun, moon, and stars in the heavens.'

"Today, Wichahpi, you become a woman. Your vision quest will be one of great direction, not only for the Lakota, but also for people of many nations. Keep your heart open, for Wakan Tanka - Great Spirit - will always speak to you there. When you act upon the direction you hear from Great Spirit, you will join your head with your heart, and wonders will come to you beyond your human abilities. Welcome the Ancestors to join you in your vision quest. They are here to guide you in all ways. You stand on the shoulders of a great people, granddaughter. The Grandfathers smile upon you today, and Grandmother Earth is happy whenever you dance upon her back. Aho Mitakuye Oyasin."

"Aho," everyone said.

After they sang two more songs to conclude the ceremony for Wichahpi, she and her grandfather left the lodge with a buffalo robe covering her so no one could see her. The remaining people stayed behind in the sweat lodge, eventually to exchange places with others so there would be continual song and prayers of support for the duration of her vision quest.

CHAPTER
Twenty-two

The sun was low in the sky to the west, although it seemed as if only a short time had passed. Tahatan stood to the side of the lodge, holding up the buffalo robe with his back to those standing outside the lodge, while looking down at the ground. Shivering from the change of extreme heat to the cool temperatures of dusk, Wichahpi stepped to the other side of the buffalo robe. She slipped off her dress, allowing it to fall to the ground, standing naked in the coral tones of the fading sunlight. She dried off her body with a large cloth. Her grandfather gently wrapped the robe around her, allowing it to trail to the ground, again with her head covered for no one to see.

He took her by horseback to the top of the mountain overlooking the Black Hills to the west, where he previously selected a sacred place for her to enter her vision quest. During the sweat lodge, her prayers infused her 405 prayer ties. Tahatan took the ties and arranged them in a square. At the corners, marking each direction, he attached a prayer flag. He laid fresh sage on the floor of the interior as a bed for her to rest when she was weary. The area was protected and ready, where only good spirits could enter. Tahatan then prayed to each direction.

Wichahpi walked into the sacred space, where she would remain for up to four days without food or water.

She had only her buffalo robe, pipe, and bed of sage. Her grandfather rode away, leaving her alone. The sun was setting in a magnificent display, in the same coral hues of the heated basalt stones used in the Inipi ceremony, leaving her to praise how perfect her vision quest began. Before the light faded, she began by singing songs - the prayers of the Lakota - to each direction.

Throughout her vision quest, Wichahpi remained in a prayerful, altered state of mind. She felt neither hunger nor thirst. At times, she noticed animals outside the circle, but she felt no fear, for she naturally had a way with them. She was within a sacred space, where nothing of harm could enter. One time, a fox approached.

"Hello. Aren't you a beautiful being," Wichahpi said as she looked directly into the animal's stunning eyes. The fox sat down and wrapped his red tail around his body. "Thank you for coming to visit. You are welcome to stay as long as you like." The fox sat at full attention outside the prayer ties, with its beautiful red tail wrapped around its body. For what seemed like hours, Wichahpi continued to talk to the fox, for they were in communion. Another early morning, a mother wolf brought her cubs, as if she was presenting them to Wichahpi. On one afternoon, three eagles circled high overhead directly above where she sat - a very good sign.

She heard voices of wisdom speak in an unfamiliar language, but given her state of mind, she understood their direction. At times, when looking out over the mountains, she had visions of detailed scenes, some that indicated her path to follow. She envisioned a golden bowl with a great burning flame, more powerful than any forest fire, and more ancient than Grandmother Earth. She could see that the bowl originally came from the Star People. Throughout the ages, the chosen keeper of the flame - the carrier of the fire - used it to cleanse the old and bring powerful change when needed.

The query that began her vision quest regarding the blue-eyed boy or man became clear. As a man, he was renowned throughout the ages as a legendary great warrior. However, the boy in her dreams grew up to be a warrior of sorts, but instead of arrows and guns, he used his intelligence, wise words, learned books, and sacred ceremony to overcome conflict. He was a spiritual warrior of the future. The details of this vision would guide her through the remainder of her days.

One night, the moon slept and the stars burst through the darkness, for it was their chance to dance in the heavens in their brilliance. She journeyed into the band of starlight that traveled directly overhead. There, she felt at home, unlike anything she knew before that moment. From there, she saw many other worlds, far in the distance and yet only a thought away. From her celestial viewpoint, she looked down upon Grandmother Earth and watched her children, some in conflict and others in peace. A voice told her it was her task to be a peacekeeper, a healer, a sage.

She briefly closed her eyes, and when she opened them again, she was the radiant center of all things, where all the directions converged. North met south, east met west, and the earth and sky joined together, all at one center point. This was a place of remembrance, knowing all things were one. It was the heart of all existence, the entirety of everything. From that point, all creation began, spiraling outward into eternity. In that sacred space, she was one with the Great Mystery of all life where she felt a joyful peace beyond her imagining. When she returned to her people, all she had to do was remember what she felt in that moment to recall the all-knowing, ever present, abundant power of Wakan Tanka.

The third night, the moon left dancing shadows, forming images in her mind of the vastness of all eternity, which left her with a knowing that any dream could come to life. Anything was possible within the width, breadth, and depth of Wakan Tanka - anything.

After three nights and four days, at sundown, Tahatan returned on horseback to bring her back from her vision quest. When he arrived on the mountaintop, she looked at him as if he was a ghost. A part of her wished to remain, but she reluctantly returned to her people with a sense of longing for the deeper mystery. Her grandfather immediately brought her to the sweat lodge, where she shared everything in her experience atop the mountain. Tahatan was astounded at the visioning power of his young granddaughter.

She mentioned the animals she saw, and the meaning of their visit that came to her. To that he said, "You have no single animal totem. It appears that whatever four-legged, winged one, finned one, or small being - they meet with you at your center. They have trust in you. Without trust, there is nothing. Always look to animals for their wisdom. They are your teachers, my granddaughter. They know Grandmother Earth in ways we do not know. Watch to see how they respond to you. Then you will know if you are living in a good way."

Every message she received, she relayed to her grandfather. Each vision beyond that of her earthly experience, she shared in detail. She told him of how she journeyed into the stars, high into the heavens. Every word she heard, each bit of guidance, she passed on to the wicasa wakan.

She saved the best for last, that of the revelation of the blue-eyed boy or man. "The blue-eyed man is a different person, in a way, than the boy. In another way, they are the same. The man is my ancestor, Crazy Horse. I saw him in battle, painted with war paint - a yellow lightning bolt on his right cheek, and the white spots that looked like hail stones on his shoulders and upper chest. While riding his beloved horse, he waved his pipe high above his head. No bullet could touch him. He was invincible in battle. The U.S. Cavalry thought his pipe was a magic wand, and were mightily afraid of him."

Tahatan smiled and shook his head in wonder. "Wakan Tanka has given you good sight, my Granddaughter, for your vision of Crazy Horse is correct. He is your ancestor, as was I, through my mother's family. As a young man, I fought beside him against the great white warrior they called Custer. All that is said about his great medicine is true. He kept to himself, not living in the same way as his people. Crazy Horse was a quiet man, alone with his thoughts that ran deep into his heart. It was there where Wakan Tanka lived within him, making him a protector of his people. His spirit will remain as the protector until the sun no longer rises."

"I entered his thoughts," Wichahpi said, "and saw *his* vision as if it were my own. Crazy Horse saw himself enter the body of another, many years past his death. This way he knew he would live on in a good way for eternity. This vision gave him peace.

"The boy with blue eyes and yellow hair will be my son. The spirit of Crazy Horse will come to life again within the boy, who will also become a protector of our people. Unlike Crazy Horse, who died because of the white man, the boy will grow up and learn much in the white man's world. He will be wise - teaching by example how to walk the Red Road. As a grown man, he will travel to lands beyond the great waters and will teach the ways of our people, keeping our traditions alive. Wherever he journeys, the respect of others will follow, including the respect of the white man.

"The boy will have an additional calling, which will increase as he matures. As an elder, he will be a wisdom keeper for a yellow-haired woman - a great seer and healer. He will pass along a golden bowl that holds a flame of power. She will be the new keeper of the flame. He will teach and guide her, and help her speak to the Grandfathers. Wakan Tanka will live within this woman, too, and in that way, Crazy Horse will also live in her. The elder and the woman will belong to a group of thirteen people from all the big lands on Grandmother Earth. Their council will hold the good way for all beings. Their work will bring healing to many hearts.

"The Ancestors have told me that my son will be known as Tatanka Ska - White Buffalo." When she told Tahatan this, she heard her grandfather cry tears of joy. He was pleased.

"My granddaughter, when a white buffalo calf is born to the Lakota, it is the most sacred of all beings, bringing about hope for good things to come. The white buffalo signifies the purity of body, mind, and spirit, unifying all people of all nations. It is a symbol of abundance and manifestation, meaning that the struggle to survive does not have to be a way of life for our people, as so many believe. If the boy grows up to use his education, taking right action in harmony with right prayer, he will find good ways to unite the world - with that of the Great Spirit - Wakan Tanka. He will live without want, with all his needs well provided. In this way, we are all guided to live.

"You have an important calling, Wichahpi, to be the mother of a great man. You are a sacred vessel for Wakan Tanka, so White Buffalo can grow up to be a man remembered. You will also be the carrier of the fire, caring for the eternal flame until it is time to give it to your son. When he is an elder, he will return the flame to the yellow-haired woman, for she is the one to whom it belongs. We are only the caretakers.

"The boy's father - the man you marry, and you will be his teachers. You must pass on to the boy our Lakota ways. Teach him our songs and our ceremonies, and help him learn how to pray in a good way. A day will come when we will again openly celebrate what the Ancestors have left us through their wisdom. White Buffalo will help the world to know of our Lakota way. Tell him your visions, and help him grow into the man who the Grandfathers foresee."

Tahatan handed her the golden chalice, which held the eternal flame. Her eyes widened as she looked into the fire, where she saw her son, as a boy, then as a man, and again as an elder. She was pleased. Her heart was full.

For the next two days, after drinking plenty of fresh water and eating lightly, Wichahpi slept, where her dreams took her away to worlds without end.

It was not long before Wichahpi married Howahkan, a young Lakota from a good family, for they grew up together and complemented each other well. They lived in the hills near Spearfish, South Dakota, where Wichahpi had grown up among other Lakota, away from the reservation life. A year later, they had a daughter, whom they named Little Deer. She was a precocious, happy child who sought adventure from when she took her first steps. Wichahpi had to watch Little Deer constantly, for the girl would disappear far from home, when later they found her in the woods playing with the animals. More than once, they had to organize a search party to find the brilliant little voyager. Tahatan was secretly concerned that his great-granddaughter was too much like her grandmother, Mika.

The next family members were twins, who were born prematurely, both tiny and weak. They lived for several months, but both died of influenza during the harsh winter of 1937, bringing great grief to their family. Wichahpi, suffering significantly from melancholy and soon found herself under the care of her elderly grandfather, Tahatan, who could not bear to watch his once happy granddaughter suffer so. Neither Howahkan nor Wichahpi wanted another child for fear of the tremendous loss that brought them into dark times.

Tahatan called on the other elders, and together they held a special Inipi ceremony for both of the young parents to cleanse them of the dark spirits. Diminished by their grief, they had very little resistance, and during the ceremony, they both easily journeyed to the place of their ancestors. There, they witnessed the happy spirits of their twin babies, leaving them to know that all was well. After the sweat was over, both Wichahpi and Howahkan felt lighter. Some of the burden had lifted from their spirits, and they were more readily able to move onward.

Later that night, Tahatan reminded his granddaughter of her vision quest. "Granddaughter, the Ancestors want you to remember who you are. When you feel your grief, take yourself to the place of heart, where the four directions meet with the center point of the earth and sky. All is possible there. Know this again, my granddaughter.

"Do you recall that you are the keeper of the light? You are the carrier of the fire. The flame in the golden bowl is also yours to use. Grandpa Napayshni directs you to sit each night at sundown in front of the flame, while holding an eagle feather. Look into the bowl's fire to help you heal your mind, body, and spirit. Let the fire burn away your sorrow. The eagle will carry your prayers to Great Spirit. Do this for 30 days and let the darkness within you become the light where the shadows will no longer follow. Remember your calling to be the mother and teacher of White Buffalo. Until you no longer feel the sadness, you cannot be his mother. Remember what Great Spirit directed you to do, Wichahpi, for you are of great importance to both the memory and the future of our people."

Tahatan then turned to Howahkan. "You, my grandson, are the protector of Wichahpi. Although you have not yet had the vision of your son, he will be a great man. You will help him to grow up in a good way. He will have great strength, because you will teach him how to live well in his body, mind, and spirit. Be happy in your days, and talk to Great Spirit in all things - from the dawning light to when the moon is high. Keep Wakan Tanka at the center of your lives, and all will be well, for you and your family will not want.

"Howahkan, your son, White Buffalo, is already on the wings of eagles. He is coming to you soon. He will be born with curly hair, the color of the sun, and his eyes will be as blue as the skies at midday. He will possess the spirit of

Crazy Horse, and the boy will also grow to be a great spiritual warrior. So, do not be alarmed at his appearance. You must prepare to be an even stronger husband and devout father, for both your children have lives that will bring great healing to our people and to the world. Because they will be significant to the people and the world, you and Wichahpi must be strong so you will guide them to live in a good way."

Three months later, Wichahpi found that she was again with child. In 1939, the baby boy was born with curly yellow hair and blue eyes, like that of his ancestor, Crazy Horse. She and Howahkan named him White Buffalo, but because of his coloring, Wichahpi called him Blue Feather.

Both his mother and father taught him the ways of their Lakota ancestors. From very early on, his mother told him stories from her vision quest. She told him of his relatives, mostly of his great-grandfather Tahatan, who only knew him for two years before he traveled the Great Ribbon of Stars and went into the Spirit World. The boy heard many tales of Crazy Horse and somehow already felt the spirit of the great warrior within him, for young White Buffalo was wise beyond his years.

CHAPTER
Twenty-three

White Buffalo rose out of bed as the sun awakened the new day. He showered and pulled his long white hair into a ponytail, and dressed warmly for the winter day ahead. He met the rest of the family at the breakfast table, as everyone hungrily awaited some of Michael's famous omelets, served with slices of crispy bacon, English muffins, and plenty of freshly brewed hot coffee. They talked of the upcoming weekend wedding events, for Chayton and Irina would arrive soon, along with their immediate family members and all of the members of Apeiros. White Buffalo, however, sat quietly, rather lost in thought.

"You are especially quiet this morning, White Buffalo. Is anything on your mind?" Darius asked.

"I am still caught in the dream world. This morning, I awoke from dreaming of my childhood. What came to me was the history of my mother, grandmother, and my maternal great-grandfather, who was a great man. Some of what I dreamt were stories my mother told me when I was young, but other parts were events I never heard. It was as if I was watching a movie of my life, and I am sure I was smiling through most of the night in my dreams."

"Welcome to my world, Uncle," Sophia said, smiling with a twinkle in her eye. "That is how my past lives come to me."

"It is a wonderful way of time-travel. I wish I had done more of it over the years," White Buffalo said.

"Would you share with us some of what you dreamt?" Darius asked.

"Indeed, tell us the juicy parts, or something dark and mysterious," Gaston said. "We all love a bit of intrigue now and again."

"What comes to mind is my education in the mission school on the reservation," White Buffalo said. "I suppose that was one of the darkest times of my life. Why don't we eat our breakfast, and then I will tell you about it."

When they finished eating, Sophia got up from her seat. "Before you begin, let me clear the table and get us more coffee." She was the one to clean up after their meals, since Michael did most of the cooking - an even trade, she thought. Sophia returned to the table with a pot of hot coffee and some wickedly rich, freshly baked cinnamon rolls, oozing with gooey pecans. "Presenting - the best of brown food. Now we're listening, Uncle. Tell us of your dreams," Sophia said. Everyone filled their cups and had a sticky cinnamon roll on their plate with forks at the ready.

In his mind's eye, the images of White Buffalo's childhood easily came to him out of the gray murky past of many decades before. White Buffalo shifted in his seat. "It was 1944. Little Deer, my sister, was ten years old, and I was five. Our parents were concerned about our education, believing if they moved to the reservation, we would be able to go to the mission school. Living in a tipi in the Black Hills was more difficult each year. The city of Spearfish was growing, and the white people there were less tolerant of Indians living in the hills nearby, even though we lived on private land, far from the city. Conditions suggested that it was time for a change.

"We had only one horse that pulled a cart with all our belongings. Only when Little Deer and I were very tired did we ride on the cart. My mother and father walked alongside with our dog. It took several long days before we eventually arrived at the Rosebud Reservation in the southern part of South Dakota. In the fall of 1945, Little Deer and I attended boarding school on the reservation. Federal funding helped subsidize the boarding of students, making it much easier for children to attend.

"We had no choice but to wear uniforms, and we were given new white names. They named Little Deer, Sarah, and me, Jeremiah. Boys with long hair or braids had their hair cut short, so my hair turned out to be short, blonde, and curly."

"I bet you were so cute, with those blue eyes of yours," Sophia said.

"My mother certainly thought so. Her nickname for me was Blue Feather," White Buffalo said.

"How precious!" Sophia said.

"You must have been a shock to your parents - having a baby with blonde curly hair and blue eyes," Darius said.

"That would have been true, but my mother saw me in her dreams many years before I was born. She saw a blonde boy with blue eyes. My great-grandfather was a very wise man. He helped her understand who I was through her vision quest. Later, he also counseled with my father, so he would be accepting of my appearance. I stood out among all my people until my hair became dark, and even then, my blue eyes set me apart.

"So, getting back to our short hair - back in the day of

the Indian Scout, the U.S. military required Native men to cut their hair short, but what they found was quite interesting. Natives made especially good scouts, not only because of their tracking abilities and their knowledge of the land and nature, but because they were highly intuitive. When their hair was cut off, they noticed that they lost some of their ability to sense well. Long hair acts as an antenna, connecting to the surrounding magnetic field. Therefore, the military allowed them to grow out their hair again, and their intuitive nature returned, making them even better scouts than when their hair was cut to military standards.

"I was only six years old, and I didn't understand that my short hair stunted my intuition, but I knew something was missing. In the summer, my hair grew out, and there seemed to be a freedom in my awareness, but I thought that was only because I was back in the comfort of home again. Of course, when school began, they cut my hair. When I left college, I grew my hair long again, often wearing it in a braid or pulled back, as I do now. Only then did I realize how much more I could perceive beyond the physical world. I later read about the Indian scouts and put two-and-two together. The same was true for me."

"That reminds me of the Biblical story of Sampson and Delilah," Sophia said. "His hair gave him his strength. When Delilah cut his hair, Sampson lost all his strength and was no longer a threat to her people. It was only when his hair grew long again that he possessed the needed strength to destroy hundreds of Philistines. Maybe it wasn't a fable after all."

"When we first met, your hair was short and black," Gaston said, "and you kept it that way through college. I thought when you finally grew out your hair, it was to return to your Native appearance for when you traveled the world to give your lectures," Gaston said.

"That was the original thought," White Buffalo said, "but when the strength of my intuition returned, I began to wonder if the story about the Indian scouts was true. Not only were the mission schools trying to make us white, they took away our powers in every way possible. Life at school was different from the way we grew up when we had such freedoms. Our first year in school was very difficult - I think even more for Little Deer, because she was older when we began.

"The school was regimented right down to the minute. We ate according to the clock, and brushed our teeth afterwards with only minutes to spare before we attended class. We had only three minutes to get from one class to the next. We made our beds, dressed and undressed, and went to bed in their model of strict semi-military scheduling. When we were not in classes, we were going about the day doing our chores. We were given very little time for play or recreation.

"We learned basic reading, writing, and math, along with specific skills geared for boys and girls. Girls learned the skills of cooking, sewing, cleaning, laundry, and office work, while boys chopped wood, milked cows, did the gardening and farming duties. We also became blacksmiths and shoemakers. The students basically operated the entire school. Very few adults performed duties, other than teaching and discipline. The idea was to train us with all the skills necessary to become successful American farmers. The only time we returned to our families was during allotted vacation times at Christmas, and in the summer months, never on weekends. We spent the majority of the year living at the school. We were to assimilate into the white man's world, forced to forget everything we knew of our Native culture.

"When we were disciplined, many times we were confined and deprived of privileges, and often we were restricted from meals. The intimidation of corporal punishment forced us to follow commands. Speaking in our native tongue brought severe retribution, beginning with having our mouths washed out with soap, and then we were forced to eat the soap made with lye, or wood ash, tallow from beef fat, and water, which made us violently sick to the stomach. Some of us were tied up in a public place to bring us shame, so other students would witness our punishment. At some of the mission schools, students had no choice but to wear marbles in their shoes, which was very painful. Many children died in the institutions from influenza and other communicable diseases. Some of the schools did not provide a healthy diet, and many became malnourished. Fortunately, for us, that was not the case.

"But we no longer ate our Native foods. We learned to use the knife, fork, spoon, and napkin when eating at tables draped with tablecloths. We could only speak English. Not even amongst ourselves could we speak our native Lakota. It had been over 60 years, since 1882, when the law deemed it illegal to celebrate our Native ceremonies and dances, which forced all Native Americans to go underground, even to pray to Wakan Tanka. Overall, the idea was essentially to wipe out our Native traditions and our historic way of life."

"How could a school treat little children so?" Sophia said.

"It was not about teaching, but more about control and the destruction of our Native lifestyle," White Buffalo said.

"My Catholic upbringing had similar disciplines," Gaston said. "I spent too many days standing in the corner of the room. The nuns would take that long pointer stick and whack us on the head or the back of our hands if we talked out of turn."

"That must be why your fingers are so crooked," Darius said with a smirk.

"Well, dear brother, it's a good thing that you have a good head of hair, or we would be forced to see all the knots on your skull from the many times you were walloped," Gaston said.

"I must admit, I have a lumpy head," Darius said. "Unfortunately, all too often I opened my mouth at the wrong time, sometimes getting a bar of soap wedged between my teeth, but never did I have to eat it. My father occasionally punished me without supper, but my dear mother would sneak me a sandwich and a glass of milk later in the evening."

"According to my mom, I never learned how to shut up," Michael said. "Today, if I say anything out of turn, I get that certain look from my lovely Sophia, which is the worst punishment of all."

"Yeah, you have it so bad," Sophia said as she crinkled an eyebrow and looked at him with a mocking glare, then winked with a smile.

"There *were* some benefits to attending the mission school," White Buffalo said. "Some of the boarding schools had clean facilities with clean running water. We learned teamwork through sports and games, and we developed deep and lasting friendships that remained well beyond our school years.

"In spite of the many restrictions, Little Deer and I thrived, both being of good mind and heart. When we were home during summer vacation, our parents encouraged us to speak English, so when we returned to school we would experience less difficulty adapting. We taught our parents much of what we learned during the year away from home, yet we returned to our Native way of life in every other way.

"Little Deer benefitted from the school's order and discipline. It seemed to calm her inquisitive nature, helping her find ways to organize order and balance for our family's home life. We were both good students from the start. Fortunately, I loved to learn everything I could. I used logic and reasoning well throughout the years of my entire education. Once I learned to read, I could not find enough books to fill my mind. As a youth, I often walked to the woods to read Emerson and, especially, Thoreau's *Walden*. If I got in trouble at school, it was because I had my head buried in a book, often getting slapped on the side of the head with the very book I was reading."

"I recall when we discussed indentured servants, and you were so quiet," Darius said. "How difficult it must have been to be forced, against your will, to assimilate into a life that was not only foreign to you, but by those who had taken away your lands, ancient traditions, your way of life, and the religion of your people."

"Unfortunately, that has been the way of the world since its inception. 'What is yours is now mine, including your women and children. My god is better than yours,'" White Buffalo said. "That is why I pursued teaching about the Lakota throughout the world, so our traditions are not forgotten. For the generations of my people who were stifled, muted, and killed, I wanted to give them a voice. And new generations are remembering their ancestors, as they, too, are living in a good way. Wherever I went, I met many other indigenous people. Together, we sought to help the world remember that we are all blessed beings of Grandmother Earth. We are not placed on her back to bring destruction to her, or to ourselves, or to anyone..."

CHAPTER
Twenty-four

Everyone from Apeiros arrived the next day, having hailed a transport van from the airport. That night, they all gathered at the Riverside Inn restaurant for their first meal together. Including Chayton, they were fourteen.

Those who had not seen White Buffalo for some time were shocked and saddened by his appearance. He had gone from a powerfully strong and fit elder, to a sick and withered old man in only a few months time. They were all so glad that they came for the wedding of Chayton and Irina, but more so to spend valued time with their beloved friend and colleague.

They were enjoying appetizers and cocktails when Jameson let Michael behind the bar to conjure up something special for White Buffalo. When Michael took his seat at the table again, Jameson arrived with a round tray holding a tall hurricane glass filled with something that looked like light blue milk, topped with whipped cream.

"What's this?" White Buffalo asked as Jameson placed the glass in front of him.

"A Blue Feather Froth," Jameson said, "a custom-made mocktail by Michael here."

"What's in it?" White Buffalo said, almost afraid to ask. "You know blue food isn't on my bucket list."

"It's pineapple juice, coconut milk, vanilla ice cream, ginger ale, and a drop or two of blue food coloring, all blended to a froth, topped with whipping cream and a white chocolate curl, which is supposed to look like a feather," Michael said.

"I've never had a drink named after me before."

"How's that?" Markos asked.

"Until I was older, my hair was light blonde, and of course, I had blue eyes, so my mother called me Blue Feather. Michael has honored me with my very own mocktail."

"A little earlier," Lestari said, "Darius was telling us about your upbringing. Please tell us more, White Buffalo. We never heard your story the last time we were together."

He first took a sip of his drink, approving of Michael's creation, and passed the glass around the table, offering a sip to anyone who was interested.

"Before we begin, I just want to say that I know my appearance may be a shock to those of you who just arrived, but the White Buffalo that you know is fully here." He sensed that they eased a bit. "Well, let me see..." White Buffalo paused for a moment to recall a story of interest. "When I was born, my sister, Little Deer, was nearly five years old. At that time, we lived high in the Black Hills in a deerskin tipi tucked between the woods. To this day, it remains my favorite home of all the places I have lived in my seven decades of life.

"Most of the time, Little Deer was of great help to our parents in helping to care for her baby brother, but she was quite the adventurer. She played well with me by introducing me to many of the animals she brought home. As the story goes, I crawled after her as best I could and learned to walk long before I was one year old.

"One autumn, when we still lived in the Black Hills, Little Deer watched our father build a travois for the horse to bring home fallen trees for firewood. Being quite an independent child, she decided to build one to attach to our dog for a planned outing for the two of us. She thought she was doing my mother a favor by taking me away from the tipi for the afternoon. After all, she was a big girl. Our mother and father often told her how clever and smart she was, and she was going to prove it to them." White Buffalo paused with a slight smile, remembering the simplicity of his early years.

"When our mother stepped away from the tipi, Little Deer found me asleep. She wrapped me in blankets and placed me on the travois, tying me to the stick framework of the sled before I awoke from my nap. Knowing I would be hungry when I woke up, she took a deerskin bag, filled it with bread and berries, and tucked it next to me on the sled. Little Deer tied a rope to the harness attached to the dog and led us down by the stream, quite a distance away from where we lived. She later told me how I laughed while I was bouncing along in the sled, but when we stopped, I began to wail. I was furious because my sister left me tied up. She knew enough not to let me loose, because I might have fallen into the stream, or I could have run away. The dog was not happy either. Evidently, my sister was beside herself, trying to feed me so I would stop fussing, but all I did was scream after spitting out the food she stuffed into my mouth."

He laughed with the others. "Luckily, the poles of the travois left tracks, which were easy for our parents to trace. By the time they caught up with us, I was red-faced and crying up a storm. My father told the story, saying, 'Oh my little man, what has your sister done?' as he held back a smile.

He took his knife with the deer antler handle and cut the cords that were bound to the dog. Finally liberated, the dog quickly ran away. Then he cut the ropes that strapped me to the sled, and unwrapped the blankets that were tightly tucked around my body. As a two-year-old boy, I scrambled to my feet, clearly angry. I ran over to my sister and hit her on the leg as hard as I was able, yelling some strong words in my toddler language that only *I* understood.

"My mother bit her lip to keep from laughing while she picked me up, still squirming. 'My little Blue Feather, you have a good, strong arm and a temper, too.' They knew well enough not to make much of the event, giving it very little attention, but later they made sure that Little Deer understood not to take me away from home again, for our own safety.

"They walked us back to the tipi while my father, Howahkan, gently held the hand of his daughter. Neither of our parents punished her, for Little Deer was trying to help our mother. Instead, they gave her more responsibility around the tipi to keep her occupied and out of trouble. By the end of each day, she was exhausted and ready to fall asleep, wrapped snugly in her buffalo robe. She soon became a strong and wise girl, having learned so many tasks at such a young age.

"In spite of my sister, I grew up without much wear or tear. Her manipulations taught me to be quite cunning as I learned how to keep clear of my sister's exploitations as we grew older."

"I could listen to your stories anytime, especially about living off the land in a tipi," Anja said. "I grew up in a hut with a dirt floor, with two siblings, raised by our loving mother and grandmother. We were very poor, but we didn't know any different, and we were happy. These stories are rich in the tales that take me far beyond the ways of civilization."

"Anja, you must share your stories with us sometime," Shoshana said.

"I will. There are many."

"Is Little Deer still with us?" Michael asked.

"No," White Buffalo said. "She passed peacefully a few years ago, but she had a rich and wonderful life."

Having enjoyed White Buffalo's tale, a few chatted back and forth while they finished their meal. Everyone soon returned to the cabin, dressed in white for the initial ceremony of Apeiros. White Buffalo contacted the others before everyone arrived, requesting that they initiate Chayton into the Order of Apeiros. Of course, everyone agreed, yet for Chayton, this would be quite the surprise.

Everyone stood in a circle in front of the burning fireplace, with White Buffalo standing at the center. Chayton stood off to the side.

"We gather together, again in celebration of life," Darius said. "Chayton, we would like for you to join us tonight. White Buffalo has something to share with you."

Chayton joined the circle and stood next to his beloved Irina.

"Chayton, my boy, you are like a son to me. I have watched you grow over the years," White Buffalo said with tears in his eyes. "Tonight, all of us are here to welcome you as the next member of the auspicious Order of Apeiros. If you choose to accept, you will honor us with your gifts and talents, as you hold the sacred space for the world and for the universe, at large. Your deeper calling will always be in doing your inner work to raise your personal vibration, so you can be your best self. This is the work of all of us, for in this we teach love. Natural entrainment occurs, bringing greater change for good - for Great Spirit to prevail - while using the attributes of the Divine in your daily walk. You will hold this task until the end of your days. Will you join us?"

"I am humbled that you all should honor me so," Chayton said. "Since I was last with you, I have held Apeiros in my heart. I have tried, to the best of my ability, to embody and practice the Divine attributes, because I believe so strongly in the work that you do in the world. So, without a doubt, I humbly accept."

They all applauded, so pleased to welcome Chayton into the Order of Apeiros. They soon quieted down as White Buffalo stood in front of the younger man. He looked deeply into Chayton's eyes as he removed his aquamarine ring from his right ring finger. He then took Chayton's hand in his and placed the ring on his finger. Everyone knew this was the passing of the torch, from a light bearer of great wisdom to one of life-giving vitality, who would carry on their sacred ancient tradition in a new way - in a good way. All were in tears.

White Buffalo took his place in the circle and stood next to Chayton.

"Join with me by turning into the circle with your right hand pointed toward the center," Darius said, choking back a tear. He took a deep breath to come from the depth of his inner strength. Now standing behind his elder, Chayton placed his left arm around the waist of White Buffalo, who stood in front of him, supporting his body next to his own. Chayton held White Buffalo's right hand on top of his to help support his arm, for his elder had little strength to stand in the circle much longer.

"Hold in the center of your being Love and Absolute Awareness, which includes all the Divine attributes," Darius continued. "Deeply feel the ecstasy of Joy, and the calm serenity of Peace. Compassion is yours through kindness of your tender heart. Beauty surrounds you in the magnificent splendor of our mountain surroundings and within the hearts of all who are here tonight. Abundance and prosperity are within the wealth of the plentitude we all enjoy. Never are we without. Health, well-being, and strength comes in forms that include the nature of our physicality, mental and emotional state, and spirituality, but we are not limited by that which is in our earthly existence, for life is eternal in all ways.

"Order is our alignment with whatever name we call our god or gods. Balance brings us poise, while Harmony is the synthesis that we hold when we honor all life around us. Oneness is our unification with all there is, knowing we are truly just one Being. Truth is always evident, being genuine in its reality, which sets all spiritual principles by which we live. And Grace is the elegance of the Divine, always loving and ever honoring of others within the evolutionary expanse of life's enfoldment. Feel this deep into your heart center, knowing you are filled with the energetic frequency from on high as you join with the God of your belief, which fills this room with Love."

The familiar golden white light began to form a vertical column at the center of their circle.

"Visualize the energy filling this beautiful mountain valley?" Darius continued. "Extend it into the surrounding counties, and now into the entire state of Colorado. This light extends throughout the United States, and into the Americas - through the western hemisphere, to the eastern hemisphere - and now throughout the world. See the areas where you live filled with this brilliant golden light. Envision the people, the animals, sea creatures, birds, and all beings filled with this light of Love. Now extend this Love throughout the galaxy and beyond, as far as your imagination will allow.

"Know that, in this expansion of consciousness, you extend who you are, as the cause of all unity and the measure of all things to all territories, every dimensional field, and to all awareness. In this, past transgressions are released and healed, leaving a bright future, because we stand in strength and clarity, grounded in the presence of the here and now - the almighty Infinite Intelligence - that which we know as Love. Feel the power. Know it is yours, as you share this Love with all of existence."

The column of light became so brilliant, all those in the group could not look at it with the exception of White Buffalo. He calmly looked into the glowing light, as it became the radiance of his being. They each remained for a few moments more, for it was not about time, but about their rise in consciousness in which they attuned through the ritual.

Darius continued. "Now pull your hand away, allowing the light to dissipate, knowing that its golden splendor is always present, and ever within each and every one of us to use for the greater good."

Chayton helped White Buffalo take a seat on the couch, noticing his elder's gleaming smile as he observed tiny golden lights floating throughout the room.

They all joined in the ceremony, officially welcoming Chayton into the Order of Apeiros, with each giving him a personal blessing as they anointed him with rose oil. The final one to bless him was White Buffalo. Chayton knelt down in front of him as White Buffalo dipped his finger into the rose oil and placed it on Chayton's forehead, at his third eye.

"I pass on the wisdom of the Grandfathers as you begin your journey," White Buffalo said. "You will continue with my work, teaching the ways of the Lakota, bringing your own expertise into the Order of Apeiros. Always begin by asking the Ancestors for guidance. Trust that Wakan Tanka is present in everything. Stay in your heart center, where all the directions come together. From that point, you will think, speak, and take action from the Sacred Way of the Heart. Be your best, with my blessings, my son." He leaned over and lightly patted Chayton on the cheek. The ceremony was complete.

Following Chayton's initiation into the Order of Apeiros, all gathered around the dining table to enjoy a scrumptious carrot cake, called the OrangeEllo, White Buffalo's favorite dessert made by the Ello sisters, of the *Two Sisters and their Husbands B, B &B*, who came all the way from Buena Vista for the week to cater the wedding. Everyone sat in anticipation of the tête-à-tête most likely awaiting the grand confabulation between the two sisters and Michael.

"Well hello, Michael, who is like God," Lou Ella said as Mary stood by her side.

"Why, Lou Ella, it's good to see you. In addition, you as well, Mary. Here you are side-by-side. You typically do a single."

"Yeah, she's been breathing down my neck all afternoon," Lou Ella said.

"I thought you looked a bit hot under the collar. So, what 'cha got for us tonight?"

"Besides a quick quip, we brought some of our famous

Ellos for your enjoyment. For the nervous bride, we have Mello Ellos, with a surprise ingredient."

"What's the surprise ingredient?" Michael asked.

"Well now, if we told you, it wouldn't be a surprise anymore, now would it?" Mary said.

"Okay, what's next?"

"We understand that the groom likes to sing. So, we created the Accapello Fello, just for him," Mary said.

"What are the special ingredients in that bakery item?"

"It's a cookie bar with dark and light chocolate chips, coconut, caramel, and an Irish Cream drizzle - a truly wicked harmony of flavors."

"Well, that's on the top of my list," Michael said.

"Wait, we haven't gotten to the good stuff yet," Lou Ella said.

"Can't wait!"

"I said, *wait!*"

"Okay, okay!"

"Tomorrow, for the wedding, we have the NovEllo," Mary said.

"I'm still waiting. What's the NovEllo?"

"NovEllo is a young wine. We created a luscious cheesecake with a delectable wine sauce. You all are the first to try it."

"I can't wait!"

"Hey! What did I say? You can try it *tomorrow* for the wedding feast."

"Is there anything else?"

"Why yes! For the happy couple on their wedding night, we created the Bord Ello." Both the sisters stood there with big smiles on their faces.

"I'm afraid to ask -"

"Don't be afraid, sport," Lou Ella said. "Man up."

"Alright," Michael said. "What is a Bord Ello?"

"It's another surprise that's certain to please the happy couple," Mary said. "Let's just say that there's plenty of whipped cream involved." With that, they left the room.

The morning sun rose with clear skies. There, in the valley, they couldn't see storms approach until they were nearly overhead, but they hoped they would have good weather for the outdoor ceremony, set for five o'clock.

Chayton's mother and father arrived early, and Irina's brother and his wife came in a few hours later. They checked into their rooms and enjoyed a casual lunch with Michael, Gaston, and Darius, at the Riverside Inn. Sophia put the finishing party touches on the cabin with floral arrangements filled with bright red roses, pine and spruce boughs, and seeded eucalyptus. The weather forecast reported a heavy winter storm on its way, which Sophia and Michael chalked up to Murphy's Law, but everyone else seemed a bit giddy in anticipation of a genuine Colorado mountain blizzard. They all kept their fingers crossed that the storm would take its time and not arrive until after the ceremony.

Just as the sun was setting in the winter sky, they all waited on the bridge framed with the tall blue spruce and mountains all around. The river trickled softly around the river rock beneath white patches of snow and ice. The valley was touched with the coral sunset, as shades of blue took their place in the evening twilight. A crystalline mist gathered overhead, ushering in colder air – a certain sign of the impending storm.

Carrying a small bouquet of bright red roses in full bloom, Irina walked along the curved path to the bridge lined with white luminarias. She was dressed in an elegant, long winter white velvet gown, over which she wore a matching velvet cape with a hood that gently draped over her head. Her long dark curls framed her face and fell over her shoulders. Chayton wore a beautiful black suit and tie, with an ivory shirt and black polished boots. His long black braid fell far down his back. He gazed at his ravishing bride, beaming with pride, so happy to marry such an amazing woman.

Michael braced White Buffalo, who could not stand for long, so the ceremony was short and yet tremendously meaningful. He opened with a prayer spoken in Lakota. For the heart of the ceremony, he spoke in English, as he charged all in attendance to hold Love and its truths for the couple during the upcoming years of their union. Irina and Chayton spoke their vows to each other in her native language of Romanian. To conclude the service, White Buffalo sang a song - a Lakota prayer - while Chayton joined him. Their deep voices resonated throughout the valley, echoing a song of love - love for Great Spirit, love for each other, and love for life itself.

Afterward, they all enjoyed dinner at the cabin, catered by the Ello sisters. After they cut the cake, White Buffalo took his leave, for he was exhausted from all the activity. It was not long before he returned to his dreams in the recall of his life.

CHAPTER
Twenty-five

*L*ittle Deer and White Buffalo caught the attention of an anonymous benefactor, who offered them each a college education when Little Deer was in her senior year of school. Five years older than her brother, she departed to attend Haskell Institute in Lawrence, Kansas, becoming the first member of her family to attend college. It was also the first time she and White Buffalo were apart. The school's vocational studies fit her career desires to support organized farming at the reservation. During that time, she also worked for five years on several Kansas farms, learning about farming and animal husbandry before returning to the reservation. Just as she returned to South Dakota, White Buffalo left to attend college in the South. Many years passed before they saw each other again.

At the time, a college education for a Native American was limited. There were few opportunities for an education beyond earning a high school diploma. Therefore, to beat the system, White Buffalo posed as an American youth seeking a higher education. After all, he came from many generations of Americans. When it came time for him to apply to colleges for admission, his career counselor put a bug in his ear about getting an education in New Orleans. He researched the city of the Old South and its rich history and was intrigued. It was one of the most diverse cities of the United States. There, he thought he might be able to blend in, but it was necessary that he change his name to something more suitably American, so he came up with the name Scott T. Anka.

His anonymous benefactor financed his room and board, in addition to his college tuition to Tulane University, his application accepted to attend in the fall. A nameplate on the door to his dorm room read, *S. Anka, G. Delacroix*, the two paired as roommates before classes began. The day after White Buffalo settled in, a lawyer by the name of André Rousseau came to his dorm room. Prior to his arrival, they had corresponded for several months through the exchange of letters. Rousseau brought him a checkbook, his first personal checking account, under the name of Scott T. Anka.

Rousseau earlier referred White Buffalo to a good forger that created all the necessary identification papers under his new name. Rarely did White Buffalo break the rules, but given that the U.S. government all but destroyed the identity of his people, he had no problem calling himself Scott Anka, as he weaseled into the system, albeit illegally.

At his dorm, when White Buffalo opened the door, the lawyer was surprised to find standing before him a very tall, fit, sophisticated, handsome young man. He was not certain what he anticipated, but the young man before him was beyond his expectations. He found White Buffalo to have a calm, humble demeanor and cultured erudition of high intellect. He held his gaze with a confidence rarely found among young men his age. Rousseau heard that the young man came from a long line of chiefs and warriors, most notably Crazy Horse. Upon their first meeting, it was clear to Rousseau that White Buffalo represented his ancestral line well. There was nothing false about him, with the exception of his new name. Rousseau's client would be pleased to hear of his first impressions.

Rousseau was a slightly built man, with grey hair and a goatee, and quite exquisitely dressed. He wore his glasses far down on his nose, looking up at White Buffalo while peering over the rims. White Buffalo thought he looked the part of a Southern lawyer, and wondered how he could possibly discern such a thought, having never been to the South until then.

"It is nice to meet you, Monsieur Rousseau. Please come in," White Buffalo said in a deep timbre corresponding with his vaulted height. "Thank you for arranging all my legal documents under my new name. I appreciate your handling all the details so I am able to attend Tulane." He smiled, showing his perfect white teeth, contrasted by his olive skin.

"It is my pleasure, Mr. Anka, or may I call you Scott, to keep it official? You may address me as André, please."

"Very well, then, André. Will there be an opportunity to meet my benefactor? I would like to extend my gratitude."

"For the time, your benefactor wishes to remain anonymous. However, I will say, you will not be disappointed when you *do* finally meet. Until then, I will be your contact. If there is anything you need, please do not hesitate to call. With that, I believe you have everything you need for now. Allow me to leave you my card."

White Buffalo looked at the business card, and then he shook André's hand. He opened the door for him. "Thank you for coming by."

"Until we meet again, sir." Rousseau tipped his hat as

he backed out of the room to leave.

White Buffalo was 21, older and more mature than the average freshman student who began their college career at eighteen. He was careful not to over-spend, to honor his patron's generosity. Following a budget, he kept a record of all of his expenses. Once he settled into his class schedule, he would find a part-time job. He intended to prove himself to Wakan Tanka and his people, and to work hard in his pursuit of a doctorate in Psychology. He hoped to soon meet his patrons, in gratitude, and eventually reimburse them for their generosity.

It was 1960, and White Buffalo went all out to adopt the latest styles for men. To attend classes in cooler months, he wore lightweight wool, high-waist trousers, and a white cotton shirt with a lightweight hound's-tooth blazer. As the weather became warm, he wore cotton slacks and a matching jacket, and at times, a seersucker suit, always with a tie to match. He topped off his outfit with a leather belt and matching cordovan wingtip shoes. For casual dress around campus, he wore blue jeans with rolled cuffs, and a white tee shirt under his red cotton casual jacket with the sleeves rolled to the elbow. Loafers with white socks were all the rage. On occasion, he wore his black leather jacket to make a statement, and oh, what a statement he made.

The look was not complete without a good haircut to pull it off. From the time he was small and blonde, his hair gradually turned to nearly black, and his eyes became deep blue. He wore a pompadour, using Royal Crown pomade as a styling aid. It only took a dime-sized dab, worked well through his thick hair. With a fine-toothed comb, he parted his hair on the side and sculpted the top into a perfect wave. He finished by brushing the sides straight back into a ducktail at the base of his neck that would have made Elvis Presley jealous. With his nearly black hair, striking deep blue eyes, and gleaming smile, he definitely caught the eyes of the ladies.

Although he spent most of his time diligently studying, one young woman by the name of Evangeline Chevalier happened to turn his head more than once. Her name alone caught his attention, for he believed that names and their meanings said much about a person. Evangeline meant *bringer of good news*, and Chevalier meant *knight, or horse-riding warrior*. Having come from a legacy of horse-riding warriors himself, he took it as a good omen that the woman who captured his heart was so named.

One day, on his way to class, she passed by and he heard her say, "Well, hello there, tall, dark, and handsome."

Although he was quite shy, White Buffalo surprised himself when he replied, "Hello yourself - petite, fair, and gorgeous."

Evangeline giggled with her girlfriends as they headed in the opposite direction for class.

White Buffalo was smitten. Never would he be the same again.

Although a native of New Orleans, Evangeline's father, Gregory Chevalier, was a Geology professor at the School of Mines in Golden, Colorado. Her mother, Colette, owned a bakery near their home in the foothills, just west of Denver. Evangeline grew up as an only child, and spent her summers working in her maternal grandparents' bakery, *La Petite Boulangerie Patisserie*, in New Orleans' French Quarter. When Evangeline was 16, she moved with her parents to Colorado, but her heart remained in Louisiana, where she elected to attend college.

After they dated for a few weeks, White Buffalo found himself in the early morning hours, working at the bakery and making bread and pastries alongside Evangeline. For the remaining years they attended Tulane, rarely were they apart.

From the beginning, White Buffalo and his roommate, Gaston, instantly became good friends. Although they were the same age, Gaston was a full academic year ahead of White Buffalo, so his experience in college and familiarity with New Orleans was of great benefit to his newfound friend and roommate. With the exception of occasional female intervention, the two were virtually inseparable, for together the two frequented the college bars, football games, college events, and parties. Gaston came from a rich ancestry of Cajun and Creole background, as well as French, Spanish, African and Indian bloodlines. Many of his people had been in New Orleans since the early 1800's.

"My father's father came from France," Gaston said. "My paternal grandmother hails from the origins of American history. Her ancestral grandparents came over on the Mayflower. On my mother's side, you might be interested to know that my grandmother is an American Indian."

"Yes? Of what tribe?" White Buffalo asked.

"I don't know," Gaston said. "She does not speak of the past very often. She's rather sensitive about it, so I don't ask. Now, her husband, my grandfather, is from the Caribbean - Jamaica. He is of African and Spanish descent, and Calusa Indian, which lived until the late 1700's on the southwest tip of Florida. The combinations of all these people here in New Orleans make up the Creole. My Cajun background comes from eastern Canada, and before that from France. I suppose you could say I am a man of the world," Gaston said, with his good-natured laugh.

"And you don't even shave yet," White Buffalo said.

Gaston rubbed White Buffalo's chin. "You're one to talk. I see very little peach fuzz on that face of yours."

White Buffalo was relieved to make a good friend he instantly trusted, finally able to reveal his origins that he too was Indian."I am a full-blooded Lakota," he said. "For most of my childhood, I grew up on a reservation in South Dakota and was educated in schools designed to assimilate the Native people into the white man's world. I appreciate what I learned, but what I want most is to be who I was born to be - a Lakota. When I earn my doctorate in Psychology, I want to educate the world about my people and our history, so they will remember us. As indigenous people, we have so much to offer those who no longer remember their own roots."

"It seems the United States is a homogenized blending of cultures," Gaston said. "What I have learned about my grandmother is that she was from the north. She once told my mother that she was the daughter of a warrior chief and holy man. Beyond that, she rarely speaks of her heritage. We believe she had a difficult childhood."

"Many Native children did," White Buffalo said. "They grew up not knowing who they were, or where they came from."

"Indeed," Gaston said. "It so frustrates us, because she once said she thought that Crazy Horse was related to her father."

"She did?" White Buffalo said. "I am told that I am also related to him. That would most likely make your grandmother Lakota. I wonder if my family knew her."

"One can only wonder," Gaston said.

White Buffalo shrugged. "It is not likely, since the Lakota are spread out with great distances of uninhabited land between them." He sat back in his chair, considering the possibility that Gaston's grandmother was one of his relations. He knew stranger things happened.

Gaston invited White Buffalo to spend Thanksgiving with him and his family at their elegant plantation house. "I do believe you might enjoy my extended family," he said. "We are rather delightfully eccentric, you might say. My father owns an antique store in the Quarter. My mother passed away when I was a child, and he later remarried a most wonderful and very wealthy widow. My stepmother owns the Delaney Hotel chain."

White Buffalo blew a sigh. "You didn't mention that you were filthy rich."

"Oh, we bathe regularly, so we are more appropriately rich in a squeaky clean sort of way."

"I hope they won't mind a poor Native kid who grew up on dirt floors."

"Not to worry," Gaston said. "My father has kept every nickel he ever made, and with the exception of their beautiful plantation home, the MacPhaidin clan lives quite unpretentiously. The hotel chain is now run by my stepbrother, who although just a year or two older than us, is insanely intelligent – and a bit of a lovable pompous ass. But his wife, who also happens to be my sister, keeps him in line."

"Wait," White Buffalo said. "Your brother is married to your-"

"*Step*brother," Gaston said. "Yes, he married my sister.

We all were rather young when our parents remarried, so I suppose he was just naturally accustomed to her underwear hanging in the bathroom. Whatever the case, their hormones just naturally seemed to mix, and before you knew it, they had a beautiful baby girl and were married."

White Buffalo quizzically looked at Gaston.

"Well," Gaston said, "I might have gotten the order backwards on that. We never really did the math, but I assure you it all worked out for the best..."

White Buffalo gladly accepted Gaston's invitation since Evangeline was planning to go to Colorado for the break, and White Buffalo could not afford to go with her. On Thanksgiving Day, he arrived with Gaston, his mouth agape at the stunning plantation house. There, ready to meet them at the front door, was Gaston's stepbrother.

"Welcome, please come on in." He stepped aside, allowing them to enter, and then shook White Buffalo's hand.

"Darius MacPhaidin, my stepbrother," Gaston said, "meet my new roommate, Scott Anka."

"How do you do, Scott. I am so happy to finally meet you. Gaston speaks so highly of you." An exquisite young woman came to his side to greet White Buffalo. "May I introduce my lovely wife, Lianne. Darling, this is Scott Anka." Darius placed his arm around his wife's shoulders.

"It is my pleasure to make your acquaintance." White Buffalo slightly bowed his head.

"Oh, the pleasure is mine," Lianne said, marveling at how handsome their guest was. A beautiful blonde three-year-old girl suddenly ran by, squealing, "Toot! Toot!" as she passed. She was gone in an instant.

"My," What Buffalo said. "Who was that?"

Darius laughed. "That bolt of lightning is Elizabeth, our daughter."

White Buffalo smiled. "I hope to meet her sometime."

"Oh, she'll be back," Lianne said, "but you have to look quickly!"

White Buffalo met the remainder of the family, present that evening. Siobhan, Darius' mother, came into the room and introduced herself. "Welcome to our home, Scott. My husband will be a bit late, but he should be here in time for dinner, which will be ready soon. Darius, darling, why don't you offer Scott something to drink."

"Yes, of course. What can I get you? A glass of our finest bourbon, perhaps?" Darius asked.

"Thank you, that sounds wonderful."

"Gaston?"

"Need you ask?"

"Only if you promise to keep your clothes on," Darius dryly said as he walked to the bar.

Gaston nudged White Buffalo with a wink. "I told you."

They all chatted mostly in small talk while waiting for dinner. White Buffalo discreetly glanced about the room, taking in the antique splendor of generations past. Never had he seen such opulence. He spent most of his life living in a deerskin tipi. He thought, *I will have to learn to be comfortable with this lifestyle if I am to travel the world.* He took note of the different styles and art throughout the home.

Just then, the butler entered the parlor. "Dinner is served."

As dinner began, Gaston's father came into the room and took his place at the head of the table.

"Forgive me for being late. Some special clients asked if they could come to the store this morning. Normally, the store would not be open on Thanksgiving, but they were leaving town and wanted to make a few holiday purchases before they left. I must say, they chose some beautiful pieces."

White Buffalo stood and extended his hand.

"Ah, you must be Scott. Dylan Delacroix, at your service."

"How do you do, sir," White Buffalo said.

Siobhan leaned over to White Buffalo as he sat. "Dylan owns an antique store down on Royal Street. You must visit sometime."

"Yes?" White Buffalo said. "What kind of antiques, Mr. Delacroix?"

"A little of this, a little of that."

"Don't let him kid you," Gaston said. "The place is enchanting, and the pieces are stunning. I'll take you there."

"And please, you must call me Dylan. May I call you White Buffalo?" He mischievously smiled.

"Well, Papa," Gaston said, "let's not beat around the bush, shall we?"

Dylan rubbed his hands together. "I do so love intrigue, and Gaston has told us all about you."

White Buffalo looked at Gaston, who shrugged. "Did I forget to mention I am the family blabbermouth?"

"Oh, no, not to worry!" Dylan said. "I assure you, your

secret is safe with us. We are so honored to have you here. So, if you please, how did you come to call yourself Scott Anka?"

White Buffalo shifted in his chair, not certain if he should reveal his origins, but, he thought, *here we go.* "I could not attend Tulane as a Lakota, so I made up a name to sound more – uh-"

"Vanilla?" Dylan said.

White Buffalo laughed. "Yes, you might say that. In the Lakota language, the word for white is *ska*. Likewise, the word for buffalo is *tatanka*. My Lakota name is Tatanka Ska. On my college application, I combined the two words and called myself Scott T. Anka. So, in a way, people call me White Buffalo without knowing it."

"How delightful!" Dylan said. "Very clever of you, but if you would prefer that we call you White Buffalo, we would be most pleased."

"Yes. Thank you. I appreciate that. Scott just doesn't seem right, but it is necessary that I go by that name at Tulane." He guardedly looked at Gaston. "That goes for blabbermouths, in particular."

"Lips are sealed," Gaston said.

"Ah, perchance to dream," Darius said.

White Buffalo was quite relieved, and felt right at home.

"Tatanka Ska is such a lovely name," Siobhan said.

"It is a shame that you have to attend Tulane under an alias," Dylan said, "but unfortunately we, as a people, are not yet advanced enough to not judge cultural differences. Someday, that will change."

"Tell us more about your people," Darius said. "We

know a bit about the Native American lifestyles, but we would love to hear about you and where you grew up."

"What most people know of the Native American is not who we are," White Buffalo said. "My people have lost their identity. By law, we cannot worship the Creator - Wakan Tanka - in the ways of our ancestors. We can no longer speak our native tongue, eat our native foods, or live in the way of our grandfathers. As a child, in the Black Hills, I grew up in a tipi and loved every minute of it. Today, my parents live on a reservation in a house to fit government standards. It became mandatory that all Native people of the United States assimilate into the white man's ways to forget who we are, but the government's prohibition only forces us to follow our native ways in secret.

"I want to use my education, so I can teach the world the ways of the Lakota - to teach the Seven Lakota Virtues as a peaceful, responsible way of life. Our culture is rich. We are the original Americans, and we are not to be forgotten. And so, I am here to pass along the ways of my people." He was a bit embarrassed at being so outspoken, but the opportunity was ripe.

"I would love to learn more," Dylan said.

"I would, too," Siobhan said. The others nodded in agreement.

"You are welcome to teach us some of your ways," Dylan said. "Would that be of interest to you?"

"Why yes, of course," White Buffalo said.

"What if you performed that sweat lodge ceremony you told me about," Gaston said. "What did you call it - an epee?"

White Buffalo laughed. "Inipi ceremony."

"What did I say?" Gaston said.

"Epee," Darius said. "Handy only if the ceremony involves a swordfight."

"Inipi, that's it," Gaston said, his eyes gleaming in anticipation. "And, Papa, don't you think Grandmamma, in particular, would be interested?"

"She just might," Dylan said. "We must invite the entire family."

"That is a capital idea!" Darius said.

"Oh, if only Patrick were here," Dylan said. "This would be right up his alley."

White Buffalo looked at Gaston. "My Uncle Patrick."

"My adventurous little brother," Dylan said. "He once lived in a tipi in Wyoming for a year when he was just 22."

"Where is he now?" White Buffalo asked.

"Who knows? In the wind. Patrick doesn't let the grass grow under his feet."

"Last we heard from him, he was moving to Colorado," Lianne said.

"Anyway," Dylan said, "I simply cannot wait to have this – what is it, Inipi?"

"Yes," White Buffalo said. "It is a sweat lodge."

"But, let me get this straight," Dylan said. "It's illegal, correct?"

White Buffalo shrugged. "It is."

"Splendid!" Dylan said, rubbing his hands together.

Lianne joined the excitement. "Oh, I can't wait!"

White Buffalo hoped he was not getting himself into

something that would cause trouble, but he looked forward to practicing his sacred ceremonies again. It had been too long.

"Well, that being settled, let's eat!" Dylan said.

During the scrumptious dinner, they all sat around the table enjoying each other's company with small talk.

"The rest of the family wanted to be here tonight," Siobhan said, "but they will be here at Christmas. We would love to have you join us, if you are not going home for the holidays."

"I would like that," White Buffalo said. "I am not planning to return home until the summer break, but if I can work at my girlfriend's grandparents' bakery, I will most likely also remain during the summer."

"When that time comes, if you so choose, you are welcome to stay with us for the summer - here at the plantation - rent free," Dylan said.

"Yes, we would be happy to have you as our guest," Siobhan said.

"I am honored, thank you. That will be my great fortune if I stay," White Buffalo said, not believing his good luck. Just so he didn't have to remember how everyone was related, with half-brothers, stepsisters, second wives, husbands, and all their ancestral origins - he would be just fine if he could remember their names.

"Wonderful then," Siobhan excitedly said. "Since you will be here for the holidays, you will be here for the Christmas Eve bonfires."

"Bonfires?" White Buffalo asked.

"Along the Great River Road," Siobhan said, "between New Orleans and Baton Rouge, we have thirty- to forty-foot pyramids of logs and leaves, which burn on top of the levees of the Mississippi River. They light the way for the Christ Child, and for Papa Noël, who will ride his sleigh, led by twelve alligators." Everyone laughed. "In between each bonfire, families and friends gather to cook and celebrate Christmas Eve together."

"Sounds like a well anticipated event," White Buffalo said.

"Yes it is, especially for children," Lianne said. "Elizabeth is getting old enough to enjoy it now."

"Papa, tell White Buffalo about how Grandmother and Grandfather first met." Gaston leaned across the table, looking at White Buffalo. "You're going to love this."

"My father was a stowaway on the *Titanic*," Dylan said, "and my mother was a First Class passenger traveling back to the United States."

"Your parents were on the *Titanic?*" White Buffalo said.

"For awhile, as my father loves to say," Dylan said. "Mama's first husband died of influenza while they were visiting his family in Wales. She was sailing back to New York to resume her career in fashion design. After several, shall we say unusual encounters on the ship, they fell in love - before it sank, of course."

"You'll love my grandfather," Gaston said.

"He was a stowaway?" White Buffalo said.

"Through unfortunate circumstances," Dylan said. "Papa's first wife had passed away suddenly in Paris, and he was broke, but he had a lucrative job offer in New York. He was a brilliant architect, and also a bit of a con artist, who worked and charmed his way into a First Class cabin and drank bourbon and smoked cigars with none other than John Jacob Astor. He and my mother met and fell in love, and all was a grand fairytale until the terrible tragedy struck.

"My mother was among the survivors, having been on one of the lifeboats. However, my father perished, or so she thought. Because he was a stowaway, there was no record of him on board, and she had no way of finding out if they recovered his body. Her heart was broken twice - first, being a widow at such a young age, and then at the loss of my father, her new love, just when the flame was sparked again. They originally made plans to meet for dinner at the end of April, at a hotel restaurant in New York City. My mother went to the restaurant in his honor, when to her surprise, she found my father there waiting for her."

"How did he survive?" White Buffalo asked.

"He was thrown in the water when the ship foundered, but he managed to cling to an overturned lifeboat with many others until a ship rescued them. He was injured and hospitalized, and my mother, thinking he went down with the ship, didn't know he survived until he was released. Anyway, they married a few months later at the home of the unsinkable Molly Brown, who they met and befriended on the cruise, and, as they say, the rest is history. Having been conceived on the ship, I was born January 15, 1913, nine months to the day after *Titanic* met her demise."

White Buffalo's eyes were wide with wonder at the story. "Well, that is a piece of history that very few people can claim. There were about 700 survivors, were there not? But I have to say, I have never heard of anyone conceived on the *Titanic*. If I am not mistaken, Dylan means 'son of the sea.'"

"It does," Dylan said. "How did you know that?"

"My people acquire their names with intention, so I find the meaning of people's names of interest, especially if they are suitable to their personality. Tell me, how did your parents come to settle here in New Orleans?"

"My mother was a fashion designer for *Lucile Ltd*, a famous fashion house from London. My father worked for the same company. In fact, they met the owner of *Lucile* while they were on *Titanic*. She offered them jobs, and they jumped at the opportunity. My father designed *Lucile's* buildings all over the world. The company built one of their establishments down here, and since my father would be here for a year, Lady Duff-Gordon, the owner of *Lucile*, asked my mother if she would be interested in opening the New Orleans' location. They liked it so much, they decided to make this their permanent home."

"I look forward to meeting them," White Buffalo said.

"Oh, they will love you," Siobhan said. "Jocelyn is a bit of a mystic herself, and she will be very interested in your culture."

"You have some interesting ancestors," Gaston said. "Tell everyone about your family."

"My grandfather's name was Tahatan. He was a warrior chief and wicasa wakan - a holy man and a dream interpreter. Through our sacred ceremonies, he helped people understand their visions and dreams. My mother, Wichahpi, participated in a ceremony called a vision quest when quite young, where she was able to see into the past and future. There, she saw one of our ancestors, Crazy Horse."

"You are related to Crazy Horse, dear boy?" Dylan said.

"Yes. Although the direct lineage of our people was passed down through storytellers and not recorded on paper, Great-grandfather told my mother that Crazy Horse was a distant cousin on his mother's side. He was a teenager when he fought alongside Crazy Horse at the battle of the Little Big Horn."

"Dear me," Darius said.

"Oh, this is as good as *Titanic*," Dylan said. "I can't *tell* you right now how much this delights me!"

"I have read that, in addition to one of the most formidable Sioux warriors, Crazy Horse was a great mystic and seer," Lianne said.

"He was. My mother's vision quest also revealed me, as a child, long before I was born. Tahatan died when I was two years old, but it was my mother and father who taught me the ways of my people."

"Oh, this is delightful," Dylan said, rubbing his hands together. "I so look forward to the Inipi, where we shall learn so much more about your people – and, I dare say, you may learn more about us." He gave White Buffalo a wink.

White Buffalo smiled and glanced at Gaston, who said, "Did I not tell you that you would love my family?"

"We look forward to learning more about your culture," Lianne said. "You can practice on us as the first people you educate." Everyone at the table was abuzz, anticipating what they would learn from the experience.

CHAPTER
Twenty-six

*O*ver the next two weeks, with the help of Dylan, Gaston, and Darius, White Buffalo built a sweat lodge deep on the plantation in a clearing among the trees, away from any neighbors' curiosities. They draped blankets and quilts over the willow framework, with the door facing west.

The mid-December temperatures were ideal, in the cool mid-60's, for the chilly air would be welcome during the extreme heat of the lodge. White Buffalo met with Gaston's family the night before to give an overview of what to expect. Everyone came with the exception of Gaston's maternal grandparents, who planned to come the next day.

Jocelyn and François, both in their mid-seventies, attended that night. White Buffalo found them to be a handsome, distinguished older couple, yet of a quite youthful countenance. Although retired, François was still a principle partner of his prominent architectural firm, *Metamorphosis.* Jocelyn, of course, was dressed with impeccable taste, still an active and well-known fashion designer. White Buffalo found her a stunningly beautiful woman. Jocelyn owned, *En Vogue,* her own fashion house, having bought out *Lucile's* New Orleans branch many years before.

Both Jocelyn and François were ready and willing to explore a new form of spirituality, which would be refreshing, as opposed to the Catholic tradition and staunch Southern Baptists prevalent in their part of the country. At the time, White Buffalo had no idea they had a mystic way very similar in nature to the spirituality of his people.

White Buffalo's beloved Evangeline also joined them that evening, with plans to participate the next day. White Buffalo thought it a fortuitous opportunity to introduce her to some of his Native ways, for very few occasions came about for him to celebrate his origins openly. Evangeline was brought up in an open-minded Christian home that embraced love and respect for all faiths, so White Buffalo revealed his secret to her very early in their relationship.

They all sat around the dining table, engrossed in making prayer ties of tobacco, held in small pieces of cotton fabric tied together with string. Each person made as many ties as they desired to take their prayers to Great Spirit during the ceremony. White Buffalo answered many questions about what to expect the next day. Most everyone was excited, with the exception of an apprehensive Siobhan, who was a genteel southern woman.

"I declare, I'm embarrassed to admit," she said, "that I've never spent much time outdoors in my bare feet."

"Not to worry, my dear, you have exquisite toes," Dylan said.

"Oh, stop," she said.

"The heat is very intense inside the lodge," White Buffalo said. "You will be glad you dressed modestly."

"You may see the world in a new light with your feet *au naturel*, no?" François said.

"Well, I wouldn't miss this for the world," Siobhan said.

"The sweat lodge has the effect on the body like a

sauna," White Buffalo said. "While in the lodge, sitting in complete darkness, the intense heat and steam purifies the mind, body, and spirit."

"How long does the Inipi last?" Darius asked.

"We could be there for some time, but you will find, inside the lodge, that time becomes irrelevant," White Buffalo said. "As we go deeper into the songs and our prayers, you may be surprised how easily you endure the heat and the darkness, because we transcend beyond our human minds. But if anyone becomes too uncomfortable, please speak up and feel free to exit and take a break. There is no dishonor in leaving, and you are welcome to come back when the next door opens."

"How do you generate the heat?" Jocelyn asked.

"Earlier this week, I asked Mr. Delacroix and Darius if any of their plantation employees might be willing to help serve as our firekeeper, which is a job that takes quite a bit of fortitude and energy. The firekeeper must be willing to work from dawn until about 4:00 p.m., stoking a fire outside the lodge that heats many large rocks we bring into the lodge. After that, he would be welcome to join the family in a feast of thanksgiving."

A young man named Jacques volunteered. He was an inquisitive Cajun man, brought up in the Catholic tradition, but he was curious about other philosophies. White Buffalo sensed he would be the perfect person to handle the very important job of firekeeper. After Jacques agreed, White Buffalo told him he would pay him well, far more than his typical hourly wage. He stressed to Jacques that his job as firekeeper was essential to the success of the Inipi ceremony, which the man was very eager to do well.

The morning of the ceremony, White Buffalo was up at

6:00 a.m., forty minutes before dawn. Shortly afterward, he met Jacques, who was already at the fire pit dug deep into the ground to avoid the wind catching a spark. The roofed pit, surrounded by a frame wrapped in chicken wire, kept cinders from straying into the nearby woods. Jacques had been there since 5:00 a.m., stacking kindling, small sticks, and larger logs in the fire pit, about ready to light the fire.

Nearby was a tall pile of wood that Jacques and White Buffalo chopped the day before, which would keep the fire burning for hours. Large cantaloupe-sized limestone rocks sat next to the fire pit, ready to be placed in the fire once it was burning well. White Buffalo brought a knapsack and two large buckets of water with a ladle. One bucket was for the ceremony participants, and the other was for Jacques to drink. The knapsack contained plenty of sandwiches, apples, cheese, and cake for Jacques, for he would need to be available and ready the entire day.

The Inipi began at noon, as scheduled. Everyone came, including Gaston's maternal grandparents, who arrived about 11:45 a.m. White Buffalo noticed they were a bit younger than Jocelyn and François, most likely in their mid to late sixties. Gaston's grandfather was a dignified dark-skinned man, tall and stately. His wife was petite. Her once black hair, now generously laced with gray, was tied in a simple knot at the base of her neck. White Buffalo could not help but notice her beauty, albeit she was much older than he. There was something noble about her, beyond her physicality. He was so busy getting everyone organized with further instructions, he did not get a chance introduce himself properly. He made a mental note to be sure to take some time to visit with them after the sweat was over, for he was very curious about her Native American lineage.

Everyone followed his instructions on how to enter the lodge after he cleansed them with the smoke of burning sage. Once they were all in place, seated on a thick bed of fresh Louisiana sage, they breathed in its fresh clean perfume. White Buffalo took in the scent, ready to proceed.

"We will sing songs throughout the ceremony. Each song is a prayer to the Creator - the Great Spirit. It does not matter to Great Spirit if you do not know the words to the songs. Do the best you can to follow along. What does matter is that you leave your ego outside the door and allow yourself to let go. Allow yourself to be humble. We are all here in support of each other. Nothing spoken here today will leave the lodge, for the Inipi is a sacred purification rite. If you are in agreement please say, 'Aho.'"

"Aho," they all agreed.

"Inipi means, 'to live again.' What we will experience today is a cleansing of the mind, body, and soul - a spiritual rebirth. The songs we will sing, and the prayers we will speak, will draw on all the forces and powers of the universe, which we know as earth, wind, fire, water, and ether. Time will disappear. If you get too hot, lie down on the bed of sage and place your face close to where the lodge meets the earth. There, you will find cool air coming in. Is everyone all right?"

"Aho," they responded.

"If anyone needs to leave, or if you become too uncomfortable, whatever the reason, do not hesitate. Before you leave, first say, 'Aho Mitakuye Oyasin' or 'All my Relations.' Jacques will open the flap, and you can safely crawl out. Okay?"

"Okay," they all said.

"Jacques, please bring in the first of the Grandfathers."

Jacques slid a large pitchfork though the door with a red-hot rock that he carefully rolled into the fire pit. After Jacques brought in four more rocks, one at a time, White Buffalo rearranged them in the fire pit with deer antlers. He threw sweet grass on the fiery stones, filling the darkened dome with the smoke and pleasant aroma to clear the senses and open the mind and heart.

Jacques exited and closed the door flap, and darkness settled in. All they could see was the red-hot glow of the stones at the center. White Buffalo spoke a prayer to Great Spirit in his native language of the Lakota. His heart sang out, not having spoken the sacred words for several months. Those in the lodge could not help but feel the resonant quality of the prayer in the ancient language of White Buffalo's people. They immediately felt a shift in the energy of the lodge. Outside, even Jacques sensed a change take place.

White Buffalo instructed both Gaston and Darius how to strike their deerskin drums in unison with an even, steady beat. They all sang several songs together. In the darkness, White Buffalo took notice of one of the women, who seemed to sing in perfect accord with him. When the pipe ceremony took place, he passed the pipe at the heart level to the person to his left, instructing them to hold the stem in the right hand and the bowl of the pipe in the left, keeping the pipe intact. Each person gently took in some of the tobacco smoke. When they released the smoke into the air, it represented a visible prayer to Great Spirit.

When it came time for individual prayers, White Buffalo began.

"Wakan Tanka - Great Spirit - this is your grandson,

Takanka Ska - White Buffalo. I come before you today with a grateful heart. Thank you, Wakan Tanka, for your guidance and for being with me in all ways. Help me so I may see with both eyes, and hear with both ears. May I be wise to speak only half as much as I see and hear. Today, I honor all the Grandfathers and all my relations. I pray for peace, for joy, for health, and for the wisdom to hear your voice. I pray to love others as you show your love for the entire world in all its beauty and wonder. Bless all people in need - those who are sick, incarcerated, and unable to help themselves. Bless all the four-legged ones, the winged ones, the finned ones, and the creepy crawlies - all those of the land, sea, and sky. Great Spirit, may I be of service so I may use my talents in a good way, and may I walk the Red Road. Aho Mitakuye Oyasin."

All responded, "Aho."

It was then time for everyone to offer their individual prayer, beginning with the men on White Buffalo's left, eventually leading in a sunwise direction to the women on White Buffalo's right. Each took their turn, some saying a prayer aloud, while others chose to pray in quiet meditation. Each concluded, speaking aloud the phrase "Aho Mitakuye Oyasin." As each prayer was spoken, the temperature continued to rise to nearly 180 degrees, intensifying the energy in the pitch black lodge.

Toward the end of the prayers, one woman spoke eloquently, "Wakan Tanka, it is I, your granddaughter. I am so grateful to celebrate with the Grandfathers today. It has been many years since I last came before you. Great Spirit, I ask your forgiveness, for I have not honored you as I should. I have not honored my birth family, but I desire to live in a good way. May I learn to pray well to you again, asking for support in everything I do. May I give generously of my time, talents, and abundant means. May I be honest in all my thoughts, words, and actions, and may I be respectful of all others. I have not been a woman with a humble heart, Great Spirit. Help me to open to love so I may live within your greatness, in humility. May I be a woman of greater compassion, seeing those who stand before me with your eyes and heart. Wakan Tanka, may I possess wisdom to make choices that serve Grandmother Earth and all that walk upon her back, to the best of my ability. I am so grateful for the privilege of being here today in more ways than I can say. Aho Mitakuye Oyasin."

"Aho."

White Buffalo noted in the back of his mind that the woman mentioned all seven of the Lakota Virtues. He then spoke directly to her, not as himself, but in the same way as his great-grandfather Tahatan, with the words that came through to him as the wicasa wakan - the holy man.

"Granddaughter, you are always welcome. Even though you may not see it, you have lived in a good way. You have given many years to help people along their path. You began with the wind at your back, but your roots have anchored deep in your life here. Remember, Granddaughter, living in a good way affects everyone. If you are happy, that becomes part of your generosity, as you respectfully and compassionately give of yourself to others from the heart. Wakan Tanka is always with you. Ask for support and it will be yours. You are much wiser now. Be kind to yourself. Love yourself first, and then all that you give to others will come from your whole self - from the wisdom of your heart. You are a good woman, Granddaughter. You have lived well. Aho Mitakuye Oyasin."

"Aho," they all responded.

White Buffalo called out for Jacques to bring the remaining heated rocks into the lodge, after which the heat increased to its highest level. Shortly after, the weather outside developed into an unusual winter thunderstorm, and it was apparent they were located at the heart of the storm. If they were standing out in the open, they would most certainly run for cover. Outside, Jacques fled to his sturdy pickup truck, where he marveled at the intensity of the storm over a steaming cup of coffee from his coffee pot, kept hot on the fire all day long.

White Buffalo assured them that they would be safe in the lodge. They were in a sacred circle, and nothing could harm them, for Wakan Tanka and all the elements were present. Thunder boomed and lightning struck simultaneously. Inside the lodge, in total darkness, they could see the flashes of lightning where the base of the domed structure met the ground. Barely could they hear themselves sing, but White Buffalo encouraged them to sing even louder. The drumbeat became more commanding with the songs, the heat, and the thunder and lightning. The energy could not have been more powerful.

As the storm passed, the ceremony ended as they sang two songs in conclusion. "Jacques, open the door," said White Buffalo.

No one was there. White Buffalo pushed open the flap and stepped outside. Everyone crawled out of the lodge and came outside into the cool rain in awe that the lodge was completely intact. Not a spark hit the blankets wrapped around the domed structure, but trees around them were still in flames. The ground all around the lodge was charred black from lightning strikes and steaming from the falling rain. The group looked at each other in silence, completely awestruck that no harm came to them. They gathered their rain-soaked belongings and quickly walked back to the plantation house where they found Jacques.

"I know you told me to stay, Mr. White Buffalo, sir," Jacques said, clearly upset, "but I feared I was gonna get char-broiled out there."

White Buffalo laughed. "Well, we could not have that happen. Come inside." White Buffalo smiled as he put his arm around the man's soggy shoulder. He asked the butler if he could find some dry clothes for Jacques. "When you get dried off and changed, come back downstairs to join us in the feast and I will pay you."

Everyone else silently went to their rooms to change into dry clothes. They all came together in the parlor to celebrate an experience of a lifetime, looking rather red-faced from the heat that still radiated from their bodies. They ate their meal in celebration, quite famished, and when they finished, they retired to the library and sat around the hearth, watching the fire burn in the fireplace. Oddly enough, they felt a chill in the winter night air, even though they had been in searing heat with lightning all around them only hours before.

Before Jacques left that night, White Buffalo gave him a twenty-dollar bill, more than twice his normal wages for a ten-hour day. "Oh, thank you, sir. I didn't expect this much. I can really use it."

"Would you be interested in helping us do this again sometime? I truly do not think the storm will be a regular event," White Buffalo said, laughing with the young man.

"Yes sir! Just let me know." Jacques fervently shook

White Buffalo's hand.

"Thank you, Jacques. You did an excellent job. I will call on you again." Jacques left the house with a smile on his face and his wet clothes in a sack.

White Buffalo came back into the library with the intention to speak with Gaston's grandmother. He suspected that she was the woman who prayed at the end of the lodge. She saw him enter the room and stood up as he approached her. Everyone in the room grew silent.

He offered his hand to her. "May I officially introduce myself. I am White Buffalo, of the Rosebud Reservation in South Dakota."

She looked up into his deep blue eyes. "Tatanka Ska, I am your grandmother, Mika. I am the daughter of Tahatan. Your mother, Wichahpi, is my daughter."

Astonished, he stood with tears that matched those pouring down her face. Mika was more than a foot shorter than he was. She reached up and gently touched her grandson's face, as he bent down and wrapped his big arms around her to receive his grandmother's embrace.

"It is true," he softly said. "When I heard your voice, Great Spirit whispered your name to me in the darkness." He hugged her again and wept in gratitude.

Everyone else shared in their moment, with not a dry eye in the room.

"When Gaston told me his grandmother was a distant relative of Crazy Horse, I wondered if you were also my grandmother, but I thought that would be too much of a coincidence. When I heard you sing and pray today, I knew we must come from the same people. I am so pleased, and my mother will be so happy to know you are still alive." He held her close again.

Mika's husband stepped forward, and she introduced him. "This is my husband, and your grandfather, Jelani Menard."

They warmly embraced. "It is my honor, sir," White Buffalo said.

"As it is mine, Grandson," Jelani said.

White Buffalo then looked at Gaston, whose eyes were alight. "Then we must be – cousins?"

"Half first cousins," Gaston said, "but who's counting? And, by the way, there are no coincidences." He gave him a wink.

"And so," White Buffalo said, "Grandmother, you are also Gaston's grandmother, correct?"

"Yes," Mika said. "Our daughter, Juliette, married Dylan, and they had two children – Gaston and Lianne. We sadly lost our sweet Juliette to pneumonia shortly after Gaston was born, but Great Spirit smiled on our beloved son-in-law when he later met Siobhan, Darius' mother, who also lost her husband – Darius' father."

White Buffalo quizzically looked at Gaston again. "Wait a minute. And you, *cousin* Gaston, just happened to become my roommate at school?"

"Kismet!" François said, wrapping his arm around a smiling Jocelyn.

White Buffalo simply stood with eyes wide open. "Grandmother, Grandfather, *you* must be my benefactors?"

"We all are, my grandson. The whole family." They all stood around him. He embraced every one of them.

"I do not know how to thank you all. I am speechless."

"Well, as you said during the ceremony, you asked to speak half as much as you see and listen," Gaston said.

Mika took his hands in hers and looked into his eyes. "Several years ago, Jelani and I came up to South Dakota, where you and Little Deer went to school. You were both exceptional students, and I told Jelani that I wanted to do something for you both. We work in the oil industry, and I could finally afford to give back to my heritage by helping you."

"Work in the oil industry," Gaston said with smirk. "They own an oil refinery outside Baton Rouge. Grandfather is a petroleum engineer, and Grandmother keeps the books and runs the place. They have more money than-"

"Gaston, dear," Mika calmly said. "I know the Inipi was an hour ago, perhaps well beyond your attention span, but may I remind you that Humility is among the seven Lakota virtues?"

"Yes ma'am," Gaston said, dropping his head.

"You may be 21 now, but you are not too old for me to turn you over my knee."

"No, ma'am."

"Oh, I just love how you do that!" Siobhan said in her lovely southern drawl.

"Hear! Hear!" Darius chimed in.

Mika turned back to White Buffalo, who tried not to laugh. "My grandson, when we returned back to New Orleans and told the family about you, we all came up with the idea to be your patrons, to help you and your sister get an education."

"So, Gaston, you knew about this?" White Buffalo said.

"I *can* keep a secret when it is important," Gaston said. White Buffalo embraced Gaston, patting him on the back.

"Thank you all. You will not regret your investment. My sister is already using her education to bring successful farming on the reservation, growing crops that can help to sustain them economically. You must meet her."

Mika nervously looked at Jelani. "We would like to travel up there, but I wanted to try this out on you first."

"What do you mean?" White Buffalo said.

"Your grandmother has been very apprehensive about meeting you," Jelani said.

"Why?"

Mika bowed her head. "I disgraced my family. I abandoned your mother. I have spent much of my life ashamed and regretful."

"I have heard the story," White Buffalo said. "You were young, and you made mistakes as we all have. You have given back to Little Deer and me, which would make both my great-grandfather and my mother happy. My mother forgave you long ago, soon after she realized the challenges of being a mother herself, so perhaps it is time that you forgive yourself."

Mika's eyes filled with tears as she tenderly touched his cheek. "You are so wise for a man so young."

"My sister, Little Deer, will be just as excited and grateful to meet you as I am. I just received a letter from her last week. She wrote how she loves what she is doing. If she were here, I know that she would also express her gratitude."

They embraced, and the entire room again filled with tears.

"Mon Dieu!" François said, dabbing a tear, "I do so love happy endings!"

Dylan agreed. "White Buffalo, you have already added so much to our family. In addition to being Mika's grandson and my first wife's nephew, that means we truly are related. You are always welcome here."

"What do you think about that?" Gaston said.

"I always wanted a brother," White Buffalo said. "You are about as close as I will get. My only problem is figuring out how I am related to Darius and the rest of you. I guess that makes you my half-cousin, half-uncle, half-sister-in-law, half-grandparents, and so on."

They all broke out in laughter.

Jocelyn put her hands on his shoulders. "Let us simply call ourselves family, dear."

They embraced, but White Buffalo couldn't help himself. "Mr. and Mrs. Delacroix, I must ask. You were on the *Titanic?*"

"Yes," François said. "At least, for-"

"Awhile!" everyone said in unison.

"Oh," François said, embarrassed, "you heard that one."

"A thousand times now," Gaston said.

"I would love to ask you more about it sometime," White Buffalo said.

"Well," François said, looking at Jocelyn, "I don't know about you, my dear, but that thunder and lightning storm over the lodge today was almost as exciting, yes?"

"I have to agree," Jocelyn said. "We have lived a relatively quiet life since that night so long ago, but today could go down in my journal as one of the two more exciting days of my life."

"Welcome to the family!" Darius said as he shook White Buffalo's hand.

Jelani came up to him, shook his hand, and placed his left hand on his grandson's shoulder. Lianne and Siobhan stood on their tiptoes to kiss him on the cheek. Evangeline stood back in the shadows and smiled, happily witnessing the union of White Buffalo with his newfound family.

"Well, everyone, I think we've had enough excitement for one day," Dylan said. "Let us all get a good night's rest. We will resume in the morning for breakfast."

Everyone left the room, but before Mika and Jelani departed, White Buffalo gave her a hug that lifted her off her feet. He smiled from ear to ear, so happy to finally meet his grandmother. "Grandmother and Grandfather, I did not get the chance to introduce to you my girlfriend, Evangeline Chevalier."

"It is a pleasure to meet you ma'am, sir," Evangeline said as they all shook hands.

"Chevalier. Is there not a wonderful bakery in the French Quarter run by the Chevalier family?" Mika asked.

"Yes, the Boulangerie is owned by my grandparents."

"We know it well. Your grandparents are good people. We have purchased our bread and pastries there for years."

"They will be pleased to hear that we met. Your grandson has become quite a baker himself. Each day, he works with me in the early morning hours as a baker making bread and pastries."

"It is a good thing that I walk to work from the dorm, so I can work off much of what I eat when I am there," White Buffalo said.

"We will see you in a couple of weeks for Christmas, I hope?" Mika said.

"Yes. I look forward to seeing you again," White Buffalo said as he reached down to hug his grandmother again. Mika and Jelani took their leave as White Buffalo sighed at the wonderful turn of the day's events.

White Buffalo drove Evangeline home and then returned to the plantation. Waiting for him was Darius, Gaston, François, and Jocelyn. Everyone else had gone to bed.

"If we could take another minute of your time before you retire for the evening," Darius said.

"Of course, what can I do for you?"

"Tomorrow afternoon, we would like to meet with you, privately. We have a very interesting proposal that we think you will want to take advantage of."

"I am intrigued," White Buffalo said, curiously looking at the others. "Just when I thought nothing could keep me awake tonight."

"We will explain tomorrow," Darius said. "Shall we say one o'clock? Let us meet here, and I will drive us down to my office, where we can have some privacy…"

CHAPTER
Twenty-seven

The five of them met at the Delaney Hotels headquarters. Although his mother remained as Chairman since her husband's death many years earlier, Darius became President and took full control of the day-to-day management of the business when he turned 21. He grew up assisting his mother wherever possible, but she insisted he finish college, a priority before he would take the reins and eventually succeed her as Chairman of the family business. Darius was highly gifted with an extraordinarily high IQ, having graduated from high school after only two years, and graduating with honors - summa cum laude - after achieving a perfect academic record in three years at Tulane. He attained his master's degree in business administration at the age of 20, and he married Lianne that same year. Baby Elizabeth followed shortly thereafter.

Darius' corner office overlooked the Mississippi River, ever a reminder of what true power meant. Whenever he had a business issue, he sat looking out the window at the water flowing past, and an answer to the problem would come to him, often with ease. Water always found a way to overcome any obstacle. Its power always prevailed. With that knowledge, he knew he too could do the same. Like his ancestors before him, Darius became an extremely successful hotelier at a remarkably young age.

"I believe my stepbrother was 40 when he was born," Gaston once told White Buffalo. No academic slouch himself, Gaston marveled at Darius' maturity and good sense. "I kept up with him in the classroom, but he often had to extract me from schoolyard scrapes when I got a little too big for my britches."

In very short order, White Buffalo recognized that Darius and Gaston, despite their obvious differences in temperament, were very close – an affection that seemed to draw White Buffalo into the circle, for he felt a very strong spiritual connection to both young men.

Darius' secretary, Winona, was already at the office to welcome them. Darius called her earlier that Sunday morning, and she agreed to come in as she did for all of his special meetings. That morning, Winona prepared afternoon tea for the group's enjoyment, with tea sandwiches, teacakes, and scones with clotted cream and strawberry preserves, all nicely laid out on a three-tiered ceramic cake plate. She placed it at the center of the coffee table in the corner of the room, surrounded by five easy chairs. Before she left, Winona poured the tea and handed each of Darius' guests a porcelain cup and saucer held in a napkin.

"Will there be anything else, Mr. MacPhaidin?" Winona asked.

"You have handled everything beautifully, Winona, as usual," Darius said. "Please leave us a full pot of tea on the side table with the cream and sugar cubes. Then, I think that will be all. I appreciate your taking the time to prepare all this for us, and for coming in on a Sunday. You may take the day off tomorrow, if you like."

"Thank you, Mr. MacPhaidin, I certainly appreciate it. I will see you Tuesday morning. Good day to you all." Winona closed the French doors as she backed out of the room.

"I was born too late," Gaston said with a sigh. "Otherwise, I would have courted and married that wonderful woman."

"Don't worry, darling, the right woman will come along," Jocelyn said, patting Gaston's hand.

"Yes," Darius said, "Mardi Gras is right around the corner."

"Don't," White Buffalo said, grabbing Gaston's arm as he was about to retort. "Not in front of your grandmother."

François chuckled, quite enchanted by White Buffalo.

"We appreciate your hosting the meeting, Darius," Jocelyn said. She poured cream into her coffee and stirred it, placing the spoon back onto the saucer.

"I am so glad you all could be here," Darius said. "White Buffalo, we are all very impressed by the way you handle yourself. Yesterday's Inipi ceremony will continue to have a positive effect on our lives. During that incredible storm, I am not sure how everything around us burned and we did not. On another level, I completely understand how we remained safe. The Great Mystery is far beyond our comprehension, but it is here for us to use."

"Yes, this is so true," Jocelyn said. She turned to White Buffalo. "You possess a rare spiritual quality that we look for. François, would you please explain to White Buffalo about Apeiros?"

"Yes, of course," François said in his refined French accent. "We belong to the Order of Apeiros, which began in Ancient Greece over three thousand years ago. We are a small, confidential group of thirteen sages, spiritual leaders, teachers, and healers - each gifted with specific spiritual and psychic abilities. We utilize the universal energies, which are individual and collective attributes of the Divine."

White Buffalo sat back in wonder. "I am intrigued." He looked at Darius and Gaston. "You both take part?"

Gaston smiled. "And you always thought of me as a bit of a goof, didn't you?"

"Well," White Buffalo said with a laugh, "it is just that - Mr. and Mrs. Delacroix, you are clearly very experienced people of the world, but the three of us are so young."

"We have no age requirement, dear," Jocelyn said with a gentle smile.

"While there is no substitute for experience," François said, "we recognize the value of fresh young minds, particularly in those as gifted as the three of you. Young Darius here is possessed of extraordinarily intuitive business instincts for a man his age, while our dear grandson Gaston is a very gifted medium."

White Buffalo cocked his head at Gaston. "Oh? Now I *am* intrigued."

"In essence, each of us has a calling, by which we support the world," Jocelyn said.

"Well, you certainly have been more than generous philanthropists on my behalf," White Buffalo said.

Gaston interjected, "What we do is more of an energy that we maintain and live within. Actually, I like that! I suppose you could call it energetic philanthropy."

"Our purpose is simple," François said. "We hold and maintain a high energetic frequency for the world, so that lower frequencies will attune with it, causing a vibrational shift of energy for the greater good. Yesterday, during the

Inipi ceremony, we all experienced this with the drumbeat, songs, and prayers. We call it entrainment - where lower energy frequencies shift to a higher level."

"Yes. It is what we hear in the unified rhythm of crickets or cicadas," White Buffalo said.

"Exactly!" Gaston said. "You see, this is why we so want you to consider joining us. You are clearly a gifted sage, and we can learn so much from you."

For the next hour, they all shared the details about the Order of Apeiros with White Buffalo.

"One of our people recently passed on, and we have a vacancy, I guess you might call it," Darius said. "We maintain the group with thirteen people, and we invite you to join us. As you can guess, being a member of the Order will most likely be one of the most important choices you will ever make, as it will affect your entire life. It is an important decision - a lifetime commitment. We would like you to consider our proposal and get back to us as soon as possible."

White Buffalo immediately responded. "I am greatly honored that you would consider me for such a position in your esteemed group. While I was in the Inipi ceremony yesterday, I had a vision of working with the very people you describe, doing good work for the greater good of the world. When I receive such visions from Wakan Tanka, I pay attention. If I do not, I soon regret it. I can tell you right now, it would be my honor to accept your invitation."

"Wonderful! We are thrilled!" Jocelyn said.

"You will add so much to our group," Darius said. "You might be pleased to know that our next annual gathering will be in Dublin, Ireland, early next summer for two weeks. When you and Gaston have finished the school year, we will take the train to New York. From there we will sail the Atlantic to Ireland aboard the Queen Mary."

"While in Ireland, we will honor you with a special induction ceremony," Gaston said. "The only thing you have to bring is a white suit. We all wear white the first evening. The rest of the time, be prepared for rain."

"In the meantime, you can practice holding the energy of Harmony," François said, "which was the mission of our member who recently passed on. We can talk in greater detail about this as the months pass."

White Buffalo sat in silent wonder at his good fortune, and yet he also felt a bit overwhelmed.

"Is something wrong, dear boy?" François said.

"It is just that – I have no money. I am indebted to my scholarship, and I cannot afford-"

"Oh, you need not worry, the Order covers all your expenses," Jocelyn said. "For thousands of years, we have had a financial overflow that continues to gain in value over time, so monetary concerns for Apeiros are never a concern."

"Again, I am so very grateful for everyone's generosity," White Buffalo said.

They all stood, each giving White Buffalo a warm handshake, while Jocelyn gave him a hug. "Welcome, Tatanka Ska. We shall all benefit from what has happened this day."

"Oui," François said, "as will the world."

As they departed, White Buffalo asked if he could take a few minutes to walk down by the river. Everyone agreed, and they waited for him in the car.

He stood on the riverbank, watching the magnificent Mississippi flow by. What an astounding six months it had been. He already knew his making the decision to join the Order of Apeiros granted him life opportunities he would otherwise not experience. He could already envision his role in Apeiros, serving all over the world in his capacity as a Lakota spiritual leader.

The river was ever his guide. He squatted down to his knees in prayer. "Good afternoon, Great River, this is your grandson, Tatanka Ska. Thank you for teaching me how you flow with ease around any obstacle. May I always move with the current as you do. May I nourish those I serve, as you do so selflessly. Help me to be the cleansing power of your waters, for I too am made of water. Help me to love others with my entire being, in the way that you give of yourself to the parched earth. Thank you for your power, and for what you continue to teach me. I am truly grateful, Great River, and so very blessed."

With a humble heart, White Buffalo joined the family at the plantation house for dinner, and later that evening he returned to the dorm with Gaston.

Five years later, earlier than he originally planned, White Buffalo graduated from Tulane University with a PhD in Psychology. His parents, Little Deer and her family, and the entire Delacroix/MacPhaidin family attended his graduation ceremony. Afterward, they all went to the plantation house to celebrate his accomplishments. During those years, Mika and Wichahpi took many opportunities to spend time with each other, reunited as mother and daughter.

The same weekend, the entire family celebrated the wedding of White Buffalo to his beloved Evangeline, officiated by White Buffalo's father, Howahkan.

While his parents were still in New Orleans, White Buffalo gave an offering of tobacco to his father, requesting that he assist him in his vision quest, for he was desirous of greater spiritual direction for his life's purpose. Of course, Howahkan accepted the gift, and they made their preparations for the sacred ritual. The entire family participated in the Inipi ceremony during his four-day vision quest.

It took place in a clearing in the woods, far from any people. He remained there in the sacred space for four days and three nights. There, he saw and heard the Ancestors convey to him the direction of Wakan Tanka, in which he was to create a center where he could teach the ways of the Lakota. White Buffalo envisioned thousands, perhaps millions of people who were eager to learn about the Lakota and all Native Americans. He saw himself meeting indigenous people from all over the world, melding cultures through common bonds.

He already was one of the thirteen of the Order of Apeiros, each with their unique qualities and talents. Together, they joined in their work of holding higher consciousness for the world, but White Buffalo's individual calling was strong - not meant for a feeble heart. He left his vision quest with a burning desire that would fuel the spark of his task for the remainder of his days.

A center, he thought, *but I have no money to build such a place and I do not necessarily possess the business acumen needed.* White Buffalo pondered the direction given, knowing that the means would appear as he took forward steps to be about his work. In the meantime, he would accept invitations to speak and teach.

As White Buffalo originally intended, he and Evangeline traveled together, while he lectured about

Native Americans, specifically the ways of the Lakota. On rare occasions, he stayed in a location for a two-week period, offering small groups the opportunity to participate in an Inipi ceremony. He led the ceremony as the wicasa wakan, in the same way as his great-grandfather, in which he felt the spirits of Tahatan, Crazy Horse, Sitting Bull, and other great chiefs and warriors of his people. They smiled upon him and were happy.

All the while, the thought of building a center dwelled in the back of his mind. After a few years, in order to gain greater clarity, he went to see a well-known psychic located in the French Quarter, just down the street from Dylan and Gaston's shop, *Nothing but Tyme*.

When he entered her domain, the atmosphere was as he imagined, for the tourist trade would expect no less. Colorful glass beads hung in the doorways, while the room contained various antique furniture and draperies in fabrics of rich colors and textures, some in woven paisley patterns. All the lighting was indirect, with low-lit lamps placed here and there about the room. Incense burned, leaving a mystical scent in the air. In the corners were tall palm trees placed in large Chinese porcelain jardinières that sat in ornate brass-footed stands. At the center of the candlelit room, on top of a thick Persian rug, sat a draped round table with two chairs.

Already feeling the effects of sensory overload, White Buffalo sat in the corner of the room on the loveseat in anticipation of meeting the medium. He thought she would be old and overdone, imagining her with a scarf tied around her head with thick curls trailing down past her shoulders. He expected her to wear gold coined jewelry around her neck - big gold hoop earrings, and too many clanging bangle bracelets. Heavy make-up, specifically black eyeliner and bright red lipstick would be the least of his presumption, as influenced by the classic films about gypsy lore. It would not have surprised him to see a man with a swarthy complexion walk into the room, wearing a big-sleeved colorful shirt unbuttoned enough to show layers of gold chains dangling over a sweater of chest hair, sporting a well-worn fedora while playing the violin.

However, when the medium entered, White Buffalo was surprised to find her an alluring bohemian-type woman. She was young, beautiful, and mysterious, as she seemed to float into the room in her long flowing skirts, holding a black cat. *What a surprise*, he thought with a bit of sarcasm. Her waist-length blonde hair in thick waves fell off her shoulders and down her back, but what most called his attention was the intensity of her green eyes. When she spoke, her full red lips seemed to say more than the words that came to his ears.

Holding out her hand, she said, "Welcome. My name is Angelina. This beautiful being is Ebony, and you are- ?"

"Scott. Scott, ahh Anka," he said as he feebly shook her hand.

She placed her cat on a ruby-colored pillow on the floor next to her chair. Ebony sat upright, wrapping her tail around her silken body, fully at attention of what was about to take place.

"Well, Scott," Angelina looked directly into White Buffalo's eyes, "I don't think you are telling me the truth. What is your true name?"

He thought, *she must be the real deal*. His shy nature took over, for her beauty unnerved him and he found himself stuttering. "Um, my name is White Buffalo."

Angelina was clearly aware of her effect on men. She motioned toward the table as she smiled. "That is a much better name for you, but it is not your true name."

"My Lakota name is Tatanka Ska."

"Now we can begin. Please take a seat." After she settled in, she said, "So, tell me, Tatanka Ska - White Buffalo, why do you call yourself Scott?"

After he explained his situation, she responded, "From this point forward, you are to call yourself White Buffalo. To your Native people, you are Tatanka Ska, but to the world, you are to be White Buffalo. It is a sacred name, for the white buffalo, as you know, has significant meaning to Native Americans. The world will identify with your name as White Buffalo, but you are no longer to call yourself Scott."

He nodded, knowing she was right.

"Tell me, what is the reason you came here today?"

"In a sacred Lakota ceremony, I was given direction to create a center where I can teach. I seek more clarity to understand that path. And, of course, if there is anything else that comes to mind, I would welcome whatever you have to say."

"Very well, then. Just relax. What I do is quite painless. Let us begin. I use Tarot cards, only as a tool, because they help insight come to me during the reading. Are you ready?"

"Yes," White Buffalo said.

"Please take three deep calming breaths with me." She gave him a warm smile, which helped ease his nervousness.

She shuffled the deck with graceful hands, her nails

painted bright red. "Please cut the deck."

After he did, she laid out the cards in an unusual pattern, her silver bangle bracelets clinking together. White Buffalo took notice that they were the only thing about her appearance that was predictable.

"I have laid out the Celtic Cross spread, which will tell of your past, present, and future," Angelina said. She took some time to look over the cards before she began her reading.

She spoke to him of his upbringing, which convinced him that she was genuine."You come from a strong lineage. I see in your ancestry a powerful man, his spirit has come back into the world to live through you. He was a warrior, and you are one as well - not one of conflict and war, but of peace and compassion. *Instead*, you are a spiritual warrior. I see you have been directed to teach the world of your Native ways, so the story of your people lives on."

"Yes, that's true."

"Please do not speak unless I direct you to do so, for it interrupts my connection with the spirits," Angelina said. "The spirits tell me that you are to create a center. You think this center is a physical place - a building or locale, where you will stand on the stage to speak and teach." She paused, taking her time. "However, this center that you are guided to create is within you, White Buffalo."

She paused and looked into his eyes to emphasize the importance of her direction. "Wherever you speak and teach, *you* are the center, and from this centered place, you will radiate what it is you have to teach, for it is not only about the words, but the way of your being. This center is not a physical structure, but one of Great Spirit that lives within you."

He was greatly surprised by this news. All along, he was certain he should do his work while headquartered in a building that he would personally finance and control. He was relieved, knowing that such an undertaking would be too much responsibility, and far too expensive, taking the emphasis from his teaching.

"This center is where your people believe the four directions meet with the earth and sky - at the singular point in the here and now," Angelina said. "The center is not the past, nor in the future, but only in the present, aligned with the One, whom you call Great Spirit - Wakan Tanka."

She placed her hands on the cards and closed her eyes. After a moment, she looked at him. "You are married, yes?"

"Yes," White Buffalo said.

"I see that she is lovely. You both want children?"

"Yes, we have been trying."

"I am sorry to tell you, but your wife is barren. You will not have children of your own."

White Buffalo slumped back in his chair and looked down, crushed by her words. He feared Evangeline would be devastated by the news.

"All things have reasons behind them. In this case, you are both to travel the world, for the world is your family, White Buffalo. You both will be welcomed with wide-open arms wherever you venture, and you will embrace those whom you serve. The world is waiting for you, White Buffalo, for you and your wife will be at home wherever your journeys take you. Everywhere you travel, you will have people who will become family of choice."

Angelina shifted in her seat and took another deep

breath. "I see that you possess an ancient golden chalice. You are the keeper of the flame, yes?"

"I am."

"Use your chalice to gain greater clarity of your vision. Before you enter sleep each night, sit in a dark room and look directly into the flame. If you do this for 30 consecutive days, you will receive insight about your future ventures. Do not break the momentum. If you do, start over until you have completed the 30 successive days. You can do this with any concern, for when the 30 days conclude, your intuition will bring you insight beyond your expectations."

She paused and closed her eyes, listening to what she was guided to tell him. "The spirits emphasize to me that what I am about to tell you is of utmost importance for you to remember." She looked at him with her penetrating green eyes. He shifted in his seat and nodded. "Far into your future, there will be a time when you will be cleansed by water. Your Inipi ceremonies cleanse you by fire and water, but when the opportunity arises, you are to say yes to the water's wisdom. Are you clear on this direction, for this is quite important for you to understand?"

"Yes, I understand."

"This cleansing will be like no other. Do not anticipate it happening, for you will know when the time comes."

She paused yet again. "Until you leave the Earth plane, you will live a long, healthy, and fulfilling life surrounded by twelve others who hold the consciousness of the world. These people are your intimate family of heart. The work of this group is crucial to the well-being of our world's evolution. Do you understand your importance within this group?"

"We are all integral parts of the whole," White Buffalo said. "Yes, I know I am as important as anyone else, and no less than another. That is one of the key philosophies of our group. We see the unity and oneness of all beings."

"Yes, and I can see this particular part of your importance will occur in your elder years," Angelina said. "You will be a sacred sage for a new member of your group, who will be like a granddaughter to you. Without you, she cannot be that which her soul guides her to be. So, please understand the magnitude of your calling. You are of great value to your people and their history, to your wife, to the group of thirteen, and for the world. Most of all, you will be of primary influence in this young woman's life, whose calling is of great significance to the world. She will be the greatest Oracle of all time. Her teachings and prophecies will initiate the ages to come.

"Not long after you meet this young woman, you will pass along the golden chalice, for it belongs to her. You and your ancestors have been the keeper of the flames, but she will be the carrier of the life force, using the chalice, among other spiritual talismans, to assist in her life's calling."

Angelina paused and sat back in her chair, waiting for several minutes in silence. "That is all I can see for now. The spirits' guidance is complete for the time being. Is there anything else you would like to know?"

"I cannot think of anything at this time. I can always return if questions come up," White Buffalo said.

"I am at your service," Angelina said, concluding his reading. "It was my pleasure to meet you, White Buffalo. You are a great man, and the world is a better place because you live in a good way as you walk the Red Road."

"I appreciate your guidance," White Buffalo said. "I

now know how it is that your reputation precedes you."

"Now, don't blow smoke, for it will blur my vision," Angelina said, and they both laughed.

White Buffalo paid her and then said his goodbyes, saddened at the news of not having children, but the remainder of the reading gave him clarity and hope for a promising future. That night, he would record in his journal everything she told him while it was fresh in his mind. As for Evangeline being barren, he would suggest they both get a check-up so she would hear the news from a medical professional.

For many years together, White Buffalo and Evangeline lived in New Orleans, where Evangeline eventually inherited her grandparents' boulangerie. They lived out in the country, near Darius' plantation. There, White Buffalo built a tipi in the center of a wooded area. When he needed solace or sought direction from Wakan Tanka, he spent hours there while sitting on the floor in front of the flame that burned eternally in the golden chalice.

When Evangeline's parents became elderly, they sold the boulangerie in the French Quarter and moved to Golden Gate Park in Colorado, where they could be near her folks. As they traveled the world together, they were always happy to return to their home in the Colorado Mountains.

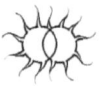

CHAPTER
Twenty-eight

White Buffalo's dream ended that night as he found Digit curled up under his arm, sleeping soundly with a tiny snore. He woke up to a morning of white, after a nighttime of snowfall. Nothing was more beautiful than gentle snow falling in the mountains, covering everything with crystalline layers. His dream left him feeling that his life was complete. He had lived in a good way.

Snow fell the entire day, leaving the valley blanketed in serenity and peace. The river was a mere trickle beneath the layers of blue ice and snow. The branches on the majestic blue spruce trees were heavily laden with snow, like the most perfect images on a Christmas card.

Everyone who was staying at the Riverside Inn remained there, happily snowed in and gathered together by the fireplace, where Jameson prepared a delicious brunch. The weather report stated that the snow would continue for at least another 24 hours. Outside, there was at least two feet of snow on the ground with no end in sight.

The group was more than comfortable, with the restaurant, indoor pool, Jacuzzi, pool table, and a theatre to relax and enjoy a film or two. The Ello sisters were also staying at the Inn, for it was an unexpected holiday from their hospitality duties. As for the newly married couple, Chayton and Irina stayed in the honeymoon suite at the Inn, and probably would not come out for at least another day.

During their candlelight dinner that night, White Buffalo told Michael, Sophia, Darius, and Gaston about the memories he recalled.

"If I understand all of what you say, then you and I are also related, correct?" Sophia asked.

"All my relations," White Buffalo said with a weak smile.

"Yes," Gaston said, "because White Buffalo and I share the same grandmother, Mika – but not the same grandfather, we are half first cousins. That makes you two half first cousins twice removed."

"But Mika is my great-great-grandmother, right?" Sophia said. "And Tahatan, my three-times great-grandfather, which makes me part Lakota?"

"You are," White Buffalo said.

"And he fought Custer at the Little Big Horn alongside Crazy Horse, who by the way is also a distant relative."

"He did, and he is," White Buffalo said.

"And you also knew my mother, and both Jocelyn and François, my great-great-grandparents, who just happened to go down with the *Titanic?*"

"I did," White Buffalo said.

"These relations I never knew all these years, you think *somebody* might have told me something," Sophia mumbled as she quickly cleared the remaining dishes from the table and wandered into the kitchen. "Of course, I must remember that I *was* Jocelyn...let's not forget Nostradamus, another ancestor...Oh, and Patrick, my father, who of course wasn't really my father at all, but my great-great uncle..."

"There is one thing I still haven't figured out," Gaston said. "Are we supposed to respond when she walks out of the room talking?"

"No, it's alright," Michael said. "She's talking to herself. She does that all the time – it's how she processes."

"You know," Darius said, "overall, she has dealt with all of this remarkably well."

Sophia hollered from the kitchen, "I would have done a lot better if one of you might have at least sent me a postcard or something!"

"For the most part, yes," Michael said.

White Buffalo managed a weak smile. "She is doing just fine."

She returned with a tray of homemade chocolate chip cookies, staying true to her culinary skills of a presentation in varied browns. "Come and join me in the great room. I built a fire, and we'll be more comfortable there."

"Now that sounds delightful," Darius said.

Sophia put her arm out for White Buffalo to hold while she led him to the best chair in the house.

"Michael," Gaston said. "We have a little surprise for you."

"Oh?" Michael said.

"You have generously served us for so long now that we thought we'd try to at least repay you a bit. If you look in the cabinet, you will find a lovely 50-year-old Glenfiddich with your name on it."

"You're kidding?" Michael said. He went to the cabinet and retrieved the scotch. "Oh, my gosh," he said, gently turning the bottle to look at it. "I've never held a bottle of scotch that was older than me – and probably worth more, too."

"Don't drop it, dear boy," Darius said.

"What a surprise!" Sophia said. "Thank you so much!"

"No, thank you, my dear ones," Gaston said.

"Yes," Darius agreed, "I cannot say when White Buffalo, Gaston, and I have spent more meaningful times together."

"I don't know what to say," Michael said.

"Say nothing," Gaston said. "Just pour."

"Yes," Darius said. "Rocks for Sophia, and neat for my esteemed brother and I. White Buffalo, dear boy, what can Michael get you?"

White Buffalo rubbed his chin, "I hear the call of a steaming cup of cocoa, extra chocolate."

Michael simply stared for a moment and then turned for the bar, mumbling, "At least I have the security of knowing nothing changes around here."

"Whipped cream and a cherry on top, if you don't mind," White Buffalo said...

They sat for hours while White Buffalo recounted the many moments in his life that brought him to who he was in the world. Digit climbed up in his lap, purring the entire time he told his tale. Then, White Buffalo told them about Evangeline. Of course, Gaston and Darius knew her well, but after she died, never had White Buffalo spoken of his only love until that night.

"She was a beauty of auburn hair and hazel eyes," he said. "The first time I saw her, I knew she would be mine. All those years that I traveled, she was by my side, able to utilize her degree in International Studies to enhance our teaching. She was fluent in many languages, which helped, because I only spoke Lakota and English. We built wonderful memories traveling throughout the world that very few have had the privilege to call their own."

He looked down with a shadow of grief that overcame his calm demeanor.

"Six years ago, we were concluding our lecture tour of Europe with our last stop in Switzerland. We had traveled so much that neither of us were paying attention to the signs left by a tired body. After several days of lectures, we were taking it easy, sitting in our hotel suite. I was watching one of my favorite movies recorded on my computer - something I rarely had a chance to do - and she was reading a book when I heard her slightly whimper. Thinking that she fell asleep while dreaming, I looked over at her, but something was terribly wrong. I called out her name and got up from my chair to take her hand. Her head fell to one side. She had passed on."

"Oh, White Buffalo, how very sad," Sophia said.

Gaston and Darius both pulled handkerchiefs and dabbed their eyes, while Michael simply put his hand to his mouth to help sway his tears.

"Before she was taken away, I sat with her for two hours, just holding her hand and remembering the beautiful life we had all those years. I spoke to her as if she could still hear me. My Evangeline was a great beauty in all ways. She was the love of my life - my only love. One of the funny things about her was that she always called me Scott, and never White Buffalo. I have loved only one woman, and I am fortunate that she agreed to marry me and live with me the remainder of her days."

"How long were you married?" Sophia said.

"45 years."

"We're so glad to hear about her," Michael said. "You never spoke of her until now."

"Some memories should be kept secreted away in the heart, where they remain precious forever," White Buffalo said. "Two nights after she died, I talked to her as if she was in the room. I said, 'I know you are alright, but I would feel so much better if you could let me know that you are okay - in a way that I will have no doubt that the message is from you.' The next afternoon, I checked my cell phone for messages. Among them was a voicemail that came from Evangeline."

"No!" Sophia said. "How could that be?"

"That is exactly what I wondered. Her voicemail message said, 'Hello my darling. Just a reminder to let you know I am right here, waiting for you. I love you. See you soon.'"

"I guess you couldn't have gotten a clearer message than that," Michael said.

"Actually, she had left the message a couple of days before she died, as a reminder to meet her for lunch that day, but it did not show up on my phone until three days after her death. Several times since then, I have asked her questions, and I receive answers in many different ways, always without a doubt that it is my Evangeline. The veil is very thin between the worlds. We just have to be willing to pay attention, for those who have gone on before us are ever reaching out to us.

"Hearing from her helped me, but I continued to feel such tremendous grief - there was a hole in my heart that would not mend. Many of my days, I wondered if it would be better if I too would leave this earth to join her, but still I carried on."

"I cannot imagine your pain, my friend," Michael said.

"About two years after her death, I traveled to Mexico to meet with other sages and shamans. Michael, you will appreciate this - we traveled to Ancient Mesoamerican sites: Toltec, Aztec, and Mayan sites, such as Monte Albán, Tulum, Chichén Itzá, Teotihuacán, and Yaxchilán, near Guatemala."

Michael smiled and nodded. "I know them well."

"At each location, we participated in sacred ceremony. At the conclusion of our tour, a few people in the group invited me to join them at a beautiful sun-heated natural pool and waterfall. What they did not tell me was that the waterfall was deep inside a cave. Years ago, a well-known New Orleans psychic told me that I was to undergo a cleansing by water, and I knew this was the time and place to fulfill that destiny.

"I ventured into the cave alone. The rest of the group waded in the sun-heated waters outside the cave opening. Luckily, there was a rope anchored on the left interior wall, which led to the waterfall toward the back. The tour guide stressed the importance of not venturing beyond the guide rope, for no light reached into the darkness that far back into the cave. I carefully followed the rope as the water became deeper the farther I went, but at the end, I had not yet come to the waterfall. I estimated the falls were ahead another ten feet or so. At that point, the water was up to my shoulders. The only sound I could hear was the rushing waters that beckoned me into the darkness. I knew I was to stand beneath the waterfall, so I let go of the rope and waded toward the falls. Under the waterfall, I turned around to face the cave entrance so I wouldn't become disoriented.

"It was like nothing I ever experienced, as the powerful waters washed over me, cleansing me of all my grief and anything I had been holding onto. Time disappeared, but I thought I must have stayed under the falls for several minutes at the most. When I tried to step away to find the guide rope in the dark, the falls forced me beneath the water. The force was so strong it knocked me off my feet, churning me under and making it difficult for me to rise to the surface. I tried several times, attempting to reach out to my right for the rope anchored to the wall, only to find myself churned under again. After several attempts, I grew weak and thought I would most certainly come to my death, but my intuitive voice then spoke to me loud and clear. *Go to your left!* And so I did. I soon found my way, holding onto the rope, now on my right, leading me toward the cave entrance to join my group, who all that time didn't even know I was gone. Knowing that, I was grateful they didn't leave me there. I thought I had been gone for no more than 30 minutes, but they said I was in the cave over two hours.

"What came from that experience was that I no longer had thoughts of leaving Grandmother Earth to join with my beloved Evangeline, and I no longer feared death. I have wondered, since then, if the two were connected - the fear of death, with thoughts of death constantly calling me at the same time. It is certainly a conundrum, and in an odd way, it makes sense. After being cleansed by the waters, I emerged with the knowing that life is precious, and how very blessed I am to have lived so well.

"And so, that being said, I want all four of you to know how much I love you. Gaston and Darius, you have been the brothers that I never had growing up. For more years than I can remember, you have entertained me with your bantering, bickering, and the deep and true love that you share. You accepted me into the family immediately, and welcomed me into Apeiros, which gave me a deeper purpose beyond that of my love for the Lakota.

"Sophia and Michael, Evangeline and I never had children, but I could not have loved them more than I love you. Thank you for allowing me to stay here with you. Being in the love that you share with each other has been a gift for me. I am truly a blessed man."

White Buffalo picked up Digit from his lap. He cradled her and then kissed her on the top of her head. He gently placed the tiny black cat on the cushion next to him. Michael helped him rise from his seat as the others stood to wish him well before he went to bed.

Darius stepped forward and gave White Buffalo a warm embrace. "From the beginning of our days together, I thought of you as family. You taught me humility and compassion, without which I might have never enjoyed this blessed life so well. I thank you, for my life has been so much better because of your wise counsel. I love you deeply, my brother."

Gaston was in tears, while the rest of them, by that time, were doing their best not to cry. Gaston held White Buffalo in his arms for quite a long time, unable to speak. Finally, he said, "I cannot imagine what my life would be without your companionship, your love, and your wise insight. My love for you is as deep as the ocean, my cousin - my brother - Aho Mitakuye Oyasin."

White Buffalo smiled and nodded at both Darius and Gaston as he turned towards Michael and Sophia. Michael wrapped his elder in his big arms and gave him a gentle hug. "You are my shaman, my warrior chief, my sacred sage. I love you." Michael kept his arm around White Buffalo, supporting him as he stood.

Sophia stepped forward and looked up into White Buffalo's eyes while placing her hands gently on his arms. He accepted her loving gaze. "You immediately captured my heart from the first time I met you when you spoke to me from the stage. Thank you for being another grandfather to me. My life could not be more blessed. I now know, without a doubt, that we have traveled lifetimes together, through many dimensions.

"When Michael and I were in Ireland, I had a vision of you and me, right here at the river's edge. You guided me with your immeasurable wisdom, just as you did the first time when we sat together in my library, at my little house. I remember all you have taught me as if we just spoke yesterday.

"So rest well, my beloved, knowing that you remain cradled in my heart, within the profound love that I have for you." Sophia tenderly placed her arms around him in a gentle embrace and kissed him on the cheek.

"My dearest Sophia, *Know Thyself*," White Buffalo said as tears flowed down Sophia's face. "To *Know Thyself* is to love yourself wholly, for love is the answer to every question, to each moment of disquiet. Love is where all directions meet at the center, where the spiral of creation takes hold. In this love, I will never be gone from your journey. You and I will recognize each other again within the continuum of life's passage, for our soul's existence is within this center place of Love's embrace, where all is known." He gently placed his hand on her tear-stained cheek.

"You are all my soul family. We will know each other again. I love you all. Aho Mitakuye Oyasin." White Buffalo touched his closed fist gently to his chest, and then opened his hand, raised with his palm facing them as a blessing. He then took Michael's arm as they walked to the elevator. Sophia, Darius, and Gaston watched in silence as Michael tenderly walked White Buffalo along the balcony to his room.

At the door, Michael smiled. "Can I bring you anything before bed - more cocoa maybe?"

"No, thank you, my son."

"Then I'll say goodnight, Uncle. Rest well."

White Buffalo briefly looked into the window of Michael's soul with a loving gaze of his deep blue eyes, and then he smiled. He quietly closed the door. Michael placed his hand flat on the door and paused for a moment before he turned and walked away. All time seemed to stop. Michael again became aware of the infinite nature of the eternal that had just taken place in that singular moment.

In his bedroom, White Buffalo changed into his nightshirt and carefully hung up his clothes, neatly placing his shoes in the closet before closing the door. He looked around at the significant memorabilia he had collected from around the world. In the corner hung Tibetan prayer flags, and on the dresser sat a brass singing bowl that rang out the clearest tone that ears could hear. He shook his turtle rattle, hearing the echo of his people through its resound. He picked up his eagle feather fan, and with a flick of his wrist, he sent a plentitude of silent prayers to Great Spirit on the wings of eagles. Photos of people he loved and places of remembrance were all over the walls. He took the Irish woolen throw from the end of the bed and draped it over the big armchair in the corner of the room.

On the nightstand, beside a framed picture of Evangeline, was his flute with many eagle feathers attached. He sat on the edge of the bed and played the flute for a short time, seeing in his mind's eye his life of freedom when he was a young boy living in the Black Hills. He then laid the flute next to a beautifully beaded deerskin pouch, which contained his sacred pipe. He removed the pipe from the pouch, unwrapping it from its protective cloth. He held the bowl of the pipe in his left hand and the stem in his right, raising his sacred chanupa up to the heavens.

In Lakota he said, "Wakan Tanka, this is your grandson, Tatanka Ska. I thank you for my life, for you have greatly blessed me with your goodness. I pray only one prayer - please continue to bless my loved ones, who remain here on Grandmother Earth, for they live in a good way with every intention to walk the Red Road - the Sacred Way of the Heart. I thank you for this life, Great Spirit, for all my blessings. Aho Mitakuye Oyasin."

He wrapped his pipe in the protective cloth and gently placed it back into the deerskin pouch. Lighting a wooden match to the dried sage that sat in an abalone shell, he waved the smoke over his body to cleanse and purify himself before he laid his head down.

From under his nightshirt, he pulled out a chain that held both his and Evangeline's gold wedding bands. He brought the rings to his lips and kissed them. As he switched off the light on the nightstand, he looked out the window. He smiled, for his heart was full as he observed the pristine beauty of gently falling snow settled into shadowed shades of blue in thick layers over the mountains' sentinels of pine and spruce. A white-tailed buck stood still in the deep snow, looking up in his direction as if it was sending him a blessing of grace. White Buffalo took notice that the deer left no tracks in the snow. He smiled. Again, he silently thanked Great Spirit for his many blessings.

White Buffalo snuggled under the covers and easily fell

asleep that night, dreaming of being in a pitch-black sweat lodge. The searing heat engulfed him. The drumbeat, songs, and prayers lifted him beyond his body, beyond that of Grandmother Earth, to the familiarity of the spiritual rebirth of the lodge. And now, as Tatanka Ska, he truly knew the meaning of Inipi - *to live again*.

Through the darkness, his beloved family members appeared, who had collectively come with the great love they shared for him. He recognized his great-grandfather immediately, even though Tahatan left the world when White Buffalo was only two years old. Tahatan stood next to White Buffalo's parents, Wichahpi and Howahkan. Little Deer and her husband, along with Evangeline's parents and her grandparents were all present. Mika and Jelani were there with Patrick, Elizabeth, Tommy, as well as Jocelyn and François. Many came, but the one whose presence honored White Buffalo most was Crazy Horse, whose humble fortitude of the great warrior remained. Evangeline stepped forward and spoke for all.

"You have lived well, my love. The Grandfathers and all the Ancestors are pleased, for your walk has been one of the heart's yearnings. You have lived in a good way with your soul's work in this life, and you will accomplish even more as you move on. Come. We invite you to join us now, but it is up to you. Do you want to come with us to join with the Ancestors, or remain on Grandmother Earth?"

"I am ready," he said as he reached out for their extended hands that took him into their loving embrace - to travel the Great Ribbon of Stars to the Spirit World... into *Síoraí*... as White Buffalo breathed his last breath.

Up next:

OUROBOROS
Continuum Book Four

the journey continues...

Available in paperback and E-book at Amazon.com,
BarnesAndNoble.com, and other online stores.

Visit ardyce.org for updated information on the
Continuum Series.

Acknowledgements

About ten years ago, most everything in my life that could change did. Simultaneously, the void left by my divorce, the death of many loved ones, and the change in my career was filled by several people who entered my life. These people made a lasting, positive impact, which remains in the continuum of my life today.

Among them were Luke and Patty Luckenbach, who introduced me to the Lakota through the Inipi ceremony. They live the ways of the Lakota through their humility, wise counsel, humor, and generously kind hearts. Through them, I had the great honor to meet Chief Homer White Lance of the Rosebud Reservation in South Dakota, who is the grandson of Grandpa Jessie, my gentle spirit guide since my early childhood. The healing wisdom of Homer remains in each step I take. I deeply resonate with the heart and spirit of what I know about the culture of the Lakota. And so, as I humbly write about some of their sacred practices to the best of my understanding, I do so with deep respect, conveying a heartfelt story from the love I feel when in company of those I know as my Lakota family.

Several opportunities arose, which started me on my journey of being a writer. Taryn Browne invited me to join her in free-writing sessions, where we met weekly at a coffee shop for two hours. We began with a starting statement, then we wrote for ten-minute segments, and followed with each one reading to the other what creatively developed, ending in a brief critique. Over many months, Taryn helped me to find my voice in my writing, and for this, I am so very appreciative for her friendship at the time.

During a workshop, Dr. Judith Orloff opened me up to the understanding of my quiet inner strength of wisdom, that of being an intuitive empath. Until then, I thought of my sensitivities as a detriment. She helped me to understand that, all along, my intuitive abilities have been my strength, propelling me forward and gracefully guiding me... that is, when I am paying attention to my intuitive guidance - my inner voice - my inner wisdom. At the time, she gently told me to visit Delphi, Greece, and long-story-short, a year and a half later, I did. The trip was a phenomenal life-changing opportunity. For several years, I have studied most of her works, which was partly what inspired me to write about the Continuum Series characters' inner strengths of intuition as they tap into the Divine wisdom within. If it weren't for her taking the time to talk with me during that significant several minutes of conversation, I may not have written the Continuum Series. I will always feel such gratitude for her lifetime of transformational work, and for her being so very present with me that day. Sometimes the seemingly smallest events shift our lives toward our greatest achievements.

During my two-year pursuit of becoming a minister, through Holmes Institute School of Consciousness Studies, I discovered my love for writing, in reading numerous texts, researching, in addition to writing paper after paper. At the time, I had no idea that what I was doing would become my way of life as a writer. I left my ministerial pursuits, because I felt my best talents could be used in being a writer and an artist. Shortly after, my writing career began when we published *I Never Heard You Cry - A Compassionate Journey Through Abortion*. Had it not been for the depth of study that I gained from Holmes Institute with the phenomenal instructors' wisdom and knowledge, I would not be living the life I love and loving the life I live as a writer and an artist. I am tremendously grateful for what those two years taught me. I continue to glean what I learned at that time, with insights that continue to teach me, and through many loving friendships gained.

The sacred friendship with Reverend Carol Righthouse has grown over the years into a spiritual connection that continues to support me during my growth through times of challenge, as well as in triumphant celebration. I so appreciate her heartfelt wisdom, grace, and strength of humble service. What I learn from her counsel helps me to write and speak from Love's power - that of the open heart's vulnerability.

I am fortunate to be a member of a monthly book group, *Reading Between the Wines*, made up of amazing, intelligent, and diverse women who first invited me to present *Apeiros - Continuum Book One*, then *Aeternalis - Continuum Book Two*, as books for their reading and review. These women are now among my growing number of readers, whom I greatly appreciate their friendships, opinions, and insights, which encourages me to become a better writer.

For all my readers and supporters, I thank you! You further inspire me to craft the next enticing tale of significance, storytelling, and art. For your enjoyment, may I present adventure and depth of thought through the lives of the characters in *Síorai*, so as you read, you may enjoy the journey into your own personal evolution.

Oftentimes, I have been fortunate to observe some of Nature's most brilliantly colored sunsets while driving westbound through western Kansas toward Colorado. I am ever grateful to witness such beauty, as seen on the cover of *Siorai*, which was the most magnificent sunset I have ever captured.

I am grateful to my unwavering writing partner, Digit. Most days, she tirelessly listens for hours to the tap, tap, tap of the keyboard as I read aloud repeated sections throughout the book, all the while sleeping comfortably near my chair, or better yet, keeping my lap warm.

I greatly appreciate the multitude of talents of my husband, Kevin. Having written and published four of his own books, he is a well-crafted writer, patient editor, and determined publisher who just will not quit until the book we are producing is as perfect as can be. Life is much easier because of Kevin's generously big heart, wit, and rock-solid way of being. His never-ending support helps me to be a better writer, illustrator, photographer, and self-editor so the next book will be a finer work of heArt than the last. Kevin's expertise continues to astound me in how he takes what I present to him and molds it into a beautiful book that makes my words and art shine at their best. May I just say, with Kevin, I won the proverbial lottery, realizing daily just how truly blessed I am!

To all those I have mentioned, and to so many more, I am tremendously grateful for how you teach me to be.

Author's Note

The question most asked of me by my readers is, what inspired me to write the Continuum Series? The reasons are multifaceted.

Many years ago, within a few months of each other, I took a couple of unexpected journeys through two different near-death-experiences, one of which was during a surgical procedure, and the other, from a car accident. While in the next dimension, after witnessing an abundantly beautiful, joyful, and peace-filled existence beyond human description, where it was made known to me that I knew everything there was to know, I then heard what sounded like my intuitive voice clearly ask, "Do you want to stay or go back?" My soul self immediately responded, "Oh no, I must go back. I have too much to do."

It was only upon my return to my earthly existence did I realize there was absolutely nothing of any negativity in the realm from which I just returned. Only Love and all its qualities were everywhere present, as I was left with a portal into the expanded awareness of the eternality of the cosmic universe. After years of pondering my soul's reason for my return - while in the question of *Just what was it that I returned to do?* - I began to put pen to paper.

I now write the best way I am able to convey, from my human perspective, what I witnessed while in the timeless realm of the Divine without the veils of my earthly existence. Everything I experienced "there" is here. The eternal *is* here, around us, within us, always and in all ways. It is in every moment - in each timeless moment of now. We experience it in the smallest moments - a tender gaze into the eyes of another as a gentle exchange of the heart, in the laughter of children, and when we take notice of nature's beauty. Each heart-filled experience adds on to the next, creating the sacred way of Love's eternal exchange, which beckons us on to the next moment of grace. We have access to the entire universe, which exists within each of us, and it is up to us to say yes to this magnificence within our own potential. From that place of knowing, we then take positive steps, which lead to giant leaps within the celestial enfoldment - the eternality of our lives.

Each of us is of importance, as in the metaphor of the big cosmic jigsaw puzzle. Each elemental being is an individual piece of the puzzle, shaped differently, in varied colors and textures - all fitting together perfectly to make the grand picture we know as our greater selves - as One. No piece is more important than another, and yet each is crucial in the importance of their individuality and to the whole.

The characters in the Continuum Series are everyday heroes, who face real life challenges while living in their individual part of the world, raising the vibratory frequency, both as individuals, and as a collective body of thirteen. They are wisdom keepers, oracles, light workers, sages, and shamans, some who have joined yet again in this lifetime as they all hold the high watch for the world - and for the universe as a whole. As we journey through each character's life story and witness his or her human challenges, it is my intention to illustrate that no one is without significance or value.

As a lover of history, I wanted to find a way to research and write about historic events and people of interest who have made a profound impact in the metaphysical (beyond the physical) nature of the world. Although I personally believe in past lives, it is not my intention for my readers to do so. I chose to tell the story of Sophia, the main character throughout the series, through her past lives so I could incorporate endless historic accounts for this ongoing tale, while weaving the sacred way of Love's qualities through-out the series. Those same attributes are the basis for the Order of Apeiros, enabling the thirteen to remember their individual soul's journey as they hold fast the highest con-sciousness for the world.

I have experienced many rich and diverse lifetimes in this singular life, at times through the dark night of the soul. I am so very grateful, for my life has rarely been boring. I live a life of great fortune, for I do what I love, and love what I do, through my writing, my art, and as a spiritual practitioner, life coach, and speaker. Each day I am ever more aware of how blessed I am to have people of tremendous value sur-rounding me. Everyone I meet is a sacred soul upon this pre-cious planet. This is why I returned - to help people remem-ber who they came here to be, so they can embrace and express their utmost potential, using their individual gifts and talents, which already exist within them.

With my highest intentions, I reach out through the writ-ten word, through my illustrations, and my photography, to create stories that bring to the reader joy, peace, hope, harmony, grace, compassion - all wrapped in love... some-times with a bit of added intrigue and mystery as well.

Knowing for you that love lights your way,

~Ardyce West

About the Author

Ardyce West is an optimum blend of spirituality and transformation. She is a Licensed Practitioner for United Centers for Spiritual Living in Colorado, as well as a certified Life Mastery Consultant and DreamBuilder Coach. Ardyce has expertly chaired large retreats and facilitated transformative healing workshops, assisting others in living a full spectrum wholehearted life through the brilliant guidance and intuition she provides for individuals and groups. Also an extremely accomplished artist, Ardyce has conducted many art and jewelry workshops.

Through captivating storytelling, Ardyce presents an empowering workshop featuring her two near-death experiences, which have resulted in her fascinating life, living through the grace of the Eternal Now.

She is the author of the metaphysical Continuum historical fiction series, including *Apeiros - Continuum Book One, Aeternalis - Continuum Book Two, Síoraí - Continuum Book Three, and Ouroboros - Continuum Book Four,* as well as the beautifully written poignant non-fiction book, *I Never Heard You Cry - A Compassionate Journey Through Abortion,* written to give a voice to the many who are affected by abortion, either through personal experience or through that of a loved one. With *Réalta - Continuum Book Five* in the works, Ardyce also wrote and illustrated her first children's book, *There Once Was a Kitty Name Digit.*

Visit ardyce.org for updated information.

Praise for
I Never Heard You Cry -
A Compassionate Journey Through Abortion

"*I Never Heard You Cry* . . . never approaches political edict or social commentary regarding abortion. Ardyce West focuses rather on the substantial number of people who do struggle with complex and deeply emotional post-abortion issues." - *Publisher*

"For me, a great book is one that leaves me moved and tingling when I complete its final passages. Ardyce West's book, '*I Never Heard You Cry*', did precisely that for me. Not only will you be supported and inspired, you will find numerous springs of healing in this book. It is poignant as well as practical, offering compassion and insight in a controversial and troubled arena. Read this book and let your heart be touched." - *Dr. Roger W. Teel, Senior Minister and Spiritual Director, Mile Hi Church, Lakewood, Colorado*

"Ardyce West courageously shares her vulnerability in exposing her soul's journey of healing after her experience of abortion. Her insights give us all strength in moving forward after irreplaceable loss into greater awareness. '*I Never Heard You Cry*' is a significant and much needed work that will heal lives." - *Rev. Christian Sorensen, D.D., Seaside Center for Spiritual Living, Encinitas, CA*

"This is a book that will support healing and transform the way people look at abortion if they are willing to suspend fearful concepts. I highly encourage you to read this book and share it with your family, friends and even counseling clients. It will make a difference in how they view the experience of abortion and hopefully encourage them to open their hearts." - *Cynthia James, Author, What Will Set You Free, Revealing Your Extraordinary Essence*

"This extraordinary book isn't about pro-life, pro-choice, politics or religion. It's about people - the vast majority of us who understand that abortion is not a black-and-white issue that can only be addressed in absolutes. While it is an essential book for those who are struggling with unexpected and unattended post-abortion grief, it's also an excellent book for parents to share with their kids to help them learn about consequences and accountability." - *Kevin Cahill, Author, Sand Creek, Letters to a Rose, The Last Cafe, Knights of Harvest*

What reviewers are saying on Amazon.com:
"Few know how to heal the emotional wounds that accompany abortion. We don't talk about it much. This book is a good place to begin. It speaks with compassion, and offers signposts to acceptance, forgiveness, and healing." - *T. Nash*

"This book attempts to sort it out without all the screaming, finger-pointing and useless drama. I applaud this author for bringing some peace to all the pain on both sides of this serious and divisive issue." - *Jane*

"It has been written with such care and compassion while elevating us beyond the false oversimplification of this being a matter merely of either pro-life or pro-choice." - *Bruce*

"It was like finding Spring water in the desert of judgment that surrounds abortion and other such life decisions that many face in this complicated world." - *Suzanne*

"This book should be given to anyone considering or has been through an abortion." - *Susan*

"The book is about so much more than the journey through abortion, it speaks to me on many different levels about my own experiences in life." - *Frannie*

"I would highly recommend *"I Never Heard You Cry"* for anyone facing a healing process or anyone who works in an area of healing or spiritual counseling." - *Carol*

I Never Heard You Cry -
a Compassionate Journey Through Abortion
by Ardyce West

Available in paperback
and e-book at Amazon.com,
BarnesAndNoble.com,
and other online book stores

* * *